E HIM

lly

"Thrilling."
—Louise Penny

"Brilliant."
—Jeffery Deaver

"Watch for those twists—
they'll get you every time."
—Ian Rankin

"Edge-of-your-seat,
heart-in-your-throat suspense."
—Tess Gerritsen

"The novels of Peter Robinson are chilling,
evocative, deeply nuanced works of art."
—Dennis Lehane

CRITICS LOVE HIM

"Devilishly good."
—*New York Times Book Review*

"Superb."
—*Wall Street Journal*

"First-rate."
—*Washington Post*

"Atmospheric."
—*Los Angeles Times*

"Exquisite."
—*USA Today*

"Rewarding."
—*Seattle Times*

"The equal of . . . P. D. James."
—*St. Louis Post-Dispatch*

YOU'LL LOVE HIM

One of the world's most popular and acclaimed writers, **PETER ROBINSON** grew up in the United Kingdom, and now divides his time between Toronto and England. The bestselling, award-winning author of the Inspector Banks series, he has also written two short-story collections and three standalone novels, which combined have sold more than ten million copies around the world. Among his many honors and prizes are the Edgar Award, the CWA (UK) Dagger in the Library Award, and Sweden's Martin Beck Award.

BLOOD AT THE ROOT

BY PETER ROBINSON

BLOOD AT THE ROOT

AN INSPECTOR BANKS NOVEL

Peter Robinson

wm

WILLIAM MORROW

An Imprint of HarperCollins*Publishers*

This book is a work of fiction. The characters, incidents, and dialogue are drawn from the author's imagination and are not to be construed as real. Any resemblance to actual events or persons, living or dead, is entirely coincidental.

A hardcover edition of this book was published in 1997 by William Morrow, an imprint of HarperCollins Publishers.

FIRST WILLIAM MORROW PAPERBACK EDITION PUBLISHED 2016.
FIRST AVON BOOKS PAPERBACK EDITION PUBLISHED 1998.

Library of Congress Cataloging-in-Publication Data has been applied for.

ISBN 978-0-06-243123-3

17 18 19 20   DIX/RRD   10 9 8 7 6 5 4 3 2

For Sheila

BLOOD AT THE ROOT

ONE

I

The boy's body sat propped against the graffiti-scarred wall in a ginnel off Market Street, head lolling forward, chin on chest, hands clutching his stomach. A bib of blood had spilled down the front of his white shirt.

Detective Chief Inspector Alan Banks stood in the rain and watched Peter Darby finish photographing the scene, bursts of electronic flash freezing the raindrops in mid-air as they fell. Banks was irritated. By rights, he shouldn't be there. Not in the rain at half past one on a Saturday night.

As if he didn't have enough problems already.

He had got the call the minute he walked in the door after an evening alone in Leeds at Opera North's *The Pearl Fishers.* Alone because his wife, Sandra, had realized on Wednesday that the benefit gala she was supposed to host for the Eastvale community center clashed with their season tickets. They had argued—Sandra expecting Banks to forgo the opera in favor of her gala—so, stubbornly, Banks had gone alone. This sort of thing had been happening a lot lately—going their own ways—to such an extent that Banks could hardly remember the last time they had done anything together.

The limpid melody of the "Au fond du temple saint" duet still echoed around his mind as he watched Dr. Burns, the young police surgeon, start his *in situ* examination under the canvas tent the scene-of-crime officers had erected over the body.

Police Constable Ford had come across the scene at eleven forty-seven while walking his beat, community policing being a big thing in Eastvale these days. At first, he said, he thought the victim was just a drunk too legless to get all the way home after the pubs closed. After all, there was a broken beer bottle on the ground beside the lad, he seemed to be holding his stomach, and in the light of Ford's torch, the dark blood could easily have passed for vomit.

Ford told Banks he didn't know quite what it was that finally alerted him this was no drunk sleeping it off; perhaps it was the unnatural stillness of the body. Or the silence: there was no snoring, no twitching or muttering, the way drunks often did, just silence inside the hiss and patter of the rain. When he knelt and looked more closely, well, of course, then he knew.

The ginnel was a passage no more than six feet wide between two blocks of terrace houses on Carlaw Place. It was often used as a short cut between Market Street and the western area of Eastvale. Now onlookers had gathered at its mouth, behind the police tape, most of them huddled under umbrellas, pajama bottoms sticking out from under raincoats. Lights had come on in many houses along the street, despite the lateness of the hour. Several uniformed officers were circulating in the crowd and knocking on doors, seeking anyone who had seen or heard anything.

The ginnel walls offered some protection from the rain, but not much. Banks could feel the cold water trickling down the back of his neck. He pulled up his collar. It was mid-October, the time of year when the weather veered sharply between warm, misty, mellow days straight out of Keats and piercing gale-force winds that drove stinging rain into your face like the showers of Blefuscuan arrows fired at Gulliver.

Banks watched Dr. Burns turn the victim on his side, ease down his trousers and take the rectal temperature. He had already had a glance at the body himself, and it looked as if someone had beaten or kicked the kid to death. The features were too severely damaged to reveal much except that he was a young white male. His wallet was missing, along with whatever keys and loose change he might have been carrying, and there was nothing else in his pockets to indicate who he was.

It had probably started as a pub fight, Banks guessed, or perhaps the victim had been flashing his money about. As he watched Dr. Burns examine the boy's broken features, Banks imagined the scene as it might have happened. The kid scared, running perhaps, realizing that whatever had started innocently enough was quickly getting out of control. How many of them were after him? Two, probably, at least. Maybe three or four. He runs through the dark, deserted streets in the rain, splashing through puddles, oblivious to his wet feet. Does he know they're going to kill him? Or is he just afraid of taking a beating?

Either way, he sees the ginnel, thinks he can make it, slip away, get home free, but it's too late. Something hits him or trips him, knocks him down, and suddenly his face is crushed down against the rainy stone, the cigarette ends and chocolate wrappers. He can taste blood, grit, leaves, probe a broken tooth with his tongue. And then he feels a sharp pain in his side, another in his back, his stomach, his groin, then they're kicking his head as if it were a football. He's trying to speak, beg, plead, but he can't get the words out, his mouth is too full of blood. And finally he just slips away. No more pain. No more fear. No more anything.

Well, maybe it had happened like that. Or they could have been already lying in wait for him, blocking the ginnel at each end, trapping him inside. Some of Banks's bosses had said he had too much imagination for his own good, though he found it had always come in useful. People would be surprised if they knew how much of what they believed to be painstaking, logical police work actually came down to a guess, a hunch, or a sudden intuition.

Banks shrugged off the line of thought and got back to the

business in hand. Dr. Burns was still kneeling, shining a penlight inside the boy's mouth. It looked like a pound of raw minced meat to Banks. He turned away.

A pub fight, then? Though they didn't usually end in death, fights were common enough on a Saturday night in Eastvale, especially when some of the lads came in from the outlying villages eager to demonstrate their physical superiority over the arrogant townies.

They would come early to watch Eastvale United or the rugby team in the afternoon, and by pub chucking-out time they were usually three sheets to the wind, jostling each other in the fish-and-chip-shop queues, slagging everyone in sight, just looking for trouble. It was a familiar pattern: "What are you looking at?" "Nothing." "You calling *me* nothing!" Get out of that if you can.

By midnight, though, most of the boozers had usually gone home, unless they had moved on to one of Eastvale's two night-clubs, where for a modest entrance fee you got membership, an inedible battered beefburger, a constant supply of ear-splitting music and, most important of all, the chance to swill back watery lager until three in the morning.

It wasn't that Banks had no sympathy for the victim—after all, the boy was *somebody's* son—but solving this case, he thought, would simply be a matter of canvassing the local pubs and finding out where me-laddo had been drinking, whom he'd been upsetting. A job for Detective Sergeant Hatchley, perhaps; certainly not one for a wet detective chief inspector with Bizet's melodies still caressing his inner ear; one whose only wish was to crawl into a nice warm bed beside a wife who probably still wasn't speaking to him.

Dr. Burns finished his examination and walked over. Burns did on-scene examinations when the local Home Office pathologist, Dr. Glendenning, was unavailable. He looked far too young and innocent for the job—in fact, he looked more like a farmer with his round face, pleasant, rustic features and mop of chestnut hair—but he was quickly becoming conversant with the different ways in which man could dispatch his fellow man to the hereafter.

"Well, it certainly looks like a boot job," he said, putting his black notebook back in his pocket. "I can't swear to it, of course—that'll be for Dr. Glendenning to determine at the postmortem—but it looks that way. From what I can make out on first examination, one eye's practically hanging out of its socket, the nose is pulped and there are several skull fractures. In some places the bone fragments might possibly have punctured the brain." Burns sighed. "In a way, the poor bugger's lucky he's dead. If he'd survived, he'd have been a one-eyed vegetable for the rest of his days."

"No sign of any other injuries?"

"A few broken ribs. And I'd expect some severe damage to the internal organs. Other than that . . ." Burns glanced back at the body and shrugged. "I'd guess he was kicked to death by someone wearing heavy shoes or boots. But don't quote me on that. It also looks as if he was hit on the back of the head—maybe by that bottle."

"Just one person?"

Burns ran his hand over his wet hair and rubbed it dry on the side of his trousers. "I'm sorry, I didn't mean to imply that. It was more likely two or three. A gang, perhaps."

"But one person *could* have done it?"

"As soon as the victim was down on the ground, yes. Thing is, though, he looks pretty strong. It might have taken more than one person to *get* him down. Unless, of course, that was what the bottle was used for."

"Any idea how long he's been there?"

"Not long." Burns looked at his watch. "Allowing for the weather conditions, I'd say maybe two hours. Two and a half at the outside."

Banks made a quick back-calculation. It was twenty to two now. That meant the kid had probably been killed between ten past eleven and eleven forty-seven, when PC Ford found the body. A little over half an hour. And a half hour that happened to coincide with pub-closing time. His theory was still looking good.

"Anyone know who he is?" Banks asked.

Dr. Burns shook his head.

"Any chance of cleaning him up enough for an artist's impression?"

"Might be worth a try. But as I said, the nose is pulped, one eye's practically—"

"Yes. Yes, thank you, Doctor."

Burns nodded briskly and walked off.

The coroner's officer directed two ambulance attendants to bag the body and take it to the mortuary, Peter Darby took more photographs and the SOCOs went on with their search. The rain kept falling.

Banks leaned back against the damp wall and lit a cigarette. It might help concentrate his mind. Besides, he liked the way cigarettes tasted in the rain.

There were things to be done, procedures to be set in motion. First of all, they had to find out who the victim was, where he had come from, where he belonged, and what he had been doing on the day of his death. Surely, Banks thought, someone, somewhere must be missing him. Or was he a stranger in town, far from home?

Once they knew something about the victim, then it would simply be a matter of legwork. Eventually, they would track down the bastards who had done this. They would probably be kids, certainly no older than their victim, and they would, by turn, be contrite and arrogant. In the end, if they were old enough, they would probably get charged with manslaughter. Nine years, out in five.

Sometimes, it was all so bloody predictable, Banks thought, as he flicked his tab-end into the gutter and walked to his car, splashing through puddles that reflected the revolving lights of the police cars. And at that point, he could hardly be blamed for not knowing how wrong he was.

II

The telephone call at eight o'clock on Sunday morning woke Detective Constable Susan Gay from a pleasant dream about visiting Egypt with her father. They had never done anything of the kind, of course—her father was a cool, remote man who had never taken her anywhere—but the dream seemed real enough.

Eyes still closed, Susan groped until her fingers touched the smooth plastic on her bedside table, then she juggled the receiver beside her on the pillow.

"Mmm?" she mumbled.

"Susan?"

"Sir?" She recognized Banks's voice and tried to drag herself out of the arms of Morpheus. But she couldn't get very far. She frowned and rubbed sleep from her eyes. Waking up had always been a slow process for Susan, ever since she was a little girl.

"Sorry to wake you so early on a Sunday," Banks said, "but we got a suspicious death after closing time last night."

"Yes, sir." Susan raised herself from the sheets and propped herself against the pillows. "Suspicious death." She knew what that meant. Work. Now. The thin bedsheet slipped from her shoulders and left her breasts bare. Her nipples were hard from the morning chill in the bedroom. For a moment, she felt exposed talking to Banks while she was sitting up naked in bed. But he couldn't see her. She told herself not to be so daft.

"We've got scant little to go on," Banks went on. "We don't even know the victim's name yet. I need you down here as soon as you can make it."

"Yes, sir. I'll be right there."

Susan replaced the receiver, ran her fingers through her hair and got out of bed. She stood on her tiptoes and stretched her arms toward the ceiling until she felt the knots in her muscles crack, then she padded to the living room, pausing to note the thickness of her waist and thighs in the wardrobe mirror on her way. She would have to start that diet again soon. Before she went to take a shower, she started the coffeemaker and put some old Rod Stewart on the CD player to help her wake up.

As the hot water played over her skin, she thought of last night's date with Gavin Richards, a DC from Regional Headquarters. He had taken her to the Georgian Theatre in Richmond to see an Alan Bennett play, and after that they had found a cozy pub just off Richmond market square, where she had eaten cheese and onion crisps and drunk a half pint of cider.

Walking to her car, both of them huddled under her umbrella because it was raining fast and, like a typical man, Gavin hadn't bothered to carry one, she had felt his warmth, felt herself responding to it, and when he had asked her back to his house for a coffee she had almost said yes. Almost. But she wasn't ready yet. She wanted to. Oh, she wanted to. Especially when they kissed good-night by her car. It had been too long. But they had only been out together three times, and that was too soon for Susan. She might have sacrificed her personal life for her career over the last few years, but she wasn't about to hop into bed with the first tasty bloke who happened to come along.

When she noticed she had been standing in the shower so long that her skin had started to glow, she got out, dried herself off briskly and threw on a pair of black jeans and a polo-neck jumper that matched her eyes. She was lucky that her curly blond hair needed hardly any attention at all. She added a little gel to give it luster, then she was ready to go. Rod Stewart sang "Maggie Mae" as she sipped the last of her black, sugarless coffee and munched a slice of dry toast.

Still eating, she grabbed a light jacket from the hook and dashed out the door. It was only a five-minute drive to the station, and on another occasion she might have walked for the exercise. Especially this morning. It was a perfect autumn day: scrubbed blue skies and only the slightest chill in the air. The recent winds had already blown a few early lemon and russet leaves from the trees, and they squished under her feet as she walked to her car.

But today Susan paused only briefly to sniff the crisp air, then she got in her car and turned the key in the ignition. Her red Golf started on the first try. An auspicious beginning.

III

Banks leaned by his office window, his favorite spot, blew on the surface of his coffee and watched the steam rise as he looked out over the quiet market square. He was thinking about Sandra, about their marriage and the way it all seemed to be going wrong. Not so much wrong, just nowhere. She still hadn't spoken to him since the opera. Not that she'd had much chance, really, with him being out so late at the crime scene. And this morning she had barely been conscious by the time he left. But still, there was a discernible chill in the house.

Last night's rain had washed the excesses of Saturday night from the cobbles, just as the station cleaning staff disinfected and mopped out the cells after the overnight drunk-and-disorderlies had been discharged. The square and the buildings around it glowed pale gray-gold in the early light.

Banks had his window open a couple of inches, and the sound of the church congregation singing "We plough the fields, and scatter" drifted in. It took him back to the harvest festivals of his childhood, when his mum would give him a couple of apples and oranges to put in the church basket along with everyone else's. He often wondered what happened to all the fruit after the festival was over.

The "Dalesman" calendar on his wall showed Healaugh Church, near York, through a farm gate. It wasn't a particularly autumnal shot, Banks was thinking, as he heard the tap on his door.

It was Susan Gay, first to arrive after Detective Superintendent Gristhorpe, who was already busy coordinating with Regional HQ and arranging for local media coverage.

As usual, Susan looked fresh as a daisy, Banks thought. Just the right amount of makeup, blond curls still glistening from the shower. While no one would describe Susan Gay as an oil painting, with her small button nose and her serious, guarded expression, her clear, blue-gray eyes were intriguing, and she had a beautiful, smooth complexion.

Not for Susan, Banks thought, the wild, boozy Saturday nights favored by Jim Hatchley, who followed hot on her heels looking like death warmed over: eyes bleary and bloodshot, lips dry and cracked, a shred of toilet paper stuck over a shaving cut, thinning straw hair unwashed and uncombed for a couple of days.

After the two of them had sat down, both nursing cups of coffee, Banks explained how the boy had been killed, then he walked over to the map of Eastvale on the wall by his filing cabinet and pointed to the ginnel where the body had been discovered.

"This is where PC Ford found him," he began. "There are no through roads leading west nearby, so people tend to cut through the residential streets, then take the Carlaw Place ginnel over the recreation ground to King Street and the Leaview Estate. Thing is, it works both ways, so he could have been heading in either direction. We don't know."

"Sir," said Susan, "you told me on the telephone that he'd probably been killed shortly after closing time. If he'd been out drinking, isn't it more likely that he was heading *from* Market Street? I mean, that's quite a popular spot for young people on a Saturday night. There's a fair number of pubs, and some of them have live bands or karaoke."

Karaoke. Banks felt himself shudder at the thought. The only other words that had a similar effect on him were "country and western music." An oxymoron if ever there was one.

"Good point," he said. "So let's concentrate our survey on the

Market Street pubs and the Leaview Estate to start with. If we draw a blank there, we can extend the area."

"How much *do* we know, sir?" Sergeant Hatchley asked.

"Precious little. I've already had a look at the overnight logs, and there are no reports of any major shindigs. We've talked to the occupants of the terrace houses on both sides of the ginnel, as well as the people across the street. The only one with anything to say was watching television, so he didn't hear anything too clearly, but he was sure he did hear a fight or something outside during the Liverpool-Newcastle game on 'Match of the Day.'"

"What exactly did he hear, sir?" Susan asked.

"Just some scuffling and grunting, then the sound of people running away. He thought more than one, but he couldn't say how many. Or which direction. He thought it was just the usual drunken yobs, and he certainly had no intention of going outside and finding out for himself."

"You can hardly blame him, these days, can you?" said Sergeant Hatchley, picking gingerly at the tissue over his shaving cut. It started to bleed again. "Some of these yobs'd kill you as soon as look at you. Besides, it were a bloody good match."

"Anyway," Banks went on, "you'd better check with Traffic, too. We don't know for certain whether the attackers ran home or drove off. Maybe they got a parking ticket or got stopped for speeding."

"We should be so lucky," muttered Hatchley.

Banks pulled two sheets of paper from a folder on his desk and passed one each to Susan and Hatchley. It showed an artist's impression of a young man, probably in his early twenties, with thin lips and a long, narrow nose. His hair was cut short and combed neatly back. Despite his youth, it seemed to be receding at the temples and looked very thin on top. There was nothing particularly distinctive about him, but Banks thought he could perceive a hint of arrogance in the expression. Of course, that was probably just artistic license.

"The night-shift attendant at the mortuary came up with this," he said. "A few months back, he got bored with having no one to talk to on the job, so he started sketching corpses as a way of passing the time. 'Still lifes,' he calls them. Obviously a man of hidden talents. Anyway, he told us this was mostly speculation, especially the nose, which had been badly broken. The cheekbones had been fractured, too, so he was guessing about how high and how prominent they might have been. But the hair's right, he says, and the general shape of the head. It'll have to do for now. The only things we know for certain are that the victim was a little over six feet tall, weighed eleven stone, was in fine physical shape—an athlete, perhaps—and he had blue eyes and blond hair. No birthmarks, scars, tattoos or other distinguishing features." He tapped the folder. "We'll try to get this on the local TV news today and in the papers tomorrow morning. For now, you can start with the house-to-house, then, after opening time, you can canvass the pubs. Uniform branch has detailed four officers to help. Our first priority is to find out who the poor bugger was, and the second is to discover who he was last seen with before he was killed. Okay?"

They both nodded and stood up to leave.

"And take your mobiles or personal radios and stay in touch with one another. I want the right hand to know what the left hand's doing. All right?"

"Yes, sir," said Susan.

"As for me," said Banks with a grim smile, "Dr. Glendenning has kindly offered to come in and do the postmortem this morning, so I think one of us should pay him the courtesy of being present. Don't you?"

IV

A lot of detectives complained about house-to-house inquiries, much preferring to spend their time in scummy pubs with low-life informers, getting the *real* feel of the Job, or so they thought. But

Susan Gay had always enjoyed a good house-to-house. At the very least it was good exercise in patience.

Of course, you got the occasional nutter, the boor, and the lecherous creep with his Hound of the Baskervilles straining at the end of its chain. Once, even, a naked child had toddled out to see what was happening and peed all over Susan's new shoes. The mother had thought it hilarious.

Then there were those endless hours in the rain, wind and snow, knocking at door after door, your feet aching, the damp and chill fast seeping right into the marrow of your bones, wishing you'd chosen some other career, thinking even marriage and kids would be better than this.

And, needless to say, every now and then some clever-arse pillock would tell her she was too pretty to be a police*man,* or would suggest she could put her handcuffs on him anytime she wanted, ha-ha-ha. But that was all part of the game, and she didn't mind as much as she sometimes pretended she did to annoy Sergeant Hatchley. As far as Susan was concerned, the human race would always contain a large number of clever-arse pillocks, no matter what you thought. And the greatest percentage of them, in her experience, were likely to be men.

But on a fine morning like this, the valley sides beyond the town's western edge crisscrossed with limestone walls, slopes still lush green after the late-summer rains, and the purple heather coming into bloom up high, where the wild moorland began, it was as good a way as any to be earning your daily crust. And there was nothing like a house-to-house for getting to know your patch.

The morning chill had quickly given way to warmth, and Susan guessed Eastvale might hit seventy before the day was over. Indian summer, indeed. She took her jacket off and slung it over her shoulder. At that time of year in the Dales, any good day was a bonus not to be wasted. Tomorrow might come rain, flood and famine, so seize the moment. Children played football in the streets, or rode around on bicycles and skateboards; men with their shirtsleeves rolled up flung buckets of soapy water over their cars, then waxed them to perfection; groups of teenagers stood around street corners smoking, trying to look sullen and menacing, and failing on both counts; doors and windows stood open; some people even sat on their doorsteps reading the Sunday papers and drinking tea.

As Susan walked, she could smell meat roasting and cakes baking. She also heard snatches of just about every kind of music, from Crispian St. Peters singing "You Were on My Mind" to the opening of Elgar's Cello Concerto, which she only recognized because it was the same excerpt as the one on the CD she got free with her classical-music magazine last month.

The Leaview Estate had been built just after the war. The houses, a mix of bungalows, semis and terraces, were solid, their style and materials in harmony with the rest of Swainsdale's limestone and gritstone architecture. No ugly maisonettes or blocks of flats spoiled the skyline the way they did across town on the newer East Side Estate. And on the Leaview Estate, many of the streets were named after flowers.

It was almost noon, and Susan had already covered the Primroses, the Laburnums and the Roses without any luck. Now she was about to move on to the Daffodils and Buttercups. She carried a clipboard with her, carefully ticking off all the houses she visited, putting question marks and notes beside any responses she found suspicious, keeping a keen eye open for bruised knuckles and any other signs of recent pugilism. If someone wasn't home, she would circle the house number. After every street, she used her personal radio to report back to the station. If Hatchley or any of the uniformed officers got results first, then the communications center would inform her.

A boy came speeding around the corner of Daffodil Rise on Rollerblades, and Susan managed to jump out of the way in the nick of time. He didn't stop. She held her hand to her chest until her heartbeat slowed to normal and thought about arresting him on a traffic offense. Then the adrenaline ebbed away and she got her breath back. She rang the bell of number two.

The woman who answered was probably in her late fifties, Susan guessed. Nicely turned out: hair recently permed, only a touch of lipstick, face powder. Maybe just back from church. She wore a beige cardigan, despite the heat. As she spoke, she held it closed over her pale pink blouse.

"Yes, dearie?" she said.

Susan showed her warrant card and held out the mortuary attendant's sketch. "We're trying to find out who this boy is," she said. "We think he might live locally, so we're asking around to find out if anyone knows him."

The woman stared at the drawing, then tilted her head and scratched her chin.

"Well," she said. "It *could* be Jason Fox."

"Jason Fox?" It sounded like a pop star's name to Susan.

"Yes. Mr. and Mrs. Fox's young lad."

Well, Susan thought, tapping her pen against her clipboard, that's enlightening. "Do they live around here?"

"Aye. Just over the street." She pointed. "Number seven. But I only said it *might* be. It's not a good likeness, you know, love. You ought to get a proper artist working for you. Like my lad, Laurence. Now there's an artist for you. He sells his prints at the craft center in town, you know. I'm sure he —"

"Yes, Mrs. . . . ?"

"Ingram's the name. Laurence Ingram."

"I'll bear him in mind, Mrs. Ingram. Now, is there anything you can tell me about Jason Fox?"

"The nose isn't right. That's the main thing. Very good with noses, is my Laurence. Did Curly Watts from 'Coronation Street' down to a tee, and that's not an easy one. Did you know he'd done Curly Watts? Right popular with the celebrities is my Laurence. Oh, yes, very—"

Susan took a deep breath, then went on. "Mrs. Ingram, could you tell me if you've seen Jason Fox around lately?"

"Not since yesterday. But then he's never around much. Lives in Leeds, I think."

"How old is he?"

"I couldn't say for certain. He's left school, though. I know that."

"Any trouble?"

"Jason? No. Quiet as a mouse. As I said, you hardly ever see him around. But it *does* look like him except for the nose. And it's easy to get noses wrong, as my Laurence says."

"Thank you, Mrs. Ingram," said Susan, glancing over at number seven. "Thank you very much." And she hurried down the path.

"Wait a minute," Mrs. Ingram called after her. "Aren't you going to tell me what's happened? After all the help I've given you. Has summat happened to young Jason? Has he been up to summat?"

If Jason's the one we're looking for, Susan thought, then you'll find out soon enough. As yet, he was only a "possible," but she knew she had better inform Banks before barging in on her own. She went back to the corner of the street and spoke into her personal radio.

V

Banks walked quickly through the narrow streets of tourist shops behind the police station, then down King Street toward Daffodil Rise. Beyond the Leaview Estate, the town gradually dissolved into countryside, the sides of the valley narrowing and growing steeper the farther west they went.

Near Eastvale, Swainsdale was a broad valley, with plenty of room for villages and meadows, and for the River Swain to meander this way and that. But twenty or thirty miles in, around Swainshead, it was an area of high fells, much narrower and less hospitable to human settlements. One or two places, like Swainshead itself, and the remote Skield, managed to eke out an existence in the wild landscape around Witch Fell and Adam's Fell, but only just.

The last row of old cottages, Gallows View, pointed west like a crooked finger into the dale. Banks's first case in Eastvale had centered around those cottages, he remembered as he hurried on toward Daffodil Rise.

Graham Sharp, who had been an important figure in the case, had died of a heart attack over the summer, Banks had heard. He had sold his shop a few years ago, and it had been run since by the Mahmoods, whom Banks knew slightly through his son, Brian. He had seen them down at the station, too, recently; according to Susan, someone had lobbed a brick through their window a couple of weeks ago.

In what used to be empty fields around Gallows View, a new housing estate was under construction, scheduled for completion in a year's time. Banks could see the half-dug foundations scattered with puddles, the piles of bricks and boards, sun glinting on idle cranes and concrete mixers. One or two streets had been partially built, but none of the houses had roofs yet.

Number seven Daffodil Rise really stood out from the rest of the houses on the street. Not only had the owners put up a little white fence around the garden and installed a paneled, natural pine-look door, complete with a stained-glass windowpane (lunacy, Banks thought, so easy to break and enter), they also had one of the few gardens in the street that lived up to the flower motif. And because it had been a long summer, many of the flowers usually gone by the end of September were still in blossom. Bees droned around the red and yellow roses that still clung to their thorny bushes just under the front window, and the garden beds were a riot of chrysanthemums, dahlias, begonias and gladioli.

The front door was ajar. Banks tapped softly before walking in. He had told Susan Gay over the radio that she should talk to the parents and try to confirm whether the drawing might be of their son before he arrived, but not to tell them anything until he got there.

When Banks walked in, Mrs. Fox was just bringing a tea tray through from the kitchen into the bright, airy living room. Cut flowers in crystal vases adorned the dining table and the polished wood top of the fake-coal electric fire. Roses climbed trellises on the cream wallpaper. Over the fireplace hung a framed antique map of Yorkshire, the kind you can buy in tourist shops for a couple of quid. Along the narrowest wall stood floor-to-ceiling wooden shelving that seemed to be full of long-playing records.

Mrs. Fox was about forty, Banks guessed. Sandra's age. She wore a loose white top and black leggings that outlined her finely tapered legs, with well-toned calves and shapely thighs—the kind you only got at that age from regular exercise. She had a narrow face, and her features seemed cramped just a little too close together. Her hair was simply parted in the middle and hung down as far as her shoulders on each side, curling under just a little at the bottom. The roots were only a slightly darker shade of blond.

Mr. Fox stood up to shake hands with Banks. Bald except for a couple of black chevrons above his ears, with a thin, bony face, he wore black-rimmed glasses, jeans and a green sweatshirt. He was exceptionally skinny, which made him appear tall, and he looked as if he had the kind of metabolism that allowed him to eat as much as he wanted without putting on a pound. Banks wasn't quite as skinny himself, but he never seemed to put on much weight either, despite the ale and the junk food.

Tea poured, Mrs. Fox sat down on the sofa with her husband and crossed her long legs. Husband and wife left enough space for another person to sit between them, but Banks took a chair from the dining table, turned it around and sat, resting his arms on the back.

"Mr. and Mrs. Fox were just telling me," Susan Gay said, getting her notebook out, "that Jason looks like the lad in the drawing, and he didn't sleep here last night."

"She won't tell us anything." Mrs. Fox appealed to Banks with her small, glittering eyes. "Is our Jason in any trouble?"

"Has he ever been in trouble before?" Banks asked.

She shook her head. "Never. He's a good boy. He never caused us any problems, has he, Steven? That's why I can't understand you coming here. We've never had the police here before."

"Weren't you worried when Jason didn't sleep here last night?"

Mrs. Fox looked surprised. "No. Why should I be?"

"Weren't you expecting him?"

"Look, what's happened? What's going on?"

"Jason lives in Leeds, Chief Inspector," Steven Fox cut in. "He just uses our house when it suits him, a bit like a hotel."

"Oh, come on, Steven," his wife said. "You know that's not fair. Jason's grown up. He's got his own life to live. But he's still our son."

"When it suits him."

"What does he do in Leeds?" Banks cut in.

"He's got a good job," said Steven Fox. "And there's not many as can say that these days. An office job at a factory out in Stourton."

"I assume he's also got a flat or a house in Leeds, too?"

"Yes. A flat."

"Can you give DC Gay the address, please? And the name and address of the factory?"

"Of course." Steven Fox gave Susan the information.

"Do either of you know where Jason was last night?" Banks asked. "Or who he was with?"

Mrs. Fox answered. "No," she said. "Look, Chief Inspector, can't you please tell us what's going on? I'm worried. Is my Jason in trouble? Has something happened to him?"

"I understand that you're worried," Banks said, "and I'll do everything I can to hurry things up. Please bear with me, though, and answer just a few more short questions. Just a few more minutes. Okay?"

They both nodded reluctantly.

"Do you have a recent photograph of Jason?"

Mrs. Fox got up and brought a small framed photo from the sideboard. "Only this," she said. "He was seventeen when it was taken."

The boy in the photo looked similar to the victim, but it was impossible to make a positive identification. Teenagers can change a lot in three or four years, and heavy boots do a great deal of damage to facial features.

"Do you know what Jason did yesterday? Where he went?"

Mrs. Fox bit her lip. "Yesterday," she said. "He got home about twelve o'clock. We had sandwiches for lunch, then he went off to play football, like he usually does."

"Where?"

"He plays for Eastvale United," Steven Fox said.

Banks knew the team; they were only amateur players, but he'd taken Brian to see them once or twice, and they had demonstrated the triumph of enthusiasm over talent. Their matches had become quite popular with the locals, and they sometimes managed to draw two or three hundred to their bumpy field on a few acres of waste ground between York Road and Market Street.

"He's a striker," said Mrs. Fox with pride. "Top goal scorer in North Yorkshire last season. Amateur leagues, that is."

"Impressive," said Banks. "Did you see him after the game?"

"Yes. He came home for his tea after he'd had a quick drink with his mates from the team, then he went out about seven o'clock, didn't he, Steven?"

Mr. Fox nodded.

"Did he say whether he'd be back?"

"No."

"Does he normally stop here on weekends?"

"Sometimes," Mrs. Fox answered. "But not always. Sometimes he drives back to Leeds. And sometimes he doesn't come up at all."

"Does he have his own key?"

Mrs. Fox nodded.

"What kind of car does he drive?"

"Oh, my God, it's not a car crash, is it?" Mrs. Fox put her hands to her face. "Oh, please don't tell me our Jason's been killed in a car crash."

At least Banks could assure her of that honestly.

"It's one of those little Renaults," said Steven Fox. "A Clio. Bloody awful color, it is, too. Shiny green, like the back of some sort of insect."

"Where does he park when he's here?"

Mr. Fox jerked his head. "There's a double garage round the back. He usually parks it there, next to ours."

"Have you looked to see if the car's still there?"

"No. I'd no call to."

"Did you hear it last night?"

He shook his head. "No. We usually go to bed early. Before Jason gets back, if he's stopping the night. He tries to be quiet, and we're both pretty heavy sleepers."

"Would you be kind enough to show DC Gay where the garage is?" Banks asked Steve Fox. "And, Susan, if the car's there, see if he left the keys in it."

Steven Fox led Susan out through the back door.

"Does Jason have a girlfriend?" Banks asked Mrs. Fox while they were gone.

She shook her head. "I don't think so. He might have someone in Leeds, I suppose, but . . ."

"He never mentioned her or brought her here?"

"No. I don't think he had anyone steady."

"Do you think he would have told you if he had?"

"I can't see any reason why he wouldn't."

"How do you and Jason get along?"

She turned away. "We get along just fine."

Susan and Steven Fox came back from the garage. "It's there all right," Susan said. "A green Clio. I took the number. And no keys."

"What is it?" Mrs. Fox asked. "If Jason wasn't in a car crash, did he hit someone? Was there an accident?"

"No," said Banks. "He didn't hit anyone." He sighed and looked at the map over the fireplace. He couldn't really hold back telling them any longer. The best he could do was play up the uncertainty aspect. "I don't want to alarm you," he said, "but a boy was killed last night, probably in a fight. DC Gay showed you the artist's impression, and someone suggested it might resemble Jason. That's why we need to know his movements and whereabouts."

Banks waited for the outburst, but it didn't come. Instead, Mrs. Fox shook her head and said, "It *can't* be our Jason. He wouldn't get into fights or anything like that. And you can't really tell from the picture, can you?"

Banks agreed. "I'm sure you're right," he said. "He's probably gone off somewhere for the weekend with his mates without telling you. Kids. No consideration sometimes, have they? Would Jason do something like that?"

Mrs. Fox nodded. "Oh, yes. Never tells us owt, our Jason, does he, Steven?"

"That's right," Mr. Fox agreed. But Banks could tell from his tone that he wasn't quite as convinced as his wife about Jason's not being the victim. He wondered why. In his experience, mothers often held more illusions about their children than fathers did.

"Does Jason have any friends on the estate he might have gone out with?" Banks asked. "Anyone local?"

Mrs. Fox looked at her husband before answering. "No," she said. "See, we've only been living in Eastvale for three years. Since we moved from Halifax. Besides, Jason doesn't drink. Well, not hardly."

"When did he get this job in Leeds?"

"Just before we moved."

"I see," said Banks. "So he hasn't really spent much time here, had time to settle in and make friends?"

"That's right," said Mrs. Fox.

"Does he have any other relations in the area he might have gone to visit? An uncle, perhaps, someone like that?"

"Only my dad," said Mrs. Fox. "That's why we moved here, really, to be nearer my dad. My mam died two years ago, and he's not getting any younger."

"Where does he live?"

"Up in Lyndgarth, so he's not far away, in case of emergencies, like. Eastvale was the closest town Steven could get a transfer."

"What kind of work do you do, Mr. Fox?"

"Building society. Abbey National. That big branch on York Road, just north of the market square."

Banks nodded. "I know the one. Look, it's just a thought, but does Jason spend much time with his grandfather? Might he be stopping with him?"

Mrs. Fox shook her head. "He'd have let us know, Dad would. He's got a telephone. Didn't want one, but we insisted. Besides, Jason's car . . ."

"Would your father know anything more about Jason's friends and his habits?"

"I don't think so," said Mrs. Fox, fidgeting with her wedding ring. "They used to be close when Jason were a young lad, but you know what it's like when kids grow up." She shrugged.

Banks did. He well remembered preferring the company of his grandparents to that of his mother and father when he was young. They were more indulgent with him, for a start, and would often give him a tanner for sweets—which he'd usually spend on sherbet, gobstoppers and a three-penny lucky bag. He also liked his grandfather's pipe rack, the smell of tobacco around the dark-paneled house, the tarnished silver cigarette case with the dint where a German bullet had hit it, saving his grandfather's life—or so his grandfather had told him. He had loved the stories about the war—not the second, but the first—and his grandfather had even let him wear his old gas mask, which smelled of rubber and dust. They had spent days walking by the River Nene, standing by the railway tracks to watch the sleek, streamlined Flying Scotsman go by. But all that had changed when Banks entered his teens, and he felt especially guilty about not seeing his granddad for a whole year before the old man died while Banks was at college in London.

"Are there any other family members?" he asked. "Brothers or sisters?"

"Only Maureen, my daughter. She's just turned eighteen."

"Where is she?"

"Nurses' training school, up in Newcastle."

"Would she be able to help us with any of Jason's friends?"

"No. They're not particularly close. Never were. Different as chalk and cheese."

Banks glanced over at Susan and indicated she should put her notebook away. "Would you mind if we had a quick look at Jason's room?" he asked. "Just to see if there's anything up there that might help us find out what he was doing last night?"

Steven Fox stood up and walked toward the stairs. "I'll show you."

The tidiness of the room surprised Banks. He didn't know why—stereotyping, no doubt—but he'd been expecting the typical teenager's room, like his son Brian's, which usually looked as if it had just been hit by a tornado. But Jason's bed was made, sheets so tightly stretched across the mattress you could bounce a coin on them, and if he had dirty washing lying around, as Brian always had, then Banks couldn't see it.

Against one of the walls stood shelving similar to that down-stairs, also stacked with long-playing records and several rows of 45s.

"Jason likes music, I see," Banks said.

"Actually, they're mine," said Steven Fox, walking over and running his long fingers over a row of LPs. "My collection. Jason says it's okay to use the wall space because he's not here that often. It's mostly sixties stuff. I started collecting in 1962, when 'Love Me Do' came out. I've got everything The Beatles ever recorded, all originals, all in mint condition. And not only The Beatles. I've got all The Rolling Stones, Grateful Dead, Doors, Cream, Jimi Hendrix, The Searchers . . . If you can get it on vinyl, I've got it. But I don't suppose you're interested in all that."

Banks *was* interested in Mr. Fox's record collection, and on another occasion he would have been more than happy to look over the titles. Just because he loved opera and classical music in general didn't mean he looked down on rock, jazz or blues—only on country and western and brass bands. This latter opinion was regarded as a serious lapse of taste in Yorkshire, Banks was well aware, but he felt that anyone who had had to endure an evening of brass-band renditions of Mozart arias, as he once had, was more than entitled to it.

Apart from Steven Fox's record collection, the room was strangely Spartan, almost an ascetic's cell, and even on such a warm day it seemed to emanate the chill of the cloister. There was only one framed print on the wall, and it showed a group of three naked women. According to the title, they were supposed to be Norse goddesses, but they looked more like bored housewives to Banks. There was no television or video, no stereo and no books. Maybe he kept most of his things in his flat in Leeds.

Steven Fox stood in the doorway as Banks and Susan started poking around the spotless corners. The dresser drawers were full of underclothes and casual wear—jeans, sweatshirts, T-shirts. By the side of the bed lay a set of weights. Banks could just about lift them, but he didn't fancy doing fifty bench presses.

In the wardrobe, he found Jason's football strip, a couple of very conservative suits, both navy blue, and some white dress shirts and sober ties. And that was it. So much for any clues about Jason Fox's life and friends.

Back downstairs, Mrs. Fox was pacing the living room, gnawing at her knuckles. Banks could tell she was no longer able to keep at bay the terrible realization that something bad might have happened to her son. After all, Jason hadn't come home, his car was still in the garage, and now the police were in her house. A part of Banks hoped, for her sake, that the victim wasn't Jason. But there was only one way to find that out for certain.

TWO

I

Frank Hepplethwaite reached for his inhaler, aimed it at the back of his throat and let off a blast of nitro. Within seconds the pain in his chest began to abate, along with that suffocating sense of panic that always came with it.

Frank sat completely still in his favorite armchair, the one that Edna had been constantly nagging him to get rid of. True, the seat cushion was worn, and it bulged like a hernia through the support slats underneath; and true, the frayed upholstery had long since lost whatever pattern it might have had and faded to a sort of dull brown with a worn, greasy spot where he had rested the back of his head year after year. But he had never found anywhere else quite so comfortable to sit and read in all his seventy-six years—and though he was seventy-six, his eyes were as good as they'd ever been. Well, almost, if he put his reading glasses on. Better than his teeth and his heart, at any rate.

When he felt steady enough again, he rested his palms on the threadbare patches of fabric and pushed himself up, slowly, to standing position. Five foot ten in his stockinged feet, and he still weighed no more than ten stone.

Face it, though, Frank, he told himself as he wrapped his scarf around his neck and reached for his tweed jacket on the hook behind the door, you won't be able to go on like this by yourself much longer. Even now, Mrs. Weston came in once or twice a week to tidy up and make his meals. And his daughter Josie came over from Eastvale to do his washing and to vacuum.

He could still manage the little domestic tasks, like boiling an egg, washing what few dishes he used, and remaking his bed in the morning—but he couldn't change the sheets, and any sort of elaborate meal was well beyond him. Not that he lacked the ability—he had been a passable cook in his time—he merely lacked the stamina. And for how much longer would he be able to manage even the little necessities? How long would it be before a simple visit to the toilet was beyond him, a bowel movement too much of a strain on his heart?

Best not think about that, he told himself, sensing the abyss that awaited him. Beyond this point be monsters. At least Edna had gone first, bless her soul, and while he missed her every minute he continued to live, at least he wouldn't have to worry about her coping after he'd gone.

Frank went into the hall and paused at the front door. He rarely got any letters these days, so he was surprised to see one lying on the carpet. It must have arrived yesterday, Saturday. He hadn't been out since Friday, hadn't even had cause to go into the hall, so it was no wonder he hadn't noticed it. Bending carefully, knees creaking, he picked it up and slipped it in his inside pocket. It could wait. It wasn't a bill. At least, it didn't look official; it didn't have one of those windows.

He opened the door, sniffed the air and smiled. Well, well, another taste of summer, with just a hint of peat smoke from the village. What strange weather the dale had been having these past few years. Global warming, the papers said, damage to the ozone layer, greenhouse effect. Whatever all that was. Bloody grand, anyway.

He decided to be devil-may-care today and took off his scarf, then he walked down the road toward the green, pausing by the whitewashed facade of the Swainsdale Heifer to watch out for traffic hurtling across the blind corner, the way it did despite the warning signs. Then he walked on the broad cobbled area in front of the gift shop, the small Barclay's Bank branch and the estate agent's office, past the King's Head to the third pub in the village, the Black Bull.

It would have to be the bloody farthest pub from his house, he always grumbled to himself, but the Black Bull had been his local for over forty years, and he was damned if he was going to change it now, even if the walk did sometimes put him out of breath. And even if the new landlord didn't seem to give a toss for anyone but tourists with plenty of readies to flash around.

Frank had seen a dozen landlords come and go. He was all right in his way, was old Jacob—a London Jew born of one of the few families lucky enough to escape to England from Germany just before the war—and he had his living to make, but he was a tight old skinflint. A drink or two on the house now and then would make an old man's pension go a lot farther. The last landlord had understood that. Not Jacob. He was as close with his brass as old Len Metcalfe had been over ten years back.

Frank pushed the heavy door, which creaked as it opened, and walked across the worn stone flagging to the bar. "Double Bell's, please," he said.

"Hello, there, Frank," said Jacob. "How are you today?"

Frank touched his chest. "Just a twinge or two, Jacob," he said. "Just a twinge. Other than that I'm right as rain."

He took his drink and wandered over to his usual small table to the left of the bar, where he could see down the corridor to the machines and the billiard table on the raised area at the far end. As usual, he said hello to Mike and Ken, who were sitting on stools at the bar agonizing over a crossword puzzle, and to that poncy southern windbag, Clive, who was sitting a stool or two down from them puffing on his bloody pipe and pontificating about sheep breeding, as if he knew a bloody thing about it. A few of the other tables were occupied by tourists, some of them kitted out for a day's walking or climbing. It was Sunday, after all. And a fine one, at that.

Frank took a sip of Bell's, winced at the sharpness and hoped the burning he felt as it went down was just the whiskey, not the final heart attack. Then he remembered the letter he had put in his pocket. He put on his reading glasses, reached his hand in and slipped it out.

The address was handwritten, and there was no indication of who had sent it. He didn't recognize the writing, but then he hardly ever saw handwriting these days. Everything you got was typed or done on computers. He couldn't make out the postmark clearly, either, but it looked like Brighouse, or maybe Bradford. It could even be Brighton or Bristol, for all he knew. Posted on Thursday.

Carefully, he tore the envelope open and slid out the single sheet of paper. It had type on both sides, in columns, and a large bold heading across the top. At first he thought it was a flyer for a jumble sale or something, but as he read, he realized how wrong he was.

Confused at first, then angry, he read the printed words. Long before he had finished, tears came to his eyes. He told himself they were Scotch tears, just the burning of the whiskey, but he knew they weren't. He also knew who had sent him the flyer. And why.

II

Some of the more modern mortuaries were equipped with video cameras and monitor screens to make it easier for relatives to identify accident or murder victims from a comfortable distance. Not in Eastvale, though. There, the attendant still slid the body out of the refrigerated unit and slipped back the sheet from the face.

Which was odd, Banks thought, as the mortuary was certainly the most recently renovated part of that drafty old pile of stone known as Eastvale General Infirmary.

Steven and Josie Fox had at first been unwilling to come and view the body. Banks could see their point. If it *was* Jason, they would have to face up to his death; and if it *wasn't,* then they would have gone through all the unpleasantness of looking at a badly beaten corpse for nothing.

Reluctantly, though, they had gone, refusing Banks's offer of a police car and choosing to walk instead. Susan Gay had returned to the station.

Because the hospital was small and old and too close to the tourist shops, another, much larger, establishment was under construction on the northern edge of the town. But, for now, Eastvale General was all there was. Every time he walked up the front steps, Banks shuddered. There was something about the dark, rough stone, even on a fine day, that made him think of operations without anesthetic, of unsterilized surgical instruments, of plague and death.

He led the Foxes through the maze of high corridors and down the stairs to the basement, where the mortuary was. Banks identified himself to one of the attendants, who nodded, checked his files and touched Mrs. Fox lightly on the arm. "Please, follow me," he said.

They did. Along a white-tiled corridor into a chilled room. There, the attendant checked his papers again before sliding out the tray on which the body lay.

Banks watched the Foxes. They weren't touching one another at all, not holding hands or clutching arms the way many couples did when faced with such a situation. Could there really be such distance between them that even the possibility of seeing their son dead at any second couldn't bridge? It was remarkable, Banks had often thought, how people who no longer have any feelings for one another can keep on going through the motions, afraid of change, of loneliness, of rejection. He thought of Sandra, then pushed the thought aside. He and Sandra were nothing like the Foxes. They weren't so much separate as *independent;* they gave one another space. Besides, they had too much in common, had shared too much joy and pain over the years simply to go through the motions of a failed marriage, hadn't they?

The attendant pulled back the white sheet to reveal the corpse's face. Josie Fox put her hand to her mouth and started to sob. Steven Fox, pale as the sheet that covered his son, simply nodded and said, "It's him. It's our Jason."

Banks was surprised at what a good job the mortuary had done on the boy's face. While it was clear that he had been severely beaten, the nose was straight, the cheekbones aligned, the mouth shut tight to cover the shattered teeth. The only wrong note was the way that one eye stared straight up at the ceiling and the other a little to the left, at Mr. and Mrs. Fox.

Banks could never get over the strange effect looking at dead people had on him. Not bodies at the crime scene so much. They sometimes churned his guts, especially if the injuries were severe, but they were essentially *work* to him; they were human beings robbed of something precious, an insult to the sanctity of life.

On the other hand, when he saw bodies laid out in the mortuary or in a funeral parlor, they had a sort of calming effect on him. He couldn't explain it, but as he looked down at the shell of what had once been Jason Fox, he knew there was nobody home. The pale corpse resembled nothing more than a fragile eggshell, and if you tapped it hard enough it would crack open, revealing nothing but darkness inside. Somehow, the effect of all this was to relieve him, just for a few welcome moments, of his own growing fear of death.

Banks led the dazed Foxes out into the open air. They stood on the steps of the hospital for a moment, silently watching the people come out of the small Congregationalist church.

Banks lit a cigarette. "Is there anything I can do?" he asked.

After a few moments, Steven Fox looked at him. "What? Oh, sorry," he said. Then he shook his head. "No, there's nothing. I'll take Josie home now. Make her a nice cup of tea."

His wife said nothing.

They walked down King Street, still not touching. Banks sighed and turned up toward the station. At least he knew who the victim was now; first, he would let his team know, and then they could begin the investigation proper.

III

Detective Sergeant Jim Hatchley would normally have enjoyed nothing more than a pub crawl any day of the week, any hour of the day or night, but that Sunday, all he wanted to do as he walked into his fifth pub, the Jubilee, at the corner of Market Street and Waterloo Road, was go home, crawl into bed and sleep for a week, a month—nay, a bloody year.

For the past two weeks, his daughter April, named after the month she was born because neither Hatchley nor his wife Carol could agree on any other name, had kept him awake all night, every night, as those bloody inconvenient lumps of calcium called teeth bored their way through the tender flesh of her gums with flagrant disregard for the wee bairn's comfort. Or for his. And he hadn't been well-enough prepared for it. In fact, he hadn't been prepared for it at all.

The first year or so of April's life, you would never have known she was there, so quiet was she. At worst, she'd cry out a couple of times when she was hungry, but as soon as Carol's tit was in her mouth she was happy as a pig in clover. And why not, thought Hatchley, who felt exactly the same way about Carol's tit himself, not that he'd been getting much of *that* lately, either.

But now April had suddenly turned into a raging monster and put paid to his sleep. He knew he looked as if he'd been on the piss every morning he went into work—he could see the way they were all looking at him—but if truth be told, he hadn't had a drink in weeks. A real drink in a pub, that was.

He remembered some story, an old wife's tale, probably, about rubbing whiskey on a teething baby's gums to quieten it down. Well, Carol wouldn't let him do that—she said she had enough on her plate with one boozer in the family—so he had rubbed it on his own gums, so to speak, or rather let it caress them briefly and gently on its way down to his stomach. Sometimes that helped him get a ten-minute nap between screaming sessions. But he never had more than two or three glasses a night. He hadn't had a hangover in so long that not only had he almost forgotten what they felt like, he was actually beginning to miss them.

So it was with both a sense of nostalgia and a feeling that he'd rather be anywhere else, especially asleep in bed, that Sergeant Hatchley entered the Jubilee that Sunday lunchtime.

Contrary to rumors around the station, Hatchley didn't know the landlord of every pub in Eastvale. Apart from the Queen's Arms, the station's local, he tended to avoid the pubs near the town center, especially those on Market Street, which always seemed to be full of yobs. If there was trouble on a Saturday night, which there often was these days, you could bet it would be on York Road or Market Street.

The Jubilee was also a chain pub: all fruit machines, theme nights, trivia and overpriced food. Overpriced ale, too. Rock bands played there on Friday and Saturday nights, and it had a reputation for getting some of the best up-and-coming bands in Yorkshire. Not that Hatchley gave a toss about rock music, being a brass-band man himself. The Jubilee was also reputed to be a fertile hunting ground for birds and drugs.

On Sunday lunchtimes, though, it became a family pub, and each family seemed to have about six children in tow. All of them screaming at once.

Hatchley leaned over the bar and presented his warrant card to the barmaid as she pulled someone a pint.

"Any trouble here Saturday night, love?" he asked.

She jerked her head without looking up at him. "Better ask His Nibs over there. I weren't working."

Hatchley edged down the bar and shoved his way through the drinkers standing there, getting a few dirty looks on the way. He finally caught the barman's attention and asked for a word. "Can't you see I'm rushed off my feet?" the man protested. "What is it you want?" Like everyone else behind the bar, he wore black trousers and a blue-and-white-striped shirt with THE JUBILEE stitched across the left breast.

When Hatchley showed his card, the man stopped protesting that he was too busy and called one of the other bar staff to stand in for him, then he gestured Hatchley down to the far end of the bar where it was quiet.

"Sorry about that," he said. "I hate bloody Sunday lunchtimes, especially after working a Saturday night." He scratched his thinning hair and a shower of dandruff fell on his shoulders. How bloody hygienic, Hatchley thought. "My name's Ted, by the way."

"Aye, well, Ted, lad," Hatchley said slowly, "I'm sorry to disturb you, but we all have our crosses to bear. First off, was there any trouble in here on Saturday night?"

"What do you mean, trouble?"

"Fights, barneys, slanging matches, hair-pulling, that sort of thing."

Ted frowned. "Nowt out of the ordinary," he said. "I mean, we were busy as buggery, so there was no way I could see what were going on everywhere at once, especially with the bloody racket that band were making."

"I appreciate that," said Hatchley, who had had the same conversation five times already that morning and was getting steadily sick of it. He slipped the sketch from his briefcase. "Recognize him?" he asked.

The barman squinted at the drawing, then passed it back to Hatchley. "Could be any number of people, couldn't it?"

Hatchley wasn't sure why, but he felt the back of his scalp prickle. Always a sign something wasn't quite right. "Aye, but it's not," he said. "It's an amateur artist's reconstruction of a lad's face, a face that were booted to a bloody pulp after closing time last night. So any help you could give us would be much appreciated, Ted."

Ted turned pale and averted his eyes before answering. "Well, seeing as you put it like that . . . But I'm telling you the truth. Nothing happened."

Hatchley shook his head. "Why don't I find myself believing you, Ted? Can you answer me that?"

"Look." Ted held his hand up, palm out. "I don't want any trouble."

Hatchley smiled, showing stained and crooked teeth. "And I'm not here to give you any."

"It's just . . ."

"Frightened of something?"

"No. It's not that." Ted licked his lips. "I mean, I wouldn't want to swear to owt, but there were a lad looked a bit like that in last night. It could've been him."

"What was he doing?"

"Having a drink with a mate."

"What did this mate look like?"

"About my height. That's five foot six. Stocky build. Tough-looking customer, you know, like he lifted weights or summat. Short fair hair, almost skinhead, but not quite. And an earring. One of them loops, like pirates used to have in old films."

"Had you seen them before?"

"Only the one in the drawing, if it is him. Sometimes comes in on a weekend after a match, like, just for a quick one with the lads. Plays for United."

"Aye, so I've heard. Troublemaker?"

"No. Not at all. Not even much of a boozer. He's usually gone early. It's just . . ." Ted scratched his head again, sending more flakes of dandruff onto the polished bar. "There was a bit of a scuffle Saturday night, that's all."

"No punches?"

He shook his head. "Far as I can tell, the lad in the picture bumped into another lad and spilled some of his drink. The other lad said something and this one replied, like, and gave him a bit of a shove for good measure. That's all that happened. Honest. Pushing and shoving. It were all over before it began. Nobody got beat up."

"Could it have continued outside?"

"I suppose it could have. As I said, though, it seemed like summat and nowt to me."

"This other lad, the one whose drink got spilled, did he have any mates with him?"

"There were three of them."

Hatchley pointed to the sketch again. "Did you see this lad and his mate leave?"

"Aye. I remember them because I had to remind them more than once to drink up."

"Were they drunk?"

"Mebbe. A bit. They weren't arse over tit, if that's what you mean. They could still walk in a straight line and speak without slurring. Like I said, I'd seen the one in the picture a few times before, and he weren't much of a drinker. He might have had a jar more than usual, but who hasn't had by closing time on a Saturday night?"

"And it wasn't till after eleven o'clock that you got rid of them, right?"

"Aye. About quarter past. I know some places are a bit lax, but there's no extension of drinking-up time in the Jubilee. The manager makes that clear."

"What about the other three?"

"They'd gone by then."

"Were they drunk, too?"

"No. At least they didn't act it."

"Anything else you can tell me about them?"

Ted looked away.

"Why do I get the impression you're still holding something back, Ted?"

"I don't know, do I?"

"I think you do. Is it drugs? Worried we'll close the place down and you'll lose your job?"

"No way. Look, like I said . . . I don't want to cause any bother."

"What makes you think you'd be causing bother by telling me the truth, Ted? All right. Let me guess. If it's not drugs, then you're probably frightened these three hooligans are going to come back and wreck your pub if they find out you ratted on them. Is that it?"

"Partly, I suppose. But they weren't hooligans."

"Oh? Who were they, then? Did you recognize them?"

"Aye. I recognized them. Two of them, anyroad."

"Names?"

"I don't know their names, but one of them's that lad from the shop off Cardigan Road. You know, the one opposite the bottom of the Leaview Estate. And the other one's dad owns that new restaurant in the market square. The Himalaya."

Hatchley raised his eyebrows.

"See what I mean?" Ted went on. "See what I'm worried about, now? I don't want to get stuck in the middle of some bloody racial incident, do I? The lad in your picture called one of them a 'Paki bastard' and told him to get out of the fucking way. That's what happened."

IV

Gallows View, *déjà vu,* Banks thought, as he pulled up outside the Mahmoods' shop. Of course, the street had changed a lot in six years, and the wire mesh that covered the display windows was one of the changes. Inside, the smell of cumin and coriander was another.

The Mahmoods were one of three Asian families in Eastvale. In these parts of Yorkshire north of Leeds and Bradford you saw very few visible minorities, even in the larger cities like York and Harrogate.

Mahmood had enlarged the shop, Banks noticed. Originally, it had occupied the ground floor of only one cottage, and the Sharps had used the other as their living room. But now the shop had been extended to take up the frontage of both cottages, complete with extra plateglass window and a new freezer section. The Mahmoods sold a whole range of products, from bread, eggs, cigarettes, milk and beer to washing-up liquid, tights, magazines, lipstick, stationery and toothpaste. They also rented out videos. Pretty soon, when the new estate was finished, the shop would be a little gold mine.

Unlike most people the racist bigots refer to as "Pakis," Charles Mahmood actually did hail from Pakistan. Or rather, his father, Wasim Mahmood, did. Wasim and family emigrated to England in 1948, shortly after partition. Charles was born in Bradford in 1953, around the time of Queen Elizabeth's coronation, and he was, naturally, given the name of her only male child because the Mahmoods were proud of their new country and its royal heritage.

Unfortunately for Charles, when his own son was born in 1976, the Prince of Wales had yet to marry and produce offspring. To name his child, Charles had to take the devious route of stealing one of the prince's middle names. He chose George. Why he didn't choose Philip, which might have been easier on the lad at school, nobody knew. As for George himself, he said he was only glad his dad hadn't called him Arthur, which would have seemed even more old-fashioned than George to his classmates.

Banks knew all this because George had been a contemporary of his own son, Brian, at Eastvale Comprehensive, and the two had become good friends during their last couple of years there. George had spent quite a bit of time at the Banks household, and

Banks remembered his love of music, his instinctive curiosity about things and his sense of humor. They had all laughed at the story of the family names, for example.

Now the kids seemed to have lost touch, drifted apart as people do, and Banks hadn't seen George for a while. Brian had just started his third year at college in Portsmouth, and George was still in Eastvale, pretty much unemployed, as far as Banks knew, apart from helping his dad out at the shop. Even though they hadn't see one another in a while, Banks still felt a little uneasy about interviewing George in connection with a criminal matter.

Charles Mahmood greeted Banks with a smile of recognition; his wife, Shazia, waved from the other side of the shop, where she was stacking shelves with jars of instant coffee.

"Is it about that brick-chucking?" asked Charles in his broad West Yorkshire accent.

Banks told him it wasn't, but assured him that the matter was still under investigation.

"What's up, then?" Charles asked.

"George in?"

"George?" He flicked his head. "Upstairs. Why, what's happened?" Banks didn't think she could have heard, but Shazia Mahmood had stopped putting jars on shelves and seemed to be trying to eavesdrop.

"We don't know yet," Banks said. "There's nothing to worry about. I'd just like to talk to him. Okay?"

Charles Mahmood shrugged. "Fine with me."

"How's he doing these days?"

Charles nodded toward the stairs. "You'd better ask him. See for yourself. He's in his room."

"Problems?"

"Not really. Just a phase he's going through. Another seven-day wonder."

Banks smiled, remembering the way his father used to say that about every hobby he took up, from Meccano to stamp collecting. He'd been right, too. Banks still felt that he lurched restlessly from interest to interest. "What particular phase is this one?" he asked.

"You'll find out soon enough."

"I'd better go talk to him, then," said Banks. "The curiosity's killing me."

He walked upstairs, aware of Shazia Mahmood's eyes drilling into his back, and didn't realize until he got to the top that he didn't know *which* room was George's. But it didn't matter by then. At the end of the hallway, beside the bathroom, a door stood slightly ajar, and from inside the room Banks could smell sandalwood incense and hear piano music.

It was jazz, certainly, but not Monk, Bill Evans or Bud Powell. No one like that. It didn't even resemble the wild flights of Cecil Taylor, one of whose records Banks had made the mistake of buying years ago on the strength of a review from a usually reliable critic. This music was repetitive and rhythmic, a sort of catchy, jangling melodic riff played over and over again with very few changes. It was vaguely familiar.

He tapped on the door and George Mahmood opened it. George was a good-looking boy with thick black hair, long eyelashes and loam-brown eyes. He looked at Banks a moment, then said, "You're Brian's dad, aren't you? The copper."

It wasn't exactly the warm welcome Banks had hoped for; he had thought George might have remembered him with more affection. Still, attitudes change a lot in three years, especially when you're young. He smiled. "Right. That's me. The copper. Mind if I come in?"

"Is this a social call?"

"Not exactly."

"I didn't think so." George stood aside. "Better come in, anyway. I don't suppose I could stop you even if I wanted."

Banks entered the bedroom and sat on a hardback chair at

the desk. George slouched in an armchair. But not before he had turned down the music a couple of notches. He was wearing baggy black trousers and a white top with a Nehru collar.

"Who is that playing?" Banks asked.

"Why?"

"I like it."

"It's Abdullah Ibrahim. He's a South African pianist."

Now that George mentioned the name, Banks realized he had heard of Ibrahim and his music before. "Didn't he used to be called Dollar Brand?" he asked.

"That's right. Just like Muhammed Ali used to be called Cassius Clay."

Banks hadn't heard of Cassius Clay in years, and he was surprised that someone as young as George had ever heard of Ali's old name at all. They made a little uneasy small talk about Brian, then Banks got quickly to the point he had come for. "George," he said, "I've come to ask you about Saturday night."

"What about it?" George looked away toward the window. "And my name's not George anymore. That's a stupid name, just my father's post-Colonial genuflection. My name's Mohammed Mahmood."

As he spoke, George turned to look at Banks again and his eyes shone with defiant pride. Now Banks saw what Charles Mahmood meant. Now it made sense: Dollar Brand/Abdullah Ibrahim, the Koran lying on the bedside table. George was exploring his Islamic roots.

Well, Banks told himself, be tolerant. Not all Muslims support death threats against writers. He didn't know much about the religion, but he supposed there must be as many different forms of Islam as there are of Christianity, which runs a pretty broad spectrum if you include the Sandemanians, the Methodists, the Quakers and the Spanish Inquisition.

Why, then, did he feel so uncomfortable, as if he had lost someone he had known? Not a close friend, certainly, but a person he had liked and had shared things with. Now he was excluded—he could see it in George's eyes—he was the enemy. There would be no more music, laughter or understanding. Ideology had come between them, and it would rewrite history and deny that the music, laughter and understanding had ever happened in the first place. Banks had been through it once before with an old school friend who had become a born-again Christian. They no longer spoke to one another. Or, more accurately, Banks no longer spoke to *him*.

"Okay, Mohammed," he said, "did you go to the Jubilee with a couple of mates on Saturday night?"

"What if I did?"

"I thought Muslims weren't supposed to drink?"

Banks could swear he saw George blush. "I don't," he answered. "Well, not much. I'm stopping."

"Who were you with?"

"Why?"

"Is there any reason you don't want to tell me?"

George shrugged. "No. It doesn't matter. I was with Asim and Kobir."

"Are they from around here?"

"Asim is. Asim Nazur. His dad owns the Himalaya. They live in the flat above it."

"I know the place," said Banks, who had eaten there on more than one occasion. He also knew that Asim Nazur's father was some sort of bigwig in the Yorkshire Muslim community. "And the other lad?"

"Kobir. He's Asim's cousin from Bradford. He was just visiting, so we took him out to listen to some music, that's all. Look, why are—"

"What time did you leave the pub?"

"I wasn't looking at my watch."

"Before closing time?"

"Yes."

"Where did you go?"

"We bought some fish and chips at Sweaty Betty's, just down Market Street, then we ate them in a shop doorway because it were pissing down. After that we went home. Why?"

"You went your separate ways?"

"Course we went separate ways. You'd have to do, wouldn't you, if you lived in opposite directions?"

"Which way did you walk home?"

"Same way I always do from up there. Cut through the Carlaw Place ginnel over the rec."

"What time would this be?"

"I'm not sure. Probably elevenish by then."

"Not later?"

"No. A bit before, if anything. The pubs hadn't come out."

"Mum and Dad still up?"

"No, they were asleep when I got back. They close the shop at ten on a Saturday. They'd been up since before dawn."

"Did you see anyone on your way?"

"Not that I remember."

"Doesn't it worry you, walking alone across the rec at night?"

"Not particularly. I can handle myself."

"Against how many?"

"I've been taking lessons. Martial arts."

"Since when?"

"Since some bastard chucked a brick through our window and cut me mum. *They* might accept what's going on, but I won't."

"What do you mean, 'what's going on'?"

There was scorn in his voice. "Racism. Pure and simple. We live in a racist society. It doesn't matter that I was born here, and my mum and dad before me, it's the color of your skin people judge you on."

"Not everyone."

"Shows how much you know. The police are part of it, anyway."

"Geor— sorry, Mohammed, I didn't come here to argue the

politics of racism with you. I came to find out about your movements on Saturday."

"So what's happened? Why are you picking on me?"

"I understand there was an altercation in the Jubilee?"

"Altercation?"

"Yes. A disagreement."

"I know what it means. I'm not some ignorant wog just got off
the boat, you know. I'm trying to remember. Do you mean that
stupid pillock who bumped into me and called me a Paki bastard?"

"That's right."

"So what?"

"What do you mean, 'So what?' You're telling me you just let it
go at that? You? With all your martial-arts training?"

George puffed up his chest. "Well, I was all for doing the pair of
them over, but Asim and Kobir didn't want any trouble."

"So you just let it go by, a racial slur like that?"

"When you look like I do, you get used to it."

"But you were angry?"

George leaned forward and rested his palms on his knees. "Of
course I were bloody angry. Every time you hear something like
that said about you, you just get filled with anger and indignation.
You feel dehumanized." He shrugged. "It's not something you'd
understand."

"Because I'm white?"

George slumped back in his chair. "You said it."

"But you listened to your friends this time?"

"Yes. Besides, we were in a crowded pub. Just about everyone
else in the place was white, apart from a couple of Rastas selling
drugs. And the last thing those bastards would do was come to our
aid if anything happened. They'd probably join in with the whiteys."

"What made you think they were selling drugs?"

"That's what they do, isn't it?"

Talk about racism, Banks thought. He moved on. "Did you
know the lad who insulted you?"

"I've seen him around once or twice. Arrogant-looking pillock, always looked down his nose at me. Lives on the Leaview Estate, I think. Why? You going to arrest him for racism?"

"Not exactly," said Banks. "He's dead."

George's jaw dropped. "He's wha—?"

"He's dead, Mohammed. His name was Jason Fox. Someone unknown, or several someones unknown, kicked seven shades of shit out of him in the Carlaw Place ginnel sometime after eleven o'clock last night."

"Well, it wasn't me."

"Are you sure? Are you sure you weren't so upset by what Jason called you that you and your friends waited in the ginnel? You just admitted you knew Jason lived on the Leaview Estate, so it would be a pretty good guess that he'd take the same short cut home as you, wouldn't it? You waited there, the three of you, and when Jason came along, you gave him what-for. I'm not saying you in-tended to kill him, just teach him a lesson. But he *is* dead, George, and there's no remedy for that."

George looked so stunned he didn't even bother to correct Banks over his name. "I'm not saying owt more," he said. "I want a solicitor. This is a fit-up."

"Come on, George. It doesn't have to be like this."

"Like hell it doesn't. If you're accusing me and my mates of killing someone, then you'd better arrest us. *And* get us a lawyer. And I told you, my name's Mohammed, not George."

"Look, Mohammed, if I do what you're asking, I'll have to take you down to the station. And your mates."

George stood up. "Do it then. I'm not afraid. If you think I'm a killer you'd be taking me anyway, wouldn't you?"

Oh, bloody hell, Banks thought. He didn't want to do this, but the silly bugger had left him no choice. He stood up. "Come on, then," he said. "And we'd better take the shoes and clothes you wore last night along with us too."

THREE

I

The crosswinds on the A1 just south of Aberford almost blew Banks off the road. He felt relieved at last when he was able to edge out from between the two juggernauts that had him sandwiched and exit onto Wakefield Road.

It was another of those changeable days, with gale-force winds blowing a series of storms from the west. Between the bouts of rain, the sky would brighten, and Banks had even seen a double rainbow near the Ripon turnoff.

Even though Wakefield Road was busy, Banks still felt able to relax a little after the ordeal of the A1. He had been playing a Clifford Brown tape, finding the sound of the trumpet suited the weather, but he had hardly been able to listen for concentrating on the road. "The Ride of the Valkyries" would have been more apt for his drive so far, with the big vans and lorries spraying up dirty rain all over his windscreen. Now, however, he found "Gertrude's Bounce" a fine accompaniment for the wind blowing the leaves off the distant trees.

It was Monday morning, and Banks was on his way to Leeds to talk to Jason Fox's employer. George Mahmood and his friends were in custody at Eastvale station, where they could be kept for another six or seven hours yet, all claiming racial discrimination and refusing to say anything.

Though Banks felt sorry for them, especially for George, he was also bloody irritated by their attitude. And it was Jason Fox who deserved his pity, he reminded himself, not the cowardly bastards who had booted him to death. *If* they had done it. Banks couldn't see George Mahmood as a killer, but then he had to admit he was prejudiced. And George had changed. Nevertheless, he was willing to keep an open mind until an eyewitness or forensic evidence tipped the balance one way or the other. In the meantime, he needed to know more about Jason Fox's life, starting with where he worked and where he lived. He could have phoned the factory, but he really wanted a face-to-face chat with someone who knew something about Jason.

Banks entered the industrial landscape of southeast Leeds. He turned down Clifford Brown and concentrated on traffic lights and directions as he headed toward Stourton.

Just off Pontefract Road, he found the long, fenced laneway that led to the plastics factory where Jason had worked. Ahead, the horizon was a jumble of factory buildings and warehouses. A row of power-station cooling towers, the hourglass shape of which always reminded Banks of old corsets adverts, spewed out gray smoke into the already gray air. Between the factories and the power station ran the sluggish River Aire, delivering its load of industrial effluent to the Humber estuary and the North Sea beyond.

Banks identified himself to the guard at the gate and asked where he could find the Personnel Department. "Human Resources," the guard told him, pointing. "Over there."

He should have known. Everyone used to call it Personnel a few years back, but now even the North Yorkshire police had their Human Resources Department. Why the change? Had "personnel" suddenly become insulting to some pressure group or other, and therefore exiled to the icy wastes of the politically incorrect?

A hundred yards or so farther on, Banks pulled up in front of the three-story office block.

The Human Resources office was much like any other—untidy

desks, computers, filing cabinets and constantly ringing tele-phones. A dark-haired young woman looked up and smiled as Banks walked in.

"Can I help you?" she asked.

"Hope so." Banks showed her his card.

If she was surprised, she didn't show it. "What is it?" she asked. "My name's Mary, by the way. Mary Mason."

"I've come about one of your employees. A lad called Jason Fox. I'd like to speak to his boss and workmates, if I can."

Mary Mason frowned. "I don't believe I know the name. Still, there's a lot of people work here, and I'm quite new to the job." She smiled. "Do you know what department he's in?"

The Foxes hadn't been that specific, Banks remembered. All he knew was that Jason worked in an office.

"Well," Mary said, "at least that lets out the shop floor, doesn't it? Just a minute." She tapped away at her computer. A few mo-ments later, she swiveled away from the screen and said, "No. It's not just me. We don't have a Jason Fox working here."

Banks raised his eyebrows in disbelief. "Are you sure?"

"According to payroll records."

"Computers make mistakes sometimes."

Mary laughed. "Don't I know it. Every once in a while my mouse starts running wild, all over the place. Nobody's managed to work out why yet, but they call it 'mad mouse disease.' In this case, though, I'd tend to believe the computer. Are you sure he was on the clerical staff?"

Banks scratched the scar beside his right eye. He wasn't sure of anything now. "That's what I was told. Would it be too difficult to check all your employees?"

Mary shook her head. "No. It'll take just a little longer. One of the benefits of computers. They do things fast, then you can spend the rest of your time varnishing your fingernails."

"I'll bet."

Mary tapped a few keys and did the Ouija-board thing with her mouse, which wasn't running wild today as far as Banks could tell, then clicked the buttons a few times and squinted at the screen.

"Nope," she said, shaking her head. "No Jason Fox anywhere in the company. Maybe he worked for another branch?"

"You have other branches?"

"Rochdale. Coventry. Middlesbrough."

"No. His parents definitely said he lived and worked in Leeds. Look, are there any back records you can check, just in case?" It was probably pointless, but it was worth a look while he was here.

"I can search the files for the past few years, if you've got a bit of patience left."

Banks smiled. "If you would, please. I've got plenty of patience."

Mary returned to her computer. Banks found himself tapping his foot on the floor as he waited. He wanted a cigarette. No chance in here; you just had to sniff the air.

Finally, with a frown creasing her brow, Mary whistled and said, "Well, what do you know . . . ?"

"You've found him?"

"I have indeed."

"And?"

"Jason Fox. Can't be two, I don't suppose?"

"I doubt it."

"Well, according to our records, he left the company two years ago after working for us for only one year."

Now it was Banks's turn to frown. "He left? I don't understand. Why?"

Mary stared at the screen and pressed her lips together in thought, then she looked at Banks with her warm, dark eyes, smiled and said, "Look, I appreciate that you're a policeman, and a pretty senior one at that. I also appreciate this might be important, even though you haven't told me a thing. But personnel records are private. I'm afraid I can't just go around giving people any information they want at the drop of a hat, or a warrant card. I'm sure you could get a court order, if you really want to know. But I'm only doing my job. I'm sorry. I couldn't tell you any more, even if I knew."

"I appreciate that," said Banks. "Can you tell me anything at all about his time here, about his friends?"

She shook her head. "As I said, it was before my time. I've never heard of him." She turned to face the others in the office. "Anyone remember a Jason Fox used to work here?"

All she got in return was blank stares and shaking heads. Apart from one woman, who said, "The name sounds familiar."

"You're thinking of Jason Donovan," someone else said, and they laughed.

"Can you at least tell me what department he worked in?" Banks asked.

"That I can tell you," Mary said. "He was in sales. Domestic. You'll find them in the old office building, across the yard. And," she said, smiling, "you should also find some of the people he worked with are still there. Try David Wayne first. He's one of the regional sales managers now."

"Just a minute," came a voice from the back of the office. "Jason Fox, you said? Now I remember. It was a couple of years back. I'd just started here. There was some trouble, some sort of scandal. Something hushed up."

II

The sound of the car pulling up woke Frank from his afternoon nap. Slowly, he groped his way back to consciousness—it seemed to take longer every time, as if consciousness itself were slowly moving farther and farther away from him—and walked over to the window. There they were: the three of them, struggling up the path against the wind. Well, he supposed they would have to come sometime; Josie had already telephoned and told him what had happened to Jason.

He answered the knock, let them in and told them to make themselves comfortable while he went to put the kettle on. The good old English custom of a nice cup of tea, he thought, had helped people avoid many an embarrassing moment. Not that they should be embarrassed about what had happened, of course, but Yorkshire folk, especially, often fell short of words when it came to strong emotions.

Josie gave him a silent hug when he came through from the kitchen, then she sat down. Grief suited her in a way, he thought; she had always looked a bit pinched to him. These days, she had also started to look more like mutton dressed as lamb, too, with that makeup, her roots showing, and those figure-hugging outfits she wore. At her age. Her mother would have been ashamed of her.

Steven looked as lackluster as ever. Couldn't Josie, he wished again, have chosen someone with a bit of spunk in him?

Then there was Maureen. Good-natured, bustling, hardworking, no-nonsense Maureen. The best of the lot of them, in his book. A proper bonny lass, too; she'd break a few hearts in her time, with her laughing eyes and smiling lips and hair like spun gold all the way down to her waist. Well, not today. But that was how he remembered her. She had cut her hair short just after she started nurses' training. A real shame, that, he thought.

"When's the funeral?" he asked.

"Thursday," Josie answered. "Oh, you should have seen what they'd done to him, Dad." She sniffled. "Our poor Jason."

Frank nodded. "Nay, lass . . . Police getting anywhere?"

"Even if they were," Josie sniffed, "they wouldn't tell us, would they?"

The kettle boiled. Frank moved to rise, but Maureen sprang to her feet. "I'll get it, Granddad. Stay where you are."

"Thanks, lass," he said gratefully, and sank back into his armchair. "What *have* they told you?"

"They've got some lads helping them with their inquiries," Josie said. "Pakistanis." She sniffed. "They think it might have started as an argument in a pub, and that these lads followed our Jason, or waited for him in the ginnel and beat him up. The police think they probably didn't mean to kill him."

"What do *you* think?" Frank asked.

Maureen came back with the teapot and raised her eyebrows at the question. "We haven't really had much time to think about it at all yet, Granddad," she said. "But I'm sure the police know their business."

"Aye."

"What is it?" Steven Fox said, speaking for the first time. "You don't think they'll do a good job?"

"I wouldn't know about that," Frank said.

"Well, what is it, then?" Josie Fox repeated her husband's question. Maureen started pouring milk and tea into mugs, spooning in sugar.

"Nowt," said Frank. He fingered the folded, creased sheet of paper in his top shirt pocket and pulled it out.

"What's that, Granddad?" Maureen asked.

"Just something I got in the post."

Maureen frowned. "But what . . . I don't . . ."

"Oh, for crying out loud," said Frank, his patience with them finally snapping. "Don't you know what happened? Don't you know anything? Did you all turn your bloody backs?" He turned toward Maureen. "What about you?" he snapped. "I'd have expected more of you."

Maureen started to cry. Frank felt the familiar pain, almost an old friend now, grip his chest. Hand shaking, he tossed the sheet toward Josie. "Go-on," he said. "Read it."

III

Banks crossed the factory yard, dodging puddles rainbowed with oil. Crates and chunks of old machinery were stacked up by the sides of long one-story buildings with rusty corrugated iron roofs. Machine noises buzzed and roared from inside. Forklifts beetled back and forth across the uneven yard, carrying boxes on pallets. The place smelled of diesel oil and burned plastic.

He soon found the old office building, which had probably been adequate in the early days, before the company grew. There was no receptionist, just a large open area with desks, computers, telephones and people. Filing cabinets stood against the walls. At the far end of the room, several small offices had been partitioned off, their lower parts wood and the upper parts, above waist height, glass.

A woman dashed by Banks on her way to the door, a couple of file folders stuffed under her arm. When he asked her if David Wayne was around, she nodded and pointed to the middle office. Banks walked between the rows of desks, attracting no attention at all, then knocked on the door that bore the nameplate DAVID C. WAYNE.

The man who invited him in was younger than Banks had expected. Late twenties, early thirties at the most. He wore a white shirt with a garish tie, wavy brown hair falling over his collar. He had one of those high foreheads with little shiny red bumps at each side that made his hairline seem to be prematurely receding, and he smelled of Old Spice. A dark sports jacket hung over the back of his chair.

He frowned as he studied Banks's warrant card, then gestured to the spare chair and said, "How can I help you?"

Banks sat down. "I'm making inquiries about Jason Fox," he said. "I understand he used to work here?"

Wayne's frown deepened. "That's going back a bit."

"But you *do* remember him?"

"Oh, yes. I remember Jason all right." Wayne leaned back in his chair and put his feet on the desk. The telephone rang; he ignored it. In the background, Banks could hear the hubbub of the office through the flimsy partition. "Why do you want to know?" Wayne asked.

Much as Banks hated parting with information, it would do no harm in this case, he thought, and it might get Wayne to open up more quickly. He could already sense that something was not quite right, and the woman in the Human Resources Department had implied some sort of cover-up. So he told Wayne that Jason had been found dead, and that his parents had said he worked for this company.

"After all this time." Wayne shook his head slowly. "Amazing."

"Why did he leave?"

"He didn't leave. Not exactly."

"He was fired?"

"No."

"Made redundant?"

"No."

Banks sighed and shifted position. "Look, Mr. Wayne," he said, "I didn't come here to play a guessing game. I came to get information that might be important in a serious police investigation."

"I'm sorry," said Wayne, scratching his head. "It's all still a bit embarrassing, you see."

"Embarrassing? In what way?"

"I wasn't in management back then. I was just one of Jason's co-workers. I had more experience, though. In fact, I was the one who trained him."

"Was he a poor worker?"

"On the contrary. He was very good at his job. Bright, energetic, quick to learn. Showed an extraordinary aptitude for computers, considering he'd had no formal training in that area. Still, that's often the case."

"Then what—"

"The job isn't everything, Chief Inspector," Wayne went on quickly. "Oh, it's important, I'll grant you that. You can put up with a lot of idiosyncrasies if someone's as good as Jason was. We've had our share of arseholes in our time and, by and large, if they're competent, hardworking arseholes, you just tend to put up with them."

"But it was different with Jason?"

"Yes."

"In what way?"

"It was his *attitude*," Wayne explained. "I suppose you'd call it his political beliefs."

"Which were?"

"To put it in a nutshell, Jason was a racist. White power and all that. And it didn't take a lot to get him on his hobby horse. Just some item in the newspaper, some new opinion poll or crime statistics."

"What exactly did he say?"

"You name it. Asians and West Indians were his chief targets. According to Jason, if something wasn't done soon, the immigrants would take over the country and run it into the ground. Anarchy would follow. Chaos. The law of the jungle. He said you only had to look around you to see what damage they'd done already. AIDS. Drugs. Unemployment. He put them all down to immigrants." Wayne shook his head again. "It was disgusting, really sick, some of the things he came out with."

"Is that why he left?"

Wayne nodded. "As I said, he didn't exactly leave. It was more of a mutual parting of the ways, maybe a little more desired on our side than his. But the company paid him off adequately and got rid of him. No blemish on his references, either. I suppose whoever employed him next found out what the bugger was like soon enough. I mean, it's all very well to crack the odd . . . you know . . . off-color joke, have a bit of a laugh. We all do that, don't we? But Jason was serious. He didn't have a sense of humor about these things. Just hatred. A palpable hatred. You could feel it burning out of him when he spoke, see it in his eyes." Wayne gave a little shudder.

"Do you know where he got it from?"

"No idea. Where *do* people get these things from? Are they born like that? Do we blame the parents? Peers at school? The recession? Society?" He shrugged. "I don't know. Probably a bit of everything. But I do know that it was always there with Jason, always just beneath the surface, if it wasn't actually showing. And, of course, we have a number of Asian and West Indian employees here."

"Did he ever insult anyone to their face?"

Wayne rubbed his forehead and glanced away from Banks, out at the bustling business activity through his window. "Mostly he just made them feel uncomfortable," he said, "but once he went too far. That was enough. One of the secretaries. Milly. Nice woman. From Barbados. Jason usually kept her at arm's length. Anyway, she got pregnant, and at some point—so she said—when it started to show, Jason made some remark to her about all her kind could do was procreate, and there were too many of them already. Milly was upset, understandably, and she threatened to report him to the Race Relations Board. Well, the directors didn't want that . . . you know . . . the whole operation under the microscope, racism in the workplace and all that . . . so they asked Jason to leave."

"They offered him money?"

"A fair settlement. Just what he would have got if he'd been made redundant."

"And he went quietly?"

Wayne nodded.

"Could I speak to Milly?"

"She's no longer with the company."

"Do you have her address?"

"I suppose I can tell you. I shouldn't, but given the circumstances . . ." He got up, pulled out a file from one of the cabinets against his wall, and told Banks the address. Then he sat down again.

"Do you know where Jason went after he left here?" Banks asked.

Wayne shook his head. "Not a clue. He never got in touch again, and I can't say I was exactly eager to seek him out."

"So when he left here he disappeared from your life?"

"Yes."

"Did he have any close friends here?"

"Not really. I wasn't even particularly close to him myself. He was a bit of a loner. Never talked about his outside interests, family, girlfriends, that sort of thing. He had no patience with the usual office chitchat. Except football. He loved to talk about football. Mad about it. On a Monday morning he'd talk about the weekend games for so long, it was sometimes hard to get him working at all."

"People listened, then? The same ones who were sickened by his racism?"

Wayne spread his hands. "What can I say? There's nothing like an enthusiasm for sports to make a person seem more human. And we seem able to overlook an awful lot in our sports heroes, don't we? I mean, look at Gazza. The bugger beats up his wife and he's still a national hero."

"What about enemies?"

Wayne raised his eyebrows. "Probably just about every immigrant in the country. At least the ones who knew what he was."

"Anyone in particular?"

"Not that I can think of."

"What was he like as a person? How would you describe him?"

Wayne put a pencil against his lips and thought for a moment, then he said, "Jason was one of those people who can frighten you with their intensity. I mean, mostly he was withdrawn, quiet, in his own world. On first impressions, he seemed rather shy, but when he did come out, whether to talk about a football game or comment on some political article in the paper, then he became very passionate, very fervent. He had charisma. You could imagine him speaking to groups, swaying their opinions."

"A budding Hitler, then? Interesting." Banks closed his notebook and stood up. He could think of nothing more to ask. "Thanks for your time," he said, holding out his hand. "I might want to talk to you about this again."

Wayne shook hands and nodded. "I'll be here."

And Banks walked through the busy office, back out into the bleak factory yard, the oil smell, the machinery noise, overflowing skips, the rainbowed puddles. Just as he got to the car, his mobile beeped.

IV

"No, Gavin, I can't possibly go out for a drink with you tonight. We're very busy."

"The boy wonder got you working overtime, then?"

"I wish you wouldn't call him that."

Susan heard Gavin chuckle over the line. "Who's he got pegged for this one, then? Our local MP? Leader of the hunt?" He laughed again.

Susan felt herself flush. "That's not very funny." She hated it when Gavin made fun of Banks.

"How about Saturday? We can go—"

"Maybe," Susan said. "Maybe Saturday. I'll have to see. Got to go now, Gavin. Work to do."

"Okay. See you Saturday."

"I said *maybe*. Just a minute . . . what's that?" Susan could hear sounds of shouting and scuffling, and they seemed to be coming from downstairs. "Got to go, Gavin," she said. "I'll ring you back."

"Susan, what's—"

Susan dropped the receiver on its cradle and walked to the top of the stairs. The scene below was utter chaos. Every Asian in Eastvale—all nine or ten of them—seemed to be pushing through the front doors: George Mahmood's parents, Ibrahim Nazur, owner of the Himalaya, and a handful of students from Eastvale College. A number of uniformed officers were holding them back, but they wanted to see the detectives, and Susan was the only CID officer in the station.

"Would you *please* not all shout at once!" Susan yelled from halfway down the stairs.

"What are you going to do about our children?" asked an angry Charles Mahmood. "You can't just lock them up for nothing. This is racism, pure and simple. We're British citizens, you know."

"Please believe me, Mr. Mahmood," said Susan, advancing down the stairs. "We're only keeping them until we get—"

"No!" yelled Ibrahim Nazur. "It's not fair. One law for whites and another law for us."

That met a chorus of agreement and they surged forward again.

Suddenly, the front doors opened and a loud voice bellowed, "What in God's name is going on here?" It had enough authority to command silence. Then Susan saw over the crowd the shiny, bald head of Chief Constable Jeremiah "Jimmy" Riddle, and for the first time ever, she was grateful for the sight.

"Sergeant Rowe," she heard Riddle say, "would you please order your officers to remove these people from the police station? Tell them if they'll kindly wait outside we'll have some news for them in just a few minutes." Then Riddle made his way through the silent crowd, cutting a swath rather like Moses parting the Red Sea.

Behind him, Sergeant Rowe muttered, "Yes, sir," and ordered three constables to usher the group out onto the street. They went without putting up a fight.

"That's better," said Riddle, approaching Susan. "It's DC Gay, isn't it?"

"Yes, sir."

"Where's DCI Banks?"

"Leeds, sir. Pursuing inquiries."

" 'Pursuing inquiries,' is he? Shopping, more bloody like. That Classical Record Shop of his. Anyone else here?"

"No, sir. Just me."

Riddle jerked his head. "Right, you. Upstairs."

Susan turned and started walking up the stairs, feeling, she imagined, somewhat like a prisoner being sent down by the judge.

It could hardly be a worse time to piss off Jimmy Riddle.

Susan had passed the first parts of her sergeant's exam, the written, almost a year ago. But police promotion is a long-drawn-out process. The last stage consisted of an appearance before the promotion board—presided over by an assistant chief constable and a chief superintendent from Regional HQ.

That was six months ago now, but Susan still broke into a cold sweat every time she remembered the day of her board.

She had spent weeks reading up on policy, national guidelines and equal opportunities, but none of it prepared her for what lay behind the door. Of course, they kept her waiting in the corridor for about half an hour, just to make her extra nervous, then the chief superintendent came out, shook her hand and led her in. She could have sworn there was a smirk on his face.

First they asked her a few personal questions to get some idea of her overall bearing, confidence and articulateness. She thought she managed to answer clearly, without mumbling or stuttering, except when they asked what her parents thought of her choice of career. She was sure that she flushed, but rather than flounder around trying to explain, she simply paused to collect herself and said, "They didn't approve, sir."

Next came the scenarios. And her interviewers added complications, changed circumstances and generally did everything they could to confuse her or get her to change her mind.

"One of the men on your shift is regularly late in the morning," the ACC began, "putting extra pressure on his mates. What do you do?"

"Have a private word with him, sir, ask him why he's being late all the time."

The ACC nodded. "His mother's dying and she needs expensive care. He can't afford it on a copper's salary, so he's playing in a jazz band until the wee hours to make a bit extra."

"Then I'd tell him he needs permission to work outside the force and advise him to get help and support from our Welfare Department, sir."

"He thanks you for your concern, but he keeps on playing with the band and turning up late."

"Then I'd think some disciplinary action would be in order, sir."

The ACC raised his eyebrows. "Really? But his mother is dying of cancer. He *needs* the extra income. Surely this is a reasonable way of earning it? After all, it's not as if he's taking bribes or engaging in other criminal acts."

Susan stuck to her guns. "He's causing problems for his fellow officers on the shift, sir, and he's disobeying police regulations. I think disciplinary action is called for if all other avenues have been exhausted."

And she passed. Now she was due to go up before the chief next week for her *official* promotion. And that chief, of course, was Chief Constable Riddle.

Still, she reminded herself as she walked into the small office she shared with Sergeant Hatchley, there was nothing Riddle could do now to block her promotion. She had already earned it, and the next step was purely a formality, a bit of pomp and circumstance. Unless, of course, she *really* screwed up. Then, she supposed, he could do whatever he wanted. He was, after all, the chief constable. And, if nothing else, he could certainly make her life uncomfortable.

The office seemed crowded with Riddle in it. The man's restless, pent-up energy consumed space and burned up the oxygen like a blazing fire. Susan sat in her chair and Riddle perched on the edge of Hatchley's desk. He was a tall man, and he seemed to tower over her.

"Who authorized the arrest?" he asked.

"They're not exactly under arrest, sir," Susan said. "Just detained for questioning."

"Very well. Who authorized their detention?"

Susan paused, then said softly, "I think it was DCI Banks, sir."

"Banks. I knew it." Riddle got up and started to pace, until he found out there was not enough room to do so, then he sat down again, his pate a little redder. Banks always said you could tell how angry Riddle was by the shade of his bald head, and Susan found herself stifling a giggle as she thought she could see it glow. It was like one of those mood rings that were a fad when she was a child, only Riddle's mood never softened to a peaceful green or calm, cool blue.

"On what evidence?" Riddle continued.

"There'd been some trouble earlier in the pub, sir, the Jubilee. It involved the Mahmood boy and the victim, Jason Fox. When DCI Banks questioned George Mahmood about it, he refused to cooperate. So did his friends. They asked for a lawyer."

"And did they get one?"

"No, sir. Well, not until this morning. It was Sunday."

"Any rough stuff?"

"No, sir."

Riddle slid his hand across his head. "Well, let's at least be thankful for small mercies. Have you any idea who Ibrahim Nazur *is?*"

"Owner of the Himalaya, sir."

"More than that. He owns a whole bloody chain of restaurants, all over Yorkshire, and the Himalaya's just the latest. He's also a highly respected member of the Muslim community and one of the prime movers in that new mosque project down Bradford way."

"Ah," said Susan.

" 'Ah,' indeed. Anything from forensics?"

"Nothing conclusive, sir. Not yet."

"Witnesses?"

"None, sir. Not so far. We're still looking."

Riddle stood up. "Right. I want the three of them out of here. Now. Do you understand?"

Susan stood too. "Yes, sir," she said.

"And tell Banks I'll be seeing him very soon."

Susan nodded. "Yes, sir."

And with that, Jimmy Riddle straightened his uniform and marched downstairs to face his public.

V

Late that afternoon, Banks walked up to the bar of the Black Bull in Lyndgarth and ordered a double Bell's for Frank Hepplethwaite and a half of Theakston's XB for himself.

According to Susan, who had phoned Banks earlier, Hepplethwaite was Jason Fox's granddad, and he said he had some information about Jason. He insisted on talking to the "man in charge." Banks had phoned Frank and, finding out that he didn't own a car, agreed to meet him in the Black Bull.

Before setting off back for Swainsdale, though, Banks had called at the Leeds address Jason Fox's parents had given him and found that Jason hadn't lived there for at least eighteen months. The flat was now occupied by a student called Jackie Kitson, and she had never heard of Jason Fox. There the trail ended.

The barman of the Black Bull was a skinny, hunched, crooked-shouldered fellow in a moth-eaten, ill-fitting pull-over. His greasy black hair and beard obscured most of his face, except the eyes, which stared out in a way reminiscent of photos of Charles Manson. He served the drinks without a word, then took down

Banks's order for one chicken-and-mushroom pie and one Old Peculier casserole. The Black Bull was one of those rare exceptions to the no-food-after-two-o'clock rule that blights most pubs.

Banks took the drinks and joined Frank at a round table by the door. At the bar, one man started telling the barman how much more cozy it was now most of the tourists had gone. He had a whiny, southern accent, and actually lowered his voice when he said "tourists." The barman, who clearly knew it was the tourist business that kept the place going, grunted "Aye" without looking up from the glass he was drying.

Two other barstool regulars working at a crossword puzzle seemed overjoyed to discover that "episcopal" was an anagram of "Pepsi Cola." To the left, down the far end where the billiard tables were, two American couples were stuffing coins in the fruit machine, shifting occasionally to the video trivia game opposite.

"You must know Mr. Gristhorpe, young lad?" said Hepplethwaite after thanking Banks for the drink.

Banks nodded. "He's my boss."

"Lives here in Lyndgarth, he does. Well, I suppose you know that. Can't say I know him well, mind you. I'm a fair bit older myself, and he's been away a lot. Good family, though, the Gristhorpes. Got a good reputation around these parts, anyroad." He nodded to himself and sipped his Bell's.

Frank Hepplethwaite had a thin, lined face, all the lines running vertically, and a fine head of gray hair. His skin was pale and his eyes a dull bottle-green. He looked as if he had once had quite a bit more flesh on his bones but had recently lost weight due to illness.

"Anyway," he said, "thank you for coming all the way out here. I don't get around so well these days." He tapped his chest. "Angina."

Banks nodded. "I'm sorry. No problem, Mr. Hepplethwaite."

"Call me Frank. Of course," he went on, tapping his glass, "I shouldn't be indulging in this." He pulled a face. "But there's limits to what a sick man will put up with." He glanced at the table, where Banks had unconsciously rested his cigarettes and lighter. "Smoke if you like, lad. I like the smell of tobacco. And second-hand smoke be buggered."

Banks smiled and lit up.

"Nice state of affairs, isn't it," said Hepplethwaite, "when a man has to indulge his vices by proxy."

Banks raised his eyebrows. The words sounded familiar, but he couldn't place them.

"Raymond Chandler," said Hepplethwaite with a sly grin. "General Sternwood at the beginning of *The Big Sleep*. One of my favorite films. Bogey as Philip Marlowe. Must have seen it about twenty times. Know it by heart."

So that was it. Banks had seen the film on television just a few months ago, but he had never read the book. Ah well, another one for the lengthening list. As a rule, he didn't read detective fiction, apart from Sherlock Holmes, but he'd heard that Chandler was good. "I'm sorry about what happened to your grandson," he said.

The old man's eyes misted over. "Aye, well . . . nobody deserves to die like that. He must have suffered like hell." He took a folded sheet of paper from his pocket and passed it to Banks. "This is why I asked you to come."

Banks nodded. He took the sheet, opened it and spread it on the table in front of him. It looked professionally printed, but most things did these days, with all the laser printers and desktop publishing packages around. Banks could remember the time—not so long ago—when all the copying in a police station was done from "spirit masters" on one of those old machines that made your fingers all purple. Even now, as he remembered it, he fancied he could smell the acrid spirit again.

The masthead, in very large, bold capitals, read THE ALBION LEAGUE and underneath that, it said in italics, *"Fighting the good fight for you and your country."*

Banks drew on his Silk Cut and started to read.

Friends, have you ever looked around you at the state of our once-great nation today and wondered just how such terrible degradation could have come about? Can you believe this nation was once called Great Britain? And what are we now? Our weak politicians have allowed this once-great land to be overrun by parasites. You see them everywhere—in the schools, in the factories and even in the government, sapping our strength, undermining the fabric of our society. How could this be allowed to happen? Many years ago, Enoch Powell foresaw the signs, saw the rivers of blood in our future. But did anyone listen? No ...

And so it went on, column-inch after column-inch of racist drivel. It ended:

And so we ask you, the true English people, heirs to King Arthur and Saint George, to join us in our struggle, to help us rid this great land of the parasite immigrant who crawls and breeds his filth in the bellies of our cities, of the vile and traitorous Jew who uses our economy for his own purposes, of the homosexual deviants who seek to corrupt our children, and of the deformed and the insane who have no place in the new order of the Strong and the Righteous. To purify our race and reestablish the new Albion in the land that is rightfully ours and make it truly our "homeland" once again.

Banks put it down. Even a long draft of Theakston's couldn't get the vile taste out of his mouth. Reluctantly, he turned back to the pamphlet, but he could find no sign of an address, no mention of a meeting place. Obviously, whoever wanted to join the Albion League would first have to find it. At the bottom of the pamphlet, however, in tiny print in the far right-hand corner, he could make out the letters *http://www.alblgue.com/index.html*. A web-site address. Everyone had them these days. Next, he examined the envelope and saw that it had been posted in Bradford last Thursday.

Their food arrived and they continued to speak between mouthfuls.

"What makes you think Jason sent you this?" Banks asked, tapping the sheet.

Frank Hepplethwaite turned away to face the dark wood partition between their table and the door. One of the Americans complained loudly that too many of the trivia questions dealt with English sports. "I mean, how the hell am I supposed to know which player transferred from Tottenham Hotspurs to Sheffield Wednesday in 1976? What game do they play, anyway? And what kinda name is that for a sports team? Sheffield *Wednesday*." He shook his head. "These Brits."

Frank turned back to Banks and said, "Because it arrived only a couple of days after I let something slip. For which may God forgive me."

"What did you let slip?"

"First you have to understand," Frank went on, "that when Jason was just a wee lad, we were very close. They used to come up here for summer holidays sometimes, him, Maureen and my daughter Josie. Jason and I would go for long walks, looking for wildflowers on the riverbanks, listening for curlews over Fremlington Edge. Sometimes we'd go fishing up the reservoir, or visit one of the nearby farmers and help out around the yard for an afternoon, collecting eggs or feeding the pigs. We always used to go and watch the sheep-shearing. He used to love his times up here, did little Jason."

"You mentioned his mother and sister. What about his father?"

Frank took a mouthful of casserole, chewed, swallowed and scowled. "That long streak of piss? To be honest, lad, I never had much time for him, and he never had much time for Jason. Do you know he never listens to those records he collects? Never listens to them! Still wrapped in plastic. I bloody ask you, what are you supposed to think of a bloke who buys records and doesn't even listen to them?"

Not much, Banks thought, chewing on a particularly stringy piece of chicken. Frank was obviously going to tell his story in his own time, his own way. "Sorry to interrupt," he said. "What happened?"

Frank paused for breath before continuing. "Time, mostly. That's all. I got old. Too old to walk very far. And Jason got interested in other things, stopped visiting."

"Did he still come and see you occasionally?"

"Oh aye. Now and then. But it were only in passing, like, more of a duty."

"When was the last time you saw him?"

"He drove out here the weekend before last. It'd be just a week before he died."

"Did he ever talk about his life in Leeds? His job? Friends?"

"Not really, no. Once said he was learning about computers or something. Of course, I know nowt about that, so we soon changed the subject."

"Did he say *where* he was learning about computers?"

"No."

"His parents told me he worked in an office."

Frank shrugged. "Could be. All I remember is him once saying he was learning about computers."

"And in all his visits," Banks went on, "didn't he ever talk about this sort of thing?" He tapped the pamphlet with his knuckle.

Frank closed his eyes and shook his head. "Never. That was why it came as such a shock."

"Why do you think he never spoke to you about it?"

"I can't answer that one. Perhaps he thought I'd be against it, until I said what I did and gave him his opening? Perhaps he thought I was an old man and not worth converting? I *am* his granddad, after all, and we had a relationship of a kind. We didn't say much to each other when we did meet up these past few years.

I'd no idea what he was up to. Mostly he'd just have time to drop by and buy me a drink and ask if I was doing all right before he was off to his football or whatever."

Banks finished his pie. "What makes you think you gave Jason an opening to send you this pamphlet?" he asked. "What was it you said?"

"Aye, well . . . We were sitting in here one day, just like you and me are now." Frank lowered his voice. "The landlord here's called Jacob Bernstein. Not that fellow there. Jacob's not in right now. Anyway, I made a remark about Jacob being a bit of a tight-fisted old Jew."

"What did Jason say?"

"Nowt. Not right away. He just had this funny sort of smile on his face. Partly a smile, partly a sort of sneer. As soon as I said it, I felt I'd done wrong, but these things slip out, don't they, like saying Jews and Scotsmen have short arms and deep pockets. You don't think about it being offensive, do you? You don't really mean any harm by it. Anyways, after a minute or so, Jason says he thinks he might have something to interest me, and a few days later, this piece of filth turns up in the post. Who else could have sent it?"

"Who else, indeed?" said Banks, remembering what David Wayne had told him that morning in Leeds. "Did you ever meet any of Jason's circle?"

"No."

"So there's no way you can help us try and find out who killed him?"

"I thought you already had the lads who did it?"

Banks shook his head. "We don't know if it was them. Not for sure. At the moment, I'd say we're keeping our options open."

"Sorry, lad," said Frank. "It doesn't look like I can help, then, does it?" He paused and looked down into his glass. "It was a real shock," he said, "when I read that thing and knew our Jason were responsible. I fought in the war, you know. I never made a fuss about it, and I don't want to now. It were my duty, and I did it. I'd do it again."

"What service?"

"RAF. Tail gunner."

Banks whistled between his teeth. His father had been a radio operator in the RAF, so he had heard what a dangerous task tail gunner was, and how many had died doing it.

"Aye," said Frank. "Anyroad, like I said, I don't want to make a fuss about it. I said something terribly wrong about someone I consider a friend, and it shames me, but it shames me even more when my grandson thinks I'd have the time of day for this sort of rubbish. I fought the bloody Nazis, for crying out loud. And for what? So my own grandson could become one of them?"

There were tears in his eyes and Banks feared for his heart. "Calm down, Mr. Hepplethwaite," he said, putting his hand on Frank's skinny wrist.

Frank looked at him through the film of tears, then gave a small nod and took a sip of Bell's. He coughed, patted his chest and forced a smile. "Don't worry, lad," he said, "It's not quite time, gentlemen, please, for this old codger yet."

VI

An emergency meeting of the Albion League had been called for that Monday evening. Not everyone was invited, of course, just the cell leaders and one or two of Neville Motcombe's current favorites, like Craig. About fifteen in all, they came from Leeds and Bradford, from Halifax, Keighley, Cleckheaton, Heckmondwike, Batley, Dewsbury, Brighouse and Elland. Skinheads, for the most part, aged between sixteen and twenty-four, racists all.

And these fifteen were the pick of the crop, Craig knew. Each cell had between five and twelve members. These were the drones—

football hooligans and otherwise violent skins—and Motcombe hardly ever came into contact with them except at rallies and at other large gatherings, when he addressed them from a distance. Mostly, he relied on his cell leaders to make sure his orders were communicated and carried out and, maybe more important still, to make sure the cash kept trickling in. After all, the league was an expensive operation to run.

They met in the upstairs room of a pub in Bingley, and as he sat sipping his lager, Craig wondered if the landlord knew exactly what was going on up there. If he did, he might not have been so quick to let them use it. On the other hand, the prospect of selling a few extra pints on a slow Monday night might tempt even the best of us to leave our ethics and politics at the door. Nothing much surprised Craig anymore. Not after what Motcombe had drawn him into.

Even though the window was half open, the place was still full of smoke. Craig could hear rain falling in the street outside. A pale streetlight halo glowed through the gauze of moisture. Occasionally, a car sloshed through the gathering puddles.

Meanwhile, Nev himself, erstwhile leader of the league, clad in his usual shiny leather jacket, was on his feet whipping his members into a frenzy. He didn't need to shout and wave his arms around like Hitler; there was enough power and conviction in his regular speaking voice. Mostly it was the eyes; they were the kind that trapped you and wouldn't let you go unless they were certain of your loyalty. They'd even made Craig tremble once or twice in the early days, but he was too good at his job to let it get to him.

"Murdered," Motcombe repeated, disgust and disbelief in his tone. He slapped the table. "One of us. Three of them. Three to one. They say one of his eyes was hanging out of its socket by the time the Paki bastards had finished with him."

Stirrings and mumblings came from the crowd. One skin started rattling his glass on the table. Motcombe shushed him with an economic hand gesture, then pulled a slip of paper out of his pocket and started to read.

"George Mahmood," he began, with the accent on *mood*. "Asim Nazur." This time, the name sounded like a sneer. People began to snicker. "And Kobir Mukhtar. Sounds about right, that one, doesn't it? Mucky-tar?"

Sycophantic laughter came from the cell leaders.

"And do you know what happened?"

Several of them, Craig included, shook their heads.

"The police let them go. That's what."

Howls of outrage.

"Oh yes, they did. This very afternoon. Our glorious warrior Jason is probably lying on some mortuary table, cut open from th'nave to th'chops as we speak, and the three bastards who put him there, the three *brown* bastards who put him there, are out walking the streets." He slammed the table again. "What do you think about that?"

"Ain't fair," one of the cell leaders chimed in.

"Typical," claimed another. "Get away with bloody murder they do these days."

"What we gonna do?" asked another.

Craig lit a cigarette and leaned forward. This promised to be interesting. As far as he was concerned, Jason Fox was an evil little pillock who deserved all he got.

"First off," said Motcombe, "I want a special edition of the newsletter out pronto. Black border, the lot. And I want to see some oomph in it. Ray?"

One of the Leeds cell leaders looked up from his pint and nodded.

"You see to that," Motcombe went on. "Now Jason's no longer with us, I'm afraid we're left to rely on your rather more pedestrian prose style. But you can do it, Ray, I'm sure you can. You know the kind of thing I want. Outrage, yes, but make sure you emphasize the *reason* this all happened, the underlying causes, what we're all about. And make sure your mention the Pakis' names. We'll send each of them a copy. If they know that the entire National Socialist Alliance knows who they are, that should give them a fucking sleepless night or two. Okay?"

Ray smiled and nodded.

"And print extra copies. Next, I'd like Geoff and Keith to start working on a memorial concert for Jason. A big bash. You've got the contacts, so pick some appropriate bands, four or five of them, rent a large space and make arrangements. Soon as you can, okay?"

Geoff and Keith nodded and scribbled some notes.

"Now, as soon as I find out the details about the funeral," Motcombe went on, "I'll be contacting several members to accompany me in a tribute of honor for our fallen hero. For make no mistake about it, Jason Fox is a *martyr,* and his murder should provide us with a rallying point. We've got a chance to turn adversity into fortune here, if we choose to seize it. By all means let us grieve and mourn our lost comrade—indeed, grieve we *must*—but let us also, as *he* would have wished, use his death to spur us on to greater things, to faster growth. You all knew Jason. You know what he stood for. Let's do credit to his memory."

A few of them nodded and muttered their agreement, then the Brighouse cell leader asked, "Are we gonna crack some heads open, then?"

A number of "ayes" went up, but Motcombe shushed them again. "Don't worry," he said. "That'll be taken care of. In time. But for the moment, we'll just publish their names and leave it at that. Let's think of the long-term mission, and let's use our golden opportunity to gain a bit of public sympathy. Think of the hundreds of blokes at home just sitting on the fence right now. They know we're right, but they don't want to make that final move and admit it. Something like this could increase our membership tenfold. Nice, pure Aryan lad, with his whole future ahead of him, murdered by Paki immigrant scum. That'll turn a few fence-sitters in our direction."

Several members murmured in agreement. "But we can't leave Jason's murder unavenged, can we?" one of them said. "They'll think we're weak."

"Sometimes you have to postpone your vengeance for the greater good, Mick. That's all I am saying. And there's strength in that, not weakness. Believe me. There'll be plenty of time for revenge down the road. Remember, the bastards who killed Jason got away with it because our corrupt legal system is on their side. But what would happen if one of us got picked up for clobbering a Paki right now? Eh? Answer me that one." No one did. They all looked as if they knew the answer already. Motcombe looked at his watch. "Now, I'll have to be on my way soon, I've got a lot to attend to, but there's no reason why you lot can't stay and enjoy a wake for Jason if you like. You've all got your orders. Meeting adjourned."

Then Motcombe tossed back the rest of his orange juice. Unlike the others, Craig had noticed, he never drank alcohol or smoked. People got up and moved around the room, some of them heading down to the bar to buy more pints. The last Craig saw of Motcombe, he was walking out of the room with two Bradford cell leaders, an arm draped over each one's shoulders, deep in quiet conversation.

Liked his private meetings, did Nev, keeping the left hand and the right hand separate. Whatever he was talking to them about or asking them to do, you could bet it would have nothing to do with what he and Craig had been talking about over the past few weeks.

Craig tossed his cigarette out of the window into the rainy night, took a deep breath and went over to mourn Jason's death with Ray from Leeds and Dogface Russell from Horsforth.

VII

It was late when Banks got home that evening, after stopping off at the station on his way from Lyndgarth, and he was tired.

Sandra was sitting at a table at the back of the living room sorting through some transparencies, holding them up to the desk light, scrutinizing each one in turn, her long blond hair tucked behind her ears.

"Drink?" Banks asked.

She didn't look up. "No, thanks."

Fine. Banks went to the cocktail cabinet and poured himself a finger of Laphroaig, thought about it for a moment, then added another finger. He picked up the evening paper from the coffee table and sat on the settee.

"Hard day?" he asked.

"Not bad," Sandra said, without looking away from the transparency she was holding. "Busy."

Banks looked at the paper for a few minutes without taking anything in, then went over to the stereo. He chose a CD of arias by Angela Gheorghiu. A few seconds into the first one, Sandra looked over and raised a dark eyebrow. "Must you?"

"What's wrong?"

"Do we really *have* to listen to this?"

"What harm is it doing?"

Sandra sighed and turned back to her transparency.

"Really," Banks pressed on. "I want to know. What harm is it doing? Is it too loud?"

"No, it's not too loud."

"Then what's the problem?"

Sandra dropped the transparency on the table a little harder than necessary. "It's bloody opera, is the problem. You know it gets on my nerves sometimes."

It was true that Sandra had once taken a magnet to one of his *Götterdämmerung* tapes. But that was Wagner, an acquired taste at the best of times. Who could possibly object to Angela Gheor-ghiu singing Verdi? Sandra had even been with him to see *La Traviata* last month, and she said she enjoyed it.

"I didn't think you found it *that* offensive," Banks said, walking back to the stereo.

"No, leave it," Sandra said. "You've put it on. You've made your point. Just leave it."

"What point?"

"What point? You know what point."

"No, I don't. Enlighten me."

Sandra snorted. "Opera. Bloody opera. The most important thing on your agenda. In your life, for all I know."

Banks sat down and reached for his Scotch. "Oh, we're back to that again, are we?"

"Yes, we're back to that again."

"Well, go on, then."

"Go on, what?"

"Get it off your chest."

"Oh, you'd like that, wouldn't you?"

"What do you mean?"

"You'd like me to get it off my chest. Let the little lady yell at you for a couple of minutes so you can tell your mates what a bloody fishwife she is. Pretend to listen, be all contrite, then just carry on as if nothing had happened."

"It's not like that," Banks protested. "If you've got a problem, tell me. Let's talk about it."

Sandra picked up another transparency and pushed a few loose strands of hair back behind her ears. "I don't want to talk about it. There's nothing to talk about."

Angela Gheorghiu had moved onto the "Aubade" from *Chéru-bin* now, but its beauty was lost on Banks.

"Look, I'm sorry," he said. "I didn't realize it was *that* impor-tant to you."

Sandra glanced sideways at him. "That's just it, isn't it?" she said.

"What is?"

"You never do. You never do consider how important something might be to me. It's always your needs that come first. Like bloody opera. You never bother asking me what *I* might want to listen to, do you? You just go straight to your bloody opera without even thinking."

Banks stood up again. "Look, I said I'm sorry. Okay? I'll take it off if it bothers you so much."

"I told you to leave it. It doesn't matter now. It's too late."

"Too late for what?"

"Oh, Alan, give it a rest. Can't you see I've got work to do?" She gestured at the transparencies spread out across the table.

"Fine," said Banks. "Fine. You're pissed off, but you don't want to talk about it. You hate opera, but you want me to leave it on. I'm the one who never considers your needs or feelings, but right now you've got work to do. Well, just bloody fine."

Banks tossed back the rest of his Laphroaig, grabbed his coat from the hall stand and slammed the front door behind him.

FOUR

I

Banks was first to arrive at Tuesday morning's CID meeting in the "Boardroom" of Eastvale Divisional Police HQ, shortly followed by DC Susan Gay, Superintendent Gristhorpe and, finally, Sergeant Hatchley.

Having been warned by Susan, Banks was dreading that Jimmy Riddle himself would show up. Riddle was a notorious early riser, and the thirty miles or so of country roads from Regional HQ to Eastvale at such an hour would mean nothing to him. Especially if it gave him an opportunity to cause Banks grief.

Banks knew he would have to face the CC before long—Gristhorpe said he had already received *his* bollocking for letting his DCI too far off the leash—but he just didn't want it first thing in the morning, never his favorite time of day. Especially after he'd gone down to the Queen's Arms after his argument with Sandra the previous evening and had a jar too many. He hadn't handled that situation well, he knew. He hadn't been at all reasonable. He had lived with Sandra long enough to know that when she lashed out like that—which was rare—it meant she had something important on her mind. And he hadn't bothered to find out what it was. Instead, he had stormed out like a petulant teenager.

As it happened, Jimmy Riddle hadn't turned up by the time coffee and biscuits were served. That probably meant he wouldn't come, Banks thought with relief; usually Riddle liked to be first there, sparkling and spotless, to get a jump on everyone.

"Right," said Gristhorpe. "What have we got so far? Alan, have you talked to the lab?"

Banks nodded. "Nothing yet. They're still trying, but they haven't found anything on the shoes or clothes we sent over for analysis. There's a lot of mud on George Mahmood's shoes, consistent with walking over the rec in the rain, and some sort of substance that looks a bit suspicious. But the lad was wearing trainers, for Christ's sake. Hardly what you'd choose if you were intending to kick someone's head in."

"But we don't know that he was *intending* to do anything, do we?" Gristhorpe pointed out.

"True. Still, it'd be difficult to kick someone to death wearing trainers. Dr. Glendenning specified heavy boots. Or Doc Martens, something like that."

"Wouldn't the rain have washed any traces of blood away?" Susan asked.

"Lab says not. If there's enough of it, which there was, and if it gets in the stitching and seeps between the sole and upper, they say it's damn near impossible to get rid of."

Susan nodded.

"Vic Manson's working on fingerprints, too," Banks said to Gristhorpe, "but he doesn't hold out a lot of hope."

"Fingerprints from where?"

"The broken bottle. According to the postmortem, there were fragments of broken glass embedded in the back of Jason Fox's skull, and they match the fragments we found near the body. It looks as if he was hit with a bottle and then kicked. Anyway, Vic says the rain has probably buggered up his chances, but he's busy spraying SuperGlue into aquariums and Lord knows what else."

"What did you find out yesterday?" Gristhorpe asked.

"Quite a lot." Banks told them in detail about Jason Fox's losing his job, his false address in Leeds, and the Albion League. "I also checked out this Milly and her boyfriend," he went on. "The West Indian woman Jason insulted at work. Seems she's gone back to live with her family in Barbados."

"Chalk up one victory to Jason Fox, then," said Gristhorpe. "Any idea where Jason lived when he wasn't at his parents' house?"

Banks smiled and produced an address in Rawdon.

"How did you find out?"

"Telephone directory. It doesn't seem as if Jason was making any particular secret out of where he lived. He just neglected to let his parents know he'd moved."

"For eighteen months?"

Banks shrugged. "Jason's relationship with his parents obviously wasn't close. There's a lot they don't know about him. I'm not entirely sure whether they didn't want to know, or whether he didn't want them to. From what I've seen so far, the Foxes aren't a particularly close family."

"How did he make his living these past two years?" Gristhorpe asked. "Do we know that?"

Banks shook his head. "No. But according to the DSS he wasn't on the dole. His grandfather mentioned something about him studying computers, too, so that might be something he's got into. I've asked Ken Blackstone to give us a hand down there, checking the local college courses. And we can check tax records, see if he got another job somewhere."

Gristhorpe nodded. "Know anything about this Albion League?"

Banks's only experience with neo-Nazis had been with the National Front in the seventies, when he was a young copper on the Met. He had read about the more recent, smaller and tougher groups, like Combat 18 and Blood and Honour, with all their concomitant white-power rock bands and magazines, but he hadn't actually come across any of them in the line of duty. "Not yet," he said. "And nobody else around here seems to have heard of them, either. Anyway, I faxed the Yard. They've got a special squad dealing with neo-Nazi groups."

"Let's keep our fingers crossed. Have you got anything to add, Sergeant Hatchley?"

"The uniformed lads canvassed the whole Market Street area again yesterday," said Hatchley. "Pubs, cafés, fish-and-chip shops, bed-and-breakfasts, the lot. Some people remember Georgie Mahmood and his two mates in the fish-and-chip shop, all right, but no one saw them heading for the ginnel. And no one remembers seeing Jason and his mate. We've managed to get an artist's impression of the lad who was with Jason, but I wouldn't expect too much." Hatchley scratched his nose. "I'm wondering if it was something to do with drugs, sir, the Jubilee being the sort of place it is. A deal gone wrong, maybe?"

"Have we got anything from the Drugs Squad on the victim or suspects?"

Hatchley shook his head. "No, sir. I've already checked with records. But still . . ."

"Well, we'll bear it in mind, anyway. Anything else?"

"Aye, sir. I had a chat with a couple of Jason's teammates from Eastvale United. He had a jar with them after the game, right enough, but none of them admit to seeing him Saturday night, and none of them recognize the lad in the artist's impression."

"Why hasn't Jason's mate come forward?" Gristhorpe mused aloud. "Does he even know what's happened?"

"It's possible he doesn't, sir," said Hatchley. "If he lives far off, like, doesn't watch much telly or read the papers."

Gristhorpe nodded and turned to face everyone. "Either that or he did it. Let's dig a little deeper into the background here. First off, find out if George Mahmood and Jason Fox really did know each other better than George is letting on. Maybe they'd crossed swords before. Let's also find out what we can about Asim Nazur and that cousin of his, Kobir . . . what's his name . . . ?"

"Mukhtar, sir," said Susan.

"Right. Someone get in touch with Bradford CID and find out if they've got anything on Kobir Mukhtar."

"I've already done that, sir," said Susan. "There was nothing on the computer, so I put in a request for information while we still had them in custody, just before . . . before the CC came round yesterday, sir."

"And?"

"Nothing, sir. Seems clean."

"All right." Gristhorpe frowned. "Susan, don't I recollect something about an incident involving the Mahmoods recently?"

"Yes, sir. About a month ago. Someone stole a brick from the building site by Gallows View and lobbed it through the Mahmoods' window. They'd covered the shop windows with wire mesh a while back after a previous incident, so the yob responsible chucked this brick through the bedroom window."

"Anyone hurt?"

"Mrs. Mahmood, sir. She was undressing for bed at the time. The brick missed her head by several inches, but a long sliver of glass broke free and sliced into her upper arm. She was bleeding pretty badly when her husband hurried her to Eastvale General. It took fourteen stitches, and the doctor insisted they call the police."

"They weren't going to?"

"They were reluctant, sir," Susan said. "Her husband said it would only cost them time and trouble, and they didn't expect any results in return. Apparently, this kind of thing had happened before, when they ran the shop in Bradford, and nobody ever did anything about it."

"Well, this isn't bloody Bradford," said Gristhorpe. "Any leads?"

"They'd had a customer, a teenage girl, earlier in the day who complained about getting the wrong change. When Mrs. Mahmood insisted she was right, the girl swept the newspapers and sweets off the counter and stalked out. We finally tracked her down, but she was in Penrith at the time of the incident. After that, nothing."

"Could it have been Jason Fox, given his views on immigrants?"

"I suppose so," Susan said. "It happened about half past ten on a

Saturday night, and we know Jason came to Eastvale on weekends. But we didn't know that then. I mean, we'd no reason to suspect him. And George Mahmood couldn't have known it was him."

"Couldn't he? Maybe he had his suspicions. Maybe he even *saw* him. But you're right, we should avoid too much speculation at this point. Perhaps you should have another word with Jason's family, Susan; see if they're a bit more forthcoming. After that, you can try the Mahmoods again, then the Nazurs at the Himalaya, see if they can tell you anything else about what happened on Saturday night." He looked at his watch, then smiled at Susan. "Time it right, lass, and you might be at the Himalaya just around lunch-time."

Hatchley laughed, and Susan blushed.

"That just about covers it." Gristhorpe rubbed his bristly chin. "But wherever we go," he said, "we tread carefully. On eggs. Remember that. Chief Constable Riddle is taking a personal interest in this case." He cleared his throat. "By the way, he apologized for not being with us this morning."

Banks overheard Hatchley whisper to Susan Gay, "Breakfast television."

Gristhorpe ignored them. "What we've all got to bear in mind at this point," he said, "is that while this case looked simple at first, things have changed. It's got a lot more complicated. And however odious a character Jason Fox is beginning to sound, remember, he didn't get a chance to fight back. That's voluntary manslaughter, at the very least, and more than likely it's murder. Don't forget, we've got all the ingredients of a racial incident here, too: white victim; handy Asian suspects picked up, interrogated and locked in the cells overnight. When you add to that the fact that Jason Fox was a racist, George Mahmood is busy exploring his Muslim roots and Asim Nazur's dad is a pillar of the community, then you've got a powder keg, and I don't want it going off on my patch, Jimmy Riddle or no Jimmy Riddle. Now let's get to it."

II

It was quicker to walk to the Leaview Estate than to drive around Eastvale's confusing one-way system, so Susan nipped out of the fire exit and took the winding cobbled streets behind the police station down to King Street. She passed the infirmary, then the Gothic pile of Eastvale Comprehensive on the right, with its turrets, clock and bell tower, and the weedy, overgrown rec on her left before entering the Leaview Estate. The weather was overcast today, windy, too, with occasional drizzle, but at least it wasn't cold.

The Foxes' garden looked less impressive in the dull light, Susan thought as she rang the doorbell, yet the roses still seemed to burn with an inner glow of their own. She felt like picking one to take home, but she didn't. That wouldn't look good at all. She could just see the headlines: POLICEWOMAN STEALS PRIZE ROSES FROM GRIEVING FAMILY. Jimmy Riddle would just love that. His pate would turn scarlet. And *bang* would go her promotion.

Josie Fox had her hair tied back today, and her face looked pale and drawn, lips bloodless without makeup. She was wearing a baggy olive jumper and black jeans.

"Oh, it's you. Come in," she said listlessly, standing aside.

"I'm sorry to intrude," Susan said, following her into the living room. "But I have a few more questions."

"Of course. Sit down."

Susan sat. Josie Fox followed suit, folding her long legs under her. She massaged the bridge of her nose with her thumb and forefinger.

"Where's your husband today?" Susan asked.

She sighed. "Steven's at work. I told him not to go in, but he said he'd be better off with something to do rather than just being stuck in the house all day. I can't say I'm not glad to see the back of him for a few hours. I couldn't face going in myself. My daughter

Maureen's come down from Newcastle to stay with us, so I'm not alone."

"Is she in at the moment?"

"Upstairs, yes. Why?"

"Will you call her down, please?"

Josie Fox frowned, then shrugged and went to the bottom of the stairs to call. A minute or so later, Maureen Fox joined them. Susan's first impression was of a rather bossy, probably very fastidious, sort of girl. She was attractive, too, in a sort of bouncy blond, healthy, athletic way, with a trim figure that looked good in the tight jeans she wore, and symmetrical features, plump red lips, a creamy complexion.

Though Maureen Fox was obviously grieving, there was still a kind of energy emanating from her that she couldn't hide; it showed itself in the way her foot kept tapping on the floor, or one leg jerking when she crossed them; in her constant shifts of position, as if she were uncomfortable no matter how she sat. Susan wondered if Jason had been at all like her. Probably not, if Susan's own family were anything to go by: her brother the stockbroker, who could do no wrong, and her sister the solicitor, apple of her father's eye. Susan had nothing in common with either of them, and sometimes she thought she must have been a changeling.

"Why did you let them go?" Josie asked. "You had them in jail, the ones who did it, and you let them go."

"We don't know that they did it," Susan said. "And we can't just keep people locked up indefinitely without evidence."

"It's because they're colored, isn't it? That's why you had to let them go. It would've been different if you thought Jason had killed one of *them,* wouldn't it?"

"Mother!" Maureen cut in.

"Oh, Maureen. Don't be so naive. Everybody knows what it's like these days. The authorities bend over backward to help immigrants. You ought to know that, being in nursing. It's all opportunities for ethnics, not for decent, hardworking white folks. Look what happened to your dad."

"What did happen to Mr. Fox?" Susan asked.

"Oh," said Maureen, with a flick of her head, "Dad got passed over for promotion. Blamed it on some Asian bloke."

"I see. Well, you're right in a way, Mrs. Fox," Susan went on, looking at Josie. "The police *do* have to be very careful about how they treat people these days, especially visible minorities. We try to handle everyone the same way, no matter what color they are." She knew it was eyewash. In the overall scheme of things, racism, along with sexism, was alive and thriving in the police forces of the nation. But, damn it, that was what *she* tried to do. "In this case, though," she went on, "we simply have no evidence yet to connect the suspects to the crime. No witnesses. No physical evidence. Nothing."

"Does that mean they didn't do it?" Josie asked.

"It raises doubts," said Susan. "That's all. I'm afraid I can't say any more about it at the moment."

"You haven't given up, have you?"

"Certainly not. We're investigating a number of leads. That's why I'm here." She paused. "I'm afraid we turned up a couple of disturbing facts about your son."

Josie Fox frowned. "Disturbing? Like what?"

"Did you know about Jason's racist views?"

"What do you mean?"

"Did he never talk about his opinions to you?"

"He never really talked about anything much," she said. "Especially not these past few years."

"Were you aware of what he thought about Asians and blacks?"

"Well," said Josie Fox, "let's put it this way. I knew he had some opinions that might be unpopular, you know, about foreigners, immigrants and such, but I wouldn't say they were particularly extreme. Lots of people think the way Jason does and it doesn't make them racists."

That was a new one on Susan: having racist views doesn't make you a racist? "Did Jason ever mention belonging to any sort of an organization?" she asked. "A group of like-minded people?"

It was Maureen Fox who broke the silence. "No. Jason never mentioned it, but he did. Belong to a group, that is. We only found out about it yesterday."

"Maureen!"

"Oh, Mother. Jason was a creep and you know it. That's why he could never keep a girlfriend. I don't care if I am speaking ill of the dead. I could never stomach him even when he was at school back in Halifax. All his talk about bloody racial purity making the country great again. It made me want to puke. It was those skins he hung around with at school, you know, them and their masters, the ones who prey on schoolkids in depressed areas. You should have done something, you and Dad."

"Like what?" Josie Fox beseeched her. "What could we have done to change him?"

"How do I know what you should have done? But you're his parents. You should have done *something*." She turned to Susan. "Yesterday we went to visit my granddad," she said. "He showed us a pamphlet he thought Jason had sent him in the post. He was very upset about it."

"The Albion League?"

"You know?"

Susan nodded. "Your grandfather told DCI Banks yesterday evening."

Maureen looked at her mother. "There. I told you Granddad wouldn't be able to keep it to himself." She turned to Susan. "Mum thought we should keep it in the family, to protect the family name, but . . ." She shrugged. "Well, the cat's out of the bag now, isn't it?"

"I still don't see what this has to do with anything," Josie Fox protested. "Now you're making out my Jason was the villain, but he was the victim. Are you suggesting those boys might have killed him because of his beliefs?"

"Could they have known?"

"What do you mean?"

Susan paused for a moment, then continued softly, "Jason wasn't here very often, Mrs. Fox. He didn't put down roots, didn't get to know people. Could those boys have known about him, about what he . . . believed?"

"They could have found out somehow, I suppose. They're Asians, so I suppose they have their own gangs, their own networks, don't they? Maybe he did talk to one of them, that one in the shop."

"Do you know if he ever shopped there?"

"I don't know, but he might have done. It's not far away, especially if you go to the bus stop down on Cardigan Drive."

"But Jason had a car."

"Doesn't mean he never took the bus, does it? Anyway, all I'm saying is he *might* have gone in the shop. It wasn't far away. That's all."

"Do you remember about a month ago, when someone threw a brick—"

"Now, wait a minute," said Josie. "You're not going to blame that on our Jason. Oh, no. Be nice and easy for you, that, wouldn't it, blaming a crime on someone who can't answer for himself, just so you can make your crime figures look better, write it off your books."

Susan took a deep breath. "That's not my intention, Mrs. Fox. I'm trying to establish a link between Jason and George Mahmood, if there is one. Given Jason's feelings about Asians, it doesn't seem entirely beyond the realm of possibility that he chucked the brick and George knew about it."

"Well, you'll never know, will you?"

Susan sighed. "Perhaps not. Do you know if Jason gave out any of those pamphlets to anyone on the estate?"

Josie Fox shook her head. "I shouldn't think so. No, I'm fairly certain he didn't. I'd have heard about it."

I'll bet you would, Susan thought. "Did any of Jason's colleagues ever call here?"

"I told you the other day. No. We didn't know his friends." For a moment, Susan had imagined a scene like the one in the Krays' east London home, the boys upstairs planning murder and mayhem while good old mum comes in with a tray of tea and biscuits, beaming at them. Obviously not. "You'd almost think he was ashamed of us," Josie Fox added.

"Or of them," said Susan. "Look, he was seen drinking with this lad in the Jubilee on Saturday night." She turned to face Maureen again and showed her the picture. "We're trying to trace him. He might be able to help us find out what happened. Have you ever seen Jason with anyone like that?"

Maureen shook her head. "No."

"Mrs. Fox?"

"No."

"You told us Jason was working at a plastics factory in Leeds. Did you know that he left there two years ago, that he was asked to leave because of his racist views?"

Josie Fox's jaw dropped and she could only shake her head slowly, eyes disbelieving. Even Maureen paled.

"Do you know where he went after that?" Susan pressed on.

"No," said Mrs. Fox, her voice flat, defeated. "As far as we knew, that's where he worked."

"Did he ever mention anything about studying computers?"

"Not to me, no."

"Do you know where Jason lived in Leeds?"

"I gave you the address."

Susan shook her head. "He hasn't been living there in eighteen months. He moved to Rawdon. Did you never visit him?"

Again she shook her head. "No. How could we? We were both working during the week. Jason, too. Besides, he came to visit us at weekends."

"Did you never telephone him?"

"No. He said it was a shared telephone, out on the landing, and the people in the other flats didn't like to be disturbed. He'd usually ring us if he wanted to tell us he was coming up."

"What about at work?"

"No. His boss didn't like it. Jason would always ring us. I don't understand. This is all . . . Why didn't he tell us?"

"I don't know, Mrs. Fox," said Susan.

Tears welled in Josie Fox's eyes. "How could he? I mean, where did it come from, him joining such a group, not telling us anything? We used to be such a close family. We always tried to bring him up properly, decently. Where did we go wrong?"

Maureen raised her eyes and sat rigidly, arms folded over her breast, staring at a spot high on the wall, as if she were both embarrassed and disgusted by her mother's display of emotion.

Where did we go wrong? It was a question Susan had heard many times, both in the course of her work and from her own parents when they complained about her chosen career. She knew better than to try to answer it.

A lot of prejudices were inherited. Her father, for example: to all outside appearances, he was a decent and intelligent man, a regular churchgoer, a respected member of the community, yet he would never eat in an Indian restaurant because he thought he was being served horse meat, dog or cat, and that the hot spices were used to mask the taste of decay.

Susan had inherited some of his attitudes, she knew, but she also knew she could fight against them; she didn't have to be stuck with them forever. So she went to lots of Indian restaurants and got to love the food. That was why Superintendent Gristhorpe's crack about having lunch at the Himalaya had made her blush. It was exactly what she had been thinking at the time: onion bhaji and vegetable samosas. *Mmmm.*

Whatever she did, though, it was always there, at the back of her mind: that feeling, inherited from her father, that these people weren't *quite like us;* that their customs and religious beliefs were barbaric and primitive, not Christian.

Where did we go wrong? Who knew the answer to that one? Giving up on the Foxes for now, Susan closed her notebook and walked back out onto Daffodil Rise. It had started to rain again.

III

The traffic on the Leeds ring road wasn't too bad, and Banks made it to Rawdon by eleven o'clock. Number Seven Rudmore Terrace was an uninspiring stone-clad semi just off the main road to Leeds and Bradford Airport. It had a small bay window, frosted-glass panes in the door and an overgrown garden.

First, Banks headed for number nine, where he noticed the lace curtains twitch as he walked up the path. Of course, when he knocked and a woman answered, she made a great pretense of being surprised to receive a caller, and left the chain on as she checked his warrant card before inviting him in.

"You can't be too careful these days," she said cheerfully as she put the kettle on. "A woman in the next street was attacked just two weeks ago. Raped." She mouthed the word rather than speaking it out loud, as if that somehow lessened its power. "In the middle of the day, no less. I'm Liza Williams, by the way."

Liza was an attractive woman in her early thirties, with short black hair, a smooth olive complexion and light blue eyes. She led Banks through to the living room, the carpet of which was covered with children's toys. The room smelled vaguely of Plasticine and warm milk.

"Jamie's taken the twins over to their grannie's for the morning," she said, surveying the mess. "To give me a breather, like. Two two-and-a-half-year-olds can be a bit of a handful, Mr. Banks, in case you didn't know that already."

Banks smiled. "I didn't know. There's a couple of years between my boy and girl. But believe me, *one* two-and-a-half-year-old was bad enough. I can't imagine two."

Liza Williams smiled. "Oh, it's not so bad really. I complain but . . . I wouldn't want to be without them. Now, I don't suppose you came here to talk about children. Is it about that woman in the next street?"

"No. I'm North Yorkshire CID," said Banks. "That'd be West Yorkshire."

"Yes, of course. I should have noticed the card." She frowned. "That just makes me even more puzzled."

"It's about next door, Mrs. Williams."

She paused, then her eyes widened. "Oh, I see. Yes, that's so sad, isn't it? And him so young."

"I'm sorry?"

"You mean about the boy who was killed, don't you? Jason. In Eastvale. That's North Yorkshire, isn't it?"

"You knew?"

"Well, we *were* neighbors, even if we weren't especially close ones. They say good fences make good neighbors, Mr. Banks, and you need a big one to keep that ugly garden of his out of view. But fair's fair. He was quiet and considerate and he never complained about the twins."

"Look, do you think we could just back up for a minute and get a few things straight?"

"Of course."

"Jason Fox lived next door, at number seven, right?"

"Yes. That's what I was telling you."

"Okay. And you read in the paper that Jason was killed in Eastvale on Saturday night?"

"Saw it on telly, actually. How else would I know? Soon as I heard it was him you could have knocked me over with a feather."

"How did you know it wasn't some other Jason Fox?"

"Well, it's not that common a name, is it, and even if the sketch they showed on the news wasn't very good, I could still recognize him from it."

The kettle boiled and Liza Williams excused herself to make tea. She came back with a tray, a pot and two mugs.

"Why didn't you call the police?" Banks asked.

She frowned. "Police? But why should I? Did I do something wrong?"

"No. I'm not accusing you of anything. Just curious."

"Well, I never thought. Why would I? I didn't really know anything about Jason. Anyway, I was really very sorry to hear about what happened, but it didn't have anything to do with me, did it? It's none of *my* business. I mean, I've never even *been* to Eastvale."

"But didn't you think the police might want to have a look around the house where Jason lived, maybe ask you a few questions about him?"

"Well . . . I . . . I don't know what to say. I'm sorry. I just assumed if the police wanted to ask me anything, they'd have asked me when they were round earlier. I thought you'd done what you had to do. I don't know what happens to people's houses after—"

"Just a minute," said Banks, sitting on the edge of his seat. "Did you say the police have already been around?"

"Yes. Plainclothes. Didn't you know?"

"Obviously not, or I wouldn't be asking you all these questions." Liza Williams didn't look or sound like a stupid woman. What could she be thinking of? "When was this?"

"Sunday morning. Before I'd even heard what happened. Why? Is something wrong?"

"No. No. It's all right." Banks scratched the scar beside his right eye. Liza poured the tea, meeting his eyes as she did so and splashing a little tea on the tray. She handed Banks a steaming mugful. "Did they talk to you?" he asked.

"No. They just went into Jason's house. Two of them. They seemed to have a key, seemed to know what they were doing."

"How did you know they were police?"

"I didn't. I just assumed, the way they seemed so purposeful. Then, later that night, when I saw about Jason on the telly . . . It seemed to make sense."

"What time was this, when they came?"

"Must have been about ten o'clock. Jamie had just come back from the newsagent's with the papers. We don't have them delivered bec—"

Banks tuned her out. At first he had considered the possibility, however remote, that West Yorkshire had been playing left hand to North Yorkshire's right. But Susan Gay hadn't even discovered Jason Fox's identity until lunchtime on Sunday, and the Foxes hadn't officially identified him until after that. So who had known who the victim was before the police did? And how had they found out?

Banks blew on his tea, took a sip, then leaned forward again. "This is very important, Mrs. Williams," he said. "Can you tell me anything about these men?"

IV

Steven Fox clearly wasn't expecting Susan, and his face showed surprise and suspicion when she turned up in his office at the building society.

"Time for a word?" she asked, smiling.

He looked at his watch. "I suppose so. It's almost lunchtime anyway."

"My treat," said Susan. She sighed inwardly, realizing she'd have to forgo the Himalaya.

Steven Fox put on his raincoat, and they walked along York Road to the El Toro coffee bar on the opposite side of the market square from the police station. The El Toro, with its dim lighting, castanet-clicking Muzak, bullfight posters and smell of espresso, wasn't renowned for its food, but the sandwiches were decent enough: Susan treated herself to prawn and tomato and Steven Fox settled for ham and cheese.

Once they had taken a bite or two and sipped some coffee, Susan began: "Would you be surprised to hear that Jason was no longer working where you told us he was?"

Steven Fox paused and rubbed his glasses, steamed up by the coffee. "To be honest," he said, "nothing much would surprise me about Jason. He was a law unto himself."

"His mother was surprised."

"Maybe she had more illusions."

That might explain, Susan thought, why Steven Fox had seemed quicker to accept that Jason might have met a violent end than Josie had been.

"And you?" she asked.

"Jason was a peculiar lad. We never had a very close relationship. I don't know why."

"Did you know anything about his affiliation with the Albion League?"

"Not until yesterday, no." Steven Fox shook his head slowly. "When Jason left home," he said, "that was it. We never really knew what he was up to after then. Still, I don't suppose it's the kind of thing you do tell your parents, is it? I mean, can you imagine your son sitting down at the dinner table one night and saying, 'Guess what, Mum, Dad. I joined a neo-Nazi party today'?"

"Not unless he thought you shared his views."

Steven banged his coffee cup down on the saucer, spilling some. "Now, hold on a minute, that's quite an allegation. I resent that. I'm not a racist."

Susan held her hand up. "I'm not alleging anything, Mr. Fox. I simply want to know."

"Well, he didn't get it from me or his mother."

"Do you have any ideas as to where he did get it from?"

"Well, that kind of thing . . . Do you really think it's as simple as . . . you know, just picking up or imitating someone's manner-isms or figures of speech?"

"No, I don't. But he had to start somewhere. What about this promotion business?"

"Josie told you about that?"

"Maureen, actually."

Steven Fox shrugged. "Back in Halifax, I lost out on a promo-tion to a fellow from Bengal. Nice chap, but . . . It was that, what do you call it . . . ?"

"Positive discrimination?"

"Aye, only giving jobs to immigrants and women. Sorry. But I had more experience. And I'd put in more years. Anyway, it gave us some hard times, not enough money coming in, that sort of thing. I think Jason took it more to heart than I did, maybe because he already had some problems of his own at school. There were a lot of Asians there, recent immigrants for the most part, some of them with poor language skills, and Jason got into trouble once for suggesting to a teacher that they were holding back the rest and ought to be put together in a special class."

"How long ago was that?"

"In his last year there. Just before we moved."

"Didn't that concern you?"

"Well, it . . . I mean, in a way, I suppose, he was right, wasn't he? Maybe he should have put it more diplomatically. Lord knows, as I said, I'm no racist, but it seems to me that if you keep on catering to the demands of foreign cultures and other religions over your own, then you do sort of . . . weaken . . . your own, don't you? For crying out loud, they don't even sing a hymn and say the Lord's Prayer at morning assembly anymore."

Susan moved on quickly. "Do you know the people who run the shop on Gallows View? The Mahmoods?"

"I know who you mean—I've nipped in there for a tin of soup from time to time—but I can't say I *know* them."

"Remember about a month ago when someone chucked a brick though their window?"

"I read about it in the local paper. Why?"

"Was Jason up that weekend?"

"Oh, come on," said Steven. "Surely you can't imagine he'd do something like that?"

"Why not?"

"He wasn't a hooligan."

"But he *was* a racist."

"Still . . . anyway, I don't remember if he was here or not. And aren't you supposed to be looking for his killers?"

"Every little bit helps, Mr. Fox. He wasn't living at the address you gave us in Leeds. Did you know that?"

"Not living there?" Steven Fox shook his head. "Bloody hell, no. I just assumed . . . I mean, why would he lie about that?"

"I don't think he lied. He just omitted to let you know. Maybe he thought you weren't interested."

Steven Fox frowned. "You must think us terribly neglectful parents."

Susan said nothing.

"But Jason was over eighteen," he went on. "He led his own life."

"So you said. He still visited home, though."

"He came home on weekends to get his washing done and get a free meal, like lots of kids do."

"You said earlier that you and Jason were never close. Why was that?"

"I don't know really. When he was younger, he was always more of a mother's boy. Then, in his teens, he got involved in football. I've never been much interested in sports myself. I was never very good at games at school. Always the last one to be picked, that sort of thing. I suppose I should have gone to watch him play, you know, shown more support . . . enthusiasm. It's not that I wasn't proud of him." He shook his head. "Maybe I was selfish. I had my record collection to catalog. Jason had his football. We just didn't seem to have anything in common. But I couldn't see where any of it was leading. How could I know?" He looked at his watch. "Look, I really do have to get back. I can't tell you anything more, honestly. If those boys really did kill Jason, you know, those immigrants you had to let go, I hope you find some evidence against them. If there's anything else I can do . . . ?"

And he got up to leave. Susan nodded, more than happy to see the back of him. For the second time that day she'd had to restrain herself from screaming that George, Asim and Kobir weren't immigrants, that they'd been bloody well born here, and their fathers before them. But she didn't. What was the point?

And now she had to go to the Himalaya and talk to Asim Nazur and his parents. They would certainly be thrilled to see her. Still, wicked though it sounded, maybe she still had room for a small samosa, after all. Just the one. For a simple pub fight gone wrong, she thought, this case was turning into a hell of a confusing affair.

V

The little pane of glass in the front door smashed easily enough when Banks applied his elbow. He stuck his hand through carefully and turned the lock. He had a warrant to search the place and, as Jason's pockets had been emptied of everything, including his house keys, this seemed the easiest way to get in.

Inside, the house was so quiet that all he could hear was the hissing of blood in his ears. There wasn't even a clock ticking. He imagined it wasn't always like that, not with the twins next door.

He started in the living room, to his right. Three-piece suite, upholstered in tan corduroy, wallpaper with thin green and brown stripes, mirror over the mantelpiece, fake-coal electric fire. Television and video. Selection of tapes, mostly science fiction and horror by the look of them. A few paperbacks: Ayn Rand, Tom

Clancy, Michael Crichton. And that was it. There was a sideboard against one wall and in one of the drawers Banks found a couple of bills addressed to Jason Fox. Nothing else.

The kitchen was spotless, dishes all in cupboards, mugs hanging from hooks over the counter. Very little in the fridge: a tub of I Can't Believe It's Not Butter; cheddar cheese turning blue at the edges, sliced white bread, boiled ham, limp celery, lettuce, tomatoes. More the kind of stuff for sandwiches than hot meals. Maybe Jason did most of his eating out.

There were three bedrooms, one no bigger than a cupboard really. That one was completely empty, the other two showed some signs of occupation. Just as at the house in Eastvale, Jason's bed was tightly made, and a similar selection of clothes hung in the wardrobe. The dresser drawers were full of socks, underwear and T-shirts, along with an unopened box of condoms and a bottle of aspirin. The third bedroom looked like a guest room, with single bed, empty drawers and not much else.

Except the computer.

But Banks didn't trust himself not to screw something up if he started messing around with that, so he made a note to get someone else in to give it the once-over.

Back in the hall, Banks could only marvel at the sheer *emptiness* of the place. There was no personality. You'd expect, if Jason was a member of a white power organization, at least a few Skrewdriver CDs and maybe one or two copies of *The Order* strewn around the place. But it was as if someone had been there and stripped away all signs of character, if there had been any. And maybe someone had.

Two men, Liza Williams had said, and they had left with some cardboard boxes. Unfortunately, it had been raining in Leeds that Sunday morning, and they had both been wearing flat caps. Black or navy blue. One of them wore a black leather jacket and jeans, the other a donkey jacket. The one in the leather jacket was taller than the other.

No, Liza admitted, they weren't particularly well dressed, but then she watched a lot of police programs on telly, so she didn't expect real policemen to be any better dressed than their fictional counterparts. No, she couldn't say how old they were, hadn't seen their faces, but she got the impression by the way they moved that they were probably fairly young and fit.

And that was about all she could say, she was sorry. She had, after all, only glimpsed them, and as she noticed they used a key to get in, she didn't worry about them being burglars or rapists. She first thought they were friends of Jason's—he sometimes had friends to stay—and then, after she heard of his death, she just assumed they'd been policemen come to return his belongings to his family or something. No, her husband hadn't seen them; he had already settled down with the Sunday papers, and once he did that . . .

The only thing she *had* noticed was a blue car parked outside, which she thought belonged to the men. But she didn't know what make it was, let alone the number. She did say it was clean, though.

Banks sighed as he closed the door behind him. He would have to get someone from West Yorkshire to fix the pane of glass he'd broken, and perhaps to question some of the other people in the street. Whatever they'd noticed, it had to be more than Liza Williams had.

VI

By mid-afternoon, Susan was wet, tired and no further ahead than she had been in the morning. The Nazurs and the Mahmoods had been sullen and uncommunicative, as expected, and she had flinched at the clear accusations of racism in their eyes. No, Jason Fox had never been in the Mahmoods' shop, as far as they knew, and the Nazurs had never seen him in their restaurant. And they knew nothing about any Albion League.

Sergeant Hatchley was still out pounding the streets, so at least she got the opportunity to warm herself up with a cup of coffee and take a little quiet time for herself.

She had just put her cold wet feet on the radiator to warm them when one of the staff from the murder room came in bearing a fax. "Just arrived," he said.

Susan thanked him and looked at the single sheet. All it said was:

THE ALBION LEAGUE

along with a telephone number. A London number.

Curious, Susan picked up the phone and dialed. She remembered that Banks had faxed a request for information about the Albion League to Scotland Yard, so she wasn't surprised when someone there answered. After a bit of shuttling around and a lot of waiting, she finally got to someone who knew what she was talking about when she mentioned the Albion League. His name, he said, was Crawley.

"Is your boss there, love?" he asked.

Susan bristled, gripping the receiver tightly, but she said nothing.

"Well?" Crawley repeated.

"I'm afraid Detective Superintendent Gristhorpe is out of the office at the moment," Susan finally managed between gritted teeth.

"And you're DC Gay?"

"Yes." At least he didn't make any cracks about her name.

"I suppose you'll have to do then."

Not her day. "Thanks a lot," she said.

"Don't take offense, love."

"I'll try not to, sweetie pie. Now how about the Albion League?"

She heard Crawley laugh at the end of the line, then he cleared his throat. "Yeah, well, it's a neo-Nazi organization, white power. That's why we're interested, see, in why you want to know."

"I'd have thought it was a simple enough inquiry," Susan said.

"True enough, love, but nothing to do with those bastards is simple. They're flagged."

"Flagged?"

"Any time their name comes up, certain people have to be informed."

"That sounds very mysterious."

"Does it?"

"Yes. Anyway, don't worry. I'm sure DCI Banks will send you a full report—he's heading the field investigation—but would you mind, just for the moment, humoring a poor DC? Could you give me some general idea of what this particular neo-Nazi organization is all about, what they want?"

She heard another brief chuckle down the line, then Crawley said, "Want? That's easy. Same as all the rest of them, really. The usual things. Racial purity. Repatriation of immigrants and all ethnics. Keep Britain white. Oh, and they want the trains to run on time, too."

"Some hope of that."

"Tell me about it. Seriously, though, love, it's not so much what these people *want*—that's usually predictable enough—but what they're willing to do to get it—what means they'll use, how they're organized, what connections they have with other groups, whether they're armed, what international links they have, if any. That sort of thing. See what I mean?"

"Yes," said Susan. "And the Albion League, how do they fit into all that?"

There was a pause. Then Crawley said, "I'm sorry, but I'm really not authorized to tell you any more than that. Have your boss give me a bell when he comes in, will you, love?"

And the line went dead.

VII

By the time Banks had finished coordinating with West Yorkshire police, it was late afternoon. He decided to drop by Tracy's residence and see what she was up to. She had only been at the University of Leeds for a little over two weeks, but already he missed her. Maybe he could take her for a spot of dinner or something. That way he would also avoid the rush-hour traffic on the way home.

And spending time with Tracy might also make him forget about his problems with Sandra for a short while.

When he got to the student residence building beside Woodhouse Moor, he was pleased to find that not just anyone could walk in. You had to know whom you wanted to see. Banks found a porter on duty, showed his identification and said he'd like to visit his daughter.

Impressed with Banks's credentials, the garrulous porter—who said he had been a policeman himself some years ago, before a leg injury forced him to retire—let him in.

As Banks walked up the two flights of stairs, he wondered if he should have announced himself first. What if Tracy was with a boy or something? Having sex? But he dismissed the idea. He couldn't imagine his daughter doing that. Either she'd be out at a lecture, or she'd be studying in her room.

When he got to her door, he knocked. He could hear music from down the hall, but not a sound from Tracy's room itself. He knocked again, more loudly this time. Nothing. He felt disappointed. She must be at a lecture.

Just as he was about to walk away, the adjacent door opened and a young tousle-haired girl stuck her head out. "Oh, sorry," she said in a husky voice. "I thought you were knocking on *my* door. Sometimes you can't tell, if you've got some music on or something." Then her eyes twinkled. "Hey, you *weren't* knocking at my door, were you?"

"No," said Banks.

She made a mock pout. "Pity. You looking for Tracy, then?"

"I'm her father."

"The detective. She's talked a lot about you." The girl twisted a tendril of red hair around her index finger. "I must say, though, she never told me you were quite so dishy. I'm Fiona, by the way. Pleased to meet you."

She held out her hand and Banks shook it. He felt himself blush. "Any idea where Tracy might be?"

Fiona looked at her watch. "Probably in the Pack Horse with the others, by now," she said with a sigh. "I'd be there myself, 'cept I'm on antibiotics for my throat, and I'm not supposed to drink. And it's no fun if you can't have a *real* drink." She wrinkled her nose and smiled. "It's just up the road. You can't miss it."

Banks thanked her and, leaving the car parked where it was, set off on foot. He found the Pack Horse on Woodhouse Lane, close to the junction with Clarendon Road, not more than a couple of hundred yards away. He felt too formally dressed for the place, even though he had taken off his tie and was wearing casual trousers and a zippered suede jacket.

The pub had the polished wood, brass and glass look of a real Victorian alehouse; it also seemed to be divided into a maze of rooms, most of them occupied by noisy groups of students. It wasn't until the third room that Banks found his daughter. She was sitting at a cluttered table with about six or seven other students, a pretty even mix of male and female. The jukebox was playing a Beatles oldie: "Ticket to Ride."

He could see Tracy in profile, chatting away over the music to a boy beside her. God, she looked so much like Sandra—the blond hair tucked behind her small ears, black eyebrows, tilt of nose and chin, the animated features as she talked. It made his heart ache.

Banks didn't like the look of the boy beside her. He had one of those expressions that always seem to be sneering at the world: something to do with the twist of the lip and the cast of the eyes.

Either Tracy didn't notice, or it didn't bother her. Or, worse, she found it attractive.

As she spoke, she waved her hands about, stopping now and then to listen to his response and sip from a pint glass of pale amber liquid, nodding in agreement from time to time. Her drink could have been lager, but Banks thought it was most likely cider. Tracy had always enjoyed nonalcoholic cider when they'd stopped for pub lunches during family holidays in Dorset or the Cotswolds.

But this glass of cider was probably alcoholic. And why not? he told himself. She was old enough. At least she wasn't smoking.

Then, as he stood there in the doorway, a strange emotion overwhelmed him. As he watched his daughter talk, laugh and drink, oblivious to her father's proximity, a lump came to his throat, and he realized he had lost her. He couldn't go over to the table and join the crowd—simply couldn't do it. He didn't belong; his presence would only embarrass her. A line had been reached and crossed. Tracy was beyond him now, and things would never be the same. And he wondered if that was the only line that had been crossed lately.

Banks turned away and walked outside. The wind made his eyes water as he went in search of somewhere else to enjoy a quiet smoke and a drink before setting off back home.

VIII

That Tuesday night, the Albion League was holding one of its regular bashes in a small rented warehouse near Shipley. Dim and cavernous, it was the same kind of place people went to for raves, but without the Ecstasy. Here, Craig guessed, the only drugs were the lager that flowed from the kegs like water from a hosepipe, nicotine and, maybe, the odd tab of amphetamine.

But one way or another everyone was pumped up. Guitars,

drums and bass crashed at breakneck pace, simple three-chord sequences, interrupted occasionally by a howl of unplanned feedback from the amps. The Albion League themselves were playing tonight, a makeshift white power band consisting of whoever felt like picking up the instruments at the time. At the moment the lead singer was growling,

> *White is white.*
> *Black is black.*
> *We don't want 'em.*
> *Send 'em back.*

Subtle. Craig wished he could wear earplugs.

From his table, Craig watched Motcombe work the room. He was good, no doubt about it. Slick. There must be at least a couple of hundred people in the place, Craig guessed, and Nev was walking around the tables patting a back here, leaning over for a smile and a word of encouragement there.

It was a miracle he managed to make himself heard with the band making so much bloody noise. Some of the older members, chronically unemployed factory workers and aging skins, had settled into a far corner, as far away from the source of the racket as possible. What did they expect, Craig wondered, the Black Dyke Mills Band playing "Deutschland Über Alles" or Wagner's *Ring* cycle? It was the rock bands that got the kids in, *and* got the message across through sheer volume and repetition.

The real trouble with this gig, Craig thought as he looked around, was that there was no chance of a bit of nooky. For some reason, girls didn't have much to do with white power freaks, and most of the kids, in turn, seemed content enough with a celibate existence, fueled by sheer race hatred alone.

The only females Craig could see tonight were a few peroxide scrubbers, like superannuated biker girls, hanging out with the older crowd, and a table of skinny birds with shaved heads and rings through their noses. He sighed and drank some lager. Can't have everything. A job's a job.

The music stopped and the singer said they were going to take a short break. Thank God for that, thought Craig. Trying to keep one eye on Motcombe, he turned to the three skins at the table with him.

Christ, he thought, they couldn't be more than sixteen. One of the Leeds cell leaders had spotted them causing a bit of aggro to a telephone box on their way home from a football match. He had joined in with them, then invited them to the show. Thick as two short planks, all three of them.

"What did you think of that, then?" Craig asked, lighting up.

"Not bad," said the spotty one, who went by the name of Billy. "I've heard better guitar players, mind you."

"Yeah, well," Craig said with a shrug, "they're pretty new, need a bit more practice, I'll admit. See, with this lot, though, it's the words that count most. Trouble is, most rock bands don't really pay any attention to what they're saying, know what I mean? I'm talking about the message."

"What message?" the slack-jawed one asked.

"Well, see, if you were listening," Craig went on, "you'd have heard what they were saying about that we should send all the Pakis and niggers back home and get this country on its feet again."

"Oh, yeah," said Billy. " 'White's white, black's black, we don't want 'em, send 'em back.' "

"That's right." Craig smiled. "So you *were* listening. Great. That's what I mean, Billy. Most rock music is self-indulgent crap, but this is real music, music with a purpose. It's truth-telling music, this is. It tells it like it is."

"Yeah," said slack-jaw. "I think I see what you mean."

In your fucking dreams, thought Craig. From the corner of his eye, he saw Motcombe about five tables away whispering in someone's ear. He couldn't make out who it was. How many irons did this one have in the fire? Even though the band had stopped playing, music still blared out of a sound system and the level of conversation was loud.

"So what do you think?" he asked. "The message?"

"Well, yeah," said pointy-head, speaking up for the first time. "It sounds all right. Send 'em all back, like. I mean, it sounds good to me." He grinned, showing bad teeth and looked around at his friends. "I mean, kick the fuckers out, right? Eh? Send the black bastards back to the jungle. Kick the fuckers out."

"Right," said Craig. "You've got it. Thing is, there's not much a person can do by himself, all alone, if you see what I mean."

"Except wank." Slack-jaw grinned.

Ah, a true wit. Craig laughed. "Yeah, except wank. And you don't want to be wankers, do you? Anyway, see, if you get organized, like with others who feel the same way, then there's a lot more you can achieve? Right?"

"Right," said Billy. "Stands to reason, don't it?"

"Okay," Craig went on, noticing the band picking up their instruments again. "Think about it, then."

"About what?" Billy asked.

"What I've just been saying. About joining the league. Where you get a chance to *act* on your beliefs. We have a lot of fun, too."

A screech of feedback came from the amp. Billy put his hands over his ears. "Yeah, I can see," he said.

He was clearly the leader of the three, Craig thought, the Alex of the group, the others were just his droogs. If Billy decided it was a good idea, they'd go along with him. Craig noticed Motcombe glance around the room, then walk out of the fire exit at the back with one of the Leeds cell leaders. He stood up and leaned over the three skins. "Keep in touch, then," he said, as the music started again. He pointed. "See that bloke at the table there, over by the door?"

Billy nodded.

"If you decide you want to sign up tonight, he's the man to talk to."

"Right."

He patted Billy on the back. "Got to go for a piss. See you later."

Casually, he walked toward the toilets near the front door. The band had started their tribute to Ian Stuart, late leader of Skrewdriver who, Blood and Honour claimed, had been murdered by the secret service. And now the Albion League had a martyr on their hands. He wondered how quickly someone would write a song about Jason Fox.

Anyway, the toilets were empty, and most people were either talking loudly or listening to the band, so no one saw Craig nip out the front door. Not that it mattered, anyway; the room was so hot and smoky that no one could be suspect for going out for a breath of fresh air.

Instead of just standing there and enjoying the smell of the cool, damp night, he walked around the back of the building toward the big car park. Glancing around the corner, he saw Motcombe and the Leeds skin standing by Motcombe's black van talking. The car park was badly lit, so Craig found it easy enough to crouch down and scoot closer, hiding behind a rusty old Metro, watching them through the windows.

It didn't take long to figure out that they were talking about money. As Craig watched, the Leeds skin handed Motcombe a fistful of notes. Motcombe took a box out of his van and opened it. Then he placed the bills inside. The skin said something Craig couldn't catch, then they shook hands and he went back inside.

Motcombe stood for a moment glancing around, sniffing the air. Craig felt a twinge of fear, as if Motcombe had twitched his antenna, sensed a presence.

But it passed. Motcombe opened the box, took out a handful of notes and stuffed them in his inside pocket. Then he squared his shoulders and strutted back in to work the crowd again.

FIVE

I

"The Albion League," said Gristhorpe in the Boardroom on Wednesday morning, his game leg resting on the polished oval table, thatch of gray hair uncombed. Banks, Hatchley and Susan Gay sat listening, cups of coffee steaming in front of them. "I've been on the phone to this bugger Crawley for about half an hour, but somehow I feel I know less than when I started. Know what I mean?"

Banks nodded. He'd spoken to people like that. Still, some had said the same thing about him, too.

"Anyway," Gristhorpe went on, "they're exactly what they sound like in their pamphlet—a neo-Nazi fringe group. Albion's an old poetic name for the British Isles. You find it in Chaucer, Shakespeare, Spenser and lots of other poets. Anyway, according to Crawley, this lot took it from William Blake, who elevated Albion into some sort of mythical spirit of the race."

"Is this Blake a Nazi, then, sir?" Sergeant Hatchley asked.

"No, Sergeant," Gristhorpe answered patiently. "William Blake was an English poet. He lived from 1757 to 1827. You'd probably know him best as the bloke who wrote 'Jerusalem' and 'Tyger, Tyger!'"

"'Tyger! Tyger! burning bright'?" said Hatchley. "Aye, sir, I think we did that one at school."

"Most likely you did."

"And we sometimes used to sing the other one on the coach home after a rugby match. But isn't Jerusalem in Israel, sir? Was this Blake Jewish, then?"

"Again, Sergeant, no. I'll admit it sounds an ironic sort of symbol for a neo-Nazi organization. But, as I said, Blake liked to mythologize things. To him, Jerusalem was a sort of image of the ideal city, a spiritual city, a perfect society, if you like—of which London was a pale, fallen shadow—and he wanted to establish a *new* Jerusalem 'in England's green and pleasant land.'"

"Was he green, then, sir, one of them environmentalists?"

"No, he wasn't."

Banks could see Gristhorpe gritting his teeth in frustration. He felt like kicking Hatchley under the table, but he couldn't reach. The sergeant was trying it on, of course, but Hatchley and Gristhorpe always seemed to misunderstand one another. You wouldn't have thought they were both Yorkshiremen under the skin.

"Blake's Albion was a powerful figure, ruler of this ideal kingdom," Gristhorpe went on. "A figure of which even the heroes of the Arthurian legends were mere shadows."

"How long have they been around?" Banks asked.

Gristhorpe turned to him, clearly with some relief. "About a year," he said. "They started as a splinter group of the British National Party, which turned out to be too soft for them. And they think they're a cut above Combat 18, who they regard as nowt but a bunch of thugs."

"Well, they're right on that count," Banks said. "Who's the grand Pooh-Bah?"

"Bloke called Neville Motcombe. Aged thirty-five. You'd think he'd be old enough to know better, wouldn't you?"

"Any form?"

"One arrest for assaulting a police officer during a BNP rally years back, and another for receiving stolen goods."

"Any connection with George Mahmood and his friends?" Banks asked.

Gristhorpe shook his head. "Other than the obvious, none."

"Surely the Albion League isn't based in Eastvale, sir?" Susan Gay asked.

Gristhorpe laughed. "No. That's just where Jason Fox's parents happen to live. Luck of the draw, as far as we're concerned. Their headquarters are in Leeds—an old greengrocer's shop in Holbeck—but they've got cells all over West Yorkshire, especially in places where there's a high percentage of immigrants. As I said before, they're not above using the yobs, but there's also that element of a more intellectual appeal to disaffected white middle-class kids with chips on their shoulders—lads like Jason Fox, with a few bobs' worth of brains and nobbut an a'porth of common sense."

"How strong are they?" Banks asked.

"Hard to say. According to Crawley, there's about fifteen cells, give or take a couple. One each in smaller places like Batley and Liversedge, but two or three in a larger city like Leeds. We don't really know how many members in each cell, but as a rough estimate let's say maybe eighty to a hundred members in all."

"Not a lot, is it? Where does this Motcombe bloke live?"

"Pudsey, down by Fulneck way. Apparently he's got a nice detached house there."

Banks raised his eyebrows. "La-di-da. Any idea how they're financed—apart from receiving stolen goods?"

"Crawley says he doesn't know."

"Do you believe him?"

Gristhorpe sniffed and scratched his hooked nose. "I smell politics in this one, Alan," he said. "And when I smell politics I don't believe anything I see or hear."

"Do you want Jim and me to have a poke around in Leeds?" Banks asked.

"Just what I was thinking. You could pay the shop a visit, for a start. See if there's anyone around. Clear it with Ken Blackstone first, make sure you're not treading on anyone's toes."

Banks nodded. "What about Motcombe?"

Gristhorpe paused before answering. "I got the impression that Crawley didn't want us bothering Mr. Motcombe," he said slowly. "In fact, I think Crawley was only detailed to answer our request for information because they knew down there that we'd simply blunder ahead and find out anyway. The bull-in-a-china-shop approach. He was very vague indeed. And he asked us to proceed with caution."

"So what do we do?"

A wicked grin creased Gristhorpe's face. "Well," he said, tugging his plump earlobe, "I'd pay him a visit, if I were you. Rattle his chain a bit. I mean, it's not as if we've been officially warned off."

Banks smiled. "Right."

"One more thing before you all go. These letters at the bottom of the Albion League's flyer." Gristhorpe lifted the pamphlet from the table and pointed. "*Http://www.alblgue.com./index.html.* Now you all know I'm a bloody Luddite when it comes to computers, but even I know that's a Web page address. Don't ask me what a Web page looks like, mind you. Question is, can we do anything with it? Is it likely to get us anywhere? Susan?"

"It might do," said Susan Gay. "Unfortunately, we don't have access to the Internet over the station computers."

"Oh. Why not?"

"I don't know, sir. Just slow, I suppose. South Yorkshire's even got their own Web page. And West Mercia."

Gristhorpe frowned. "What do they do with them?"

Susan shrugged. "Put out information. Community relations. Crime stoppers. Chief constable's opinion on the state of the county. That sort of thing. It's an interface with the community."

"Is it, indeed?" Gristhorpe grunted. "Sounds like a complete bloody waste of time to me. Still, if this Albion League thing's worth a try, is there some way you could have a peek? Or should I say surf?"

Susan smiled. "Browse, actually, sir. You surf the Net, but you browse the Web."

"And is there any wonder I've no patience with the bloody machines?" Gristhorpe muttered. "Whatever you call it, can you get a look at it?"

Susan nodded. "I've got a hook-up from home," she said. "I can certainly give it a try."

"Then do it, and let us know what you find. Alan, did those lads from West Yorkshire find anything on Jason Fox's computer?"

Banks shook his head. "Clean as a whistle."

"Clean as in somebody washed it?"

"That's what they said."

Gristhorpe grimaced as he shifted his bad leg and shook it to improve the circulation before standing up. "Right, then," he said. "That's about it for now. Let's get cracking."

II

Susan enjoyed the unexpected surprise of being able to go home during working hours, even though she knew she was there to work.

First, she kicked off her shoes and put on the kettle. Then she looked through her collection of different tea varieties and settled on Autumn, a black tea dotted with small pieces of apple, perfect for the drizzly, blustery day. On impulse, she put a pinch of cinnamon in the pot, too. While the tea was brewing, she put on her CD of Andrew Lloyd Webber's greatest hits, smiling as she thought how much Banks would hate it, then she poured herself a cup of tea and got down to work.

The computer was in her bedroom because her flat was so small. It was the one room where she never received visitors. At least not yet. But she wasn't going to allow herself to think about DC Gavin Richards right now.

Cup of apple-and-cinnamon-scented tea steaming beside her and "Don't Cry for Me, Argentina" drifting in from the living room, Susan curled her feet under her on the office chair and logged in. Then she typed in the address from the flyer and clicked her mouse.

The screen remained blank for a long time as the various bits and pieces of the document coming in over the telephone line added up, then suddenly it turned black.

Next, a multicolored image began to appear, line by line from the top of the screen down, and soon the Albion League's emblem, a swastika made out of burning golden arrows, appeared in full. Probably, Susan thought, remembering Superintendent Gristhorpe's words and the Blake song, it was some sort of image of Blake's "arrows of desire."

Around the top of the swastika, the words THE ALBION LEAGUE curled in a semicircle of bold Gothic script.

It took a couple of minutes for the rest of the document to transfer. When it was complete, Susan started browsing through it. "Memory" floated in from the living room.

Unlike pages in a book, Web pages have an extra dimension provided by hypertext links, highlighted words or icons you can click on to go to another, related site. At first, Susan ignored these links and concentrated on reading the text. It was much the same as the pamphlet she had seen, only there was more of it.

The first paragraph welcomed the reader to the page and explained that the Albion League was a fast-growing group of concerned citizens dedicated to ethnic purity, freedom of speech, law and order, and the establishment of the true English "homeland."

After that came a number of links. Some were closely related sites, such as the British National Party's home page or Combat 18, and some were American or Canadian, such as Stormfront, Aryan Nation and the Heritage Front. They varied from the fairly literate to the downright unreadable, but some of the graphics were imaginatively conceived. Susan had never thought members of white-power groups to be particularly creative or intelligent. She had to remind herself that, these days, you didn't have to be an Einstein to work a computer. Almost any kid could do it.

She opted for the league's "News" icon and was soon treated to a number of recent stories from the unique perspective of the Albion League.

The first item concerned the amount of public money being channeled toward the huge new mosque under construction between Leeds and Bradford, and contrasted it with the shocking state of disrepair of most of Britain's churches.

The second contended that a leading academic had "proved" humans were actually descended from pale-skinned northern tribes rather than from "hairy Africans."

And so it went on: a Tory MP known for his stand on morality and family values had been surprised by a police raid on a homosexual brothel in Sheffield, wearing only a blond wig and a tutu; Leeds City Council had voted to rename one of the city's streets after a black revolutionary "scum" . . . example after example of government hypocrisy, just deserts and cultural decay.

One story concerned a white schoolboy who had been stabbed just outside the gates of a Bradford comprehensive school by three members of an Asian gang. It was a sad-enough tale—and Susan remembered reading about it in the *Yorkshire Post* only a couple of weeks ago—but according to the Albion League, the tragic stabbing had occurred because the local council was dominated by "ethnics" and by their brainwashed, politically correct white lackeys, who had all known about the school's problems for years but had never done anything. The victim could, therefore, be seen as "a sacrifice to the multiracial society." Susan wondered what they would make of Jason Fox's death.

She paused and took a sip of cold tea to soothe her stomach. The Lloyd Webber had finished ages ago and she had been too absorbed to go into the living room and put something else on. Though she hadn't actually learned much more about the Albion League and its members from the Web page, she had learned enough to make her question how she felt about freedom of speech. These people would claim all attempts to silence them violated their basic democratic freedom. Yet given any power at all, they would silence everyone but straight white males.

At the end of the league's page, Susan found, as with many sites, a hypertext link to the page's designers. In this case, the name was "FoxWood Designs."

Curious, Susan clicked on the name. Again she was disappointed. She had expected names and addresses, but all she got was a stylized graphic image of a fox peering out from some dark trees, along with an E-mail address.

Still, she thought, as she made a note of the address, there was a slight chance that if one half of the team was Mr. Fox, then the other half was Mr. Wood. And if she could track down Mr. Wood, then she might just find *one* person who knew something about Jason Fox's life. And his death.

As soon as Susan hung up her modem, the telephone rang.

It was Gavin.

"Susan? Where've you been? I've been trying to phone you all morning. I bumped into Jim Hatchley in the station and he told me you were working at home."

"That's right," Susan said. "What do you want?"

"Charming. And I was going to invite you to lunch."

"Lunch?"

"Yes. You know, that stuff you eat to keep you alive."

"I don't know . . ." said Susan.

"Oh, come on. Even a hardworking DC needs a spot of lunch now and then, surely?"

Come to think of it, Susan *was* hungry. "Half an hour?"

"If that's all you can spare me."

"It is."

"Then I'll take it."

"And you're paying?"

"I'm paying."

Susan grinned to herself. "Right. See you at the Hope and Anchor in ten minutes."

III

The old greengrocer's turned out to be a former corner shop at the end of a street of back-to-backs between Holbeck Moor and Elland Road. The windows were boarded with plywood, on which various obscenities, swastikas and racist slogans had been spray-painted. Drizzle suited the scene perfectly, streaking the soot-covered red brick and the faded sign over the door that read ARTHUR GELDERD: GREENGROCER.

Banks wondered what Artur Gelderd, Greengrocer, would have thought if he knew what had become of his shop. Like Frank Hepplethwaite, Arthur Gelderd had probably fought against Hitler in the war. And forty years or more ago, before the supermarkets, this place would have been one of the local neighborhood meeting places, and a center of gossip; it would also have provided Gelderd and his family with a modest living. Now it was the headquarters of the Albion League.

Banks and Hatchley looked the building over in the slanting drizzle for a moment. Cars hissed by on Ingram Road, splashing up dirty rainwater from the gutters. The window in the shop door was protected by wire mesh, and the glass itself was covered with old adverts for Omo and Lucozade, so you couldn't see inside. In the center was a cardboard clock face to show the time the shop would next be open. It was set at nine o'clock, and it would probably be set at that time forever.

Sergeant Hatchley knocked with his hamlike fist; the door rattled in its frame, but no one answered. He tried the handle, but the place was locked. In the silence after the knocking, Banks thought he heard a sound inside.

"What do we do?" Hatchley asked.

"Knock again."

Hatchley did so. Harder this time.

It did the trick. A voice from behind the door shouted, "What do you want?"

"Police," said Banks. "Open up."

They heard someone remove a chain and turn a key in a lock, then the door opened.

For some reason, the new occupants hadn't removed the bell that hung on its pliant arc of metal at the back of the door, and it jangled as Banks and Hatchley walked in. The sound reminded Banks of childhood errands to his local corner shop, the way he used to watch, hypnotized, as Mrs. Bray turned the handle on the machine and the bacon swung back and forth in the slicer, making a whooshing sound every time the whirling wheel blade carved off a slice; he remembered the smoky smell of the cured meat in the air, mingled with fresh bread and apples.

What he smelled when he walked in now soon put such nostalgia out of his mind—burned carbon from the photocopier and laser printer, recent paint, smoke and fresh-cut paper.

The place didn't even resemble a shop anymore. What must have been the counter was covered with stacks of paper—more copies of the flyer, by the looks of it—and a computer hummed on a desk beside a telephone. On the walls were a framed poster of Adolf Hitler in full spate, addressing one of the Nuremberg rallies, by the look of it, and a large image of a swastika made out of burning arrows.

A short young man with lank black hair, antique National Health glasses and a spotty face shut the door behind them. "Always happy to help the local police," he said with a stupid grin. "We're on the same side, we are."

"Fuck off, sonny," said Banks. "What's your name?"

The young man blinked at the insult and stepped back a pace. "There's no need—"

"Name?" Banks repeated as he and Hatchley advanced, backing the young man up against the counter.

The kid held his hands up. "All right, all right. Don't hit me. It's Des. Des Parker."

"We're just going to have a little look around, Des, if that's all right with you," Banks said.

Des frowned. "Don't you need a search warrant? I mean, I know my rights."

Banks stopped and raised his eyebrows. He looked at Hatchley. "Hear that, Jim? Des here knows his rights."

"Aye," said Hatchley, walking toward the telephone and picking up the receiver. "Shall I do the honors, sir?"

Des looked puzzled. "What honors? What's he doing?"

"Getting a search warrant," Banks explained. "In about half an hour we'll have fifty flatfoots going over the place with a fine-tooth comb. Sergeant Hatchley and I will stay here with you until they arrive. Maybe you'd like to inform the building's owner—if it's not you—while we wait. He might want to be here to make sure *his* rights aren't violated."

Des gulped. "Mr. Motcombe . . . He wouldn't like that."

"So what?"

"What's going on, Des? Who the fuck is this? Is there a problem?"

The new speaker came out of the back room, zipping up his fly, accompanied by the sound of a toilet flushing. This one looked a few years older than Des Parker and at least fifty brain cells brighter. Tall and skinny, he was wearing a black T-shirt, jeans and red braces, and his dyed-blond hair was cut very close to his skull. He also wore a diamond stud in one ear and spoke with a strong Geordie accent. Definitely not the lad who'd been in the Jubilee with Jason Fox last Saturday.

"No problem at all," Banks said, showing his warrant card

again. "We'd just like a quick shufti around, if that's all right with you. And you are?"

The newcomer smiled. "Of course. We've got nothing to hide. I'm Ray. Ray Knott."

"But, Ray!" Des Parker protested. "Mr. Motcombe . . . We can't just let—"

"Shut it, Des, there's a good lad," said Ray with another smile. "As I said, we've nothing to hide." He turned to Banks. "Sorry about my mate," he said, pointing to his temple. "He's none too bright, isn't Des. Few bricks short of load."

Banks picked up a copy of the flyer. "What's this, then, Ray? The Albion League? A new football league, perhaps? Out to rival the Premier, are you?"

"Very funny," said Ray. But he wasn't laughing.

"Tell us about Jason Fox," Banks prompted.

"Jason? What about him? He's dead. Kicked to death by Pakis. You lot let them go."

Hatchley, still poking around, brushed against the huge stack of pamphlets on the counter. They fell to the floor, scattering all over the place. Ray and Des said nothing.

"Sorry," said Hatchley. "Clumsy of me."

Banks marveled at him. Full of contradictions and surprises was Jim Hatchley. While he'd pin photos of half-naked women on his corkboard—at least he did before Susan moved in—he hated pornographers; and while he'd join in with lads laughing at racist jokes, and was certainly a casual bigot himself, he didn't like neo-Nazis, either. Of course, none of it seemed like a contradiction to him. The way he put it, he wasn't prejudiced, he hated everyone.

"We're not sure who killed him yet," said Banks. "Where were the two of you at that time?"

Ray laughed. "You can't be serious. Us? Kill Jason? No way. He was one of us."

"So it won't do you any harm to tell me where you were, would it?"

"I were at home," Des said.

"By yourself?"

"No. I live with me mum."

"And I'm sure she's really proud of you, Des. Address?"

Des, stuttering, told him.

"What about you, Ray?"

Ray folded his arms and leaned against the counter, one leg crossed over the other, big grin on his face. "Drinking in my local."

"Which is?"

"The Oakwood. Up Gipton way."

"Witnesses?"

Ray grinned. "Six or seven at least. Local darts championship. I won."

"Congratulations. What about Sunday morning?"

"Sleeping it off. Why?"

"Alone?"

"Yes."

Banks made some notes, then said, "There was no contact address on your flyer. You're not a secret society, are you?"

"No. But we have to be careful. We have a position we want to get across, and we know it's not popular with a lot of people. So we don't exactly go around shouting about our existence to everyone."

"I'll bet you don't."

"Not everyone understands."

"I'm sure they don't. How does a person join, then?"

"Why? You interested?"

"Just answer the fucking question."

"All right. All right. No need to get shirty. Just my little joke. We recruit people."

"Where?"

Ray shrugged. "Wherever we can find them. It's no secret. Schools, youth clubs, football matches, rock concerts, the Internet. We vet them pretty thoroughly, too, of course, if they express any interest."

"Tell me, Ray, what are *your* duties?" Banks asked, pacing around the small room as he talked. "How high up the totem pole are *you?*"

Ray grinned. "Me? Not very high. Mostly, I hand out pamphlets. And I'll be doing some of the writing now Jason's dead."

"Propaganda? Was that his job?"

"One of them."

"The Goebbels of the group, eh?"

"Come again?"

"Never mind, Ray. Before your time. Anything else?"

"I do some training."

"What sort of training?"

"Country weekends. You know, survival skills—camping, hiking, physical fitness, that sort of thing."

"Real Duke of Edinburgh's Award stuff?"

"If you like."

"Weapons?"

Ray folded his arms. "Now, you *know* that would be illegal."

"Right. How silly of me to ask. Anyway, Ray, back to Jason Fox. How well did you know him?"

"Not very."

"You mean the two of you didn't share your ideas on immigration policy and sing the occasional verse of the 'Horst Wessel' song together after a couple of jars?"

"No," said Ray. "And you can sneer all you like. I'm getting fed up of this. Look, why don't you go get your search warrant and call in your bully boys. Either that or get the fuck off our property."

Banks said nothing.

"I mean it," Ray went on. "I'm calling your bluff. Either bring in the bluebottles or bugger off."

Banks thought for a moment as he engaged Ray in a staring match. He decided that there was nothing more to be learned here. Besides, he was getting hungry. "All right, Ray," he said. "We've finished with you for the time being. Jim?"

"What? Oh, sorry." Sergeant Hatchley managed to knock over a half-full mug of tea on the counter. Banks turned and watched as the dark stain spread around the bottom few pamphlets left on the counter and began to rise up as the paper absorbed it. Then, with Hatchley behind him, he opened the door and they headed out to the car. The drizzle had stopped now and a brisk wind had sprung up, allowing the occasional shaft of sunlight to slant through puffy gray clouds.

"We didn't *have* to leave, sir," Hatchley said as they got in the car. "We could have leaned on them a bit more."

"I know that. We can always go back if we need to, but I don't think we'll find any answers there."

"Think they had anything to do with Jason's death?"

"I don't know yet. I can't honestly see why they would."

"Me neither. What next?"

Banks lit a cigarette and slid the window down a couple of inches. "We'll have a word with Neville Motcombe this afternoon," he said, "but before that, how do you fancy lunch with Ken Blackstone? There was something young Adolf said back there that gave me an idea."

IV

When Susan got to the Hope and Anchor, just around the corner on York Road, Gavin was already looking over the menu, a full pint beside him. Susan waved, stopped at the bar for her usual St. Clement's and went over to join him. She put the copy of *Classic CD* that she'd bought at the newsagent's on the bench beside her.

"What brings you to town, then?" she asked.

"I had a couple of boxes of stuff to deliver to your records officer. It's not all computers, you know."

The place was fairly quiet, and soon they had both ordered the lasagna-and-chips special. Gavin raised his glass. "Cheers."

"Cheers." Susan smiled at him. A little over six foot, and only a couple of years older than her, Gavin was a good-looking fellow with a strong chin, soulful eyes and a mop of shaggy chestnut hair. He played fullback for the police rugby team.

"So," Gavin said, "you are the sergeant when a call is received that there is a small nuclear device in the Swainsdale Centre. A validated code word has been given, it is a busy time of day, and you have twenty minutes to hand over every packet of Rice Krispies in Eastvale at a designated spot. What do you do?"

Susan laughed. "Get in my car and drive like hell out of there."

"Sorry, DC Gay, you fail."

It was a running joke between them. They had met just after doing their boards, and since then they had been coming up with progressively more absurd versions of the scenarios they had been given to solve.

"What's that?" Gavin asked, pointing at the magazine.

"Just a music magazine."

"I can see that. Bring it along in case the conversation gets boring, did you?"

"Idiot." Susan grinned. "I picked it up on the way. I thought *I* might have to wait for *you*."

Gavin picked up the magazine. "Classical music? With a free compact disc? Cecilia Bartoli. Sir Simon Rattle. I say. Alan Bennett plays are one thing, but I didn't know you were such a culture vulture."

Susan snatched the magazine back. "It's something I picked up from DCI Banks," she said. "I get to hear a lot of classical stuff traveling in the car with him and I thought . . . well, some of it's really interesting. This is just an easy way of finding out more about it, that's all. You get snippets of things on the disc, and if I like them, sometimes I'll go and buy the whole thing."

"Ah, the ubiquitous DCI Banks. I should have known his hand would be in this somewhere. And where might golden boy be today?"

"He's gone to Leeds. And I told you not to call him that."

"Leeds? Again? Know what I think?" Gavin leaned forward and narrowed his eyes. "I think he's got a fancy woman down there. That's what I think."

"Don't be absurd. He's married."

Gavin laughed. "Well I've never known that to stop a bloke before. What about this violinist you told me about? Is Banks bonking her?"

"You're disgusting. Her name's Pamela Jeffreys, and she's a violist, not a violinist. For your information, DCI Banks is a decent bloke. He's got an absolutely gorgeous wife. She runs the art gallery at the community center. I'm certain he's faithful to her. He wouldn't do anything like that."

Gavin held his hand up. "All right, all right. I know when I'm beaten. If you say so. He's a saint."

"I didn't say that, either," Susan said through gritted teeth. Then she glared at him.

Their food came, and they both tucked in. Susan concentrated on her lasagna and tried to ignore the chips. Not entirely successfully.

"I'll tell you one thing, though," Gavin said, "your Banks is definitely not a saint in Chief Constable Riddle's books."

"Jimmy Riddle's a pillock."

"That's as may be. But he's also Chief Constable Pillock, and your golden boy has been pissing him off mightily of late. Just a friendly word of warning, that's all."

"Are you talking about those Asian kids we brought in?"

Gavin nodded. "Could be something to do with them, yes. That and near causing a race riot."

"A race riot? In Eastvale?" She laughed. "It was a storm in a teacup, Gavin. I was there. And we'd good reason to detain those three kids. They're still not off the hook, you know. The lab found something suspicious on George Mahmood's shoe. They're still working on it."

"Probably dog shit. I think you'll need a lot more than that to convince the CC."

"They think it might be blood. Anyway, you know as well as I do that Jimmy Riddle only ordered their release because of political pressure."

"Don't underestimate political pressure, Susan. It can be a powerful motivator. Especially in a person's career. Even so, you're probably right about his reasons." Gavin pushed his empty plate aside. "To be honest, I can't say I've ever heard the CC have a good word to say for darkies in private. But the public face is another matter. Sure they only got off because they're colored. This time. And because Mustapha Camel, or whatever his name is, is some big wallah in the Muslim community. But there's a large section of the public—especially some of the more liberal members of the press—who say they were only arrested in the first place because they were colored. Take your pick. You can't win. Anyway, you might just want to warn DCI Banks that the CC is on the warpath."

Susan laughed. "What's new? I think he already knows that." She glanced at her watch.

"Maybe *that's* why he's gone to Leeds?"

"DCI Banks isn't scared of Jimmy Riddle."

"Well, maybe he should be."

Susan wasn't certain from his expression whether Gavin was being serious or not. It was often difficult to tell with him. "I've got to go," she said, standing up.

"You can't. You haven't finished your chips."

"They're fattening."

"But I've not had my full half hour yet."

"Isn't life unfair," Susan said, smiling as she pecked him on the cheek and turned to leave.

"Saturday?" he called out after her.

"Maybe," she said.

SIX

I

DI Ken Blackstone, West Yorkshire CID, was already waiting when Banks and Hatchley arrived at the pub he'd suggested over the telephone, a seedy-looking dive near Kirkgate Market, at the back of the Millgarth police headquarters.

Most days there was an open-air market near the bus station, behind the huge Edwardian market hall, and today in the drizzle a few lost souls in macs wandered around the covered stalls, fingering samples of fabric and fruit, thumbing through tattered paperback romances and considering the virtues of buying that "genuine antique" brass door knocker.

But no one showed much enthusiasm, not even the vendors, who were usually keen to sing out the praises of their wares and draw customers to their stalls. Today most of them stood to the side, wearing flat caps and waxed jackets, drawing on cigarettes and shuffling from foot to foot.

The pub wasn't very busy, either. Blackstone had assured them the cook did a decent Yorkshire pudding and gravy, and luckily it turned out to be true. In deference to duty, Banks and Blackstone drank halves. Hatchley, unwilling to miss what was a rare opportunity these days, had a full pint of Tetley's bitter. A giant jukebox stood in one corner of the lounge bar, but it was silent at the moment, so they didn't have to shout.

"Well, Alan," said Blackstone, echoing Gavin Richards's sentiments, "you've been spending so much time down here this past year or two, I'm surprised you're not thinking of moving."

Banks smiled. "I won't say it hasn't crossed my mind. Oh, not seriously. Well, maybe just a little bit seriously. With both Brian and Tracy gone, the house just seems too big, and much as I love Eastvale . . . I think Sandra misses big-city life. And I wouldn't mind being a bit nearer Opera North." When he mentioned Sandra, he felt a pang. They hadn't talked since their argument the other night, and Opera North had certainly played its part in that.

Blackstone smiled. "It's not such a bad place. You could do a lot worse."

Banks looked at Hatchley, who had done a stint on the West Yorkshire force several years ago. "Jim?"

"He's right," Hatchley agreed. "And it might not be a bad career move." He winked. "It's a long way from Jimmy Riddle. We'd miss you, of course."

"Stop it, you'll make me cry," Banks said, pretending to reach for a handkerchief.

"All right," said Hatchley. "We won't miss you, then."

"Anyway," Banks asked, "how's crime?"

"Much the same as usual," said Blackstone. "We've had a spate of 'steamings' lately. Five or six young lads will go into a shop, then, when the shopkeeper's got his cash register open, they rush into action, create chaos all around while they grab what they want from customers and till alike. Kids for the most part. Fifteen and under, most of them. They've also taken to doing building societies and post offices the same way."

Banks shook his head. "Sounds American to me."

"You know how it goes, Alan. First America, then London, then the rest of the country. What else . . . ? We've had a few too many muggings at cash dispensers, too. And to cap it all, it looks like we're heading for another drug war in Chapeltown."

Banks raised his eyebrows.

Blackstone sighed. "Bloke goes by the name of 'Deevaughan.' Spelled like the county: Devon. Anyway, Devon came up from London about a month ago and sussed out the scene pretty quickly. Already it looks like we can put down one murder to him."

"Can't prove anything, of course?"

"Course not. He was in a pub with twenty mates when it happened. This one's bad, Alan. Crack, cocaine, the usual stuff, of course. But word also has it he's a big heroin fan. He spent the last few years in New York and Toronto, and there's rumors of death follow him around wherever he goes. Still want to move here?"

Banks laughed. "I'll think about it."

"Anyway, you didn't come to talk about *my* problems. How can I help you this time?"

Banks lit a cigarette. "Know anything about Neville Motcombe? Runs a white-power group called the Albion League. Lives out Pudsey way. Offices in Holbeck."

Blackstone shook his head. "I've heard of him, but I can't really say I know much, not off-the-cuff. Bit out of my bailiwick, to be honest."

"What is? Neo-Nazis or Pudsey?"

Blackstone laughed. "Both, I suppose." With his thinning sandy hair—still enough left to curl around his ears—wire-rimmed glasses, long, pale face and Cupid's-bow lips, Blackstone reminded Banks more of an academic than a copper. Except that he was always well-dressed. Today, he wore a dazzling white shirt, its brightness outdone only by his gaudy tie, and a pinstripe suit that looked tailor-made, not off-the-peg, with a silk handkerchief poking out of the top pocket. Banks didn't even wear a suit and tie unless he had to, and he always kept the top button of his shirt undone. Today he was wearing his favorite suede jacket again, and his tie hung askew.

"How did you come to hear about him?" Banks asked.

Blackstone laughed. "Bit of a joke around the station, actually. Seems he tried to flog a stolen stereo to one of our off-duty PCs at a car-boot sale last year. Luckily for us, it was one of our honest PCs, and he traced it to a Curry's break-in a couple of months earlier."

"What happened?"

"Nothing. Motcombe swore blind he'd bought it at the market and we couldn't prove otherwise. Got a light rap on the knuckles, and that's the lot."

"Did you know about the Albion League?"

"I've heard of it, yes. I try at least to stay abreast of possible troublemakers."

"And you think they're likely ones?"

Blackstone pursed his lips. "Mmm. I'd say they've got potential, yes. We've had a few unattributed racial incidents this past year or so. We can't tie them in to him and his group yet, but I have my suspicions."

"Anything in particular?"

"Know that big mosque they're putting up out Bradford way?"

Banks nodded.

"There's been a few small acts of sabotage. Nothing much. Stolen building materials, spray-painted racist slogans, slashed tires, scratched paintwork. That sort of thing."

"And you suspect Motcombe's lot?"

"Well, it'd be surprising if there weren't some sort of organized group behind it. What really worries me is what level of violence they're likely to rise to."

"A bomb? Something like that?"

Blackstone shrugged. "Well, if the IRA can do it . . . Anyway, it's just speculation at the moment. Want me to dig around a bit more?"

Banks nodded. "I'd appreciate it, Ken. Right now anything is better than nothing. We're getting nowhere fast."

"What about those Asian lads you had in custody?"

"They're not off my list yet."

"You said earlier you had an idea," Sergeant Hatchley prompted Banks.

"Ah, yes." Banks stubbed out his cigarette and looked at Blackstone. "It's probably just a minor thing, really. We talked to two of Motcombe's cronies in Holbeck. Ray Knott and Des Parker."

Blackstone nodded. "We know Ray Knott," he said. "Used to be a dab hand at taking and driving away."

"Used to be?"

Blackstone shrugged.

"Anyway," Banks went on. "At one point, Knott let slip that the Albion League, or Motcombe himself, actually *owned* the property. I'm wondering if that's true or whether it was simply some sort of figure of speech. You know, the way someone might say 'Get off my property' even if it's only rented?"

"And you'd like me to check it out?"

"If you would."

"May I ask why?"

"Because I'd like to know if money's involved. If Motcombe owns property and lives in a nice house in Pudsey, maybe there's some scam involved."

Blackstone nodded. "Hmmm. Good thinking. I'll do what I can. As a matter of fact, I've got a couple of mates in the town hall, and they owe me a favor or two."

Banks raised his eyebrows. "What's this, Ken? Have you been tipping them off when their brothel's going to be raided?"

Blackstone laughed. "Not exactly."

"There's an address in Rawdon I'd like you to check, too, if it's not too much trouble. Jason Fox lived there. As far as we know, he hasn't been employed this past couple of years, so we'd like to know how he could afford it."

"Will do," said Blackstone. He looked at his watch. "Look, I should get back to the station. I can make a couple of phone calls, get working on it pretty much straightaway."

"We should be moving along, too," said Banks, looking at Hatchley, who started swigging the last of his ale in expectation of an imminent departure. "We're going to pay Mr. Motcombe a visit. And there's another thing, Ken."

Blackstone raised his eyebrows.

"We still haven't been able to track down the lad Jason Fox was drinking with the night he was killed. If the Albion League, or Neville Motcombe himself, does actually own the Holbeck building, or the Rawdon house, do you think you could check and see if he owns any other property in the city? Who knows, it might lead us to Jason's mystery pal."

"Who may or may not know something?"

Banks smiled and nudged Hatchley. "Ever the optimist, our Ken, isn't he, Jim?"

Hatchley laughed. "West Yorkshire does that to you."

"Can do," said Blackstone, standing up. "I'll call you soon as I get anything."

"Appreciate it," said Banks. "I owe you one."

"I'll remember that if you ever transfer here."

II

After lunch, Susan's Wednesday afternoon was becoming every bit as frustrating as Tuesday's had been. She had telephoned the service provider that gave Internet and Web access to FoxWood Designs, but she couldn't get a name and address out of them over the phone. A court order would see to that, of course, but what grounds had she to seek one? A vague hunch that it might lead her to someone who might know something about a mysterious death?

Every once in a while she left her computer terminal, stretched, and paced around the flat for a while. She put on the disc that came with her magazine, and arias followed solo piano pieces, which in turn followed symphonic movements, from Monteverdi to Maxwell Davies. It was all very confusing.

Like Banks, she wondered about George Mahmood and his mates. Had they done it? They certainly could have. And maybe not many people would blame them. The reporters had been around the station in droves, of course, and there was sure to be an article on police racism in the weekly *Eastvale Gazette*, due out on Friday.

Susan turned back to her desk. Still working on the assumption that if "Fox" was Jason Fox, then "Wood" might turn out to be a real person, too, she phoned directory assistance and discovered, as she suspected, that in Leeds alone there were pages of "Woods."

Well, she supposed, she *could* try them all. And what would she say? Ask each one if he knew Jason Fox? If this Wood person didn't want the police to know he knew Jason, he would hardly be likely to tell her over the telephone, would he?

There had to be an easier way. Tax records? Business registries? Maybe FoxWood Designs was incorporated, or had registered their design as a trademark.

Suddenly she realized there might be an even easier way than that. Subterfuge.

She hurried back to the computer, where she typed away for a few minutes, then sat back to survey her handiwork. Not bad. She made one or two small changes, correcting a typo here and an awkward phrase there. When she had finished, the message read:

```
TO: FoxWood Designs
FROM: Gayline Fashions


I have just started my own fashion-design
business and I'm looking for ways to find a
wider audience, for my products. I noticed
your work recently on a Web page and was very
impressed by what I saw. I realized that the
```

Web is an ideal way to achieve my aims and
from what I saw I realized your company would
be more than capable of handling the graphics
necessary for the sort of page I have in mind.
I would really like to talk to you about this
as soon as possible. Do you think you could
supply me with your address so that I could
come around and discuss the possibility of our
working together? I would much appreciate the
opportunity to get myself established on the
World Wide Web without delay.

Susan Gay.
Sole Proprietor: Gayline Fashions.

Susan read it over. It wasn't perfect—English had never been
her strong point at school—but it would do.

She saved the message and logged in again. Then, when all
the preliminaries were done with, she took a deep breath, pressed
enter, and sent her message bouncing around the world's computer
systems to the E-mail address she had taken from the bottom of
the FoxWood Designs page.

III

Before Banks and Hatchley even had time to ring Motcombe's
doorbell, they saw the figure approaching through the frosted
glass.

"Mr. Motcombe?" said Banks, showing his identification.

"That's me," said Motcombe. "I'm surprised it took you so long.
Please. Come in."

They followed him through to the living room.

"You've been expecting us?" Banks asked.

"Ever since Jason's tragic demise."

"But you didn't bother to call us?"

Motcombe smiled. "Why should I have? I don't know anything that can help you. But that doesn't keep *you* away from *me,* does it? Sit down. Please."

Hatchley sat in one of the deep armchairs and took out his notebook. Banks walked over to the window at the far end of the room. The house was perched on a hillside; the back window looked over toward the village of Tong, not much more than a mile away, past Park Wood. The smoking chimneys of Bradford stood to the right and Leeds sprawled to the left.

"Yes, it's impressive, isn't it?" Banks heard Motcombe say behind him. "It's one of the things that helps me remember what we're fighting for. That all isn't lost." Motcombe was standing so close that Banks could smell peppermint toothpaste on his breath.

Banks turned and walked past him, glancing around at the rest of the room. The furniture looked solid and well-crafted—a table, chairs, sideboard and a glass-fronted cabinet, all dark, shiny wood. While there were no posters of Hitler or swastikas on the bright floral wallpaper, inside the cabinet was obviously Motcombe's collection of Nazi memorabilia: armband, bayonet, German officer's cap—all bearing the swastika—a series of dog-eared photographs of Hitler, and what was probably a wartime edition of *Mein Kampf,* again with the swastika on the front.

"Hitler was an inspiration, don't you think?" Motcombe said. "He made mistakes, perhaps, but he had the right ideas, the right intentions. We should have joined forces *with* him instead of sending our forces against him. Then we would have a strong, united *Europe* as a bulwark against the corruption and impurity of the rest of the world, instead of the moth-eaten ragbag we do have."

Banks looked at him. He supposed Motcombe was imposing enough. Tall and gaunt, wearing a black polo-neck jumper tucked into matching black trousers with sharp creases, and a broad belt with a plain, square silver buckle, he had closely cropped black hair—shorter even than Banks's own—a sharp nose, and lobeless ears flat against his skull. His eyes were brown, and there was a gleam in them like the winter sun in a frozen mud puddle. A constant sly smile twitched at the corners of his thin, dry lips, as if he knew something no one else did, and as if that knowledge made him somehow superior. He reminded Banks of a younger Norman Tebbit.

"That's all very interesting," Banks said at last, resting the backs of his thighs against the table. "But, if you don't mind, we've got some questions for you."

"Why should I mind? As far as I'm concerned, we're on the same side." Motcombe sat, crossed his legs and put his hands together in front of him, fingertips touching, as if in prayer.

"How do you work that one out?" Banks asked, thinking it odd that was the second time he'd heard the same thing today.

"Easy. Jason Fox was killed on your patch. You did your job as best you could under the circumstances. You found his killers quickly. But you had to let them go."

He narrowed his eyes and gazed at Banks. Just for a moment Banks fancied he saw a gleam of something in them. Conspiracy? Condescension? Whatever it was, he didn't like it.

"How that must have sickened you," Motcombe went on, his voice a low, hypnotic monotone. "Having to bow to political pressure like that. Believe me, I *know* how your hands are tied. I *know* about the conspiracy that renders our police ineffective. You have my every sympathy."

Banks took a deep breath. It smelled like a non-smoking room, but at this point he didn't care. He lit up anyway. Motcombe didn't complain.

"Look," said Banks, after he blew out his first mouthful. "Let's get something straight from the start. I don't want your sympathy. Or your opinions. Let's stick to the facts. Jason Fox."

Motcombe shook his head slowly. "You know, I half expected

something like that. Deep down, most people agree with us. Just listen to the way they talk in pubs, the jokes they tell about Chinks, Pakis, niggers and Yids. Listen to the way *you* talk when you let your politically correct guard down." He pointed toward the window. "There's a whole silent nation out there who want what we want but are afraid to act. We aren't. Most people just don't have the courage of their convictions. We do. All I want to do is make it possible for people to look into their hearts and see what's really there, to know that there are others who feel the same way, then to give them a way they can act on it, a goal to aim for."

"A white England?"

"Is that such a bad thing? If you put your prejudices aside for just a few moments and *really think* about it, is that such a terrible dream to pursue? Look at what's happened to our schools, our culture, our religious trad—"

"Didn't you hear me the first time?" Banks asked, his voice calm but hard. "Let's stick to the facts."

Motcombe favored him with that conspiratorial, condescending smile, as if he were regarding a wayward child. "Of course," he said, inclining his head slightly. "Please, Chief Inspector, go ahead. Ask your questions. And there's an ashtray on the sideboard just behind you. I don't smoke myself, but my guests occasionally do. Secondhand smoke doesn't bother me."

Banks picked up the ashtray and held it in his left hand while he spoke. "Tell me about Jason Fox."

Motcombe shrugged. "What is there to say? Jason was a valued member of the Albion League and we will miss him dearly."

"How long had you known him?"

"Let me see, now . . . about a year. Perhaps a little less."

"How did you meet?"

"At a rally in London. Jason was flirting with the British National Party. I had already left them as they didn't adequately serve my vision. We talked. At the time, I was just about to start setting up the league, making contacts. A few months later, when we got going, Jason and I met again at a conference. I asked him, and he joined us."

"Were you close?"

Motcombe tilted his head again. "I wouldn't say close, no. Not in the personal sense, you understand. In ideas, yes." He tapped the side of his head. "After all, that's where it counts."

"So you didn't socialize with him?"

"No."

"What was Jason's specialty? I heard he was your minister of propaganda."

Motcombe laughed. "Very good. Yes, I suppose you could put it like that. He wrote most of the pamphlets. He also handled the computer. An essential tool in this day and age, I fear."

Banks showed him the vague drawing of the boy Jason had been drinking with the night he was killed. "Do you know him?" he asked. "Is he one of yours?"

"I don't think so," Motcombe said. "It's almost impossible to tell, but I don't think I recognize him."

"Where were you on Saturday night?"

Motcombe's black eyebrows shot up and he laughed again. "Me? Do you mean *I'm* a suspect, too? How exciting. I'm almost sorry to disappoint you, but as a matter of fact I was in Bradford, at a tenants' meeting. In a block of council flats where some people are becoming very concerned about who, or should I say *what* they're getting for neighbors. Crime is—"

"You can prove this, I suppose?"

"If I have to. Here." He got up and took a slip of paper from the sideboard drawer. "This is the address of the block where the meeting was held. Check up on it, if you want. Any number of people will vouch for me."

Banks pocketed the slip. "What time did the meeting end?"

"About ten o'clock. Actually, a couple of us went on to a pub and carried on our discussion until closing time."

"In Bradford?"

"Yes."

"Have you ever been to Eastvale?"

Motcombe laughed. "Yes. I've been there on a number of occasions. Purely as a tourist, you understand, and not for about a year. It's a rather pretty little town. I'm a great lover of walking the unspoiled English countryside. What's left of it."

"Have you ever heard of George Mahmood?"

"What a ridiculous name."

"Have you ever heard of him?"

"As a matter of fact, I have. He's one of the youths responsible for Jason's death."

"We don't know that."

"Oh, come on, Chief Inspector." Motcombe winked. "There's a big difference between what you can prove and what you *know*. You don't have to soft-soap me."

"Wouldn't think of it. Did Jason ever mention any racial problems in Eastvale?"

"No. You know, you're lucky to live there, Chief Inspector. As I understand it, these Mahmoods are about the only darkies in the place. I envy you."

"Then why don't you move?"

"Too much work to be done here first. One day, perhaps."

"Did Jason ever mention George?"

"Once or twice, yes."

"In what context?"

"I honestly don't remember."

"But you'd remember if he said he chucked a brick through their window?"

Motcombe smiled. "Oh, yes. But Jason wouldn't have done a thing like that."

For what it was worth, it was probably the first positive link between Jason Fox and George Mahmood that Banks had come across so far. But what *was* it worth? So Jason had noticed George in Eastvale and mentioned him to Motcombe. That didn't mean George knew Jason was a neo-Nazi.

And everything Motcombe said could have come from the newspapers or television. There had been plenty of local coverage of the detainment and release of the three Asian suspects. Ibrahim Nazur had even appeared on a local breakfast television program complaining about systemic racism.

"What about Asim Nazur?" he asked.

Motcombe shook his head. "Doesn't sound familiar."

"Kobir Mukhtar?"

Motcombe sighed and shook his head. "Chief Inspector, you have to understand, these do not sound like the kind of people I mix with. I told you I remember Jason mentioned a certain George Mahmood once or twice. That's all I know."

"By name?"

"Yes. By name."

The Mahmood part Jason might have known from the shop sign. But George? How could he have known that? Perhaps from the report in the *Eastvale Gazette* after the brick-throwing incident. As Banks recollected, George had been mentioned by name then.

If Motcombe was lying, then he was playing it very cautiously, careful not to own to knowing *too* much, just enough. Obviously a story of a full-blown conspiracy between the three Asians to attack Jason Fox would be even better for propaganda purposes, but it would be much more suspicious. A jet flew across the valley, a bright flash of gray against the gray clouds. Suddenly, someone else walked into the room. "Nev, have you got—Sorry, didn't know you'd got company. Who's this?"

"This," said Motcombe, "is Detective Chief Inspector Banks and Detective Sergeant Hatchley."

"And now we've got that out of the way," said Banks, "maybe you'd care to tell us who you are?"

"This is Rupert," said Motcombe. "Rupert Francis. Come in, Rupert. Don't be shy."

Rupert came in. He was wearing a khaki apron, the kind Banks had to wear for woodwork classes at school. His hair was cut short, but that was where his resemblance to Jason's mystery friend ended. In his mid- to late twenties, Banks guessed, Rupert was at least six feet tall, and thin rather than stocky. Also, there was no sign of an earring and, as far as Banks could make out, no hole to hang one from.

"I'm a carpenter, a cabinetmaker," said Motcombe. "Though it's more in the form of a hobby than a true occupation, I'm afraid. Anyway, I've converted the cellar into a workshop and Rupert helps me out every now and then. He's very good. I think the traditional values of the craftsman are very important indeed in our society, don't you?"

Rupert smiled and nodded at Banks and Hatchley. "Pleased to meet you," he said. "What's it about?"

"It's about Jason Fox," said Banks. "Didn't happen to know him, did you?"

"Vaguely. I mean, I saw him around. We weren't mates or anything."

"Saw him around here?"

"Down the office. Holbeck. On the computer."

Banks slipped the drawing from his briefcase again. "Know this lad?"

Rupert shook his head. "Never seen him before. Can I go now? I'm halfway through finishing a surface."

"Go on," said Banks, turning to Motcombe again.

"You really must try believing us, Chief Inspector," he said. "You see—"

Banks stood up. "Are you sure there's nothing else you can tell us? About Jason? About his problem with George Mahmood?"

"No," said Motcombe. "I'm sorry, but that just about covers it. I told you when you first came that I couldn't tell you anything that would help."

"Oh, I wouldn't say you haven't helped us, Mr. Motcombe," said Banks. "I wouldn't say that at all. Sergeant."

Hatchley put his notebook away and got to his feet.

"Well," said Motcombe at the door, "I suppose I'll see you at the funeral?"

Banks turned. "What funeral?"

Motcombe raised his eyebrows. "Why, Jason's, of course. Tomorrow." He smiled. "Don't the police always attend the funerals of murder victims, just in case the killer turns up?"

"Who said anything about murder?"

"I just assumed."

"You make a lot of assumptions, Mr. Motcombe. As far as we know, it could have been manslaughter. Why are you going?"

"To show support for a fallen colleague. Fallen in the course of our common struggle. And we hope to gain some media coverage. As you said yourself, why waste a golden opportunity to publicize our ideas? There'll be a small representative presence at the graveside, and we'll be preparing a special black-border pamphlet for the event." He smiled. "Don't you realize it yet, Chief Inspector? Jason is a martyr."

"Bollocks," said Banks, turning to leave. "Jason's just another dead Nazi, that's all."

Motcombe tut-tutted. "Really, Chief Inspector."

At the door, Banks did his Columbo impersonation. "Just one more question, Mr. Motcombe."

Motcombe sighed and leaned on the doorpost, folding his arms. "Fire away, then, if you must."

"Where were you on Sunday morning?"

"Sunday morning? Why?"

"Where were you?"

"Here. At home."

"Alone?"

"Yes."

"Can you prove it?"

"Is there any reason I have to?"

"Just pursuing inquiries."

"I'm sorry. I'm afraid I can't prove it. I was alone. Sadly, my wife and I separated some years ago."

"Are you sure you didn't visit number seven Rudmore Terrace in Rawdon?"

"Of course I'm sure. Why should I?"

"Because that was where Jason Fox lived. We have information that two men went there on Sunday morning and cleaned the place out. I was just wondering if one of them happened to be you."

"I didn't go there," Motcombe repeated. "And even if I had done, I wouldn't have broken any law."

"These men had a key, Mr. Motcombe. A key, in all likelihood, taken from Jason Fox's body."

"I know nothing about that. I have a key, too, though." He grinned at Banks. "As a matter of fact, I happen to own the house."

Well, Banks thought, that was one question answered. Motcombe *did* own property. "But you didn't go there on Sunday morning?" he said.

"No."

"Did you give or lend a key to anyone?"

"No."

"I think you did. I think you sent some of your lads over there to clean up after Jason's death. I think he had stuff there you didn't want the police to find."

"Interesting theory. Such as what?"

"Files, perhaps, membership lists, notes on upcoming projects. And the computer had been tampered with."

"Well, even if I did what you say," said Motcombe, "I'm sure you can understand how I would be well within my rights to go to a house I own to pick up property that, essentially, belongs to me, in my capacity as leader of the Albion League."

"Oh, I can understand that completely," Banks said.

Motcombe frowned. "Then what . . . ? I'm sorry, I don't understand."

"Well, then," Banks said slowly. "Let me explain. The thing that bothers me is that whoever went there went before anyone knew that the victim was Jason Fox. Anyone except his killers, of course, that is. Bye for now, Mr. Motcombe. No doubt we'll be seeing you again soon."

SEVEN

I

It was a long time since Frank had worn a suit, and the tie seemed to be choking him. Trust the weather to brighten up for a funeral, too. It was Indian summer again, warm air tinged with that sweet, smoky hint of autumn's decay, sun shining, hardly a breeze, and here he was in the back of the car next to his daughter Josie, who was dressed all in black, sweat beading on his brow despite the open window.

The drive to Halifax from Lyndgarth, where Steven had picked him up, was a long one. And a bloody ugly one once you got past Skipton, too, Frank thought as they drove through Keighley. Talk about your "dark Satanic mills."

He had wondered why they couldn't just bury the lad in East-vale and have done with it, but Josie explained Steven's family connections with St. Luke's Church, where his forebears were buried going back centuries. Bugger yon streak of piss and his forebears, Frank thought, but he kept his mouth shut.

Nobody said very much on the journey. Josie sobbed softly every now and then, putting a white handkerchief to her nose, Steven—who for all his sins was a good driver—kept his eyes on the road, and Maureen sat stiffly, arms folded, beside him, looking out the window.

Frank found himself drifting down memory lane: Jason, aged

four or five, down by The Leas one spring afternoon, excited as he caught his first stickleback in a net made of old lace curtain and a thin strip of cane; the two of them stopping for ice cream one hot, still summer day at the small shop in the middle of nowhere, halfway up Fremlington Hill, melting ice cream dripping over his knuckles; an autumn walk down a lane near Richmond, Jason running ahead kicking up piles of autumn leaves, which made a dry soughing sound as he plowed through them; standing freezing in the snow in Ben Rhydding watching the skiers glide down Ilkley Moor.

Whatever Jason had become, Frank thought, he had once been an innocent child, as awestruck by the wonders of man and nature as any other kid. Hang on to that, he told himself, not the twisted, misguided person Jason had become.

They arrived at the funeral home on the outskirts of Halifax with time to spare. Frank stayed outside watching the traffic rush by because he could never stand the rarefied air of funeral homes, or the thought of all those corpses in caskets, makeup on their faces and formaldehyde in their veins. Jason, he suspected, would have needed a lot of cosmetic attention to *his* face.

Finally, the cortege was ready. The four of them piled into the sleek black limousine the home provided and followed the hearse through streets of dark millstone-grit houses to the cemetery. In the distance, tall mill chimneys poked out between the hills.

After a short service, they all trooped outside for the graveside ceremony. Frank loosened his tie so he could breathe more easily. The vicar droned on: "In the midst of life we are in death: of whom may we seek for succor, but of thee, O Lord, who for our sins are justly displeased? Thou knowest, Lord, the secrets of our hearts . . ." A fly that must have been conned into thinking it was still summer buzzed by his face. He brushed it away.

Steven stepped forward to cast a clod of earth down on the coffin. The vicar read on: "For as much as it hath pleased Almighty God of his great mercy to receive unto himself the soul of our dear brother here departed . . ." It should have been Josie dropping the earth, Frank thought. Steven never did get on with the kid. At least Josie had loved her son once, before they grew apart, and she must still feel a mother's love for him, a love which surely passes all understanding and forgives a multitude of sins.

All of a sudden, Frank noticed Josie look beyond his shoulder and frown through her tears. He turned to see what it was. There, by the line of trees, stood about ten people, all wearing black polo-necks made of some shiny material, belts with silver buckles and black leather jackets, despite the warmth of the day. Over half had skinhead haircuts. Some wore sunglasses. The tall, gaunt one looked older than the rest, and Frank immediately guessed him to be the leader.

They didn't have to announce themselves. Frank knew who they were. As sure as he knew Jason was dead and in his grave. He had read the tract. As the vicar drew close to the end of his service, the leader raised his arm in a Nazi salute, and the others followed suit.

Frank couldn't help himself. Before he could even think about what he was doing, he hurried over and grabbed the leader. The man just laughed and brushed him off. Then, as Frank attempted to get at least one punch in, he was surrounded by them, jostling, pushing, shoving him between one another as if he were a ball, or as if they were playing "pass the parcel" at some long-ago children's party. And they were laughing as they pushed him, calling him "Grand-dad" and "Old man."

Frank flailed out, but he couldn't break away. All he saw was a whirl of grinning faces, shorn heads and his own reflection in the dark glasses. The world was spinning too fast, out of control. He was too hot. His tie felt tight again, even though he had loosened it, and the pain in his chest came on fast, like a vise gripping his heart and squeezing.

He stumbled away from the group, clutching his chest, the pain spreading like burning needles down his left arm. He thought he could see Maureen laying into one of youths with a piece of wood. He could just hear her through the ringing and buzzing in his ears. "Leave him alone, you bullies! Leave him alone, you fascist bastards! Can't you see he's an old man? Can't you see he's poorly?"

Then something strange happened. Frank was lying on the ground now, and, gently, slowly, he felt himself begin to float above the pain, or away from it, more like, deeper into himself, detached and light as air. Yes, that was it, deeper into himself. He wasn't hovering above the scene looking down on the chaos, but far inside, seeing pictures of himself in years long gone.

A number of memories flashed through his mind: flak bursting all around the bomber like bright flowers blooming in the night, as Frank seemed to hang suspended above it all in his gun turret; the day he proposed to Edna on their long walk home in the rain after the Helmthorpe spring fair; the night his only daughter, Josie, was born in Eastvale General Infirmary while Frank was stuck in Lyndgarth, without even a telephone then, cut off from the world by a vicious snowstorm.

But his final memory was one he had not thought of in decades. He was five years old. He had trapped his finger in the front door, and he sat on the freshly scoured stone step crying, watching the black blood gather under the fingernail. He could feel the warmth of the step against the backs of his thighs and the heat of his tears on his cheeks.

Then the door opened. He couldn't see much more than a silhouette because of the bright sunlight, but as he shaded his eyes and looked up, he *knew* it was the loving, compassionate, all-healing figure of his mother bending over to sweep him up into her arms and kiss away the pain.

Then everything went black.

II

"Ah, Banks. Here you are at last."

As soon as he heard the voice behind him on his way back to his office from the coffee machine, Banks experienced that sinking feeling. Still, he thought, it had to happen sometime. Might as well get it over with. Gird his loins. At least he was on his own turf.

Their enmity went back for some time; in fact, Banks thought, it probably started the moment they met. Riddle was one of the youngest chief constables in the country, and he had come up the fast way, "accelerated promotion" right from the start. Banks had made DCI fairly young, true, but he had made it the hard way: sheer hard slog, a good case clearance record and a natural talent for detective work. He didn't belong to any clubs or have any wealthy contacts; nor did he have a university degree. All he had was a diploma in business studies from a polytechnic—and that from the days before they were all turned into second-string universities.

For Riddle, it was all a matter of making the right contacts, mouthing the correct buzzwords; he was a bean-counter, at his happiest looking over budget proposals or putting a positive spin on crime figures on "Look North" or "Calendar." As far as Banks was concerned, Jimmy Riddle hadn't done a day's real policing in his life.

Hand on the doorknob, Banks turned. "Sir?"

Riddle kept advancing on him. "You know what I'm talking about, Banks. Where the hell do you think you've been these past few days? Trying to avoid me?"

"Wouldn't think of such a thing, sir." Banks opened the door and stood aside to let Riddle in first. The chief constable hesitated for a moment, surprised at the courtesy, then stalked in. As usual, he didn't sit but started prowling about, touching things, straightening the calendar, eyeing the untidy pile of papers on top of the filing cabinet, looking at everything in that prissy, disapproving way of his.

He was immaculately turned out. He must have a clean uniform for each day, Banks thought, sitting behind his rickety metal desk and reaching for a cigarette. However strict the anti-smoking laws had become lately, they still hadn't stretched as far as a chief inspector's own office, where not even the chief constable could stop him.

To his credit, Riddle didn't try. He didn't even make his usual protest. Instead, he launched straight into the assault that must have been building pressure inside him since Monday. "What on earth did you think you were doing bringing in those Asian kids and throwing them in the cells?"

"You mean George Mahmood and his mates?"

"You know damn well who I mean."

"Well, sir," said Banks, "I had good reason to suspect they were involved in the death of Jason Fox. They'd been seen to have an altercation with him and his pal earlier in the evening at the Jubilee, and when I started to question George Mahmood about what happened, he asked for a solicitor and clammed up."

Riddle ran his hand over his shiny head. "Did you have to lock all three of them up?"

"I think so, sir. I simply detained them within the strict limits of the PACE directive. None of them would talk to us. As I said, they were reasonable suspects, and I wanted them where I could see them while forensic tests on their clothing were being carried out. At the same time, Detective Sergeant Hatchley was trying to locate any witnesses to the assault."

"But didn't you realize what trouble your actions would cause? Didn't you *think,* man?"

Banks sipped some coffee and looked up. "Trouble, sir?"

Riddle sighed and leaned against the filing cabinet, elbow on the stack of papers. "You've alienated the entire Yorkshire Asian community, Banks. Had you never heard of Ibrahim Nazur? Don't you realize that harmony of race relations is prioritized in today's force?"

"Funny, that, sir," said Banks. "And I thought we were supposed to catch criminals."

Riddle levered himself away from the cabinet with his elbow and leaned forward, palms flat on the desk, facing Banks. His pate seemed to be pulsing on red alert. "Don't be bloody clever with me, man. I've got my eye on you. One false move, one more slip, the slightest error of judgment, and you're finished, understand? I'll have you back in Traffic."

"Very well, sir," said Banks. "Does that mean you want me off the case?"

Riddle moved back to the filing cabinet and smiled, flicking a piece of imaginary fluff from his lapel. "Off the case? You should be so lucky. No, Banks, I'm going to leave your chestnuts in the fire a bit longer."

"So what exactly is it that you want, sir?"

"For a start, I want you to start behaving like a DCI instead of a bloody probational DC. And I want to be informed before you make any move that's likely to . . . to embarrass the force in any way. *Any* move. Is that clear?"

"The last bit is, sir, but—"

"What I mean," Riddle said, pacing and poking at things again, "is that as an experienced senior police officer, your input might be useful. But let your underlings do the legwork. Let them go gallivanting off to Leeds chasing wild geese. Don't think I don't know why you grab every opportunity to bugger off to Leeds."

Banks looked Riddle in the eye. "And why is that, sir?"

"That woman. The musician. And don't tell me you don't know who I'm talking about."

"I know exactly who you're talking about, sir. Her name's Pamela Jeffreys and she plays viola in the English Northern Philharmonia."

Riddle waved his hand impatiently. "Whatever. I'm sure you

think your private life is none of my business, but it is when you use the force's time to live it."

Banks thought for a moment before answering. This was way out of order. Riddle was practically accusing him of having an affair with Pamela Jeffreys and of driving to Leeds during working hours for assignations with her. It was untrue, of course, but any denial at this point would only strengthen Riddle's conviction. Banks wasn't sure of the actual guidelines, but he felt this sort of behavior far exceeded the chief constable's authority. It was a personal attack, despite the cavil about abusing the force's time.

But what could he do? It was his word against Riddle's. And Riddle was the CC. So he took it, filed it away, said nothing and determined to get his own back on the bastard one day.

"What *would* you like me to do, then, sir?" he asked.

"Sit in your office, smoke yourself silly and read reports, the way you're supposed to. And stay away from the media. Leave them to Superintendent Gristhorpe and myself."

Banks cringed. He hated it when people used "myself" instead of plain old "me." He stubbed out his cigarette. "I haven't been anywhere near the media, sir."

"Well, make sure you don't."

"You want me to sit and read reports? That's it?"

Riddle stopped prowling a moment and faced Banks. "For heaven's sake, man! You're a DCI. You're not supposed to be gadding off all over the place interviewing people. Coordinate. There are plenty more important tasks for you to carry out right here, in your office."

"Sir?"

"What about the new budget, for a start? You know these days we've got to be accountable for every penny we spend. And it's about time the Annual Policing Plan was prepared for next year. Then there's the crime statistics. Why is it that when the rest of the country's experiencing a drop, North Yorkshire's on the rise?

Hey? These are the sort of questions you should be addressing, not driving off to Leeds and treading on people's toes."

"Wait a minute, sir," said Banks. "Whose toes? Don't tell me Neville Motcombe's in the lodge as well?"

As soon as the words were out, Banks regretted them. It was all very well to want his own back on Riddle, but this wasn't the way to do it. He was surprised when Riddle simply stopped his tirade and asked, "Who the hell's Neville Motcombe when he's at home?"

Banks hesitated. Having put his foot in his mouth, how could he avoid not showing it down as far as his lower intestine? And did he care? "He's an associate of Jason Fox's. One of the people I was talking to in Leeds yesterday."

"What does this Motcombe have to do with the lad's death, if anything?"

Banks shook his head. "I don't know that he does. It's just that his name came up in the course of our inquiries and—"

Riddle began pacing again. "Don't flannel me, Banks. I understand this Jason Fox belonged to some right-wing racist movement? Is that true?"

"Yes, sir. The Albion League."

Riddle stopped and narrowed his eyes. "Would this Neville Motcombe have anything to do with the Albion League?"

No flies on Jimmy Riddle. "Actually," Banks said, "he's their leader."

Riddle said nothing for a moment, then he went back and resumed his pose at the filing cabinet. "Does this have anything to do with the Jason Fox case at all, or are you just tilting at windmills as usual?"

"I honestly don't know," Banks said. "It's what I'm trying to find out. It might have given George and his pals a motive to attack Jason."

"Have you any proof at all that the three Asians *knew* Jason Fox belonged to this Albion League?"

"No. But I did find out that Jason knew George Mahmood. It's a start."

"It's bloody nothing is what it is."

"We're still digging."

Riddle sighed. "Have you got *any* real suspects at all?"

"The Asians are still our best bet. The lab hasn't identified the stuff on George's trainers yet because there are so many contaminating factors, but they still haven't discounted its being blood."

"Hmm. What about the other lad, the one who was supposed to be with Jason Fox in the pub?"

"We're still looking for him."

"Any idea who he is yet?"

"No, sir. That was another thing I—"

"Well, bloody well find out. And quickly." Riddle strode toward the door. "And remember what I said."

"Which bit would that be, sir?"

"About tending to your duties as a DCI."

"So you want me to find out who Jason's pal was at the same time as I'm reading reports on budgets and crime statistics?"

"You know what I mean, Banks. Don't be so bloody literal. Delegate."

And he walked out, slamming the door behind him.

Banks breathed a sigh of relief. Too soon. The door opened again. Riddle put his head round, pointed his finger at Banks, wagged it and said, "And whatever you might think of me, Banks, don't you ever dare imply again that I or any of my fellow Masons fraternize with fascists. Is that clear?"

"Yes, sir," said Banks as the door closed again. *Fraternize with fascists,* indeed. He had to admit it had a nice ring to it. Must be the alliteration.

In the peace and silence following Riddle's withdrawal, Banks sipped his coffee and mulled over what he'd been told. He knew Riddle had a point about the way he did his job, and that certainly didn't make him feel any better. As a DCI, he should be more involved in the administrative and managerial aspects of policing. He *should* spend more time at his desk.

Except that wasn't what he wanted.

When he had been a DI on the Met and got promoted to DCI on transferring to Eastvale, it was on the understanding—given by both Detective Superintendent Gristhorpe *and* Chief Constable Hemmings, Jimmy Riddle's predecessor—that he was to take an active part as investigating officer in important cases. Even the assistant chief constable (Crime), also since retired, had agreed to that.

Recently, when the powers that be had considered abolishing the rank of chief inspector, Banks was ready to revert to inspector at the same pay, rather than try for superintendent, where he was far more likely to be desk-bound. But it had never happened; the only rank to be abolished was that of deputy chief constable.

Now Jimmy Riddle wanted to tie him to his desk anyway.

What could he do? Was it really time for another move?

But he didn't have time to think about these matters for very long. Not more than two minutes after Riddle had left, the phone rang.

III

Susan arrived ten minutes late for lunch at the Queen's Arms, where the object was to discuss leads and feelings about the Jason Fox case over a drink and a pub lunch. An informal brainstorming session.

Banks and Hatchley were already ensconced at a dimpled copper-topped table between the fireplace and the window when Susan hurried in. They were both looking particularly glum, she noticed.

She stopped at the bar and ordered a St. Clement's and a salad sandwich, then joined the others at the table. Hatchley had an almost-empty pint glass in front of him, while Banks was staring gloomily into a half. They scraped their chairs aside to make room for her.

"Sorry I'm late, sir," she said.

Banks shrugged. "No problem. We went ahead and ordered without you. If you want something . . ."

"It's all right, sir. They're doing me a sandwich." Susan glanced from one to the other. "Excuse me if I'm being thick or something, but it can't be the weather that's making your faces as long as a wet Sunday afternoon. Is something wrong? I feel as if I've walked in on a wake."

"In a way, you have," said Banks. He lit a cigarette. "You know Frank Hepplethwaite, Jason's granddad?"

"Yes. At least I know who he is."

"Was. I just got a call from the Halifax police. He dropped dead at Jason's funeral."

"What of?"

"Heart attack."

"Oh no," said Susan. She had never met the old man but she knew Banks had been impressed with him, and that was enough for her. "What happened?"

"Motcombe brought nine or ten of his blackshirts to the graveside and Frank took umbrage. Made a run at them. He was dead before his granddaughter could get them to back off."

"So they killed him?"

"You *could* say that." Banks glanced sideways at Hatchley, who drained his pint, shook his head slowly and went to the bar for another. Banks declined his offer of a second half. Smoke from his cigarette drifted perilously close to Susan's nose; she waved her hand in the air to waft it away.

"Sorry," said Banks.

"It doesn't matter. Look, sir, I'm having a bit of trouble understanding all this. It sounds like manslaughter to me. Are we pressing charges against Motcombe or not?"

Banks shook his head. "It's West Yorkshire's patch. And they're not."

"Why not?"

"Because Frank Hepplethwaite attacked Motcombe, and his lot were merely defending themselves."

"Ten of them? Against an old man with a bad heart? That's not on, sir."

"I know," said Banks. "But apparently they didn't punch or kick him. They just pushed him away. They were protecting themselves from him."

"It still sounds like manslaughter."

"West Yorkshire don't think they can get the CPS to prosecute."

The Crown Prosecution Service, as Susan knew, were well-known for their conservative attitude toward pursuing criminal cases through the courts. "So Motcombe and his bully boys just walk away scot-free? That's it?"

Hatchley returned from the bar. At almost the same time, Glenys, the landlord's wife, appeared with the food: Susan's sandwich, plaice and chips for Hatchley and a thick wedge of game pie for Banks.

"Not exactly," said Banks, stubbing out his cigarette. "At least not immediately. They were taken in for questioning. Their argument was that they were simply attending the funeral of a fallen comrade when this madman started attacking them and they were forced to push him away to protect themselves. The fact that Frank was an old man didn't make a lot of difference to the charges, or lack of them. Some old men are pretty tough. And they didn't know he had a bad heart."

"Isn't there *anything* we can do?" Susan turned to Hatchley.

He shook his head, piece of breaded plaice on his fork in mid-air. "It doesn't look like it." Then he glanced at Banks, who looked up from his pie and nodded. "It gets worse," Hatchley went on. "We're in no position to charge Motcombe, it seems, but Motcombe has brought assault charges against Maureen Fox, Jason's sister. It seems she attacked him and his mates with a heavy plank she picked up from the graveside and cracked a couple of heads open, including Motcombe's."

Susan's jaw dropped. "And *they're* charging *her*?"

"Aye," said Hatchley. "I shouldn't imagine much will come of it, but it's exactly the kind of insult Motcombe and his sort like to throw at people."

"And at the justice system," Banks added.

There were times, Susan had to admit, when she hadn't much stomach for the *justice system,* even though she knew it was probably the best in the world. Justice is always imperfect and it was a lot more imperfect in many other countries. Even so, once in a while something came along to outrage even what she thought was her seasoned copper's view. All she could do was shake her head and bite on her salad sandwich.

In the background, the cash register chinked and a couple of shop workers on their lunch break laughed at a joke. Someone won a few tokens on the fruit machine.

"Any more good news?" Susan asked.

"Aye," said Hatchley. "The lab finally got back to us on that stuff they found on George Mahmood's trainers."

"And?"

"Animal blood. Must have stepped on a dead spuggy or summat while he was crossing the rec."

"Well," Susan said, "this is all very depressing, but I think I've got at least one piece of good news."

Banks raised his eyebrows.

Susan explained about the message she had left with the Fox-Wood Designs page. "That's why I was late," she said. "When I first checked, the reply hadn't come through, so I thought I'd give it just a few minutes more and try again."

"And?" said Banks.

"And we're in luck. Well, it's a start, anyway."

Susan brought the folded sheet of paper out of her briefcase and laid it on the table. Banks and Hatchley leaned forward to read the black-edged message:

```
Dear Valued Customer,

Many thanks for your interest in the work of
FoxWood Designs. Unfortunately, we have had
to suspend business for the time being due to
bereavement. We hope you will be patient and
bring your business to us in the near future,
and we apologize for any inconvenience this
may have caused you.


Yours Sincerely,

Mark Wood.
```

"*Mark Wood*. So we've got a name," said Banks.

Susan nodded. "As I said, it's not much, but it's a place to start. This *could* be the lad who was with Jason in the Jubilee. At the very least, he's Jason's business partner. He ought to know something."

"Maybe," said Banks. "But he still might prove to have nothing to do with the case at all."

"But don't you think it's a bit fishy that he hasn't come forward yet, no matter who he is?"

"Yes," said Banks. "But Liza Williams didn't come forward, either. Jason's neighbor in Rawdon. She didn't see any reason to. Nor did Motcombe."

"Well, sir," Susan went on, "I still think we should try and find him as soon as possible."

"Oh, I agree." Banks reached for his briefcase. "Don't mind me, Susan, I'm just a bit down in the dumps about what happened to Frank Hepplethwaite."

Susan nodded. "I understand."

"Anyway," Banks went on, "there's one thing we can check, for a start. I got a fax from Ken Blackstone listing Motcombe's properties and tenants. I haven't had time to have a good look at it yet." He pulled the sheets of paper out and glanced over them. "Seems Motcombe owns a fair bit of property," he said after a few moments. "Four houses in addition to his own, two of them divided into flats and bed-sits, the semi where Jason Fox lived, and a shop with a flat above it in Bramley. He also owns the old grocer's shop where the Albion League operates from, as we thought." Finally, a few seconds later, he shook his head in disappointment. "There's no Mark Wood listed among the tenants. Maybe that would have been *too* easy."

"I wonder where Motcombe got his money from," Susan said.

"Members' dues?" Hatchley chipped in.

"Hardly likely," said Banks with a grim smile. "Maybe he inherited it? I'll get in touch with Ken again, see if he can work up some more background on Mr. Motcombe for us."

"You don't really think he did it, do you?" Susan asked.

"Kill Jason? Honestly? No. For a start, he doesn't seem to have a motive. And even if he did have something to do with it, he certainly didn't do it himself. I doubt he's got the bottle. Or the strength. Remember, Jason was a pretty tough customer. But let's have a closer look at him anyway. I don't like the bastard, or what he stands for, so any grief we can give him is fine with me. Even a traffic offense. Besides, I'd look a right prat if we overlooked something obvious, wouldn't I? And that's the last thing I need right now."

"The chief constable?" Susan ventured.

Banks nodded. "Himself. In the flesh. So I'd better get back to my desk and *coordinate*."

IV

Banks felt bone-weary when he arrived home that evening shortly after six o'clock. He was still upset about Frank Hepplethwaite's senseless death, his run-in with Jimmy Riddle was still niggling him, and the lack of progress in the Jason Fox case was sapping his confidence. Well, he'd done the best he could so far. If only the lab boys or Vic Manson could come through with something.

Sandra wasn't home. In a way, that made him feel relieved. He didn't think he could deal with another argument right now. Or the cold shoulder.

He made himself a cheese omelet. There wasn't any real cheese in the fridge, so he used a processed slice. It tasted fine. Shortly after eight, when Banks was relaxing with *Così Fan Tutte* and a small Laphroaig, Sandra got back. Anxious to avoid another scene, Banks turned the volume on the stereo very low.

But Sandra didn't seem to notice the opera playing softly in the background. At least she didn't say anything. She seemed distracted, Banks thought, as he tried to engage her in conversation about the day.

When he offered to take her out for a bite to eat—the omelet not having filled him up nearly as much as he'd hoped—she said she'd already eaten with a couple of friends after the arts committee meeting and she wasn't hungry. All Banks's conversational gambits fell on deaf ears. Even his story of Jimmy Riddle's bollocking failed to gain an ounce of sympathy. Finally, he turned to her and said, "What's wrong? Is this because of the other night? Are you still pissed off at me about that?"

Sandra shook her head. The blond tresses danced over her shoulders. "I'm not pissed off," she said. "That kind of thing is always happening with us. *That*'s the real problem. Don't tell me you haven't noticed how little we see of one another these days? How we both seem to go our separate ways, have our separate interests? How little we seem to have in common? Especially now Tracy's gone."

Banks shrugged. "It's only been a couple of weeks," he said. "I've been busy. So have you. Give it time."

"I know. But that's not it. We're always busy."

"What do you mean?"

"Work. Yours. Mine. Oh, that's not the real problem. We've always been able to deal with that before. You've never expected a dutiful little wife staying at home all day cooking and cleaning, ironing, sewing buttons on, and I thank you for that. But even that's not it." She took one of his cigarettes, something she did so rarely these days that the gesture worried him. "I've been thinking a lot since the other night, and I suppose what I'm saying is that I feel alone. I mean in the relationship. I just don't feel I'm part of your life anymore. Or that you're part of mine."

"But that's absurd."

"Is it? Is it, really?" She looked at him, frowning, black eyebrows crooked in the furrow of her brow. Then she shook her head slowly. "I don't think it is, Alan. What was Saturday all about, then? And the other night? I think if you're honest with yourself, you'll agree. This house feels empty. Cold. It doesn't feel like a home. It feels like the kind of place that two people living separate lives use to sleep and eat in, occasionally passing one another on the landing and saying hello. Maybe stopping for a quick fuck if they've got time."

"That's not fair, and you know it. I think you're just feeling depressed because both the kids have grown up and flown the coop. It'll take time to get used to."

"Next thing you'll be saying I'm feeling this way because it's that time of the month," said Sandra. "But you're wrong. It's not that, either." She thumped her fist on the arm of the chair. "You're not listening to me. You never really *listen* to me."

"I *am* listening, but I'm not sure I understand what I'm hearing. Are you sure this isn't still about last Saturday?"

"No, it's not about last bloody Saturday. Yes, all right, I admit I was angry. I thought for once you might just forsake your sacred bloody opera to do something that *I* thought was important. Something for *my* career. But you didn't. Fine. And then the other night you go and put your opera on the stereo. But you've always been selfish. Selfishness I can deal with. This is something else."

"What?"

"What I've been trying to tell you. We're both independent people. Always. That's why our marriage worked so well. I wasn't waiting and fretting at home for you to come back from work. Worrying that your dinner might get cold. Worrying that something might have happened to you. Though, Lord knows, that was something I never could put out of my mind, even though I tried not to let on to you too much. And if I was out and there was no dinner, if your shirt wasn't ironed, you never complained. You did it yourself. Not very well, maybe, but you did it."

"I still don't complain when dinner's not ready. I made a bloody processed-cheese omel—"

Sandra held her hand up. "Let me finish, Alan. Can't you see what's happened? What used to be our strength—our independence—now it's driving us apart. We've led separate lives for so long, we take it for granted that's how a relationship should be. As long as you've got your work, your music, your books and the occasional evening with the lads at the Queen's Arms, then you're perfectly happy."

"And what about you? Are you happy with your gallery, your photography, your committee meetings, your social evenings?"

Sandra paused a long time, long enough for Banks to pour them both a stiff Laphroaig, before she answered. "Yes," she said finally in a soft voice. "That's just it. Yes. Maybe I am. For a while I've been thinking they're all I do have. You just haven't been here, Alan. Not as a real factor."

Banks felt as if a hand made of ice had slid across his heart. It was such a palpable sensation that he put his hand to his chest. "Is

there someone else?" he asked. On the stereo, Fiordiligi was singing quietly about being as firm as a rock.

Suddenly Sandra smiled, reached out and ran her hand over
his hair. "Oh, you sweet, silly man," she said. "No, there's no one
else." Then her eyes clouded and turned distant. "There could have
been . . . perhaps . . . but there isn't." She shrugged, as if to cast
off a painful memory.

Banks swallowed. "Then what?"

She paused. "As I said, I've been thinking about it a lot lately,
and I've come to the conclusion that we should go our separate
ways. At least for a while." She reached forward and held his hand
as she spoke, which seemed to him, like the smile, an out-of-place
gesture. What the hell *was* wrong?

Banks snatched his hand back. "You can't be serious," he said.
"We've been married over twenty years and all of a sudden you
just decide to up and walk out."

"But I *am* serious. And it's not all of a sudden. Think about it.
You'll agree. This has been building up for a long time, Alan. We
hardly ever see one another anyway. Why continue living a lie?
You know I'm right."

Banks shook his head. "No. I don't. I still think you're over-
reacting to Tracy's leaving and to Saturday night. Give it a little
time. Maybe a holiday?" He sat forward and took her hand now. It
felt limp and clammy. "When this case is over, let's take a holiday,
just you and me. We could go to Paris for a few days. Or somewhere warm. Back to Rhodes, maybe?"

He could see tears in her eyes. "Alan, you're not listening to
me. You're making this really difficult, you know. I've been trying
to pluck up courage to say this for weeks now. It's not something
I've just come up with on the spur of the moment. A holiday's not
going to solve our problems." She sniffled and ran the back of her
hand under her nose. "Oh, bugger," she said. "Look at me now. I
didn't want this to happen." She grabbed his hand and gripped it
tightly again. This time he didn't snatch it away. He didn't know

what to say. The icy touch was back, and now it seemed to be creeping into his bones and inner organs.

"I'm going away for a while," Sandra said. "It's the only way. The only way both of us can get a chance to think things over."

"Where are you going?"

"My parents. Mum's arthritis is playing her up again, and she'll appreciate an extra pair of hands around the place. But that's not the reason. We need time apart, Alan. Time to decide whether there's anything left to salvage or not."

"So this is just a temporary separation you have in mind?"

"I don't know. A few weeks, anyway. I just know I need to get away. From the house. From Eastvale. From you."

"What about the community center, your work?"

"Jane can take over for a while, till I decide what to do."

"Then you might not come back?"

"Alan, I'm telling you I don't know. I don't know what to do. Don't make it harder for me. I'm at my wit's end already. The only sensible thing is for me to get away. Then . . . after a while . . . we can talk about it. Decide where we want to go next."

"Why can't we talk now?"

"Because it's all too *close* here. That's why. Pressing in on me. Please believe me, I don't want to hurt you. I'm scared. But we've got to do it. It's the only chance we've got. We can't go on like this. For crying out loud, we're both still young. Too bloody young to settle for anything less than the best."

Banks sipped more Laphroaig, but it failed to warm the icy hand now busy caressing the inside of his spine. "When are you going?" he asked, his voice curiously flat.

Sandra avoided his eyes. "As soon as possible. Tomorrow."

Banks sighed. In the silence, he heard the letter box open and close. Odd, at that time of night. It seemed like a good excuse to get out of the room for a moment, before he started crying himself, or said things he would regret, so he went to see what it was. On the mat lay an envelope with his name typed on the front. He opened the door, but it was quiet outside in the street, and there was no one in sight.

He opened the envelope. Inside he found a plane ticket from Leeds and Bradford Airport to Amsterdam Schiphol, leaving late the following morning, a reservation for a hotel on Keizersgracht, and a single sheet of paper on which were typed the words: "JASON FOX: SHHHHH."

EIGHT

I

The Dutch coast came into view: first the dull-brown sandbars where the gray sea ended in a long white thread; then the dikes, marking off the reclaimed land, protecting it from the water level.

Banks turned off his Walkman in the middle of "Stop Breaking Down." He always listened to loud music when flying—which wasn't very often—because it was the only thing he could hear over the roar of the engines. And he hadn't played *Exile on Main Street* in so long he'd forgotten just how good it was. The Rolling Stones' raucous rhythm and blues, he found, also had the added advantage of blocking out depressing thoughts.

The plane banked lower over the patchwork of green and brown fields, and Banks could soon make out cars on the long straight roads, rooftops glinting in the midday sun. It was as lovely an autumn day in the Netherlands as it had been in Yorkshire.

Banks rubbed his eyes. He had spent a sleepless night in Brian's room because Sandra had insisted it would only make things more difficult if they slept together. She was right, he knew, but still it rankled. It wasn't even a matter of sex. Somehow it seemed so unfair, when threatened with the loss of someone you had loved for over twenty years, that you didn't even get that one last night of warmth and companionship together to remember and cherish. It felt like all the things you had left unsaid when someone died.

No matter how long Sandra said that she had been grappling with the problem, her decision had come as a shock to Banks. Perhaps, as she had argued, that was a measure of how much he had turned his back, drifted away from the relationship, but somehow her words didn't soften the blow. Now, more than anything, he felt numb, a pathetic figure floating around in zero gravity.

When he thought of Sandra, he thought mostly of the early days in London, where they lived together for about a year before they got married. It was the mid-seventies. Banks was just finishing his business diploma, already thinking about joining the police, and Sandra was taking a secretarial course. Every Sunday, if he didn't have to work, they went on long walks around the city and its parks, Sandra practicing her photography and Banks developing his copper's eye for suspicious characters. Somehow, in his memory, it was always autumn on these walks: sunny but cool, with the leaves crackling underfoot. And when they got back to the tiny Notting Hill flat, they'd play music, laugh, talk, drink wine and make love.

Then came marriage, children, financial responsibilities and a career that demanded more and more of Banks's time and energy. Most of his friends on the force were divorced before the seventies were over, and they all asked in wonder and envy how he and Sandra managed to survive. He didn't really know, but he put a lot of it down to his wife's independent spirit. Sandra was right about that. She wasn't the kind of person who simply hung around the house and waited for him to turn up, fretting and getting angrier by the minute as the dinner was ruined and the kids screamed for bedtime stories from Daddy. Sandra went her own way; she had her own interests and her own circle of friends. Naturally, more responsibility for the children fell on her shoulders, because Banks was hardly ever home, but she never complained. And for a long time, it worked.

After Banks's near burnout on the Met and a long rocky patch in the marriage, they moved to Eastvale, where Banks thought things would settle down and the two of them would enjoy a rural, peaceful and loving drift into middle age together; the kind of thing that most couples married as long as they had been experience.

Wrong.

He looked at his watch. Sandra would be on the train to Croydon now, and whatever happened, whatever she finally decided, things would never be the same between them again. And there was nothing he could do about it. Not a damn thing.

He picked up that morning's *Yorkshire Post* from the empty seat beside him and looked at the headline again: "WORLD WAR TWO HERO DIES AT GRANDSON'S FUNERAL: Neo-Nazis responsible, says granddaughter." There was no photograph, but the basic facts were there: the Nazi salute, Frank Hepplethwaite's attack, Maureen Fox's spirited defense. All in all, it made depressing reading. And then there was the brief sidebar interview with Motcombe himself.

Motcombe deeply regretted the "pointless death" of "war hero" Frank Hepplethwaite, he began, while pointing out how ironic it was that the poor man had died attacking the only people who dared demand justice for his grandson's killers. Naturally, on further thought, neither he nor any member of his organization had any intention of pursuing charges against Maureen Fox, even though the head wound she gave him required five stitches; things had just got out of hand in the heat of the moment, and he could quite understand her attacking him and his friends with a plank. Grief makes people behave irrationally, he allowed.

Of course, Motcombe went on, everyone knew who had killed Jason Fox, and everyone also knew why the police were powerless to act. That was just the state of things these days. He was sympathetic, but unless the government finally decided to act and do something about immigration, then . . .

Jason was a martyr of the struggle. Every true Englishman should honor him. If more people listened to Motcombe's ideas, then things could only change for the better. The reporter, to give her due credit, had managed to stop Motcombe from turning the entire interview into propaganda. Either that or the copy editor had made extensive cuts. Even so, it made Banks want to puke. If anyone was the martyr in this, it was Frank Hepplethwaite.

Frank reminded Banks of his own father in many ways. Both had fought in the war, and neither spoke very much about it. Their racial attitudes were much the same, too. Banks's father might complain about immigrants taking over the country, changing the world he has known all his life, making it suddenly alien and unfamiliar, threatening even. And in the same way, Frank might have let slip a remark about a tight-fisted Jew. But when it came down to it, if anyone needed help, black or Jewish, Banks's dad would have been first in line, with Frank Hepplethwaite probably a close second.

As unacceptable as even these racial attitudes were, Banks thought, they were a hell of a long way from those held by Neville Motcombe and his like. Banks's dad's view, like Frank's, was based on ignorance and anxiety, on fear of change, not on hatred. Perhaps in Motcombe's case the hatred sprang from an initial fear, but in most people it never went that far. Just like a lot of people have bad childhoods but they don't all become serial murderers.

The wheels bumped on the runway, and soon Banks was drifting into the arrivals hall with the crowds. He was traveling light, with only one holdall, so he didn't have to wait at the baggage claim. The place was like a small city, bustling with commerce, complete with its shops, bank, post office and tourist-information desk. A colleague had told him a while ago that even pornography was on sale openly at Schiphol. He had neither the time nor the inclination to look for it.

The first thing Banks needed when he got off a plane alive was a cigarette. He followed the signs to the bus stop and found he had a fifteen-minute wait. Perfect. He enjoyed a leisurely smoke, then got on the bus. Soon it was speeding along the motorway under grids of electrical wires and tall street lamps.

The excitement of arrival pushed Banks's problems into the background for the moment, and he began to take some pleasure in his rebellion, his little act of irresponsibility. So that no one would feel he had disappeared completely into thin air, he had rung Susan Gay and told her he was taking the weekend off to go to Amsterdam and should be back sometime Monday. Susan had sounded puzzled and surprised, but she had made no comment. What could she say, anyway? Banks was her boss. Now, as the bus sped toward the city center, he began to savor the coming hours, whatever they might bring. It could hardly be worse than life in Eastvale right now.

He had been to Amsterdam once before, with Sandra, one summer when they were both between college and jobs. He remembered the bicycles, canals, trams and houseboats. The place was full of leftover sixties spirit back then, and they had tried it all while they could: the Paradiso, the Milky Way, the Vondelpark, the drugs—well, marijuana, at least—as well as taking in all the museums and the tourist sights.

Stationsplein looked much the same. The air was warm, tinged only faintly with the bad-drains smell from the canals. Trams clanked about in all directions. A Perspex-covered boat set off on its canal tour. Arrows of ripples hit the stone quay.

Mixed with the late-season tourists and ordinary folk were all the post-hippie youth styles: punk spikes, a green Mohawk, studded leather vests, short bleached hair, earrings, nose rings, pierced eyebrows.

Banks found the taxi rank nearby. He would have liked to walk after being cooped up on the plane and the bus, but he hadn't got his bearings yet. He didn't even know how to get to the hotel, or how far it was.

The taxi was clean and the driver seemed to recognize the name of the hotel. Soon he had negotiated his way out of the square and they were heading along a broad, busy street lined with trees, arcades, shops and cafés. The pavements were crowded with tourists, even in early October, and Banks noticed that some of the cafés and restaurants had tables out on the street. He opened the window a little and the smell of fresh-brewed coffee came in. God, it was like a summer's day.

The driver turned, crossed a picturesque bridge, then continued along one of the canals. Finally, after a few more turns, he pulled up in front of the hotel on Keizersgracht. Banks paid what seemed like an exorbitant amount of guilders for such a short trip, then hefted his holdall out of the boot.

He looked up at the unbroken row of buildings in front of him. The hotel was small and narrow, about six floors high, with a yellow sandstone facade and a gabled roof. It was wedged in a long terrace of uneven seventeenth- and eighteenth-century buildings that had once, Banks guessed, probably been merchants' houses. Some were built of red brick, some of stone; some had been painted black or gray; some had gables, some had flat roofs. All of them seemed to have plenty of windows.

Banks dodged a couple of cyclists and walked into the hotel lobby. The man at the desk spoke good English. Banks remembered from his previous trip that most people spoke good English in Amsterdam. They had to do. After all, how many English people bothered to learn Dutch?

Yes, the man said, his room was ready, and he was delighted to be able to offer a canal view. Breakfast would be served in the ground-floor lounge between seven o'clock and nine. He was sorry that the hotel had no bar of its own, but there were plenty of fine establishments within a short walking distance. He hoped Mr. Banks would be comfortable.

When Banks pulled out his credit card, the clerk waved it away, telling him the room was fully paid for until Monday morning. Banks tried to discover who had paid for it, but the clerk became extremely coy, and his English went downhill fast. Banks gave up.

Then the clerk handed him a message: a single sheet of paper bearing a typed message that read "De Kuyper's: 16:00hr."

Banks asked what "De Kuyper's" meant and was told it was a brown café—a sort of Dutch local pub—about a hundred meters to his left along the canal. It was on a quiet street corner and would probably have a few tables outside. A very nice place. He couldn't miss it.

The room was a gabled attic up five flights of narrow stairs. When Banks got there, he was panting and beads of sweat had broken out on his forehead.

Though there was hardly room to swing a dead cat and the bed was tiny, the room was clean, with black timber beams and pale blue wallpaper. It smelled pleasantly of lemon air freshener. A blue ashtray stood on the bedside table, beside the reading light and telephone. There were also a small television set and en suite facilities.

The canal view more than made up for any inadequacies. Banks particularly liked the way the ceiling and the black-painted beams sloped down toward the gabled window, drawing the eye to its perspective. And sure enough, he looked down on Keizersgracht and the tall, elegant facades of the buildings opposite. The room was a little too warm and stuffy, so he opened the window, letting in hints of distant street sounds. He looked at his watch. Just after two. Plenty of time for a shower and a nap before the mystery meeting. But first he headed for the telephone. There was always a chance that Sandra had changed her mind.

II

Susan Gay was worried about Banks. Kicking her heels back in her office with black coffee and a so-very-sinful KitKat, she thought about the brief, puzzling phone call. What the hell did he think he was doing, taking a few days off in the middle of a major investigation? Just when they were getting close to tracking down Mark Wood. All right, so it was the weekend. Or almost. But didn't he know that Jimmy Riddle would go spare if he found out? Even Superintendent Gristhorpe would be annoyed.

There had to be more to it. The way he had sounded on the phone bothered her. Abrupt. Distracted. Not like him at all.

Was it the Amsterdam thing? Is that what had him so worried? Was there some danger involved, or something illegal? Banks didn't often act outside the law, not like some coppers Susan had known, but he did sometimes—they all did—if he felt there was no other way. Was he up to something?

Well, she concluded, she didn't know, and there was probably no way of finding out until he got back and revealed all, if he did. Until then, the best thing to do was get on with her work and stop behaving like a mother hen.

She hadn't had a lot of luck tracking Mark Wood down so far. It would take her forever to check out all the listings in the telephone directory. Even then, he might not live in the Leeds area or have a telephone. Sergeant Hatchley was in Leeds today with one of his old cronies from Millgarth visiting the properties Motcombe owned. Maybe they would turn up something, but she doubted it.

She was just about to pick up the phone and start dialing down her list when it rang.

"Is that DC Gay?" the voice said. "Susan?"

"Yes." She didn't know who it was.

"It's Vic here, Vic Manson, from Fingerprints."

"Ah, of course. Sorry, I didn't recognize your voice for a moment. How's it going?"

"I was trying to call Alan, but apparently he's not in his office. All I could get at home was his answering machine. Do you know where he is?"

"I'm afraid he won't be in at all today."

"Not ill, I trust?"

"Can I help, Vic?"

"Yes. Yes, of course. Do you know much about fingerprints?"

"Not a lot. Have you got some news?"

"Well, yes, in a way. Though it's not very good, I'm afraid. Not as good as I'd hoped for."

"I'm listening."

"Right. Well, when I talked to Alan earlier in the week I was testing the glass from the broken bottle found near Jason Fox's body."

"I remember," Susan said. "He said something about spraying it with SuperGlue in an aquarium."

Manson laughed. "Yes. Cyanoacrylate fuming, as a matter of fact."

"I'll take your word for it."

"Yes . . . well, I'm sorry, but it didn't work. We found nothing on the glass. Probably because of the rain."

"And that's it?"

"Not entirely. Do you know anything at all about ninhydrin?"

"Isn't it a chemical for getting prints from paper?"

"Sort of, yes. What ninhydrin does is it makes visible the amino acids you deposit with sweaty fingers, especially on paper."

"I see. But I thought we were concerned with *glass* here, Vic, not paper?"

"Ah, yes," said Manson. "We were. That is until it got us nowhere. But I found a couple of fragments of glass that were also covered by part of the *label* and, luckily, two of them were *under* the body, label side up, but not touching the victim's clothing, quite protected from the rain. Amino acids are water-soluble, you see. Anyway, I don't want to get too technical about it, but it took a long time, and I destroyed one fragment completely, but after I brought a smudge or two out with ninhydrin treatment, I was able to get much better ridge detail under laser light."

"You got a fingerprint?"

"Now, hold on. Wait a minute," said Manson. "I told you from the start it's not a major breakthrough. What I got was a partial fingerprint. *Very* partial. Even with computer enhancement I couldn't do a hell of a lot more with it. And remember, any number of people could have handled that bottle. The cellarman, the land-lord, the bartender. Anyone."

"So you're saying it's worthless?"

"Not completely. Oh, it certainly wouldn't stand up in a court of law. Not enough points of comparison. I mean, it could almost be mine, at a pinch. Well, I exaggerate, but you see what I mean."

"Yes," said Susan, disappointed. She began to feel impatient. "Has this got us anywhere at all?"

"Well," Manson went on, "I ran it through the new computer-ized matching system and I got a list of possibles. I confined the search to Yorkshire and, of course, it only applies to people whose prints we have on file."

"And the print could belong to any person on the list?"

"Technically, yes. At least, as far as court evidence is con-cerned. I'm sorry. I can send it over, anyway, if you'd like?"

"Just a minute," said Susan, feeling her pulse quicken a little. "Do you have it in front of you? The list?"

"Yes."

"Let's try a hunch. Could you check for a name?"

"Of course."

"Try *Wood*. Mark Wood."

It was worth a try. Susan could hear her heart beating fast in the silence that followed. Finally, after what seemed like a millen-nium, Manson said, "Yes. Yes, there is a Mark Wood. I don't have all the details here, of course, but West Yorkshire have probably got a file on him."

"West Yorkshire?"

"Yes. That's where he lives. Castleford area. If he's still at the same address, that is."

"You've got the address?"

"Yes." He read it out to her.

"And let me guess," Susan said. "He was convicted for football hooliganism or some sort of racial incident?"

"Er . . . no, actually," said Manson.

"What then?"

"Drugs."

"Drugs?" Susan repeated. "Interesting. Thanks a lot, Vic."

"No problem. And tell Alan I called, will you?"

Susan smiled. "Will do."

Although Vic Manson said the evidence wouldn't stand up in court, that didn't matter to Susan at the moment. The link between the partial print on the beer bottle and Jason Fox's Web-page design partner was just too strong to be coincidence.

At first, Susan had thought the other lad must have either run away or left Jason *before* the attack. Now, though, the picture looked very different indeed. Maybe they couldn't convict Mark Wood on the basis of the fingerprint, but they could try for a confession or some sort of physical evidence. For a start, the people in the Jubilee should be able to identify him.

But first, Susan thought, reaching for her jacket and her mobile, they would have to find him. Already she was feeling tremors of excitement, the thrill of the chase, and she was damned if she was going to be stuck by herself in Eastvale while Sergeant Hatchley had all the fun and glory.

III

With his hair still damp, Banks stepped out into the late-afternoon warmth. Sandra hadn't been home when he called, hadn't changed her mind. It was what he had expected, really, though he felt a tremendous sense of disappointment when all he got was his own voice on the answering machine.

After an hour or so spent listening to some Mozart wind quintets on the Walkman, though, followed by a long hot shower, he started to feel more optimistic than he had on the plane. Sandra would come back eventually. Give her a few days at her parents' to get over the tiff, and then things would soon return to normal.

Well, almost. They'd have a lot of talking to do, a lot of sorting out, but they'd manage it. They always had.

As he walked onto Keizersgracht, he still had that disconnected feeling he had experienced on arriving, as if all this—canal, bicycles, houseboats—were somehow not quite real, not connected with his life at all. Could he be living some sort of parallel existence, he wondered, another life going on at the same time as he was back in Eastvale talking over the future with Sandra?

Or was he time-traveling? After feeling as if he'd been away for a year, would he suddenly find himself back in Eastvale only seconds after he had left? Or, worse, would he land back right in the middle of that terrible conversation last night, moments before the magic envelope arrived?

He tried to shake off the feeling as he admired the facades of the old buildings along the canal. Rows of bicycles were parked on the stone quay, and a couple of small houseboats were moored nearby. That must be an interesting existence, Banks thought, living on the water. Maybe he'd try it. Now he was a free agent once again, he supposed he could do whatever he wanted, live where he pleased. As long as he had a source of income, of course. Still, there was always Europol or Interpol.

The sun had disappeared behind a gauze of cloud, giving a slightly hazy, misty effect to the light. It was still warm, though, and he slung his jacket over his shoulder as he walked.

Two pretty young girls passed him by, students by the look of them, and the one with long hennaed hair smiled. Definitely a flirtatious smile. Banks felt absurdly flattered and pleased with himself, as well as a bit embarrassed. Here he was, in his early forties, and young girls were still giving him the eye.

He supposed he must look young enough, despite the hint of gray at the temples of his closely cropped black hair, and he knew he was in fairly good shape for his age, still lean in physique, with the suggestion of wiry, compact strength. Casually dressed in jeans, trainers and a light blue denim shirt, he probably seemed younger than he was. And while his rather long, sharply angled face was not handsome in any regular sense of the word, it was the kind of face women seemed to notice. Sandra had always said it was because of his lively, striking dark blue eyes.

He reached a small stone bridge with black iron railings. A flower vendor stood at the corner and the musky scent of roses filled the air. It took him back to a vivid memory, the way smells do, something to do with one of his walks with Sandra many years ago, but he cut it off. He stood for a moment leaning on the railings and looking down into the murky water, with its floating chocolate wrappers and cigarette packets scattered among the rainbows of diesel oil, then took a deep breath and turned back to the street.

There was the pub, De Kuyper's, right on the corner, as the desk clerk had said. It had an exterior of dark brown wood and smoked plate-glass windows with the name painted in large white letters. A few small round tables stood outside, all empty at the moment. Banks glanced inside the dark wood-paneled bar, saw no one he knew or who took any interest in him, then went out again. He patted his jacket pocket to make sure he had his cigarettes and wallet with him, then slung it over the back of a chair and sat down.

He was early for the meeting, as he had intended. While he didn't really expect any danger, not here, in the open, on a warm afternoon, he wanted to be able to cover as many angles as possible. His table was perfect for that. From where he sat, he could see all the way along the curving canal past the hotel he had walked from, and a fair distance in the other direction, too. He also had a clear view of the opposite bank. Somewhere, in the distance, he could hear an organ-grinder.

When the white-aproned waiter came by, Banks ordered a bottle of De Koninck, a dark Belgian beer he had tried and enjoyed once at Belgo, a London restaurant. With the beer in front of him, he lit a cigarette and settled back to wait, watching the people walk to and fro, laughing and talking, along the canal. He already had his suspicions about who would turn up.

As it happened, he didn't have long to wait. He had just lit his second cigarette and worked about halfway through the beer, when he noticed someone out of the corner of his eye coming down the narrow side street.

It was a familiar figure, and Banks congratulated himself for getting it right. None other than Detective Superintendent Richard "Dirty Dick" Burgess in the flesh. A little more flesh than on their previous meeting, by the look of it, most of it on his gut. And his hair was now almost as gray as his cynical eyes. Burgess worked for Special Branch, or something very close to it, and whenever he appeared on the scene Banks knew there would be complications.

"Banks, me old cock sparrow," said Burgess, putting on the Cockney accent Banks knew he'd lost years ago. Then he clapped Banks on the back and took a chair. "Mind if I join you?"

IV

A steady drizzle had settled in by the time Susan passed the Garforth exit, and she had to switch on her windscreen wipers to clean off all the muck the lorries churned up. Castleford wasn't far, though, and soon the enormous cooling towers of Ferrybridge power station came into sight. She found the road to Ferry Fryston without much trouble and, pulling over into the car park of a large pub to consult her map, pinpointed the street she was looking for.

Mark Wood lived in a "prefab" on one of the early-postwar council estates. These were houses—mostly semis or short terrace blocks—built of concrete prefabricated in the factory, then assembled on the site. In this area, they were built originally to house colliery workers, but since all the local pits had been closed during the Thatcher years, they were up for grabs, a source of cheap housing.

The houses themselves weren't up to much. They had no central heating, and the walls were damp. In the rain, Susan thought, the concrete looked like porridge.

Susan negotiated her way through the maze of "avenues," "rises," "terraces" and "drives" which curved and looped in great profusion, then she spotted Hatchley's darkgreen Astra, just around the corner from Wood's house, as they had arranged over the phone.

Susan pulled up behind him, turned off her engine, then dashed over and jumped in beside him.

"Sorry if I kept you waiting, Sarge," she said. "Three-car accident near the York junction."

"That's all right," said Hatchley, stubbing out a cigarette in the already overstuffed ashtray. "Just got here myself. Bugger of a place to find. Bugger of a place to live, too, if you ask me."

"How shall we play it?"

Hatchley squirmed in his seat and ran his pudgy fingers under the back of his collar, as if to loosen it. "Why don't you start the questioning?" he said. "It'll be good experience now you're going to be a sergeant. I'll jump in if I think it's necessary."

"Fine," said Susan, smiling to herself. She knew that Hatchley hated carrying out formal interviews unless he was talking either to an informant or a habitual criminal. With Wood, they just didn't know yet, so Hatchley would let her lead, then he would follow if she got somewhere interesting or fill in the gaps if she missed something.

As it turned out, Hatchley had even more reason for assigning the interview to Susan. When they knocked on the door, a young woman opened it, and Hatchley was useless at interviewing women. Susan finessed their way inside easily enough, showing her warrant card, after learning that Mark had just "nipped out" to the shop for some cigarettes and would be back in a few minutes. Good, she thought; it gave her a chance to talk to the girlfriend alone first.

Inside, the house was clean and tidy enough, but Susan's sense of smell, always sensitive, reacted at once to the mingled baby odors—warm milk, mushy food and, of course, the whole mess when it all comes out transformed at the other end—plus the kitty litter. Sure enough, a black-and-white cat prowled the room and a baby slept in its cot in the corner, occasionally emitting a tiny sniffle or cry, as if disturbed by dreams. One of the walls was damp, and the wallpaper was peeling off near the ceiling.

"What's it all about?" the woman asked. "I'm Shirelle. Mark's wife."

That was Susan's first shock. Shirelle was Afro-Caribbean. And she didn't look a day older than fourteen. She was small in stature, with a flat chest and slim hips, and her pale brown face was framed by long braided black hair that cascaded over her shoulders. Looking at her sitting there in the worn old armchair, it was hard to believe she was old enough to be a mother.

"We've just a few questions to ask your Mark, love," said Susan, in as reassuring a tone as she could manage. When Shirelle didn't answer, she went on, "Maybe you can help. Do you know Jason Fox?"

She frowned. "No. I've never met him. Mark mentioned him once or twice. They work together. But he's never brought him here."

I'm not surprised, Susan thought. "Did Mark ever tell you anything about him?"

"Like what?"

"What he's like, how they get on, that sort of thing."

"Well, I don't think Mark likes him all that much. They haven't been working together for long, and I think Mark's going to break with him. Apparently, this Jason has some peculiar ideas about immigrants and stuff."

You could say that again. "Doesn't that bother you?"

"I'm not an immigrant. I was born here."

"How long have they been working together?"

"A few months."

"How did they meet?"

"They were both doing a computer course in Leeds at the same time, and neither of them could get a job after. I think this Jason had a bit of money to put into starting a business. Mark was top of the class, so Jason asked if he wanted to join him. Like I say, I don't think Mark's going to stick with him. It's just a start, that's all. It's hard to get started when you don't have the experience."

"How's the business doing?" Susan asked.

Shirelle looked around her and snorted. "What do *you* think? Hardly made enough to pay for this place and you can see what a dump it is." Now she neither looked nor sounded like a fourteen-year-old.

The cat tried to climb on Susan's knee, but she pushed it away. "It's not that I don't like cats, Shirelle," she said, "but I'm allergic to them."

Shirelle nodded. "Tina, come here!" she said.

But the cat, as cats do, gave her a you-must-be-joking look and ignored her. Finally, Shirelle shot forward, scooped up Tina and deposited her in the next room, closing the door.

"Thanks," said Susan. "Have you heard of the Albion League?"

Shirelle shook her head. "What's that when it's at home?"

"Do you know where Mark was last Saturday night?"

Shirelle glanced away for just long enough that Susan knew she was going to tell a lie. Why? Had her husband told her to? Or did she want to avoid trouble with the police? With some people, it was habitual. Whatever the reason, as soon as she said, "He was here. At home," Susan asked her to think carefully about her answer.

"What time do you mean?" Shirelle asked, after a few moments' hesitation. "Because he might, you know, have nipped down the pub for a jar or two with his mates."

"Which pub would that be?"

"Hare and Hounds. At the corner. That's his local." Shirelle seemed distracted by Sergeant Hatchley, who had said nothing so

far, but just sat next to Susan on the sofa watching the whole proceedings, still as a statue, occasionally nodding encouragement
and making a note in his black book. She kept looking at him, then
turned her large, frightened eyes away, back to Susan.

"And if we were to ask there, at this Hare and Hounds," Susan
said, "then they'd remember Mark from last Saturday night, would
they?"

"I . . . I don't—"

At that moment the front door opened and a male voice called
out, "Sheri? Sheri?"

Then Mark Wood entered the room: stocky build, muscular,
short hair, loop earring and all. Early twenties. The man in the
picture.

"Hello, Mark," said Susan. "We've been wanting a word with
you ever since last Saturday."

When Mark saw Susan and Hatchley he stopped in his tracks
and his jaw went slack. "Who . . . ?" But it was obvious he knew
who they were, even if he hadn't been expecting them. He put the
packet of cigarettes on the table and sat in the other armchair.
"What about?" he asked.

"Jason. We'd have thought you might have got in touch with us,
you know, since Jason died."

"Jason what?" Shirelle burst in. She looked at Mark. "Jason's
dead? You never told me that."

Mark shrugged.

"Well?" Susan asked.

"Well, what?"

"What do you have to say? Even if your wife didn't know, *you*
knew Jason was dead, didn't you?"

"Read about it in the paper. But it's nothing to do with me,
is it?"

"Isn't it? You were there, Mark. You were in Eastvale drinking with Jason. You left the Jubilee with him shortly after closing
time. What we want to know is what happened next."

"I was never there," Mark said. "I was here. At home. Now we've got little Connor, I don't get out as much as I used to. I can't just leave Sheri alone with him all the time, can I? Besides, as you can probably tell, we're a bit short of the readies, too."

"I'll bet you own a car, though, don't you?"

"Just an old banger. A van. I need it for the business."

"Designing Web pages?"

"That's not all we do. We do a bit of retail, refurbish systems, set up networks, troubleshoot, that sort of thing."

"So you haven't been out dealing drugs for a while?"

"You know about that, do you?"

"We do our research. What do you expect?"

Mark shifted in his chair and shot a quick glance at Shirelle. "Yeah, well, it was years ago now. It's behind me. I've been clean ever since."

"Were you selling drugs at the Jubilee last Saturday night?"

"No. I told you. I wasn't even there. Besides, I served my time."

"You're right," said Susan. "Nine months, if I read the record right. It's nice to know there really is such a thing as rehabilitation. That's not what we're interested in anyway. All we care about is what happened to Jason Fox. What about the Albion League, Mark? Are you a member?"

Mark scoffed. "That bunch of wankers? That was Jason's thing. Not mine." He looked at Shirelle. "Or isn't that obvious enough to you already?"

"Did Jason ever introduce you to their leader, Neville Motcombe, or any of the other members?"

"No. He kept asking me to go to meetings, but that's all. I think he picked up that I wasn't really interested."

"But the two of you produced the Web page for them."

"Jason did that in his spare time. By himself. Thought it was a good idea to put the company's logo at the bottom. Said it could bring us more business." He shrugged. "Business is business, even if some of it does come from crackpots."

"And did it?"

"Did it what?"

"Bring in more business?"

"Nah. Not much. To be honest, I think hardly anyone even looked at it. I mean, would you?"

"But you were friends with Jason, too, weren't you?"

"I wouldn't really say that."

"I understand he provided the capital to start the business?"

Mark looked at Shirelle. Susan guessed he was probably trying to work out exactly what his wife had told them already.

"Yes," he said. "I didn't have any money, but Jason put in a few hundred quid, just to get us going. Only a loan, mind you."

"So you wouldn't say you were friends?"

"No. It's not as if we actually socialized together."

"But you *were* socializing last Saturday night in Eastvale."

"I told you, I wasn't there. I was here all evening."

"Didn't you even nip out for a jar?" Susan asked. "Shirelle here said she thought you might have done."

Mark looked to his wife for guidance. "I . . . I don't . . ." she said. "They've been confusing me, Mark. *Was* it Saturday? I don't remember. I only said he might have gone out for a few minutes."

"*Did* you go out, Mark?" Susan repeated.

"No," said Mark. Then he turned to Shirelle. "Don't you remember, love, when we went in town shopping in the afternoon, we picked up a couple of bottles at the offie, then we rented that Steven Seagal video and we just stayed in and watched it. Don't you remember?"

"Oh, yes, that's right," said Shirelle. "Yes, I remember now. We stayed in and watched a video together."

Susan ignored Shirelle; she was lying again. And she thought it interesting that no matter how poor people seemed, how short of the "readies" they were, they always had enough money for booze, cigarettes, videos and pets. Cars, even. "So you weren't in Eastvale at all last Saturday night, then, Mark?"

Mark shook his head. "No."

"I suppose the video rental shop will have a record?"

"I suppose so. They're computerized, all the latest gear, so they ought to. I never asked. I mean, I didn't think anyone would be interested."

"But you could still be lying, couldn't you?" Susan went on. "In fact, it doesn't matter at all whether you rented a video on Saturday afternoon or not, does it? You could have gone to Eastvale on Saturday evening, met Jason in the Jubilee and booted him to death. You could have watched the video after you got home."

"I told you. I didn't do anything of the sort. I wasn't anywhere near there. Besides, why would I do a thing like that? I already told you, Jason was my business partner. Why would I kill the goose that lays the golden eggs?"

"You tell me. I understand you were going to dump him?"

Again, Mark looked at Shirelle, who stared into her lap.

"Look," he said, "I'm telling you, I didn't do anything. I wasn't anywhere near Eastvale. I've never even been there in my life."

Suddenly, Hatchley lurched to his feet, making even Susan jump. "Let's cut the bollocks, lad," he said, putting his notebook back in his inside pocket. "We know you were there. People *saw* you in the pub. And we've got a clear set of your fingerprints on the murder weapon. What have you got to say about that?"

Mark looked from side to side, as if seeking an escape route. Shirelle started to cry. "Oh, Mark . . ." she wailed. "What can we do?"

"Shut up blubbering," he said, then turned back to Susan and Hatchley. "I want a lawyer."

"Later," said Hatchley. "First, we're going to fill a plastic bag with your shoes and clothes, then we're going to go back to Eastvale for a nice long chat in a proper police interview room. How do you feel about that?"

Mark said nothing.

Connor stirred in his cot and started to cry.

V

"Tell me one thing," Banks said. "Why the hell have you dragged me all the way to Amsterdam?"

Burgess smiled, flipped open his tin of Tom Thumb cigars and selected one. "Everything will be made clear in time. Shit, it's good to see you again, Banks," he said. "I knew I could rely on your curiosity to get you here. I can't think of a better man for a case like this." He lit the small cigar and blew out a plume of smoke.

"What case would that be?" asked Banks, who had learned, over the years, to trust Burgess about as much as he would trust a politician in an election year.

"Oh, don't be coy. The Jason Fox case, of course."

The waiter came out. Burgess asked Banks what he was drinking. Banks told him he'd have another De Koninck.

"Filthy stuff," said Burgess. Then he turned to the waiter. "Still, bring him another one, will you, mate, if that's what he wants. I'll have a lager. Whatever you've got on tap."

Banks noticed for the first time that Burgess had his graying hair pulled back and tied in a ponytail. Bloody typical. The aging-stud look.

"Beautiful day, isn't it?" Burgess said when the waiter came back with their drinks. "Aren't you glad I got you the ticket, Banks?"

"I'm overwhelmed with delight and gratitude," said Banks, "but I wouldn't mind knowing what it's all about. Just a hint, maybe, to start with."

"That's my Banks." Burgess jerked forward—all his motions seemed jerky—and clapped him on the shoulder. "Always anxious to get down to business. You know, you could have made super by now. Who knows, even chief super. If only you weren't such a Bolshie bastard. You never did learn to be nice to the right people, did you?"

Banks smiled. "And *you* did?"

Burgess winked. "I must've done something right, mustn't I? Anyway, enough about me. Sometime earlier this week you—or someone in your division—set off an alarm bell I'd placed on a certain file."

"The Albion League?"

"Who's a clever boy, then? Yes, the Albion League. I got a bloke called Crawley—good chap—to answer and instructed him to give away as little as possible. See, I wanted to know why *you* were so interested in the league. It's not as if they've got a big operation in North Yorkshire, after all. Then I found out about the Jason Fox killing, and things sort of fell into place."

"You knew Jason was a member?"

"Of course I bloody did. He was Neville Motcombe's right-hand man. Hotly tipped for future Führerdom himself. Now Jason getting himself killed like that was a very bad thing, because it set off all kinds of warning bells all over the place. Which is why I'm here. You, too."

A couple of young blond girls walked by. One of them was wearing a tight T-shirt and high-cut turquoise shorts. She was pushing her bicycle as she chatted with her friend. "Jesus Christ, would you look at that ass," said Burgess, lapsing into his habitual American slang. "Gives me such a hard-on I don't have enough skin left to close my eyes." He gave a mock shudder. "Anyway, where was I?"

"Warning bells."

"Yes. I don't know how much you know about him, Banks, but Motcombe is a nasty piece of work. Just because he's a fucking fruitcake it doesn't mean you should underestimate him."

"I'd have thought that *you* would have had every sympathy with him," Banks said. "In fact, I'm surprised you're not a member of the Albion League yourself."

Burgess laughed. "Oh, what a cheap shot. You know what, Banks, you're so very predictable. Do you know that? That's one of the reasons I like you. I've been waiting for a remark like that ever since I sat down." He settled back in his chair and puffed on his Tom Thumb. "Do I think we're letting too many foreigners in? Yes. Do I think we've got a problem with our immigration policy? Damn right I do. But do I think a gang of goose-stepping football hooligans are the answer? No, I don't. Look at this lot." He waved his arm around, as if to indicate the Dutch in general. "Look at the problems they've had with their darkies. And they've only got Dutch Guiana to worry about."

"Suriname," said Banks.

"Whatever."

"And I think you'll find they also colonized a lot more of the world than just that."

"Listen, Banks, stop being a bloody smart-arse. That's not the point, and you know it. You can't convince me that England wouldn't be a damn sight more civilized and law-abiding if we hadn't let so many of the buggers in to start with."

"Civilized and law-abiding as in football hooligans?"

"Oh, it's no fucking use arguing with you, is it? Got an answer for everything, haven't you? Let me put it in a nutshell. While I think this Albion League might have some pretty good ideas, I don't like getting dressed up like an idiot and hanging around with skinheads and leather-fetishists without two brain cells to rub together between them. Credit me with a bit more sense than that, Banks. Whatever I am," Burgess concluded, thrusting his thumb toward his chest, "I am not a fucking loony."

Burgess was actually wearing his trademark scuffed-up black leather jacket, but Banks let that one go by.

"Anyway," Burgess went on after a long swig of generic lager, "back to Neville Motcombe. We know he's got connections with other right-wing groups in Europe and America. Over the past four years, he's traveled extensively in Germany, France, Spain, Italy and Holland. He's also been to Greece and Turkey."

"I wouldn't have thought a neo-Nazi would find much to interest him in Turkey," Banks said.

"You'd be surprised. There are plenty of right-wing Turkish

groups with access to arms. Get them cheap off the Russians in Azerbaijan or Armenia. Very strategically located for lots of nasty things, is Turkey. And don't forget, Johnny Turk's a slimy bastard. Anyway, Motcombe has also visited a number of militia training camps in the southwestern United States, and he's been spotted entering the Nazi party headquarters in Lincoln, Nebraska. That, for your information, is where most of the instructions on bombs and explosives come from. So this guy has talked to the sort of people who blew up that government building in Oklahoma City." Burgess pointed his cigar at Banks. "Whatever you do, Banks, don't underestimate Neville Motcombe. Besides, when you get right down to it, this isn't really about politics at all. There's something else."

"What?"

"Money. One of the Turkish right-wingers Motcombe has been communicating with frequently of late, via the Internet, is a suspected international drug dealer. Heroin, mostly. And we happen to know he's looking for new outlets in England. They met when Motcombe was in Turkey during the summer, and electronic traffic between them has increased dramatically over the past three weeks. The wires are hot, you might say."

"What do these messages say?"

"Ah, well, there's the problem. Our computer whizzes have been keeping an eye on these cyber-Nazis, as they're called. We know some of their passwords, so we can read a fair bit of the traffic. Until they get on to us and change the passwords, that is. Problem is, some of the really hot stuff is encrypted. They use PGP and even more advanced encryption programs. I kid you not, Banks, these things make Enigma look like a fucking doddle."

"So you can't decipher the messages?"

"Well, maybe they're just chatting away about Holocaust denial or some such rubbish—we can't exactly decipher their messages— but knowing the Turk, I doubt it. I'd say he's found the pipeline he was looking for."

Banks shook his head. "And Jason Fox?" he said. "Do you think this could have something to do with his death?"

Burgess shrugged. "Well, it's a bit of a coincidence, isn't it? And I know you don't like coincidences. I thought you should be filled in, that's all."

"What a load of bollocks," said Banks. "And don't give me all this cloak-and-dagger shit. Encrypted E-mail. Vague suspicions. Is this what you dragged me all this way for?"

Burgess looked offended. "No," he said. "Well, not entirely. As it happens, I don't know much about it yet myself."

"So why *am* I here?"

"Because a very important person is here, *has* to be here for at least a week. Because it's essential you talk to this person before you go any further in your investigation. And because it wouldn't do for you to be seen together back home. Believe me, he'll be able to tell you a lot more than I can. Good enough?"

"What about the telephone?"

"Oh, give me a break, Banks. If they can eavesdrop on Charlie and Di, they can bloody well eavesdrop on you. Telephones aren't secure. Quit bellyaching and enjoy yourself. It won't be all work. I mean, what are you complaining about? You've got yourself a free weekend in one of the most exciting cities in the world. Okay?"

Banks thought for a moment, watching the bicycles and cars passing by on the canal side. He lit a cigarette. "So what happens next?" he said.

"Tomorrow afternoon, *I* get up-to-date on what's going on, then I'm off on my holidays, believe it or not. I think I'll just go out to Schiphol and take the first flight somewhere tropical. In the evening, *you* have a very important meeting." Burgess told him to be at a bar near Sarphatipark at eight o'clock, but not whom he would find when he got there. "And make sure you're not followed," he added.

Banks shook his head at the melodrama. Burgess just loved this cloak-and-dagger crap.

Then Burgess clapped his hands, showering ash on the table. "But until then, we're free agents. Two happy bachelors—and notice I didn't say 'gay'—with the whole night ahead of us." He lowered his voice. "Now, what I suggest is that we find a nice little Indonesian restaurant, shovel down a plate or two of rijsttafel and swill that down with a few pints of lager. Then we'll see if we can find one of those little coffee shops where you can smoke hash." He rested his arm over Banks's shoulder. "And after that, I suggest we take a stroll to the red-light district and get us some nice, tight Dutch pussy. It's all perfectly legal and aboveboard here, you know, and the girls have regular checkups. Tried and tested, stamped prime grade A." He turned to Banks and squinted. "Now, I know you've got that lovely wife of yours waiting at home—Sandra, isn't it?—but there really is nothing quite like a little strange pussy once in a while. Take my word. And what she doesn't know won't hurt her. My lips will be eternally sealed, I can promise you that. How about it?"

As usual, Banks thought, the bastard showed his unerring instinct for finding the spot that hurt, like a dentist prodding at an exposed nerve. There was no way Burgess could know what had happened between Banks and Sandra the previous evening. Nobody knew but the two of them. Yet here he was, right on the mark. Well, to hell with him.

"Fine," said Banks. "You're on." Then he raised his glass and finished his beer. "But first, I think I'll have another one of these."

NINE

I

"I'm sorry we had to take you away from your wife and child, Mark," said Gristhorpe. "Let's hope it won't be for long."

Wood said nothing; he just looked sullen and defiant.

"Anyway," Gristhorpe went on, "I'd like to thank you for sparing us the time." He balanced a pair of reading glasses on his hooked nose and flipped through some sheets of paper in front of him, glancing up over the top of his glasses from time to time. "There's just a few points we'd like to get cleared up, and we think you can help us."

"I've already told you," Wood said. "I don't know anything."

Susan sat next to Gristhorpe in the interview room: faded institutional green walls, high barred window, metal table and chairs bolted to the floor, pervading odor of smoke, sweat and urine. Susan was convinced they sprayed it in fresh every day. Two tape recorders were running, making a soft hissing sound in the background. It was dark outside by the time they actually got around to the interview. Gristhorpe had already given the caution. Wood had also phoned a solicitor in Leeds, Giles Varney, and got his answering machine. You'd be lucky to find a lawyer at home on a Friday evening, in Susan's experience. Still, he had left a message and steadfastly refused the duty solicitor. Hardly surprising, Susan thought, given that Giles Varney was one of the best-known solicitors in the county. She would have thought he was way out of Mark's league.

"Yes," said Gristhorpe, taking off his glasses and fingering the papers in front of him. "I know that. Thing is, though, that sometimes when people come into contact with the police, they lie." He shrugged and held his hands out, palms up. "Now, I can understand that, Mark. Maybe they do it to protect themselves, or maybe just because they're afraid. But they lie. And it makes our job just that little bit more difficult."

"I'm sorry, I can't help you," said Wood.

Good sign, Susan noted. Gristhorpe had the lad apologizing already.

"Now," Gristhorpe went on, "the last time you got into trouble, you told the police that you had no idea the van you were driving was used for carrying drugs, or that some of the people you were involved with were dealing drugs. Is that true?"

"Do you mean is that what I said?"

"Yes."

Mark nodded. "Yes."

"And is the *statement* true?"

Mark grinned. "Well, of course it is. It's what I told the court, isn't it? A matter of public record. It's hardly my fault if the magistrate didn't believe me."

"Course not, Mark. Innocent people get convicted all the time. It's one of the problems with the system. Nothing's perfect. But with so many lies going around, you can understand why we might be just a bit wary, a little bit overcautious, and perhaps not quite as trusting as you'd like, can't you?"

"I suppose so. Yes."

Gristhorpe nodded. "Good."

The superintendent's interview technique, Susan noticed, was in direct contrast to Banks's, with whom she had more experience of questioning subjects. Banks would sometimes needle his interviewees, and when he'd got them confused and vulnerable, he would subtly suggest possible scenarios of how they had committed the crime, and why. He sometimes even went so far as to explain to them their feelings and state of mind while they were doing it. Then, if they were new to the world of crime, he would sometimes describe in graphic detail what kind of life they could expect in jail and after. Banks worked on his subjects' *imaginations;* he used words to paint images unbearable to the hearer.

Gristhorpe seemed to concentrate more on logic and reasoned argument; he was polite, soft-spoken and unrelenting. He seemed slower than Banks, too. As if he had all the time in the world. But Susan was keen to get it over with. She had already pulled a couple favors to get the lab working overtime on Mark Wood's shoes and clothing, and if they came up with some solid forensic evidence, or if Gristhorpe got a confession, there was a good chance they could wrap things up before tonight. Jimmy Riddle would be pleased about that.

As a bonus, she would have the weekend free, for once, and she might get her Saturday night out with Gavin. She had considered phoning him earlier—even picked up the phone—but no, she told herself, it wouldn't do to seem *too* keen, *too* easily available. Let him cajole her. Seduce her. *Win* her.

"You see," Gristhorpe went on, "that's one of our main problems, sorting out the lies from the truth. That's why we have science to help us. Do you know what 'forensic' means?"

Wood frowned and tugged on his earring. "It means science, doesn't it? Like blood types, footprints, DNA and fingerprints?"

"That's a common error," Gristhorpe said, toying with his glasses on the table. "Actually, it means 'for use in a court of law.' It's from the Latin, related to the word *forum*. So one of the best systems we have to help us tell the lies from the truth is a complex and broad-ranging branch of science dedicated solely to presenting scientific evidence *in court*. Now, of course, before we get to court, we use this forensic evidence to help us identify the people who should be on trial. And in your case, I'm afraid the evidence tells us that you should be in court for the murder of Jason Fox. What do you have to say about that, Mark?"

"Nothing. What can I say? I've done nothing."

Wood was taken aback by Gristhorpe's gentle and erudite logic, Susan could tell. But he was cool. She noticed that Gristhorpe let the silence stretch until Wood started squirming in his chair.

"Well, you must have something to say, lad," Gristhorpe went on, putting on his glasses again and slipping a photograph from the file in front of him. "This is an image of a fingerprint found on the label of a beer bottle," he said, turning it around so Wood could see it clearly. "It was developed by a very painstaking process. Forensic science doesn't produce miracles, Mark, but sometimes it seems to come close. Now, I'm sure you're an intelligent-enough lad to know that fingerprints are unique. So far, no two fingers have been found to possess the same ridge characteristics. Isn't that amazing?"

Wood said nothing; his eyes were glued to the photo.

"Anyway," Gristhorpe went on, "what's particularly interesting about *that* fingerprint is that it came from a fragment of a broken bottle found at the scene of Jason Fox's murder. But perhaps I'm being precipitous in referring to it as a *murder* so soon, because that hasn't been proven yet. You do know that there's a big difference between homicide and manslaughter, don't you, Mark?"

Wood nodded. "Yes."

"Good. And there's also a big difference in jail sentences. But we won't let that detain us for the moment. Anyway, the point is that it is a close match for *your* fingerprint—one we already have on file—and that it was found in the ginnel by the rec, on a fragment of a broken beer bottle under Jason Fox's body. I'd like you to tell me how it got there."

Wood licked his lips and glanced at Susan. She said nothing. He looked back into Gristhorpe's guileless blue eyes.

"Well, er . . . I suppose I must have touched it, mustn't I, if it's got my prints on it?" He smiled.

Gristhorpe nodded. "Aye. I suppose so. When might that have happened, Mark?"

"I gave it to Jason," Wood said finally.

"When?"

"When we came out of the pub. You see, I thought I wanted another beer, so I bought a bottle from out-sales as we were leaving, but then I remembered I had to drive back down the A1, so I just gave it to Jason. He said he was walking home."

"Ah," said Gristhorpe. "So you *gave* the bottle of beer to Jason when you parted outside the Jubilee?"

"That's right. I was parked just down the street the pub was on. Market Street. Is that right?"

"That's the one." Gristhorpe looked at Susan, who raised her eyebrows.

"What's wrong?" Wood asked.

Susan scratched the cleft of her chin. "Nothing, really, Mark," she said. "It's just that you've confused me a bit. When I talked to you earlier you denied being in Eastvale at all last Saturday night. Don't you remember?" She pretended to read from the paper in front of her. "You bought a couple of bottles of beer at the off-license and rented a Steven Seagal video, which you and your wife watched that evening. You didn't even nip out to the Hare and Hounds for a quick one. That's what you said, Mark."

"Yeah, well . . . It's like he said earlier, isn't it?" He looked at Gristhorpe.

"What would that be, Mark?" Gristhorpe asked.

"About people ly— About people not telling the exact truth sometimes when the police come after them."

"So you didn't tell the truth?"

"Not exactly."

"Why not?"

"I was scared, wasn't I?"

"What of?"

"That you'd fit me up for it because I've been in trouble before."

"Ah, yes," said Gristhorpe, shaking his head. "The classic fit-up. That's another one of the problems we constantly have to fight against: the public's perception of the police, mostly formed by the media. Especially television. Well, I won't deny it, Mark, there *are* police officers who wouldn't stop at forging a notebook entry or altering a statement in order to convict someone. We're all embarrassed about the Birmingham Six, you know. That's why there are so many laws now to help people in your position. We can't beat you up. We can't force a confession out of you. We have to treat you well while you're in custody—feed you, allow you exercise, give you access to a solicitor. That sort of thing. It's all covered in the PACE guidelines." Gristhorpe spread his hands. "You see, Mark, we're just humble public servants, really, gentle custodians here to see that your rights aren't abused in any way. By the way, you must be a bit hungry by now, aren't you? I know I am. How about I send out for some coffee and sandwiches?"

"Fine with me. Long as they're not salmon. I'm allergic to salmon."

"No problem. Susan, would you ask one of the uniformed officers to nip over to the Queen's Arms and ask Cyril to do us two or three ham-and-cheese sandwiches? And have one of the lads up front bring us a pot of fresh coffee, please."

"Of course, sir."

Susan popped her head out of the door and made the request, then she went back to her chair.

"While we're waiting, though," said Gristhorpe, "and if you don't mind, Mark, let's get back to what happened last Saturday night, shall we? As I understand it, you've changed your original story—which, quite understandably, you now admit was a lie."

"Because I was scared you'd fit me up."

"Right. Because you were scared we'd fit you up. Well, I hope I've put your mind at rest about that."

Wood leaned back in his chair and smiled. "You're a lot nicer than those bastards from West Yorkshire who nabbed me on that drugs charge."

Bloody hell, thought Susan, the old man's even getting compliments out of his suspects now, let alone mere apologies.

"Well," said Gristhorpe, inclining his head modestly. "West Yorkshire have a lot more problems than we do, being a lot more urban and all. They sometimes have to cut corners a bit roughly."

"You're telling me."

"But that's all behind you now, Mark, isn't it? I see you've been a good lad since then. You took a course and then you went into business. Admirable. But now there's just this little spot of bother, and the sooner we get it cleared up, the sooner you can get back to leading a normal and productive life with your family. Did Jason ever try to interest you in the Albion League?"

"Sometimes. He'd spout a load of garbage about how the Holocaust didn't really happen—how most of the Jews died of typhoid and the showers were just ways of disinfecting them, like, not really death camps at all. I must admit, it made me a bit sick. Then I lost interest and didn't pay much attention after that. Half the time I thought he couldn't even be serious."

"I understand your wife is Afro-Caribbean?"

"Her family's from Jamaica, yes."

"How did you manage to reconcile this with doing business with a racist like Jason?"

"I never thought much about it, really, not at first. Like I said, I thought Jason spouted a load of silly rubbish. I figured he'd probably grow out of it."

"You said 'at first.' What about after that?"

"Yeah, well, it started getting to me, Sheri being Jamaican and all. We had a couple of arguments. I was on the verge of ditching him when—"

"When what, Mark?"

"Well, you know, he died."

"Ah, yes. Did you tell him you were married to a Jamaican woman?"

"Are you joking? And listen to him prattle on about that? He really had a bee in his bonnet about mixed marriages. No, I kept my private life and my business activities completely separate."

Gristhorpe adjusted his glasses again and took a moment or two to look over some sheets of paper. Then he looked back at Wood, held his glasses in his hand and frowned. "But you knew that Jason was doing this computer work for the league?"

The food came, and they took a moment's break to pass around sandwiches and pour coffee.

"Yes, I knew," Wood answered. "But what he did in his own time was up to him."

"Even if you didn't agree? It bore the trademark of the business you ran together, didn't it?"

"We could use all the business we could get."

"Right. So you let your name be used for neo-Nazi propaganda even though you found the idea loathsome. Your wife is black, for crying out loud, Mark. What do you think Jason Fox and his ilk would do with her if they got half a chance? What does that make you, Mark? Are you ashamed of her?"

"Now hold on a minute—"

Gristhorpe leaned forward. He didn't raise his voice at all, but he fixed Mark with his eyes. "No, Mark, *you* hold on a minute. You were drinking with Jason Fox on the night he got killed. Now, you've already lied to us once or twice, but we'll let that go by for the moment. Your latest story is that you *were* with Jason, but the two of you parted outside the Jubilee, at which time you gave him the bottle of beer you'd bought from out-sales because you remembered you had to drive home. Is that right?"

"Yes."

"And the two of you weren't close friends?"

"No. I've told you. We worked together. That's all."

"So what were you doing pubbing with him in the Jubilee?

Eastvale's a long way from your normal stamping ground, isn't it? Can you explain that?"

"He said he was going up to Eastvale to play football. I felt like a night out, that's all. Somewhere different. Just for a change. Sheri knew I'd been a bit down lately, like, about the business and all, and she said she didn't mind staying home with Connor. The Jubilee gets really good bands on a Saturday night, and I like live music."

"So you drove all the way up from Castleford to spend a social evening with a business associate you didn't particularly like, someone who believed your wife and all her kind should be packed off in boats back to the Caribbean?"

Mark shrugged. "I went to see the band. Jason said he'd come along, as he'd be in town anyway, that's all. I thought it might make a change from Razor's Edge and Celtic Warrior and all that other crap he listens to. Hear some decent music for once. The Jubilee's got a good reputation all over the north. Just ask anyone. And it's not that far. Straight up the A1. Doesn't take more than a hour and a half or so each way."

"That's three hours' driving, Mark."

"So? I like driving."

"Where did you go after you left Jason?"

"I drove straight back home. I wasn't over the limit, if that's what you're thinking."

"But you still came all this way knowing you'd be drinking and having to drive back?"

Wood shrugged. "I'm not a big boozer. I can handle three or four pints over the course of an evening."

"Are you sure you didn't have more than that, Mark?"

"I had three pints. Four at the most. If that put me over the limit, charge me."

"Are you sure you didn't have too much to drink and ask Jason if you could stay at his house? Are you sure you didn't walk down—"

"No. I told you. I drove straight home."

"All right, Mark. If you say so. I do, however, have one more question for you before I leave you to think over our little discussion."

"What's that?"

"If you gave Jason the beer bottle, and he drank from it on his way home, then why didn't we find *his* fingerprints on it, too?"

II

The girl was incredibly beautiful, Banks thought. Part Oriental, she had long, sleek black hair, a golden complexion, a heart-shaped face with perfect, full lips and slightly hooded eyes. She couldn't have been more than nineteen or twenty years old.

At the moment, she was sitting on a chair bathed in the red neon glow, wearing dangling silver earrings and a black lace bra and panties. Nothing else. Her slender legs were parted slightly at the inner thighs so the plump mound of her pudendum was clear to see. She had a tiny tattoo—a butterfly, it looked like—on the inside of her left thigh.

And she was smiling at Banks.

"No," said Burgess. "Not that one. She's got no tits."

Banks smiled to himself and came back to earth. Lovely as the girl was, he could no more think of sleeping with her than he could with one of Tracy's friends. Though he was quite happy to wander around the red-light district windowshopping with Burgess, he had never intended to buy anything on offer there. Nor, he suspected, did Burgess, when it came right down to it. And after three or four pils with jenever chasers, it was doubtful whether either of them was even capable of much in that direction anyway.

Amsterdam was especially beautiful at night, Banks thought, with the necklaces of lights strung over the bridges mirrored in the canals, and the glowing, candlelit interiors of glass-covered "lovers'" tour boats spilling Mantovani violins as their wake made the reflections shimmer in the dark, oily water. He wished Sandra were with him, and not Burgess. They would wander the canals all night and get hopelessly lost again, just as they had done all those years ago.

At night the red-light district had much more of an edge than during the day, when it was basically just another stop on a sight-seeing tour. Most tourists stayed away at night, but as far as Banks could tell, it wasn't any more dangerous than Soho. His wallet was safely zipped in the inside pocket of his suede jacket, and he had nothing else worth stealing. And if it came to violence, he could handle himself. Though he felt a bit light-headed, he wasn't drunk.

They wandered along, jostled by the crowds, stopping to look into the occasional window and surprised, more often than not, by the beauty and youth of the prostitutes on display. At one point someone bumped into Burgess and Banks had to step in and pre-vent a fight. Wouldn't go down well, that, he thought: SENIOR SCOT-LAND YARD DETECTIVE ARRESTED FOR ASSAULT IN AMSTERDAM'S RED-LIGHT DISTRICT. Maybe, he thought with a smile, he should have let it go on.

After a while the crowds had a claustrophobic effect on Banks, and he was thinking of going back to his hotel when Burgess said, "Fuck it. You know what, Banks?"

"What?"

"Hate to admit it, but I probably couldn't even get it up if I tried. Let's have another drink. A nightcap."

That seemed like a good idea to Banks, who fancied a sit-down and a smoke. So they nipped into a bar on a street corner, and Burgess promptly ordered pils and jenever again for both of them.

They chatted about mutual friends on the force over the loud music—some sort of modern Europop, Banks thought—and watched the punters come and go: sailors, punks, prostitutes, the occasional dealer shifting some stuff. When they'd finished their drinks, Burgess suggested another round but Banks said they should find somewhere nearer the hotel while he could still remember his way.

"Fuck the hotel. We can take a taxi anywhere we want," Burgess protested.

"I don't know where the nearest taxi rank is. Besides, it's not far. The walk'll do you good."

Burgess was truly over the top by now. He insisted on just one more jenever, which he downed in one, and then, after a bit more grumbling, he agreed to walk and stumbled out after Banks into the street. They soon got out of the redlight district and onto Damrak, which was still busy, with Burgess meandering from side to side, bumping into people. Banks remembered that Dirty Dick's second nickname on the Met was "Bambi," on account of the way his physical coordination went all to pieces when he was pissed.

"Got a joke," Burgess said, nudging Banks in the ribs. "This bloke goes into a pub with an octopus, and he says to the lads in the band, 'I'll bet any of you a tenner my pet here can play any instrument you care to give him.'"

They took one of the narrow streets that crossed the canals toward Keizersgracht. Banks found his attention wandering, Burgess's voice in the background. "So one of the lads brings him a clarinet, and the bloody octopus plays it like he was Benny Goodman. Another bloke brings him a guitar and it's Django fucking Reinhardt."

Banks fancied a coffee and wondered if he could get one at the hotel. If not, there was bound to be a café nearby. He looked at his watch. Only ten o'clock. Hard to believe they'd done so much in such a short time. A small café would actually be better than the hotel, he decided. He would dump Burgess, pick up his Graham Greene and find a place to sit, read and people-watch for a while.

"Anyway, this goes on for ages, instrument after instrument. Bongos, trombone, saxophone. You name it. Bring him a ukulele, and it's George Formby. The octopus plays them all like a virsh . . . a virsh . . . a virt-you-oh-so. Finally, one of the musicians, he's had enough and he goes out and finds a set of bagpipes. He gives them to the octopus and the octopus looks at them, frowns, turns them every which way, then back again. 'Looks like you're about to lose your tenner, mate,' the musician says. Christ, I need a piss."

Burgess tottered toward the quayside, hands working at his fly, head half-turned to look back at Banks, a crooked smile on his face. "So the guy says, 'Hang on a minute, mate. When he finds out he can't fuck it, he'll play it.' Get it? Argh! Shi-it!"

It happened so quickly that Banks didn't even have a chance to take half a step. One moment Burgess was pissing a long, noisy arc into the canal, the next, he had toppled forward with an almighty splash, followed by a string of garbled oaths.

TEN

I

By Saturday morning, Susan guessed, Mark Wood must be feeling like one of those mice that has wandered into a humane trap; it can't find its way back out, and it is just beginning to realize that it's in a trap. Even when the mice do get released, she realized, they generally find themselves a long way from home.

"Your solicitor, Mr. Varney, rang," said Gristhorpe. "He's sorry, he was out last night. Anyway, he's on his way up from Leeds. What can we do for you in the meantime? Coffee? Danish?"

Wood reached forward and helped himself to a pastry. "I don't have to talk to you until he gets here," he said.

"True," said Gristhorpe. "But remember that caution I read you yesterday? If you don't say anything now, it could go very badly for you later when you try to change your story again."

"What do you mean?"

"You know what I mean. You're a liar, Mark. You've already given us half a dozen old wives' tales. The more lies you tell, the lower your credibility rating falls. I'm offering you a chance to sweep the board clean, forget the lies and tell me the truth once and for all. What happened after you and Jason Fox left the Jubilee last Saturday night? Your solicitor will only give you the same advice. Tell the truth and I'll turn on the tape recorders."

"But I've already told you."

Gristhorpe shook his head. "You lied. The bottle. The finger-print, Mark. The fingerprint."

Susan hoped to hell that Gristhorpe did get somewhere before Giles Varney arrived, because he'd milked that fingerprint for far more than it was worth already. They couldn't be certain it was Wood's, and Gristhorpe had framed his references to it with great care when the tapes were running, saying it was a "close match" rather than an identical one.

Even "close match" was pushing it a bit. One of the first things Varney would do was look at the forensic evidence and tell his client just how flimsy it was. Then Wood would clam up. Susan had phoned the lab just a few moments ago, and while they said they might get some results before the morning was out, it cer-tainly wouldn't be within the hour.

Even then, she knew, these would only be preliminary results. But they might, at a pinch, at least be able to determine whether there was human blood on Wood's clothing and whether it matched Jason Fox's *general* type. For more specific and solid evidence, such as DNA analysis, they would have to wait much longer. Even a general grouping, Susan thought, along with an identification and statement from the landlord of the Jubilee, would be more than they had right now. And it might be enough to convince the magistrates to remand Wood for a while longer.

"Nobody touched that bottle but you, Mark," Gristhorpe went on. "The fingerprint proves that."

"What about the bloke I bought it off? Why weren't his finger-prints on it?"

"That's not important. Mark. What matters is that *your* finger-prints were on it and Jason's weren't. There's no getting away from that, solicitor or no solicitor. If you tell me the truth now, things will go well for you. If you don't . . . well, it'll be a jury you'll have to explain yourself to. And sometimes you can wait months for a trial. Years, even."

"So what? I'd be out on bail and you can't prove anything."

True, Susan thought.

"Wrong," Gristhorpe said. "I don't think you'd get bail, Mark. Not for this. It was a vicious murder. Very nasty indeed."

"You said it might not be murder."

"That depends. The way things are looking now, you'd have to *confess* to make us believe it was manslaughter, Mark. You'd have to tell us how it really happened, *convince* us it wasn't murder. Otherwise we've got you on a murder charge. Concealing evidence, not coming forward, lying—it all looks bad to a jury."

Wood chewed on his lower lip. Susan noticed the crumbs of pastry down the front of his shirt. He was sweating.

"You're a clever lad, aren't you, Mark?"

"What do you mean?"

"You know all about computers and the Internet and all that stuff?"

"So?"

"Now, me, I don't know a hard drive from a hole in the ground, but I *do* know you're lying, and I *do* know that your only way out of this tissue of lies you've got yourself well and truly stuck in is to tell me the truth. Now."

Finally, Wood licked his lips and said, "Look, I didn't kill anyone. All right, I was there. I admit it. I was there when it started. But I didn't kill Jason. You've got to believe me."

"Why do I have to believe you, Mark?" Gristhorpe asked softly.

"Because you do. It's true."

"Why don't you just tell me what happened?"

"Can I have a smoke?"

"No," said Gristhorpe. "After you've told me. *If* I believe you." He turned on the dual cassette recorder and made the usual preamble about the time, date and who was present.

Wood sulked and chewed his lip for a moment, then began: "We left the Jubilee just after closing time, like I said. I had a bottle with me. Jason didn't. He didn't drink much. In fact, he had a thing about drink and drugs. Into health and fitness, was Jason.

Anyway, we took the short cut—at least that's what he told me it was—through some streets across the road, and where the streets ended there's a ginnel that leads between two terrace blocks to some waste ground."

"The rec," said Gristhorpe.

"If you say so. I didn't know where the fuck we were."

"Why were *you* also heading in that direction? I thought you said your car was parked on Market Street."

"It was. Jason asked me back to his place for a drink. That's all. I know I shouldn't have been drinking so much when I was driving, but . . ." He grinned. "Anyway, it was like you said yesterday. If I thought I'd had too much, I would've stopped the night."

"At Jason's house?"

"His parents' house, yes."

"Carry on."

"Well, the ginnel looked a bit creepy to me, but Jason went ahead. Then, all of a sudden, they came at us, three of them, from where they'd been waiting at the other end. The rec end."

"Three of them?"

"That's right. Asian lads. I recognized them. Jason had had a minor run-in with one of them earlier, in the pub."

"What happened next?"

"I dropped the bottle and scarpered fast. I thought Jason was right behind me, but by the time I looked back he was nowhere in sight."

"You didn't see what happened to him?"

"No."

"And you didn't go back?"

"No way."

"All right. What *did* you do next?"

"I kept going until I got to the car, then I drove home."

"Why didn't you call the police?"

Wood scratched his neck and averted his eyes. "I don't know. I suppose I didn't think of it, really. And I'd been drinking."

"But your friend—sorry, your business associate—was in danger. He could at least expect a severe beating, and all you could do was scarper. Come on, Mark, you can't expect me to believe that. Surely you've got more bottle, a fit lad like you?"

"Believe what you want. I didn't know Jason was in danger, did I? For all I knew he'd run off in a different direction. I'd have been a proper wally to go back there and get my head kicked in."

"Like Jason."

"Yeah, well. I didn't know what happened, did I?"

"Did you really believe that Jason had got away too?"

"He could have done, couldn't he?"

"Okay. Now tell me: if you'd done nothing wrong, why didn't you come forward later, after you *knew* Jason had been killed?"

Mark scratched the side of his nose. "I didn't know till I read it in the papers a couple of days later. By then I thought it would look funny if I came forward."

Gristhorpe frowned. "Look funny?"

"Yeah. Suspicious."

"Why?"

"Because I hadn't said anything at the time. Isn't that something makes you blokes suspicious?"

Gristhorpe spread his hands. "Mark, we're simple souls, really. We're just thrilled to bits when someone decides to tell us the truth."

"Yeah, well . . . I must admit I wasn't too proud of myself."

"What for? Running away? Deserting your mate when he needed your help?"

Wood looked down at his hands clasped on his lap. "Yes."

"Any other reason you kept out of it?"

"Well, if they killed Jason, whether they meant to or not . . . I mean, I've got a wife and kid. Know what I mean? I wouldn't want to put any of us in danger by testifying if there were likely to be . . . you know . . . recriminations."

"Recriminations? By the three attackers?"

"By them, yes. Or people like them."

"Other Pakistani youths?"

"Well, yeah. I mean, they stick together, stand up for one another, don't they? I didn't want to put my wife and kid at risk."

Gristhorpe shook his head slowly. "This isn't making any sense to me, Mark. You look like a strong lad. Why didn't you stay and fight with Jason, give him a bit of support?"

"I told you, I was thinking of Sheri and Connor. I mean, how would they manage without me, if I got hurt, put in hospital?"

"Same way they'll have to manage without you when you get put in jail, I suppose," said Gristhorpe. "You're telling me you ran away out of concern for your wife and child?"

Wood's face reddened. "I'm not saying that's what I thought straight off. It was instinctive. I didn't have much choice, did I? And like I said, I thought Jason was right behind me. It was three against two."

"It was three against one after you ran off, Mark. What sort of choice did Jason have? The two of you could have taken those three easily. I'd have put *my* money on you."

Wood shook his head.

"Are you telling me you're a coward, Mark? Strong-looking lad like you? Bet you lift weights, don't you? Yet when it comes to the crunch you bugger off and leave your mate to die alone."

"Look, will you shut up about that?" Wood leaned forward and banged his fist down. The metal table rattled. "The point is that I *didn't do anything.* It doesn't matter whether I ran away. Or why I ran away. All that matters is that I didn't kill Jason!"

"Calm down, Mark." Gristhorpe raised his hand, palm out. "What you're saying is true. Technically, at any rate."

"What do you mean, technically?"

"Well, if what you're telling us is the truth at last—"

"It is."

"—then you didn't kill Jason in any legal, criminal sense of the word. But I'd say you're morally responsible, wouldn't you? I mean, you could have saved him, but you didn't even try."

"I told you to stop it with that. You can't prove it would have done any good if I'd stayed. Maybe I'd have got killed, too. What good would that have done anyone? I don't care about fucking *morality*. There's nothing you can charge me with."

"How about leaving the scene?"

"That's crap, and you know it."

"Maybe so," Gristhorpe admitted. "Nevertheless, deserting your mate the way you did . . . That's something you'll have to live with forever, isn't it, Mark?"

Gristhorpe went to the door and asked the two uniformed officers to come in and take Wood back to his cell, then he and Susan picked up their coffees and left the stuffy interview room for Gristhorpe's office. Up there, in a comfortable chair, with plenty of space and clean air to breathe, Susan felt herself relax.

"What do you think of his story?" Gristhorpe asked.

Susan shook her head. "He's certainly a bit of a chameleon, isn't he? I hardly know what to think. I'll tell you one thing, though, sir; I think I caught him in at least one more lie."

Gristhorpe raised his bushy eyebrows. "Oh, aye? And which lie would that be?"

"Mark told us that when they left the Jubilee, Jason invited him back to his house for a drink, and maybe to stop overnight. Jason wouldn't have done that. His parents insisted he *never* brought his friends to their house."

"Hmm. Maybe they're the ones who are lying?"

"I don't think so, sir. Why should they? If you think about it, Jason lived most of his life in Leeds. He only came home on weekends occasionally, mostly to play football for United, spend a little time with his parents, get his washing done, maybe visit his granddad. He never told any of them what he was up to in Leeds. It's easy to see why he wouldn't want to mention Neville Motcombe or explain how he got fired from the plastics factory. And that meant he couldn't mention the computer business either. He could have simply lied from the start, told them he'd left the factory of his own free will for something better, but he didn't. Didn't want to face the questions, I suppose. After that, all the lies became interconnected. Who knows what Mark might have let slip to Jason's parents?" She shook her head. "Unless Mr. and Mrs. Fox are lying, which I doubt, then it's hardly likely Jason would suddenly decide to take one of his Leeds mates back to the Eastvale house on a whim. Too risky. And there's another thing. Jason didn't keep anything to drink at the Eastvale house. In fact, according to all accounts, he hardly drank at all."

"Maybe he was intending to give Mark some of his dad's Scotch or something?"

"It's possible, sir," Susan said. "But as I say, I doubt it."

"And maybe he would have bent the rules a bit if his mate had had too much to drink and needed somewhere to sleep it off? That might also explain why Mark didn't drive down from Market Street to Jason's place."

"Again, sir," said Susan, "it's possible."

"But you're not convinced. Do you think he did it?"

"I don't know, sir. I just don't trust his story."

"Make that *stories*. All right, I'll bear your reservations in mind. I can't say I like them much, either." He shook his head slowly. "Anyway, we'd better arrange to bring in George Mahmood and his pals again."

"Even though the forensic evidence supports George's story?"

"Even so."

"Chief Constable Riddle will love that, sir."

"The way I see it, Susan, we've got no choice. Mark Wood says he saw three Asian lads attack Jason Fox. Unless we can prove he's lying, it doesn't matter what we think. We *have* to bring them in."

Susan nodded. "I know, sir."

"And give the lab another call. Ask them to get their fingers out. If all they can tell us is there's human blood on the clothes, I'd be satisfied for the time being. Because if we don't get something positive soon, Mark Wood is going to walk out of here in less than an hour and I'm still not happy with a word he's told us."

II

Banks made it down to breakfast with just minutes to spare before the nine-o'clock deadline, getting a frosty look from the stout waitress in the hotel lounge for his trouble. First, he helped himself to coffee from a table by the window, then he sat down and looked around. A large NO SMOKING symbol hung over the lace-curtained window.

He doodled away at yesterday's *Yorkshire Post* crossword while he sipped the rich black coffee and waited. Eventually, the waitress returned and, with a dour glance, she deposited a glass of orange juice and a plate in front of him. On the plate lay a few slices of cold ham, a chunk of Edam cheese, a hard-boiled egg, a couple of rolls and some butter. The Dutch breakfast. Banks tucked in.

He felt fortunate in having only the mildest of hangovers. The slight ache behind his eyes had been easily vanquished with the aid of two extra-strength paracetamols from his traveler's emergency kit, and he suspected that the minor sense of disorientation he felt was still more due to being in a foreign city than to the residual effects of alcohol. Whatever the reason, he felt fine. At least physically.

Only as he sipped the last of his coffee did he realize he hadn't thought of his domestic problems at all last night. Even now, in the morning's light, everything felt so distant, so disembodied. He could hardly believe that Sandra had really gone. Was it a question of not being there to see the tree fall in the woods, or was it what the psychologists of grief called denial? Maybe he would ask his psychologist friend Jenny Fuller when she got back from America. Jenny. Now, if Sandra really *had* gone, did that make him a free agent? What were the rules? Best not think about it too much. Maybe he would ring home again before going out, just to see if she had come back.

He was the only person sitting in the spotless lounge, with its dark wood smelling of polish, its lace doilies, ticking clock and knickknacks stuffed in alcoves. As he had hoped, Burgess had either breakfasted earlier or hadn't even got out of bed yet. Banks suspected the latter.

Thank the Lord a passer-by had stopped to help him haul Burgess out of the canal last night. Dirty Dick had stood there dripping the foul water and complaining loudly about the canal-building Dutch engineers—most of whom, according to him, had only one parent, a mother, with whom they had indulged in unspeakable sexual relations.

Banks finally managed to persuade him to calm down and walk back to the hotel before the police arrived and arrested them.

That they succeeded in doing, and their arrival attracted only a puzzled frown from the man at the desk as they traipsed through the lobby. Burgess still trailed dirty canal water as he went, his shoes squelching with every step. He held his head high, like W. C. Fields trying to pretend he was sober, and walked with as much dignity as he could muster. After that, he went straight up to his room on the second floor, and that was the last Banks had seen or heard of him.

After breakfast, Banks went all the way back up to his room and phoned home again. Still nothing. Not that he had expected Sandra to get the *first* train back home, but one lives in hope. He didn't leave a message for himself.

As he trod carefully back down the steep, narrow stairs, tiptoeing over the landing near Burgess's room, he reflected on how he had enjoyed himself last night, how, against all expectations, he had enjoyed his night of freedom. He hadn't done anything he wouldn't normally have done, except perhaps drink too much and get silly, but he had *felt* differently about it.

For the first time, he found himself wondering if Sandra wasn't, perhaps, right. Maybe they both did need a little time to maneuver and regroup after all the changes of the past few years, especially Sandra's new and more demanding job at the gallery, and the loss of the children.

Not children now, Banks reminded himself. Grown-ups. He thought back to that evening in the Pack Horse only a few days ago, when he had watched Tracy with her friends and realized he couldn't cross the lounge to be with her; then he remembered a telephone call he had once made from Weymouth to his son in Portsmouth, realizing then for the first time how distant and independent Brian had become.

Well, there was nothing he could do about it. Any of it. Except to make damn sure he kept in touch with them, helped them the best he could, became a friend and not a meddlesome irritation to them. He wondered how they would take the news of their parents' separation. For that matter, who would tell them? Would Sandra? Should he?

He walked out onto Keizersgracht. The sun glinted on the parked bicycles on the quay and on the canal, making a rainbow out of a pool of oil. Reflections of trees shimmered gently in the ripples of a passing boat.

His mysterious meeting was set for eight o'clock tonight. Well, he thought, in the meantime, on a day like this, tourist map in hand, he could walk the city to his heart's content.

III

"You've got to admit, Superintendent, that your evidence is pretty thin."

Giles Varney, Mark Wood's solicitor, sat in Gristhorpe's office later that Saturday morning, staring out over the market square as he talked.

Outside, a sunny morning had brought plenty of tourists to the bustling open market, but now it was clouding over and, to Susan's well-trained nose, getting ready to pour down before the day was out. She had already seen the gusts of wind, which would later bring the rain clouds, billowing the canvas covers of the market stalls.

Varney wasn't a pinstripe lawyer like the one they'd had to deal with last year in the Deborah Harrison murder. He was casually dressed in jeans and a sports shirt, and his very expensive light wool jacket hung on a stand in the corner. He was young, probably not much older than Susan's own twenty-seven, in good shape, and handsome in a craggy, outdoorsy kind of way. He looked as if he were on his way to go hang-gliding.

There was something Susan didn't like about him, but she couldn't put her finger on it. An arrogance, perhaps, or overconfidence. Whatever it was, it put her on her guard.

"I realize that, Mr. Varney," said Gristhorpe, "but I'm sure you can see our predicament."

Varney smiled. "With all due respect, it's not my job to see your predicament. It's my job to get my client out of jail."

Supercilious prat, Susan thought.

"And it's our job," countered Gristhorpe, "to get to the bottom of Jason Fox's death. Your client admits he was at the scene."

"Only *prior* to the crime. He couldn't have had any knowledge of what was going to happen."

"Oh, come off it, Mr. Varney. If three kids came at you in a dark alley, I think you'd have a pretty good idea what was about to take place, wouldn't you?"

"That's beside the point. And since when has saving your own skin been regarded as a criminal act? Technically, my client is not guilty of any crime. I expect you to release him immediately. I trust you have the real criminals in custody?"

"On their way. Again," muttered Gristhorpe.

Varney raised an eyebrow. "Yes, I understand you had these same chaps in custody once before and let them go?"

"Had to," Gristhorpe said. "No evidence. You'd have approved."

Varney smiled again. "Not having much luck with evidence these days, are you, Superintendent?"

"There *is* one other small matter," said Gristhorpe.

Varney glanced at his Rolex with irritation. "Yes?"

"Your client has now become an important witness. I trust you'd have no objection to his remaining here in order to identify the suspects when we've brought them in?"

Varney narrowed his eyes. "I don't know what you're up to, Superintendent. But something smells. Still, how could I have any objection? And I'm sure my client will be more than willing to help sort out this mess for you. As long as he's released from his cell this very minute and treated as a witness rather than as a criminal. He also has to know that he's free to go home whenever he wants."

Susan breathed a sigh of relief. She knew that Gristhorpe was playing for time, trying to find some reason to keep Mark Wood in Eastvale until the lab came up with something—or with nothing. This way, at least, they might get another hour or so out of him, especially if they had him write another formal statement *after* the identification. Maybe a lot more time than that if they put together an identification parade, which would mean importing a few more Asians of similar build to George, Kobir and Asim.

As it turned out, they hardly had to wait at all. Just as Gristhorpe was about to leave the office and take Varney down to release Mark Wood, the phone rang. Gristhorpe excused himself, picked up the receiver, grunted a few times, then beamed at Susan. "That's the lab," he said. "They've found traces of blood between the uppers and the soles of Mark Wood's Doc Martens, and it matches Jason Fox's blood group. I'm afraid, Mr. Varney, we've got a few more questions for your client."

Varney sniffed and sat down again. Gristhorpe picked up his phone and called downstairs. "Bert? Have young Mark Wood brought up from the cells, would you? Yes, the interview room."

Giles Varney insisted on having a private talk with Mark Wood before the interview. Susan waited with Gristhorpe in his office, where they went over all Wood's previous statements, planning their strategy. The rags of cloud had drifted in from Scotland now and the air that blew in through the partially open window was beginning to smell like a wet dog. Susan walked over and watched some of the tourists looking at the sky, then heading for the pubs or for their cars.

"Hungry?" Gristhorpe asked.

"I can wait, sir," said Susan. "A few less calories won't do me any harm."

"Me neither," grinned Gristhorpe. "But at my age you don't worry about it so much."

There was a brisk tap at the door and Giles Varney walked in.

"Finished?" Gristhorpe asked.

Varney nodded. "For the moment. My client wishes to make a statement."

"Another one?"

"Look," said Varney with a thin smile, "the blood evidence isn't much to write home about so far, you have to admit, and the fingerprint rubbish is even less. You should be grateful for what you can get."

"In a few days," Gristhorpe countered, "we'll have DNA on the blood. And I suspect your client knows that will prove it's Jason Fox's. At the moment, I think we've got enough to hold him."

Varney smiled. "That's what I thought you'd say. What you hear might change your mind."

"How?"

"After a certain amount of reflection, on the advice of his solicitor, my client is now willing to explain exactly what happened last Saturday night."

"Right," said Gristhorpe, getting up and glancing over at Susan. "Let's get to it then."

They went into the interview room, where Mark Wood sat chewing his fingernails, went through the preliminaries and turned on the tape recorders.

"Right, lad," said Gristhorpe. "Mr. Varney here says you wish to make a statement. I hope it's the truth this time. Now what have you got to say?"

Wood looked at Varney before opening his mouth. Varney nodded. "I did it," Wood said. "I killed Jason. It was an accident. I didn't mean to."

"Why don't you tell us what happened, Mark?" Gristhorpe coaxed him. "Slowly. Take your time."

Wood looked at Varney, who nodded. "We were going back to his place, like I said before. Jason was going on about those Pakis back in the Jubilee, what he thought should be done with them. We started arguing. I told him I didn't like that racist crap. Jason was going on about how I was really a racist deep down, just like him, and why didn't I admit it, join the group. I laughed and told him I'd never join that band of wankers in a million years. I was pretty mad by then, so I told him that my wife was from Jamaica. Then he started insulting her, calling her a black bitch and a whore and calling little Connor a half-breed mutant. We were getting near the ginnel now and Jason was really laying into me. Really crude stuff. Like I'd betrayed the white race by marrying a nigger, and shit like that." Mark paused and rubbed his temples. "I'd had a few drinks, more than I admitted, and more than Jason, at any rate, and sometimes I . . . well, I've got a bit of a temper when I'm pissed. I just lost it, that's all. He came at me. I had the bottle in my hand and I just lashed out with it and hit him."

"What happened next?"

"He didn't go down. Just put his hand to the side of his head and swore, then he came at me again. He was strong, was Jason, but I reckon I'm probably stronger. Anyway, we started fighting, but I think the head wound had sort of weakened him and I managed to knock him down. I thought about what he'd said about Sheri and Connor and I just saw red. The next thing I knew, he wasn't moving, and I ran off."

"And left him there?"

"Yes. I didn't know he was fucking dead. How could I? I thought I'd just put him out of action for a while."

"Why did you empty his pockets?"

"I didn't. Why would I do that?"

"Because the whole thing was a lot more deliberate than you're saying? Because you wanted to make it look like a mugging? You tell me, Mark."

"Superintendent," Varney chipped in. "My client is offering a voluntary statement. If he says he didn't empty the victim's pockets, then I suggest you believe him. He has no reason to lie at this point."

"I'll be the judge of that, Mr. Varney," said Gristhorpe. He looked at Mark again.

Mark shook his head. "I don't remember doing that. Honest."

Gristhorpe sniffed and riffled through some sheets of paper in front of him. "Mark," he said finally, "Jason Fox's injuries included a fractured skull and a ruptured spleen. Yet you say you only knocked him down?"

"That's how it happened. I admit I lost it, I was in a rage, but I didn't mean to kill him."

"All right, Mark," said Gristhorpe. "Is this the statement you want to make?"

"Yes."

"My client will be pleading to the charge of manslaughter, Superintendent," Varney said. "And I think there might be some room for mitigating circumstances."

"Plenty of time for charges later," said Gristhorpe. "Let's just go through the story again first." Gristhorpe turned to Susan and sighed. "Susan, go and make sure George Mahmood and his friends are released immediately. The poor sods won't know whether they're coming or going."

Susan nodded and got up. As she left the interview room, she heard Gristhorpe say wearily, "Right then, Mark, once more from the top."

IV

Using a street map he'd bought that afternoon, Banks walked to the address Burgess had given him. Though he felt silly doing it, he had looked over his shoulder once in a while and taken a very circuitous route.

It was another brown café, this one on a street corner by Sarphatipark. The park itself was a dark rectangle wedged between blocks of tenements. It looked familiar. He was sure he had seen it before, with Sandra. It reminded him of the kind of square you'd find in Bloomsbury or Edinburgh. The café itself wasn't the kind of place listed in the tourist guides. The wood was dark and stained with years of tobacco smoke, and most of the tables were scratched and blackened here and there where cigarettes had been left to burn.

One or two locals sitting at the bar, workingmen by the look of their clothes, turned and glanced at Banks as he walked in and found a table in the far corner. One of them said something to the man behind the bar, who shrugged and laughed, then they paid him no further attention. Only a few tables were taken, and only one of those by a young man and a woman. It was pretty much of a men's pub by the look of it. Accordion music was playing quietly behind the bar. Welcome to hell.

The table wobbled. Banks took a beer mat and placed it under one leg. That helped. Not wanting a repeat of last night, he decided he was going to stick with beer, and not even drink many of those. That jenever could be deadly. He ordered an Amstel, lit a cigarette and settled down to wait, back to the wall, eyes on the door. After a day spent walking around the city, stopping only at a café now and then for a coffee and a cigarette, Banks was also glad of the chance to rest his legs.

As he waited, he reflected on the curious and unsettling experience he had had that afternoon. One of the places he'd walked by was a canal-side coffeehouse he remembered visiting with Sandra all those years ago. The kind of place that also sold hash and grass. It didn't seem to have changed at all. At first he thought it couldn't possibly be the same one, but it was. Curious, he turned back and wandered inside.

At the back, where it was darker, piles of cushions lay scattered on the floor. You could lie back, smoke your joint, look at the posters on the wall and listen to the music. He noticed a young couple there, in the far corner, and for one spine-tingling moment, in the dim light, he felt he was looking down on himself and Sandra when they were young. And he hadn't even smoked any hash.

Shaken, he walked out into the sunshine and went on his way. It was a good five or ten minutes before he could get rid of the spooky feeling. He and Sandra had smoked some hash there with some Americans, he remembered. Dylan's *Blonde on Blonde* album had been playing, the long "Sadeyed Lady of the Lowlands." Later, they had made love in their sleeping bag in the Vondelpark, hidden away from other nighthawks by some bushes. Memories. Would he never escape them?

Just as he was lighting his second cigarette, someone walked through the door. And for the second time that day Banks felt gobsmacked.

If he wasn't mistaken, it was the man he had last seen in Neville Motcombe's house: Rupert Francis, the tall, gangly woodworker.

He obviously noticed Banks's surprise. "You can close your mouth now, sir," he said. "It really is me."

Banks shook his head slowly. "So I see. Rupert Francis, right? And what's with the 'sir'?"

"Actually, I'm DS Craig McKeracher, sir," he said, shaking hands. "That makes you my senior officer. Pleasure to make your acquaintance." He smiled sheepishly and sat down. "I'm sorry about all the cloak-and-dagger stuff, sir, but if they found out who I really am, they'd kill me."

Banks shook hands and collected his thoughts. The waiter came over and Craig ordered a beer.

"I think we can drop the 'sir,'" said Banks.

Craig nodded. "If you like. I must admit you gave me the shock of my bloody life when I saw you at Nev's place the other day. I thought the game was up right there and then."

"You didn't have to show yourself."

"I know. But I heard voices, so I thought up an excuse and came up to see what was going on. Part of my brief, after all, to keep my eyes and ears open. Just as well you'd never seen me before."

"How long have you been undercover there?"

"About five months. Nev trusts me. 'Rupert Francis' has an impeccable background with the neo-Nazi movement. BNP, fringe groups, the whole kit and caboodle. He's even been done on firearms and explosives charges. In addition to that, he's got a long and varied criminal record. Assault, burglary, drugs. You name it. That's something Nev also trusts."

"How would he know about your record?"

Craig sipped some beer from the bottle before answering. His Adam's apple bobbed in his skinny throat. "He's got a man on the inside somewhere. West Yorkshire. Some PC or DC sympathetic to the cause. Believe me, there are plenty of blokes on the Job who'd have no ax to grind with Neville Motcombe's ideas. However he does it, he has no problem checking out criminal records."

"So it's you who wants me here, not Burgess?"

"Yes. After I'd seen you, I got in touch with Dirty—with Superintendent Burgess soon as I could. He's my controller, but with things getting so hot lately we've not had the chance for much more than minimal telephone contact. And you've got to be really careful over the phone. Anyway, I told him I wanted to talk to you as soon as possible, but I didn't want to risk doing it locally. Then I thought this would be a perfect opportunity. Know why I'm here?"

"Haven't a clue," said Banks.

"I'm helping to organize an international conference on race and IQ, if you can swallow that. Anyway, Superintendent Burgess said not to worry, he'd make the arrangements." Craig grinned. "In fact, he said he'd enjoy it. You should have heard him when I told him you'd walked right into Nev's front room. I gather the two of you know each other? You and the super, that is?"

Banks stubbed out his cigarette and sipped some beer. "You could say that."

"He likes you. Honest, he does. Respects you. That's what he told me. I reckon he thinks you're a bit naive, but he was glad to hear it was you on the Fox case and not someone else."

"Maybe we should start a mutual admiration society."

Craig laughed.

"Anyway," Banks asked, "why all this interest in the Albion League?"

"Because of Neville Motcombe and his contacts with known international terrorists. When he left the BNP and decided to start his own fringe group, we thought it'd be a good idea to keep an eye on him."

Banks sipped some Amstel. "And did he live up to your expectations?"

"In some ways, yes. In others, he exceeded them. The Albion League's nowhere near as politically active as we thought it would be. As Combat 18 are, for example. I'm not saying there haven't been violent incidents, there have, and I've even heard talk of a pipe bomb to sabotage the mosque opening. Now we know about that possibility, we can tighten security and make sure it doesn't happen. But mostly, as far as revolutionary action is concerned, they've been pretty tame so far. More like a fucking boys' club than anything else."

"I wondered about that. What is it with Motcombe and these young boys? Is he gay or something?"

The waiter came over and they ordered two more beers. When he had gone again, Craig said, "No. No, Nev's not gay. I'll confess I had my own suspicions when I first met him and he invited me down the cellar to help with his woodwork. Like, come and see my etchings. But he's not. If anything, I'd say he was asexual. His wife left him. If you ask me, it was because he spent more time licking envelopes than licking her. He's that kind of person. Power is more important to him than romantic or sexual relationships. The youth thing is just part of his shtick. He actually used to be involved in church groups, youth clubs, that sort of thing. He was even a Boys' Brigade leader at one time. Always did like paramilitary organizations and uniforms."

"What happened?"

"He got kicked out for trying to recruit kids to the BNP. Anyway, a big part of his thing is the emphasis on the old British values and virtues: war games in the Pennines, crafts, camping, hiking, survival techniques, a healthy mind and healthy body. That sort of thing."

"Baden-Powell with swastikas?"

"If you like. He even throws in a bit of environmentalist stuff to hook the greenies. You know—preserve the traditional English village against pollution, that sort of thing. Thing is, to him pollution isn't only a matter of destroying the ozone layer and the rain forests or what have you, it includes most non-Aryan racial groups. Perhaps Nev's only saving grace as a human being is that his overriding trait is greed."

"What do you mean?"

Craig rubbed his cheek and frowned. "Just an observation of mine. Haven't you sometimes thought that people's vices are often the only things that make them interesting? As a pure neo-Nazi,

Nev would simply be a bore. A sick and dangerous bore, perhaps, but a bore nonetheless. Predictable. It's the other stuff that's interesting, the stuff we didn't expect."

"Burgess mentioned drugs. Is that right?"

Craig nodded, finished his beer and slid the bottle aside. "Fancy walking?"

"Why not."

They paid their bill and walked outside. There were still plenty of people on the streets, especially along Albert Cuypstraat, where they walked through the debris of that afternoon's market—wilted lettuce leaves, a squashed tomato, chicken bones, a piece of cardboard that said "f4.50" on it. The smell of fish still infused the evening air. Now Banks knew why Sarphatipark had felt so familiar. He and Sandra *had* been there; they had spent an hour or two one afternoon wandering the market stalls.

"Like I said," Craig went on, "Nev got to trust me, take me into his confidence. I think he liked the fact that according to my criminal record, I didn't mind doing anything as long as it was profitable. And it didn't take me long to work out that Nev likes profit more than anything."

"So it's money with him, not politics?"

"Mmm, not entirely. Maybe it's both at the same time, if he can get it that way. If not, then I'd say money comes out distinctly on top. Like I said, Nev's a greedy bastard. Greedy for power and greedy for cash. First thing I found out when I got involved was that he was organizing some of his younger and thicker recruits into groups of thieves, turning their gains over to him, of course, for the good of the league."

"And they did this?"

Craig snorted. "Sure they did. Let's face it, most of these kids are pretty dense. Five or six of them would go into a shop, say, and as soon as—"

"Steaming?"

"You know about it?"

"I've heard the term. And I know it's been a problem for West Yorkshire CID recently. Along with muggings at cash dispensers. I didn't know Motcombe was behind it."

"Some of it. I'm sure there are plenty of freelancers out there, too. But what Nev does is he takes these kids' anger and channels it. He gives them someone to hate. He gives their rage some structure and provides them with real targets rather than nebulous ones. So they end up believing they're committing theft, assault and vandalism for a good cause. Isn't that what terrorism is basically all about, anyway? Add a few *olde worlde* patriotic values, a lot of guff about the 'true English homeland' and a bit of green to the mix and it makes them feel like downright responsible and virtuous citizens, the only ones who really care about their country."

"You make it sound easy."

They turned right, toward the neo-Gothic mass of the Rijksmuseum, dark and solid against the night sky. Streetlights cast long shadows. A breeze stirred, wafting a smell of decay from the canal. Banks could hear music in the distance, see TV screens flickering through people's curtains.

Craig shrugged. "It's not as hard as you think, that's the sad thing. Recruiting isn't, anyway. Take rock concerts, for example. Invitation only. Makes people feel privileged and exclusive right off the bat. Then the white-power bands get the kids all worked up with their rhythm and energy, and someone like me moves in to bring the message home. And they target schools, particularly schools that have a large number of immigrant pupils. They hang around outside in the street and pass out leaflets, then they hold meetings in different venues. They also hang out in the coffee bars where some of the kids go on their way home. You know, start chatting, give them a sympathetic shoulder for their problems with Ali or Winston. They get a surprising number of converts that way."

"Some of whom Motcombe organizes into gangs of thieves?"

"Some, yes. But not all." He laughed. "One or two of the lads in the know have nicknamed him 'Fagin.'"

Banks raised his eyebrows. "'You've got to pick a pocket or two,'" he sang, a passable imitation of Ron Moody in *Oliver.* "I imagine he'd just love that."

Craig smiled. "I'll bet. Thing is, there's a lot of money to be made, one way or another. Steaming and mugging are just part of the bigger picture. These right-wing political groups finance themselves in any number of ways. Some deal in arms and explosives, for example. Then there's the rock angle. These bands record CDs. That means people produce, record, manufacture and distribute them. That can be big business. And where there's rock, there's drugs. There's a lot of money to be made out of that."

"Motcombe has an arrest for receiving, doesn't he?"

"Yes. His one big mistake. A couple of his lads broke into a Curry's and ran off with a few videos and stereos under their arms. They didn't tell Nev where they'd got the stuff from. Anyway, since then, it's been cash only. And he skims off the top, too. I've seen him stuff the notes into his own pocket." Craig shook his head. "If there's one thing worse than a Nazi, it's a bent Nazi."

"How does Jason Fox fit in? Was he one of the thieves?"

Craig paused and leaned on a bridge as they crossed to Hobbemakade, looking down at the reflections of the lights. Banks stood beside him and lit a cigarette. It was quiet now apart from a few cars and the whir of an occasional bicycle.

"No, Jason never went out steaming. Not his style. Too smart. Jason was a thinker. He was good at recruiting, at propaganda in general. The thing about Jason was, he was basically an honest kid. A straight, dedicated Nazi."

"One of those boring fascists, without vices?"

Craig laughed. "Almost. Not exactly boring, though. In some ways he was naive in his sincerity, and that made him almost likable. *Almost.* But he was also more dedicated, more driven, than most of the others. Frightening. See, when you come down to it, Nev's not much more than a petty crook with delusions of grandeur. Jason, on the other hand, was the genuine article. Real dyed-in-the-wool neo-Nazi. Probably even read *Mein Kampf.*"

"I thought even Hitler's most fanatical followers couldn't get through that."

Craig laughed. "True."

"Have you any ideas as to why Jason was killed? Was he involved in this drug deal?"

They moved away from the bridge and headed down the street. Banks flicked his cigarette end in the water, immediately feeling guilty of pollution.

"No," Craig said. "Not at all. Jason was violently antidrug. In fact, if you ask me, that's where you might want to start looking for your motive. Because he certainly knew about it."

V

"Another bottle of wine?"

"I shouldn't," said Susan, placing her hand over her half-filled glass.

"Why not? You're not driving."

"True."

"And you've just wrapped up a case. You should be celebrating."

"All right, all right, you silver-tongued devil. Go ahead."

Gavin grinned, called the waiter and ordered a second bottle of Chablis. Susan felt her heart give a slight lurch the way it did when she first jumped the Strid at Bolton Abbey as a teenager. It happened the moment her feet left the ground and she found herself hurtling through space over the deep, rushing waters, because that was the moment she had committed herself to jumping, despite all the warnings. So what had she committed herself to by agreeing to a second bottle of wine?

She took another mouthful of filo-pastry parcel, stuffed with Brie, walnuts and cranberries, and washed it down with the wine she had left in her glass. It hadn't even been there long enough to get lukewarm. Already, she was beginning to feel a little light-headed—but in a pleasant way, as if a great burden had been lifted from her.

They were in a new bistro on Castle Walk, looking west over the formal gardens and the river. A high moon silvered the swirling current of water far below and frosted the tips of the leaves on the trees. The restaurant itself was one of those hushed places where everyone seemed to be whispering, and food and drink suddenly appeared out of the silence as if by magic. White tablecloths. A floating candle in a glass jar on every table. It was also, she thought, far too expensive for a couple of mere DCs. Still, you had to push the boat out once in a while, didn't you, she told herself, just to see how far it would float.

She stole a glance at Gavin, busy finishing his venison. He caught her looking and smiled. She blushed. He really did have lovely brown eyes, she thought, and a nice mouth.

"So how does it feel?" Gavin asked, putting his knife and fork down. "The success? I understand it was largely due to your initiative?"

"Oh, not really," Susan said. "It was teamwork."

"How modest of you," he teased. "But seriously, Susan. It was you who found the killer's name. What was it . . . Mark something or other?"

"Mark Wood. Yes, but Superintendent Gristhorpe got him to confess."

"I'd still say you get a big gold star for this one."

Susan smiled. The waiter appeared with their wine, gave Gavin a sip to test, then poured for both of them and placed it in the ice bucket. Good God, Susan thought, an *ice* bucket. In Yorkshire! *What am I doing here? I must be mad.* She had finished her food now and concentrated on the wine while she studied the dessert menu. Sweets. Her weakness. Why she was a few inches too thick around the hips and thighs. But she didn't think she could resist nutty toffee pie. And she didn't.

"Chief Constable Riddle's pretty damn chuffed," Gavin said later as they tucked into their desserts and coffee. "Sunday or not, it's my guess he'll be down your neck of the woods again tomorrow dishing out trophies and giving a press statement. As far as he's concerned, this solution has gone a long way toward diffusing racial tensions."

"Well, he was certainly keen to get everything signed, sealed and delivered this afternoon."

"I'll tell you something else. Golden boy isn't exactly top of the pops as far as the CC is concerned."

"What's new?" Susan said. "And I told you, I wish you'd stop calling him that."

"Where is he, by the way?" Gavin went on. "Rumor has it he hasn't been much in evidence the last couple of days. Not like him to miss being in at the kill, is it?"

"He's taken some time off."

"Pretty inconsiderate time to do that, isn't it?"

"I'm sure he has his reasons." Susan pushed her empty dessert plate aside. "Mmm. That pie was divine."

"How very mysterious," Gavin said. "Is he often like that?"

"Sometimes. He can be a bit enigmatic when he wants, can the DCI. Anyway, I'm glad Jimmy Riddle's happy, but this just isn't the sort of solution that makes you feel exactly wonderful, you know."

"Why not?"

"I can't help feeling a bit sorry for Mark Wood."

"Sorry? I thought he was supposed to have kicked his mate to death?"

"Yes, I know."

"Isn't that about as vicious as it gets?"

"I suppose so. But he *was* provoked. Anyway, I don't mean that. It's not so much *him* I feel sorry for, it's his family. He has a young wife and a baby. Poor devils. I can't help but wonder how they're going to manage without him."

"He should have thought of that before he killed Jason Fox, shouldn't he?"

Susan drank some more wine. It tasted thin and acidic after the sweetness of her dessert. "I know," she said. "But you should have seen where they live, Gavin. It's a dump. Thin walls, peeling wallpaper, damp, cramped living space. And it's a dangerous neighborhood, especially for a young woman alone with her baby. Gangs, drugs . . . And it was partly because he was defending his wife, her race, that he ended up killing Jason."

Gavin shook his head. "I never took you for a bleeding heart, Susan. You can't allow yourself to start getting sentimental. It'll make you soft. He's a villain and you've done your job. Now let's just hope the court puts him away where he belongs. Poverty's no excuse. Plenty of people have it tough and they don't go around booting their pals to death. My dad was a miner, for crying out loud, and more often out of work than in. But that doesn't give me an excuse to go around acting like a yob. If you want anything in this life, you go out and get it, you don't idle around moaning about what a bad hand you've been dealt."

"I suppose so," Susan said. She refilled her wineglass and smiled. "Anyway, enough of that. Cheers."

They clinked glasses.

"Cheers," Gavin said. "To success."

"To success," Susan echoed.

"Why don't we pay the bill and go," Gavin said, leaning forward. His hand touched hers. She felt the tingle right down to her toes. "I'll walk you home."

Susan looked at him for a moment. Those soft, sexy brown eyes.

Long lashes he had, too. "All right," she said, her hand turning to clasp his. "Yes. I'd like that."

VI

No more than a few hundred miles away, over the North Sea, Banks and Craig McKeracher had passed the Rijksmuseum and were walking down the quiet streets toward Prinsengracht.

"Basically," Craig was busy explaining, "Nev met this right-wing loony in Turkey who had a load of heroin he wanted to shift, and he wondered if Nev could help. Nev couldn't, of course. He knows bugger-all about dealing drugs. Doesn't know a fucking joint from a tab of acid. But he's always one to leave the door a little ajar, so he tells this bloke, hang on a while, let me see what I can do. Now there's only two people he knows with any brains who have ever had anything to do with drugs. One of them's yours truly, and the other's Mark Wood."

Banks paused. "Wait a minute. Motcombe knew Mark Wood?"

"Yes."

"This is Jason's business partner?"

Craig snorted. "Some partnership that'd be. There wasn't a lot of love lost between them, as far as I could see."

"Is Mark a member of the league?"

Craig shook his head. "No, he wouldn't have anything to do with them."

"Then how—"

"Mark and Jason met on this computer course, and they got on well enough at first. They were both good at it, too. Anyway, when they finished, Mark couldn't get a job. I understand he's got a wife and kid and lives in a shit-hole out Castleford way, so he was pretty desperate by then. Nev finances Jason in the computer business—only because he knows it's something he'll be able to use to his advantage down the line—and Jason decides he'll take

Mark on as partner, seeing as he came top of the class. Naturally, because Nev's putting money into the business, he's curious about Mark, so Jason arranges a meeting. I wasn't there, but I gather Nev had got details of his record by then and quizzed him about the drug arrest."

"What were the details?"

"Mark used to be a roadie for a Leeds band, a mixed-race band, like UB40, and one of the Jamaicans, a Chapeltown bloke, was into dealing in a big way. Used the group van, and got Mark involved. They got caught. End of story. So Nev finds out that Mark has some contacts in Chapeltown who might know someone who'll be interested if the price is right."

"This wouldn't involve a bloke called Devon, would it?"

Craig raised his eyebrows. "Yeah. How'd you know about him?"

"Same source I heard about the steaming. Just a lucky guess. Carry on."

"Right. Well, like I said, living in this shit-hole with his wife and kid, Mark was definitely interested in making money, even though he didn't give a flying fuck for Nev's politics. But he made a perfect go-between. Devon and his mates probably wouldn't be any too happy if they knew their supplier was a fascist bastard who thought they should all be sent home to rot in the sun, at best. But Mark got on with the black community okay, and they seemed to accept him. And he wasn't a member of the league."

Banks nodded. "Okay. That makes sense."

They spotted a vendor at the street corner, and as neither had eaten that evening, they bought bags of chips with mayonnaise, something Banks would never think of eating back in Eastvale. Here, they tasted wonderful.

"But how did Jason square all this with his politics?" Banks asked as they walked on. "You said he was dedicated. Straight."

"He didn't. That's the point. I'll get to it in a minute. See, in general, neo-Nazis aren't only racist, they're also anti-drug, same way they're anti-gay."

"Even though many of Hitler's lot were homosexuals or junkies?"

Craig laughed. "You can't expect logic or consistency from these buggers. I'll give Nev his due, though. Normally, he could make raping and murdering old ladies sound like a good thing to do for the cause. A true politician. A week or so later, when Mark's out of the way, he has another meeting with just me and Jason, and he tells us about this idea he came up with after traveling in America and talking to fellow strugglers there. What he thinks is that by providing a steady and cheap supply of heroin, you weaken and destroy the fabric of the black community, making them much poorer and more vulnerable when the big day comes, blah-blah-blah. It's his version of the smallpox blankets the whites gave the American Indians. Or, more recently, that newspaper story about the CIA financing the crack business in south-central Los Angeles. As a bonus, the blacks become complicit in their own destruction. That's the kind of irony Nev can't resist. And all the while he makes a tidy profit out of it, too. Couldn't be better."

"Jason fell for this crap?"

Craig kicked at an empty cigarette packet in the street. "Ah, not exactly. There's the rub. Motcombe needed one of us, someone *inside* the league, just to keep an eye on Mark and make sure everything was going tickety-boo. He didn't fully trust Mark. Jason, being Mark's partner, seemed a natural choice. But Jason didn't go for it. Jason wasn't interested in profit; he'd have starved for the cause. Nev seriously underestimated his right-hand man's dedication. Jason didn't fall for all that rubbish about weakening the community from within. In fact, he saw the scheme for exactly what it was—a money-making venture on Nev's part. Apparently, he already suspected Nev of skimming for his own gain, and there was quite a little power struggle brewing between them. They argued. Jason said he knew the organization needed money, but this just wouldn't work, that there was no way they could limit the sale to blacks, that it would spread to the white community too and sap their spirit as well. He said drugs were a moral evil and a pure Aryan would have nothing to do with them. He also said heroin wouldn't encourage the immigrants to go back home, which is what the organization was supposed to be all about, and that they'd be better concentrating on making the buggers feel uncomfortable and unwelcome than plying them with opiates."

"Impressive," said Banks. "But surely Motcombe must have suspected he'd react that way? Why did he even tell Jason in the first place?"

"I think Nev really did miscalculate the intensity of Jason's reaction. It would also have been pretty hard to keep anything like that from him. Nev fell in love with what he thought was his impeccable rhetoric, and he figured the best thing was to bring Jason in right from the start. No way, he thought, could anyone not see the absolute perfection of his logic and irony. At that point also, remember, he'd no idea how violently anti-drugs Jason was. It had simply never come up before." Craig shook his head. "I was there. Nev was absolutely stunned at Jason's negative reaction."

"What happened next?"

"They argued. Nev couldn't convince him. In the end he said he'd abandon the idea."

"But he didn't?"

"No way. Too much money in it. He just cut Jason out."

"But Jason knew?"

"I think by then he was pretty certain Nev wouldn't give up potential profits that easily."

"So Jason knew about the proposed drug deal and Motcombe was worried he'd go to the police."

"That was always a possibility, yes. But even more of a threat was that he'd talk to other ranking neo-Nazis. Nev's peers and colleagues. Some of whom felt exactly the way Jason did about drugs. Think about it. If Jason could convince them Nev was nothing but a petty thief and a drug dealer, then Nev would never be able to hold his head up in the movement again. He'd be ostracized. Hypocrisy reigns in the far right every bit as much as it does in most other places. There's another thing, too."

"What's that?"

"Jason had charisma. He was popular. Nev was coming to see him as a rival for power—and power meant money for Nev. So Nev was getting paranoid about Jason. It was Jason who made first contact with most of our members. It was Jason they went to when they had problems with the ideology of beating the crap out of some poor black or Asian kid. Jason who set them straight."

"So Jason was making inroads on Motcombe's position?"

"Exactly."

Banks nodded. He found a rubbish bin and dropped his empty chip packet in it. They were near Keizersgracht now, not too far from the hotel.

"What was your role in all this?"

"Like I said, Nev wanted someone close, someone *in* the league to keep tabs on Mark. Obviously Jason wasn't going to do it, so I was the next logical choice. I hadn't been around as long as Jason, but I *did* have an impressive criminal record, including drugs charges."

"So what it comes down to is that Motcombe had a pretty good motive for wanting Jason out of the way."

Craig nodded. "Exactly. That's why I needed to talk to you. To fill you in on it all. I don't know who killed Jason. I wasn't privy to that. Nev likes to keep his left hand and his right hand quite independent from one another. But I do know the background."

They paused at a bridge. A young couple stood holding hands and looking into the reflections of lights in the water. "Where do you want me to go with this?" Banks asked.

"Wherever it takes you. I didn't have you brought here to tell you to lay off, if that's what you think. And it's not a competition, or a race. Whatever we can get Motcombe for is fine with me. And with Superintendent Burgess. That's why he agreed to arrange this meeting. All I'm asking is that you hold off moving against Nev until you've got something you're certain will put him away for a long time." He grinned. "Oh, and I'd appreciate it if you don't blow my cover. I value my life, and I might need to stick around awhile longer to see what he gets up to next."

"When is this drug deal supposed to take place?"

"The heroin's already on its way."

They reached the door of Banks's hotel. He thought for a moment, then said, "All right."

"Appreciate it, sir."

"Coming in?"

"No. Got to go. I'm staying somewhere else."

"Take care, then."

"I will. Believe me."

They shook hands, and Craig wandered off down the canal. Banks looked up at the hotel's facade. It was still early. He wasn't tired and didn't fancy sitting in a cramped room watching Dutch television. He also had a lot to think about. Zipping up his jacket against the chill, he wandered off in search of a quiet bar.

VII

Susan put her hands behind her head, rested back on the pillow and sighed.

"Was that a sigh of contentment," Gavin asked, "or disappointment?"

She laughed and nudged him gently. "You should know. You had something to do with it."

"*I* did? Little old me?"

And to think that not more than an hour ago she'd had cold feet. When they had got back to her flat, she had asked Gavin in and one thing led to another, as she had known and hoped it would when she agreed to the second bottle of wine. But when the crucial decision came out into the open, there was an embarrassing moment when it turned out that neither of them had any protection. Well, it was good in a way, Susan realized. It meant that he wouldn't think she was a slut, and she didn't think he had taken her out to dinner in the expectation of ending up in her bed. But it was bloody awkward, nonetheless.

Luckily, there was an all-night chemist's on York Road, not more than a couple of hundred yards away, and Gavin threw on his jacket and set off. While he was gone, Susan started to get nervous and have second thoughts. Instead of giving in to them, she busied herself tidying up the place, especially the bedroom, throwing clean sheets on the bed, and when he came back she found, after a little kissing and caressing, that her resolve was just as strong as before.

And now, as she basked in the afterglow, she was glad she had made the decision. One of Chopin's piano concertos—she didn't know which one—played softly from the living room.

"Well, I couldn't think of a better way to celebrate," said Gavin. His hand brushed Susan's thigh and started sliding up over her stomach.

"Mmm. Me neither."

"And I'll tell you something else," he whispered in her ear. "I'll bet we're having a better victory celebration than anyone. Even golden boy, wherever he is."

Something about the mention of Banks's name gave Susan a moment of uneasiness, the way she had felt naked talking on the telephone to Banks when the Jason Fox case started. But it passed. She smiled and stretched, feeling a little sleepy from the wine and sex. "Oh, he's probably not having such a bad time," she said. "He does all right."

"What makes you think that? You don't know where he is or what he's doing."

"I do know where he is."

Gavin's hand rested on her breast. He had soft hands, like silk brushing her warm skin. She felt her nipple harden. "You know?" His hand moved again, downward.

Susan gave a little gasp. "Yes. Amsterdam. He's gone to Amsterdam."

"Lucky devil," said Gavin. Then he did something with his hand that made Susan realize she wasn't all that sleepy after all.

ELEVEN

I

Finding Jimmy Riddle wearing out the carpet back at Eastvale Divisional HQ had about the same effect on Banks's stomach as the dodgy landing.

The plane had banked sharply and plunged into thick cloud. By the time Banks had seen the runway, they were practically on it, still at an awkward angle, and for one stomach-lurching moment he had been certain the pilot was coming in too steeply and would crash the plane, wing first. But it leveled out in time, and apart from a little more bouncing and swaying than usual, the landing had gone without incident.

And now, an hour and a half later, his stomach was going through the same cartwheels again.

It was late afternoon. Banks's flight had been delayed and he hadn't arrived at Leeds and Bradford until three o'clock; he hadn't even eaten lunch. Not much chance of a bite now. He hadn't intended calling at the station, but when he neared Eastvale, he couldn't face going back to the empty house immediately.

"Ah, Chief Inspector Banks," said Riddle. "I've been waiting for you. Nice of you to drop by."

"Sorry, sir," Banks mumbled, as Riddle followed him into his office.

Riddle tugged his trousers up at the knees to preserve the

creases and sat on the edge of the desk, looking down on Banks. Banks supposed he took that position because he thought it gave him a psychological edge. Little did he know.

"And take the bloody smirk off your face, man," Riddle said. "Have you any idea how much trouble you're in?"

"Trouble, sir?"

"Yes, Banks. Serious trouble this time. You bugger off for a weekend in Amsterdam in the middle of a major investigation and leave your underlings to do your work for you. And it so happens that while you're away, they solve the case." He smiled. "I must admit, that does give me more than a little satisfaction."

"With due respect, sir—"

"With due *nothing,* Banks." Riddle craned his neck forward. The tendons tautened and the skin around his throat flushed. "What the bloody hell did you think you were up to? Can you answer me that?"

Banks had tried to prepare himself for a moment like this on the flight back. If truth be told, though, he had expected it to come from Gristhorpe, not Riddle. And there was a big difference. It wasn't that he didn't trust Riddle. The man was squeaky-clean. It wasn't even that he suspected Riddle of "fraternizing with fascists." That had only been a joke. A bad one, at that. But whereas Gristhorpe would accept Banks's explanation at face value and let things lie, Riddle was too much of an interfering bastard to do that.

If Banks told him what he had discovered from Craig McKeracher, Riddle would be on the phone to his cronies all over the place in a matter of moments. If there was any chance of glory to result from the situation, he would want his due share. And one wrong telephone call could have serious consequences for Craig. On the other hand, if Riddle could see nothing to be gained, then he would order Banks to pass on what he knew and leave it to West Yorkshire. Riddle hadn't got to be chief constable by pursuing the

truth against all odds. The problem was, someone in West Yorkshire had already been leaking information to Motcombe.

A dilemma, then.

Banks also knew that, as far as Riddle was concerned, the case
was solved. Most satisfactorily solved.

So it was with carefully measured tones that he answered the
question, aware even as he did so that it just wouldn't wash. "I
can't tell you everything, sir," he said. "At least, not just yet. It's
very delicate. But I can assure you my trip was directly related to
the Jason Fox case."

Riddle shook his head. "Delicate? Too delicate for the likes of
me? No, Banks. That won't do. I've already told you, the Jason Fox
case was solved in your absence."

"I know, sir. I read about it in the morning paper." Banks had
picked up a copy of *The Independent* at Schiphol Airport and had
seen a full report on the arrest and confession of Mark Wood for
the murder of Jason Fox. Including a quote from Riddle to the
effect that "Fox was killed by a friend of his in a dispute after several drinks. While alcohol was certainly a factor, race was not, I
am very pleased to say." Banks didn't believe it for a moment. "But
I'm not sure that's how it happened," he went on.

"Oh," said Riddle. "You're not sure that's how it happened,
aren't you? Maybe if you'd been here doing your job, you'd have
a better idea about what's going on. Well, let me tell you, Banks,
that is *exactly* how it happened. Your fellow officers got a confession out of Mark Wood. While you were off cruising the red-light
district, no doubt."

Banks had to admit that did hit a little too close to home. "In all
fairness, sir—"

Riddle stood up and went to lean on the filing cabinet, checking
for dust first. "Don't talk to me about fairness, Banks. I've been as
fair with you as I can be. I've given you more latitude, more freedom to tilt at your own various windmills than I've allowed any

man under my direct command. And what have you done with that freedom? You've abused it, that's what you've done. Day trips to Leeds to buy classical records and meet your bit on the side, and now a weekend in Amsterdam in the middle of a major investigation. What do you have to say?"

"If you'll allow me to get a word in, sir," Banks said calmly. "In the first place, my trip was *entirely* case-related, and in the second case, you haven't *solved* the Jason Fox case."

Riddle's pate went on red alert. "And I'm telling you the case is solved. *Telling* you, Banks."

"But—"

"And who paid for this trip to Amsterdam, might I ask?"

Shit. If Banks told him it was the Met, Riddle either wouldn't believe him, or he'd be on the phone trying to find out exactly who was behind it, setting off alarms like a mad cow walking through a Cambodian minefield. Besides, Dirty Dick Burgess, the only one who could really vouch for him apart from Craig, was on holiday "somewhere tropical."

"I can't say, sir," he said.

"I trust you didn't pay for it yourself, then, out of your own pocket?"

"No, sir."

"I thought not. And your wife? Did she accompany you on this mysterious case-related mission?"

"No, sir."

"Your mistress, perhaps? Or were you out there shagging the local girls?"

Banks stood up, his irritation growing. "Look, sir, I'm beginning to resent these implications. You might be my senior officer, but I don't have to put up with personal abuse from you."

Riddle stepped forward, chin jutting out like the prow of a ship. "You'll put up with whatever I dish out, laddie, and right now I'm dishing out a suspension."

"You're what?"

"You heard me, Banks. I'm suspending you from your duties pending a disciplinary hearing into your activities."

"You can't do that."

"Yes, I bloody well can. Read the regulations. I think skiving off for a long weekend during an important investigation is grounds enough for an inquiry. Dereliction of duty. For crying out loud, man, you're a DCI. You're supposed to set an example."

Banks sat down again, a leaden weight in his chest. "I see. This is official, then?"

"Official as it gets."

Banks could hardly believe what he was hearing. Anger burned inside him. Red behind his eyes. Everything was fucked. His marriage. Now his job. For some reason, this idiot had decided to persecute him. It just didn't matter to Riddle that there might still be unanswered questions in the Jason Fox case; he'd put his blinkers on and he wouldn't take them off. No doubt pleasing the Muslim community *and* the general populace simultaneously.

"So that's it, then?" he said. "I'm free to go?"

"Yes. In fact, I order you to go." Riddle grinned. "You're suspended, Banks."

"Right. I can tell you've been looking forward to saying those words for some time."

Riddle nodded. "Oh, yes."

Banks got up, slipped his cigarettes in his top pocket and picked his jacket up from the coatrack. Next he picked up his briefcase but paused in front of Riddle and laid it down on the desk again on his way to the door. "Is that your last word on the subject, sir?" he asked.

"Yes."

Banks nodded. Then he swung his arm back as far as it would go and hit Riddle hard, right in the mouth. Riddle staggered back against the flimsy desk and slid to the floor. Which was where he lay, shaking his head and wiping blood from his mouth with the back of his hand as Banks said, "And I've been looking forward to that, too, sir. Goodbye." Then he left the station, his knuckles aching and bleeding.

II

The minute Susan heard raised voices arguing about Amsterdam, she tiptoed into the corridor like a sneaky schoolgirl to listen. Then she heard a loud crash and saw Banks stalk out of his office and out of the building through the fire exit, without even glancing in her direction.

The chief constable hadn't left, though. Puzzled, Susan crossed the corridor and pushed Banks's office door open. Then she just stood there. Chief Constable Riddle was getting up from the floor, brushing dust from his uniform and dabbing his mouth with a blood-soaked handkerchief.

He saw her standing in the doorway, pointed and said, "Get back to your office, DC Gay. Nothing happened, you saw nothing, do you understand?"

"Yes, sir . . . Er . . . what about DCI Banks . . . ?"

"DCI Banks is under suspension."

Susan's jaw dropped.

"Back to your office," Riddle said again. She noticed one of his front teeth was chipped. "And remember: If word of this gets out, I'll know exactly where it came from, and your career won't be worth two penn'orth of shit, sergeant's exam or no sergeant's exam."

"Yes, sir."

Back in her office, Susan leaned on her desk, took a deep breath and tried to collect the thoughts that were suddenly spinning in her mind, out of control. Had she really just seen Jimmy Riddle getting up off the floor in Banks's office, wiping blood from his mouth? Yes, she had. Was that why Banks had got suspended?

But Riddle wanted her to keep it quiet, so there had to be another reason. He could have Banks kicked off the force for assaulting a senior officer, but it would have to be made public then.

She could understand Riddle's desire for silence easily enough—he would look like a real wimp if he publicly accused one of his DCIs of assault. After all, as Susan well knew, the police force was still very much a man's world, and physical prowess was important to men. Riddle would feel humiliated by what had just happened; it would be a blow to his macho ego. The last thing he'd want known was that Banks, four or five inches shorter than him and slighter in build, had knocked him down. If that got out, people all over the region would be sniggering at him behind his back even more than they did now.

So he must have suspended Banks for some other reason.

Amsterdam? Was that it?

And then she realized something. At first, it was just a vague sense of apprehension, then the tumblers fell into position, one inexorably after the other. Then came the final click, and the door opened.

Susan looked at her watch. Just after five.

First, she drove the short distance to Banks's house. As she drove, she chewed on her lip wondering if she was doing the right thing. She wished Superintendent Gristhorpe were here to advise her, but he'd gone off to teach a two-week course at Bramshill that morning. She didn't even know what she was going to say to Banks. After all, he was her senior officer. What could she, a mere DC, do to help?

But there were things she wanted to know. She had worked with Banks for several years now and had come to know his moods pretty well. She had seen him angry, sad, hurt and frustrated, but she had never seen him like this. Nor would she ever have thought him the kind of person to do something as stupid and impulsive as punching Jimmy Riddle.

Call it woman's intuition, a term she had a lot more respect for than she would ever care to admit in front of a roomful of male colleagues, but she felt something was seriously wrong. And it wasn't only to do with Riddle. All she could think of was that something had happened in Amsterdam. But what?

She walked up the front path to Banks's semi. Standing on the doorstep, she took a deep breath, counted to three, and rang the bell.

Nothing happened.

She rang again.

Still nothing.

She waited a few minutes more, tried knocking and ringing the bell. Still nothing. Where the hell was he? Looking around, she couldn't see his car.

She dashed down the path and jumped back in her Golf. She was starting to feel angry now, not a good emotional state for driving, but at least anger would sustain her all the way and help her do what she had to. She headed out of town through the darkening countryside at a dangerous speed, crossed over the A1 and headed southeast, then hurtled through the dark, through villages where families were just settling down to tea and an evening with the telly.

Soon she was on the outskirts of Northallerton, pulling up outside Gavin's modest terrace house.

Gavin answered on the first ring and smiled when he saw Susan. "Come in," he said, standing aside. "This is an unexpected pleasure."

Susan walked into the hall and Gavin leaned forward to plant a kiss on her cheek. She jerked back and slapped him hard across the face. Gavin staggered back a step or two. "You bastard," Susan said. "You bastard. How could you do it?"

Gavin looked surprised. He held his hand to the reddening weal on his cheek. "Do what? What the hell did you do that for?"

"You know why."

"No, I don't. Look, take your coat off and come through. Then you can tell me what you're on about."

Susan followed him into the living room but she didn't take her coat off. "I won't be stopping," she said. "I'll just say what I have to say and go."

Gavin nodded. He leaned against the wall with his arms folded. He was wearing tartan slippers, Susan noticed, and looked ridiculous. Somehow, that helped.

"All right," he said. "I'm listening. And it'd better be good after what you just did to me."

"Oh, it's good all right," Susan said. "It took me a while. I don't know. Maybe I'm thick, maybe I'm a fool, but I worked it out in the end."

"Well, you are supposed to be a detective, after all. But look, I still don't know what you're talking about. Will you back up a little and explain?"

Susan shook her head. "You're so damn smooth, aren't you, Gavin? You used me. That's what I mean."

"How did I use you? I thought you enjoyed—"

"I'm not talking about sex. I'm talking about information. All the time we were going out together, all the things I told you in private, all the station gossip. You passed it all on to Jimmy Riddle, didn't you? Even what I told you in bed on Saturday."

"I don't know what you're talking about."

But he looked away from her eyes, down at his slippers. Susan had seen that guilty gesture in enough criminals to know it meant Gavin was lying. "Yes, you bloody well do," she went on. "How else could Riddle have known everything he did? I should have twigged much earlier, then maybe none of this would have happened."

"What?"

"Riddle suspended Banks this afternoon. Don't tell me you didn't know."

Gavin shrugged. "Oh, that. Well, it's the chief constable's pre—"

"Don't give me that crap. You got me to talk about Banks in private. Shop talk. It was me who told you he liked to call at the Classical Record Shop whenever he had to go to Leeds. When Riddle mentioned that to me a few days ago, I didn't even think at the time about where he might have got it from. It was me who told you about Pamela Jeffreys, too, the violist involved in that case a couple of years ago, the one he felt guilty about. And on Saturday night, in bed, I told you Banks was in Amsterdam. My fault for being such a fool. Blame it on the wine. But you . . . you . . . You're beneath contempt."

"Okay," said Gavin, gazing at her coolly. "So the chief constable wanted to be informed about what was going on at Eastvale. So what? He's like that. Unlike his predecessor, he likes to be in the know. Hands on. It's easy for you. *You* don't have to work close to him, day in, day out, do you?" He pointed his thumb at his chest. "I do. And we all have our careers to consider, don't we? What's so wrong with that?"

Susan could hardly believe what she was hearing, even though it was exactly what she had expected. "So you admit it? Just like that? You used me to spy on my colleagues?"

"Well, seeing as you have the evidence, there's not a lot else I can say, is there? I can hardly deny it. Yes. *Mea culpa.*"

"I don't understand, Gavin. How could you do that?"

Gavin shrugged. "I never thought it would come to anything like this," he said. "For crying out loud, it was only little tidbits, nothing important. Like I said, Riddle just wanted to be kept informed. But that wasn't why I asked you out in the first place. That only came later. When he found out I was going out with you. And believe me, I didn't tell him. He's got quite a network, has Riddle." He shrugged. "I didn't really think it would do any harm."

"Did he want to be kept informed about Eastvale in general, or DCI Banks in particular?"

Gavin shifted from foot to foot. "Well, he *did* ask about Banks in particular. He never really approved of Banks, you know. Thought he was a bit of a maverick, if truth be told."

"I know that," said Susan. "He never liked him. Right from the start. I remember the Deborah Harrison case, when Banks upset some of Riddle's important friends. He was just looking for something to use against him. And you used me to get it for him. That's what I can't forgive."

"Like I said, I didn't really think I was doing anything—"

"Oh, stuff it, Gavin. I'm not interested in your excuses. You used me to scupper Banks's career, and that's all I care about."

"If that's how you want to see it."

"Is there any other way?"

"I take it things are over between us, then?"

Susan could only look at him and shake her head. Then she turned to leave.

"What is it, Susan?" Gavin called after her. "Fancy him yourself, do you? You should listen to the way you talk about him. Like a lovesick teenager. Believe me, it wasn't very difficult to get you talking about him. The hardest thing was getting you to stop. Even in bed."

Susan slammed the door behind her and got back in her car. She couldn't move, couldn't even turn the key in the ignition. All she could do was sit there, hands gripping the steering wheel, shaking. She took deep breaths.

And then Susan did something she hardly ever did, something she always hated herself for when it happened. She started to cry. Bloody great convulsive sobs. Because, fuck it, she said to herself, Gavin was right. She had never admitted it, but she had known it for ages. It *was* Banks she cared about; it *was* Banks she fancied. And, dammit, he was a married man, he was her senior officer, and he wouldn't look at her that way in a month of Sundays. She was just another stupid girl in love with her boss and there was no way she could stay in Eastvale now, not after this.

III

It had long since turned dark when Banks got home. For hours, it seemed, he had driven around the Dales, hardly noticing where he was, or what music kept repeating on the cassette player. His knuckles still hurt, but the shaking inside had stopped. Had he really done it? Punched Jimmy Riddle? He realized he had, and he also realized that at the moment the anger had burst out of him, it was Sandra he had been thinking of, not the bloody job.

The house was quiet and empty. A different quality of silence and emptiness than he had ever felt there before. First, he had a look around to see if anything was missing. Sandra hadn't taken very much. Most of her clothes were still in the wardrobe, the scent of her hair still lingered on the pillows, and her photograph of the misty sunset above Hawes still hung over the fireplace in the living room.

It made him think how only on Sunday, yesterday, he had wandered the Amsterdam museums in the rain, a pilgrim marveling at Rembrandt's *The Night Watch* in the Rijksmuseum, unsettled by *Crows in the Wheatfield* in the Van Gogh Museum, and, finally, elated by the bright, whimsical Chagalls in the Stedelijk Museum.

All the while thinking how Sandra would have loved it, and how he would like to treat her to a visit one weekend in spring, perhaps as a belated birthday present.

But Sandra was gone.

He noticed the red light blinking on the telephone answering machine. Thinking it might be Sandra, he got up and pressed the replay button. One call was Vic Manson, two were hang-ups, but the next four were from Tracy. On the last one, she said, "Dad, are you there? It's Sunday now. I've been trying to ring you all weekend. I'm worried about you. If you *are* there, please answer. I talked to Mummy and she told me what happened. I'm so sorry. I love you, Daddy. Please give me a ring."

Banks stood by the phone for a moment, head in his hands, tears burning in his eyes. Then he did what any reasonable man would do in his situation. He cranked Mozart's *Requiem* up as loud as he could bear it and got rat-arse drunk.

TWELVE

I

When Banks stirred on the sofa at about four o'clock in the morning, Mozart's *Requiem* was still playing on "repeat." And a more fitting piece of music he couldn't imagine. It was playing loudly, too, and he was surprised that none of his neighbors had called the police. Still, he *was* the police. Or used to be.

Wishing he were still unconscious, he groaned, rubbed his stubble, rolled off the sofa and put some coffee on, turning the volume down on the stereo as he went. Then he stumbled upstairs and swallowed a handful of aspirins, washed down with two glasses of water to irrigate his dehydrated brain cells.

Back downstairs, as the coffee dripped through the filter with frustrating slowness, he surveyed the damage: twelve cigarette ends in the ashtray; no burns on the sofa or carpet; about two fingers of Laphroaig left. If he was going to keep up this rate of drinking, he would have to start buying cheaper Scotch. Still, it could have been a lot worse, he concluded, especially as he remembered the bottle had only been about three-quarters full when he started.

When the coffee was ready, he decided to switch from the *Requiem* to the C Minor Mass, something to bring a little more light and hope into his bleak world, then he tried to collect his thoughts.

He had punched Jimmy Riddle; that was the first memory to

come back. And he had skinned knuckles to prove it. Well, that had been a stupid thing to do, he realized now, and it had also probably put the mockers on his career.

Jobless, then. Also wifeless and hung over. At least the hangover would go away. It *could* be worse, couldn't it? Yes, it could, he realized. He could have been diagnosed with a terminal illness. He racked his brains to see if that had, in fact, happened, but could find no memory of it. It would probably happen today the way his lungs felt after all those cigarettes.

So what was he going to do? Become a private eye? Enter a monastery? Get a job with some security outfit? Or should he just carry on and solve the Jason Fox case on his own to run rings around Jimmy Riddle, just as Sherlock Holmes did around Inspector Lestrade? Alan Banks, Consulting Detective. Had a nice ring to it.

He poured himself a cup of black coffee and flopped back on the sofa. Looking at the misty Hawes sunset over the fireplace, for some reason he remembered Sandra telling him on Thursday that there *might have been* somebody else, but there wasn't. Remembered the faraway look in her eyes when she said it.

And that made him angry. He pictured Sandra with some strapping, bearded young artist, standing in the wind on the moors doing a Cathy and Heathcliff, looking lovingly into each other's eyes and exercising restraint. "No, my darling, we *mustn't*. There's too much at stake. Think of the children." Grand passion collides with family values and moral responsibility. It was a scene from a cheap romance. But all the same, it made Banks clench his jaw. What *might* have been. And, come to think of it, he only had her word for it that she hadn't left him to run off with someone else, someone she would only take up with publicly after a "decent" interval.

Well, two could play at that game. Banks had had his chances at infidelity in the past, too, but he hadn't taken them. He hadn't romanticized them, either. He thought especially of Jenny Fuller.

There had been a time, some years ago, when something might have blossomed between them. Was it too late now? Probably. Jenny seemed to spend most of her time teaching in America these days, and she had a steady boyfriend over there. Then there was Pamela Jeffreys, the one Riddle thought was his mistress. Banks hadn't slept with Pamela, either, but it was an appealing thought.

So many choices. So many possibilities. Then why did he feel so bloody miserable and empty? Because, he concluded, none of them was what he wanted. What he wanted, when it came right down to it, was his job back, Sandra back and his hangover gone. Perhaps if he played a country-and-western song backward . . . ? He couldn't even do that, hating country and western the way he did. Still, taking stock of himself, he realized that, depressed as he was, he felt calmer now than when he was stuck at the airport yesterday contemplating his return home. Thumping Jimmy Riddle probably had something to do with that.

After the first cup of coffee, he realized he was hungry. He hadn't eaten anything since that snack on the plane, a million years ago now. Searching through the remnants of the fridge, he managed to throw together three rashers of streaky bacon and two eggs only a week past their sell-by date. That would have to do. The one remaining slice of bread was a little stale, but it hadn't turned green yet, and it would fry up nicely in the bacon fat. Cholesterol special. So what?

As he fried his breakfast, Banks remembered Tracy's messages. He would have to ring her today and put her mind at rest. Should he explain to her about losing his job, too? Best not yet, he decided. It was bad enough his daughter should suddenly find herself the child of a broken marriage the minute she flew the coop, let alone the child of a disgraced copper. There would be time enough for that later. He would have to phone Brian in Portsmouth, too, and his own parents. They would all be upset.

Suddenly, the day ahead seemed full of things to do. None of them pleasant. The only bright spot was that he wouldn't have to worry about money for a while; the suspension was *with* pay. And Jimmy Riddle couldn't do a thing about that until *after* a disciplinary hearing.

He cursed as he broke an egg while lifting it onto the plate and yolk ran all over the counter. It would have to do. No more left. Carefully, he used the spatula to lift the one unbroken egg onto the fried bread, then patted the bacon with some kitchen roll to remove the excess grease and tucked in. When he'd finished, he poured another cup of coffee and lit a cigarette.

It was still just past five in the morning, and he hadn't a clue what to do to keep him occupied until it was a decent time to start phoning people. Sleep was out of the question now, and he knew he couldn't possibly concentrate on reading a book or listening to music. He needed something completely mindless, something to keep his thoughts off his problems for a few hours. Like television.

But there was nothing on television at that time apart from something educational on BBC2 and a studio discussion on ITV, so he started sorting through the video collection, odds and sods he'd picked up over the years. Finally, he found one that would do. It was still in its cellophane wrapper, so someone must have bought it for him as a present and he'd forgotten he had it.

Bridge on the River Kwai. Perfect. He remembered his dad taking him to see a revival of it at the Gaumont when he was about twelve. It would take him back to those days, when life was simple, and right at the moment he would give anything on earth to be that innocent twelve-year-old again, grabbing his father's hand when Jack Hawkins burned the leeches off with a cigarette, thrilling at the way all the birds flew up and the pool turned red with blood when they ambushed the Japanese patrol, and biting his nails to the quick as Alec Guiness made his final, dying, staggering way to the dynamite plunger. Yes, *The Bridge on the River Kwai* might just keep the dark hounds of depression at bay for another couple of hours, until daylight came.

II

Susan didn't know where she was going when she left the station around eleven o'clock that morning, only that she had to get out of the office for a while. Let Riddle suspend her, too, if he found out.

The next thing she knew she found herself on Castle Walk looking out over the formal gardens and the river, all framed in the branches of the beeches. It was the same view she'd had from the bistro with Gavin on Saturday night. Just thinking about that night made her burn with shame and rage.

Across the Swain, a belt of trees called the Green partially obscured the East Side Estate, but she could still make out a few of the light red brick terraces and maisonettes, and the three twelve-story blocks of flats—a crime wave in themselves—poked their ugly heads way above the trees. Beyond the estate and the railway tracks were the chocolate factory and a few old warehouses, corrugated metal roofs glinting in the sun. A local diesel rattled by and blew its horn.

She would have to leave Eastvale; there was no doubt about that. Now that she had admitted her feelings to herself, she could no longer work with Banks. She couldn't trust herself not to act like a love-struck schoolgirl; nor could she go running off in tears every time she saw him, either. And she *would* have to see him. He might be suspended for the moment, but a disciplinary hearing would probably reinstate him, she thought.

It also hadn't taken her long to work out the fact that, after what she had witnessed yesterday, Jimmy Riddle would want her as far away from North Yorkshire as possible. At least that could be easily accomplished without raising any eyebrows.

Although it *did* happen on occasion, it was rare for a DC to be promoted straight to the rank of detective sergeant within the same station. The most likely scenario was a transfer and at least a year back in uniform. This was supposed to be a safeguard against corruption: senior officers offering promotion in exchange for falsified evidence.

At first, Susan had hoped the chief constable would approve her request to stay. But being promoted within Eastvale CID didn't matter to her now. She had to leave. And the farther away, the better. Devon and Cornwall, maybe. She had fond memories of childhood holidays in that part of the world: St. Ives, Torquay, Polperro.

How could she have been so stupid? she asked herself again. In cafés, pubs and in bed she had chatted away to Gavin about Banks and his idiosyncrasies, his love of music, his guilt over the injuries to Pamela Jeffreys, and Gavin had turned it over to Jimmy Riddle, who had twisted and perverted it beyond all recognition. If anyone deserved to be suspended, it was Riddle and Gavin. Fat chance.

An old woman walking a dog passed Susan on the path and said hello. After they had gone by, Susan paused a moment to sit on a bench. She was facing north now and to her left she could see the square Norman church tower, the bus station and the glass-and-concrete Swainsdale Centre. Straight ahead was the pre-Roman site in the distance, not much more than a couple of bumps in the grassland down by the river.

Even though there wasn't a great deal to do around the station in the aftermath of the Jason Fox case, Susan didn't think she could honestly stay away too long. After all, a call might come in, something important, and if she missed it she'd have to explain why.

She remembered something else she had overheard yesterday: Banks expressing doubts about the solution. Though she couldn't quite put her finger on exactly what, there were things about Mark Wood's confession that rang false with her, too. Maybe she should have a look over the reports again. So, with a sigh, she stood up and headed back around Castle Walk.

As she went up the stairs to CID, she told herself she would have to get a grip, lock up her feelings, keep them separate and behave like a professional. She could do it; she'd done it before. On some level, being a woman in a man's world, she did it all the time. She would also have to work out how to deal with Banks's misplaced trust in her. Should she tell him about Gavin? Could she really do that?

III

Shortly after six o'clock that evening, Banks sat in Leeds Parish Church. Though not much to look at from the outside, the interior had recently been restored to all its Victorian Gothic glory; like the Town Hall, all stained glass, dark polished wood and high arches.

He wasn't there because his troubles had driven him to religion. In fact, he was listening to a rehearsal of Vivaldi's *Gloria* by the St. Peter's Singers and Chamber Orchestra. It certainly wasn't where he had expected to be, or what he had expected to be doing when he woke up on the sofa that morning.

Tracy had rung him much earlier than he would have thought of ringing her. At least he was feeling a bit more human by then. She was full of concern, naturally, and he tried to assure her that he would be okay. Tracy told him she was going down to Croydon for a while to stay with her mother and grandparents, but she assured him she wasn't taking sides. He told her to go, take care of her mother; he'd see her when she came back. Reluctantly, she hung up. Maybe he hadn't lost Tracy after all.

He felt the need to get out of Eastvale around noon, so he phoned Pamela Jeffreys. As it turned out, she had a rehearsal that evening, but Banks was welcome to attend. She was surprised to hear from him and said she would be delighted to see him. Someone pleased to see him? Music to his ears.

He drove to Leeds in plenty of time to browse the city-center record shops first. A couple of CDs would be paltry compensation for the miserable time he'd had lately, but they would be better than nothing. Like the toy soldier his mother always used to buy him after he'd been to the dentist's.

By half past six, the conductor seemed frustrated by the soprano section's inability to enter on time, so he ended the rehearsal early. Pamela packed away her viola, grabbed her jacket and walked toward Banks. She was wearing black leggings and a baggy black velvet top, belted at the waist, with a scoop neckline which plunged just above the curve of her breasts. Her long raven hair hung over her shoulders and the diamond stud in her right nostril glittered in the sidelighting. Her skin was the color of burnished gold, her eyes almond in shape and color, and her finely drawn red lips revealed straight white teeth when she smiled. Many of them were crowned, Banks knew. Looking at her now, he found it hard to believe that only a couple of years ago she had been lying in a hospital bed covered in bandages wondering if she would ever be able to play again.

Banks gave her a peck on the cheek. She smelled of jasmine. "Thank you for inviting me," he said. "Wouldn't have missed it for the world."

She turned up her nose. "We were terrible. But thanks anyway. And it's nice to see you, stranger."

"Sorry I couldn't stick around after *The Pearl Fishers,*" Banks said.

"That's okay. I was knackered anyway. Long day. What did you think?"

"Wonderful."

She grinned. "For once, you're right. Everything seemed to fit together that night. Sometimes it just does that, you know, and nobody knows why."

Banks gestured around the church. "I'm surprised you have time for this."

"St. Peter's? Oh, if the schedules work out all right, I can do it.

I need all the practice I can get. I've been recording the Walton Viola Concerto, too, with the orchestra. For Naxos. Finally the viola's getting some of the respect it deserves."

"You were the soloist?"

She slapped his arm. "No. Not me, you idiot. I'm not *that* good. The soloist was Lars Anders Tomter. He's *very* good."

"I'm really glad it's all working out for you, anyway."

Pamela smiled and made a mock curtsy. "Thank you, kind sir. So, where now?"

Banks looked at his watch. "I know it's a bit early, but how about dinner?"

"Fine with me. I'm starving."

"Curry?"

Pamela laughed. "Just because I'm Bangladeshi, it doesn't mean I eat nothing but curry, you know."

Banks held his hands out. "Whatever, then. Brasserie Forty-four?"

"No, not there," Pamela said. "It's far too expensive. There's a new pizza place up Headingley, just off North Lane. I've heard it's pretty good."

"Pizza it is, then. I'm parked just over in The Calls."

"You can have curry if you really want."

Banks shook his head, and they walked through the dimly lit cobbled backstreets to the car. They were in the oldest part of Leeds, and the most recent to be redeveloped. Most of the eighteenth- and nineteenth-century warehouses by the River Aire had been derelict for years, until the civic-pride restoration schemes of the eighties. Now that Leeds was a boom town, they were tourist attractions, full of trendy new restaurants, usually located on something called a "wharf," the kind of word nobody there would have used twenty years ago. Canary Wharf had a lot more to answer for than vanished fortunes, Banks thought.

"It's not that I think you eat curry all the time because you're Asian," he said. "It's just that there isn't a decent curry place in

Eastvale. Well, there *is* one, but I think I might be *persona non grata* there at the moment. Anyway, pizza sounds great."

"What did you get?" Pamela asked as she got into the Cavalier and picked up the HMV package from the passenger seat.

"Have a look," said Banks, as he set off and negotiated the one-way streets of the city center.

"*The Beatles Anthology*? I never would have taken you for a Beatles fan."

Banks smiled. "It's pure nostalgia. I used to listen to Brian Matthew do 'Saturday Club' when I was a kid. If I remember rightly, it came on right after Uncle Mac's 'Children's Favourites,' and by the age of thirteen I'd got sick to death of 'Sparky and the Magic Piano,' 'Little Green Man' and 'Big Rock Candy Mountain.'"

Pamela laughed. "Before my time. Besides, my mum and dad wouldn't let me listen to pop music."

"Didn't you rebel?"

"I did manage to sneak a little John Peel under the bedclothes once in a while."

"I hope you're speaking metaphorically." Banks drove past St. Michael's Church and the Original Oak, just opposite. The streetlights were on, and there were plenty of people about, students for the most part. A little farther on, he came to the junction with North Lane, an enclave of cafés, pubs and bookshops.

"Here," said Pamela, pointing. Banks managed to find a parking spot, and they walked around the corner into the restaurant. The familiar pizza smells of olive oil, tomato sauce, oregano and fresh-baked dough greeted them. The restaurant was lively and noisy, but they only had to wait at the bar for a couple of minutes before they got a tiny table for two in the back. It wasn't a great spot, too close to the toilets and waiters' route to and from the kitchen, but at least it was in the smoking section. After a while, sipping the one glass of red wine he was allowing himself that evening, and smoking one of the duty-free Silk Cuts he'd picked up at Schiphol, Banks hardly noticed the bustle or the volume level anymore.

"So, have you got a boyfriend yet?" he asked when they were settled.

Pamela frowned. "Too busy," she said. "Besides, I'm not sure I trust myself to get involved again. Not just yet. How's your wife? Sandra, isn't it?"

"Yes. She's fine."

After a while of small talk, their pizzas came—Banks's margherita and Pamela's fungi.

"How's life at the cop shop?" Pamela asked between mouthfuls.

"I wouldn't know," said Banks. "I've been suspended from duty."

He hadn't intended to tell her, certainly not with such abruptness, but it had come out before he could stop it. He couldn't seem to hold back *everything*. In a way, he was glad he'd said it because he had to confide in someone. Her eyes opened wide. As soon as she had swallowed her food, she said, "What? Good Lord, why?"

As best he could, he told her about the Jason Fox case, and about thumping Jimmy Riddle.

"Aren't you still angry?" she asked when he'd finished.

Banks sipped some wine and watched Pamela wipe a little pizza sauce from her chin. The people at the next table left. The waiter picked up the money and began to clean up after them. "Not really angry," Banks said. "A bit, perhaps, but not a lot. Not anymore."

"What, then?"

"Disappointed."

"With what?"

"Myself mostly. For being too stupid not to see it coming. And for thumping Riddle."

"I can't say I blame you, from what you've told me."

"Oh, Riddle's an arsehole, no doubt about it. He even suggested that I took *you* to Amsterdam with me."

"Me? But why?"

"He thinks you're my mistress."

Pamela almost choked on a mouthful of pizza. Banks didn't feel particularly flattered. Afterward, he couldn't tell if she was blushing or just red in the face from coughing. "Come again," she managed finally, patting her chest.

"It's true. He thinks I've got a mistress in Leeds and that's why I keep making up excuses to come here."

"But how could he know? I mean . . . ?"

"I know what you mean. Don't ask me." Banks smiled, felt his heart skip, but went on anyway, aiming for a light tone. "It didn't seem like such a bad idea."

Pamela looked down. He could see he'd embarrassed her. "I'm sorry," he said. "That was supposed to be a compliment."

"I know what it was supposed to be," Pamela said. Then she smiled. "Don't worry. I won't hold it against you."

Please do, he almost said, but managed to stop himself in time. He wondered if she would take him home with her if he told her that he and Sandra had split up. They ate some more pizza in silence, then Pamela shook her head slowly and said, "It just sounds so unfair."

"Fairness has nothing to do with it." Banks pushed his plate aside and lit a cigarette. "Oh, sorry," he said, looking at the small slice left on Pamela's plate.

"That's all right. I'm full." She pushed hers aside, too.

"This Neville Motcombe you mentioned, isn't he the bloke who was interviewed in the *Yorkshire Post* this weekend? Something to do with neo-Nazis disrupting a funeral?"

"That's the one."

"Didn't someone die there?"

"Yes," said Banks. "Frank Hepplethwaite. I knew him slightly."

"Oh, I'm sorry."

"It's okay. We weren't close friends or anything. It's just that I liked him, and I think, of anyone, he's the real victim in this whole mess. Tell me something: Have you ever come across Motcombe in any other context?"

"What, you mean with me being the sort of person this Albion League might target?"

"Partly. Yes."

She shook her head. "Not really. I've been lucky, I suppose. Oh, I've been insulted in the street and stuff. You know, called a Paki bitch or a Paki slut. It's always 'Paki.' Can't they think of anything else but that?"

Banks smiled. "That's part of their problem. Severely limited thinking. No originality."

"I suppose so. I'm not saying it doesn't bother me when it happens. It does. It upsets me. But you get used to it. I mean, it starts not to surprise you as much, so you don't get shocked by it as easily. But it still hurts. Every time. Like hot needles being stuck through your skin. Sometimes it's just the way people look at you. Am I making any sense?"

"Perfect."

"I remember once when I was a kid back in Shipley—oh, this must have been in the seventies, twenty years ago now—and I was walking back from my aunt's house with my mum and dad. We walked around this corner and there was a gang of skinheads. They surrounded us and started calling out racist insults and shoving us. There were about ten of them. There was nothing we could do. I was terrified. I think we all were. But my dad stood up to them, called them cowards and shoved them right back. At first they just laughed, but then they started to get worked up and I could tell they were getting ready to really hurt us. My mother was screaming and I was crying and they got my dad on the ground and started kicking him . . ." She trailed off and shook her head at the memory.

"What happened?"

Pamela looked up and smiled through her tears. "Would you believe it, a police car came by and they ran off? A bloody police car. About the only time the police have ever been there when I've needed them. Must have been a miracle."

They both laughed. The waiter came by and took their plates.

"What now?" Pamela asked, after she'd wiped her eyes from the mingled tears of humiliation and laughter.

"Coffee? Dessert?"

She hit him on the arm again. "I don't mean that, idiot. I mean, you. Your future."

"Looks bleak. I'd rather concentrate on dessert."

"Just a cappuccino for me."

Banks ordered two cappuccinos and lit another cigarette.

"You're smoking too much," Pamela said.

"I know. And just when I'd managed to cut down."

"Anyway, you haven't answered my question."

"What question was that?"

"You know quite well. Your future. What are you going to do?"

Banks shook his head. "I don't know yet. It's too early to say."

"Well, surely when this chief constable person has done his investigation, he'll have to reinstate you?"

"I doubt it. Even if a disciplinary hearing really does reinstate me, it doesn't matter."

"Why not?"

"Think about it," said Banks. "I hit the chief constable. Even if he does keep that just between the two of us, it still means I can't work with him anymore. He'd find ways to make my life a living hell."

"I understand it might make things difficult."

"Difficult? It was *difficult* before all this. After . . ." He shrugged. "Impossible, more like."

The restaurant was full of students now. They looked like an artsy, literary crowd, all talking excitedly about the latest music, arguing loudly about books and philosophy. They made Banks feel old; made him feel he had wasted his life. A waiter passed by carrying plates, leaving a trail of garlic and basil smells.

"But you can get a job somewhere else," Pamela said. "I mean as a policeman. In a different region. Can't you?"

"I suppose so. I don't mean to be negative, Pamela, I just haven't thought that far ahead yet."

"I understand." She leaned forward and put her hand on his. Candlelight glittered in her diamond stud, made shadows of burnished gold and lit the fine down between her breasts.

Banks swallowed and felt his excitement rise. He wanted to take her home and lick every inch of her golden skin. Or did he? There would be consequences, confidences shared, a *relationship*. He didn't think he could handle anything like that right now.

Pamela sat back and flipped a long tress of hair over her shoulder with the back of her hand. "What about this case you were working on?" she asked. "You seemed to imply that it's not over."

"Everyone thinks it is."

"And you?"

Banks shrugged.

She toyed with a gold bracelet on her arm. "Look, Alan, this person you talked about earlier. Mark Wood. *Did* he do it?"

"I don't know. He *might* have done. But not, I don't think, the way he said he did, or for the reason he claimed."

"Does it matter?"

"Yes. It could mean the difference between manslaughter and murder. And if someone else was behind it, say Neville Motcombe, I'd hate to see him get away with it while Mark Wood takes the fall alone."

"If you were still on the force, would you be working on this case?"

"Probably not. The chief constable's got his confession. Everybody's happy. Case closed."

"But you're not on the force."

"That's right."

"So that means you *can* still work on it if you want."

Banks smiled and shook his head. "What impeccable logic. But I don't think so. I can't do it, Pamela. I'm sorry. It's over."

Pamela sat back and studied him for a moment. He reached for another cigarette, thought twice about it, then lit up anyway.

"Remember when I was hurt?" she said.

"Yes."

"And thought I might never play again?"

Banks nodded.

"Well, if I'd taken your negative attitude, I wouldn't have played again. And, believe me, there were times when giving up would have been the easiest thing in the world. But you helped me then. You encouraged me. You gave me strength and courage when I was at my lowest. I'd never had a friend like . . . someone who didn't want . . ." She turned away for a moment. When she looked back, her eyes were deeply serious and intense, glistening with tears. "And now you're giving up. Just like that. I don't believe it. Not you."

"What else can I do?"

"You can follow up on your ideas. On your own."

"But how? I don't have the resources, for a start."

"Someone will help you. You've still got friends there, in the department, haven't you?"

"I hope so."

"Well, then?"

"I don't know. Maybe you're right." Banks gestured for the waiter and paid, waving aside all Pamela's attempts to contribute. "My idea, my treat," he said.

"So you *will* do something? You promise me you won't just sit around at home and mope?"

"Yes, I promise. I'll do something." He scraped his chair back and smiled. "Now, come on. Let me take you home."

THIRTEEN

I

The first thing Banks needed to do, he realized in the cold light of Wednesday morning, was spend a few hours going over *all* the paperwork on the Jason Fox case—especially that which had been generated in his absence. He realized he had missed a lot over the weekend, and there were things he needed to know if he was to make any progress on his own. But how could he get hold of it? Nobody was going to kick him out of Eastvale station, he didn't think, but neither could they let him just walk in and take what he wanted.

There wasn't even a crust of bread left in the house, and he didn't fancy eating Sandra's leftover cottage cheese, so he made do with coffee and Vaughan Williams's "Serenade to Music" for breakfast.

As he let the sensuous music flow over him, he thought about last night. When he had dropped Pamela at her flat, he had half hoped she would invite him up for a drink, but she just thanked him for the lift, said she was tired and hoped she would see him again soon. He said he would call and drove off with a pang of disappointment about not getting to do something he probably wouldn't have done anyway, even if he had had the chance. But seeing her had been good for him. At least she had persuaded him to keep working on the case.

When the music finished, he picked up the phone and called Sandra in Croydon. He had been thinking of calling last night when he got in, but decided it was too late.

Her mother answered.

"Alan? How are you doing?"

"Oh, not so bad, considering. You?"

"About the same. Look, er, I'm really sorry about what's happened. Do you want to speak to Sandra?"

"Please."

"Just a minute."

She sounded embarrassed, Banks thought as he waited. Not surprising, really. What could she say? Her daughter had left her husband and come home to sort herself out. Banks had always got on well with his mother-in-law, and he didn't expect she was going to see him as a monster now, but nor was she going to chat with him about his feelings over the telephone.

"Alan?"

It was Sandra's voice. She sounded tired. He felt the icy hand squeeze his heart. Now he had her on the line, he didn't know what to say. "Yes. I . . . er . . . I just wanted to know if you were okay."

"Of course I'm okay. I wish you hadn't called."

"But why?"

"Why do you think? I told you. I need time to work things out. This doesn't help."

"It might help me."

"I don't think so."

"I spent the weekend in Amsterdam."

"You did *what?*"

"In Amsterdam. It was strange. It brought back a lot of memories. Look, do you remember—"

"Alan, why are you telling me this? I don't want to talk about it. Please. Don't do this to me. To us."

"I'm only—"

"I'm going now."

"Don't hang up."

"Alan, I can't deal with this. I'm going now."

"Can I speak to Tracy?"

There was silence for a while, then Tracy came on the phone. "Dad, it's you. I was worried."

"I'm okay, love. Your mother . . . ?"

"She's upset, Dad. Honest, I don't understand what's happening any more than you do. All I know is Mum's confused and she says she needs some time away."

Banks sighed. "I know that. I shouldn't have called. She's right. Tell her I'm sorry. And tell her I . . ."

"Yes?"

"Never mind. Look, does Brian know about all this? I'm sorry, I haven't been very organized. Other than you, I haven't called anyone else."

"It's all right, Dad. You don't have to apologize to me. I suppose it's hard to know what to do when something like this happens. I mean, it's not exactly something you can take a course on, is it?"

God, she sounded suddenly so mature, Banks thought. Much more mature than he felt right now. "Does he?"

"Yes. We talked to him over the weekend."

"How's he taking it?"

"Cool. You know Brian. He's okay."

"When am I going to see you?"

"I'm staying the rest of the week down here. But I'll come up for the weekend if you want."

"You will?" The icy hand relaxed its grip and Banks's heart warmed a little.

"Of course. You know I love you, Dad. I love you both. I told you yesterday, I'm not taking sides. Please don't think because I came down here that I think any less of you."

"I don't. Anyway, the weekend would be great."

Tracy hesitated. "You won't be at work all the time, will you?"

"I . . . er . . . no, I don't think so," Banks answered. No point telling her about his suspension, he thought. The last thing he needed right now was his daughter feeling even more sorry for him from a distance. "I'll pick you up at the train station. What time does your train get in?"

"It gets back to Leeds mid-afternoon. But I'll need to drop by the residence first. There might be messages. I shouldn't really have taken off like that. I've only just started there."

"I'm sure they'll understand."

"I hope so."

"So why don't I come down to Leeds and pick you up at the student residence? Does that sound like a good idea?"

"That'd be great."

"What time?"

"About six be okay?"

"Fine. And we'll stop at the King's Head in Masham for something to eat on the way back."

"Great. And, Dad."

"What?"

"Take care of yourself."

"I will. See you on Friday. Good-bye."

"Good-bye."

Banks hung on to the receiver for a while after the line went dead, then he swallowed, took a deep breath and dialed Brian's number in Portsmouth.

After six rings, a sleepy voice drawled. "Uh. Yeah. Who is it?"

"Did I wake you?"

"Dad?"

"Yes."

"Well, yeah, as a matter of fact, you did. But it's all right. I should be getting up anyway. Next lecture's at ten. What's up?"

"I gather you've heard about your mother and me?"

"Yeah. It's too bad. Are you okay?"

"I'm doing fine."

"And mum?"

"I just talked to her. She's a bit confused right now, but she'll be okay."

"Great. What's going to happen?"

"I don't know. She says she needs some time away."

"She'll come back, Dad, you'll see."

"I hope so."

"Just wait and see. She's just having a mid-life crisis, that's all. She'll get over it."

Kids. Banks couldn't help but smile. "Right. And how are you?"

"Fine."

"How's your classes?"

"All right. Hey, Dad, the band's got a couple of gigs coming up next weekend. Paying gigs." Brian played in a local blues band. Banks thought he was a pretty good guitar player.

"That's great. Just don't let it get in the way of your studies."

"I won't. Don't worry. Gotta go now, or I'll be late for the lecture."

"When are you coming up?"

"I'll try to get up to see you before Christmas. Okay?"

"Fine. If money's a problem, I'll pay for your ticket."

"Thanks, Dad, that'd be a great help. Gotta go."

"Good-bye."

"Bye, Dad. And hang in there."

Hang in there. Like a kid from some American television program. Banks smiled as he hung up. Well, that was enough family business for the moment, he thought. He knew he should phone his own parents and tell them what had happened, but he couldn't face them yet. They'd be really upset. All these years they had loved Sandra like the daughter they had never had. If anyone was likely to blame him for what had happened, it would be his own parents, not Sandra's, he thought ironically. No, best wait. Maybe Sandra would come up with Tracy at the weekend, then he wouldn't have to tell them anything.

He poured some more coffee and put on the Beatles CD that he'd bought in Leeds yesterday. It was the second of the three anthologies, and he'd been thinking of buying it ever since it came out. He went straight to the second disc: outtakes from "Strawberry Fields Forever." His favorite. Singing along, he tidied up a little, but soon started to feel restless and caged. Somehow, it didn't feel right to be home during the daytime, watching neighbors walk back and forth with shopping and the unemployed bank clerk across the street wash his car for the second time in a week.

It was time for action. He picked up the telephone, dialed the station and asked to be put through to DC Susan Gay's extension.

She answered on the second ring.

"Susan?" Banks said. "It's me."

"Sir? Are you . . . Is everything all right?"

He was sure she meant it, but her voice sounded tight and cool. "I'm fine. Is Jim there?"

"No, he's out on the East Side Estate. Another break-in."

"The super?"

"Away at Bramshill."

"Good. Sorry, I didn't mean that to sound like it did. Look, I know I shouldn't ask you this, but do you think you could do me a favor?"

"Sir?"

"I need to look over the stuff on the Jason Fox case again. All of it—from the crime-scene photographs to Mark Wood's statements. Can you help?"

"Can I ask why you're still interested, sir?"

"Because I'm not satisfied. Will you help me?"

There was a long pause, then Susan said, "Why don't you come to the station?"

"Is that a good idea?"

"It's pretty quiet here right now. The super's going to be away for a couple of weeks."

"Well, if you're certain. I don't want to get you into trouble."

Banks heard a sound like a harsh cough or bark at the other end. "Are you all right?"

"Fine. Frog in my throat. That's all. It's okay, sir. Really it is."

"Are you sure? If Jimmy Riddle turns up—"

"If Jimmy Riddle turns up, I'm buggered. I know that. But there's far too much stuff to photocopy. And that would look suspicious, especially the way you have to account for every penny you spend around here these days. I'll take the risk if you will, sir."

"All right."

"But I'd still like to know why you're not satisfied."

"I'll tell you about it when I know more myself. At the moment it's mostly just a feeling. That and a few bits of information about Mark Wood I picked up in Amsterdam."

"Why don't you just come to the station as soon as you can, then. I'll be waiting." And she hung up hurriedly.

Banks grabbed his coat and left the house. It was another sunny day, with a little high cloud and a slight chilly edge. The leaves had turned a little more than last week, and some were beginning to fall already.

He needed the exercise, so he decided to walk. He plugged in his earphones and turned the Walkman on: Billie Holiday singing "Strange Fruit."

He walked along Market Street past the roundabout, the zebra crossing, garage and school, the local shopping center with its Safeway supermarket and collection of smaller shops and banks. There was a lot of traffic on Market Street today and the acrid smell of petrol and diesel fumes mingled with dry, dusty air.

He paused across from the Jubilee, whose large stone-and-red-brick frontage curved around the junction of Market Street and Sebastopol Terrace. That was where Jason Fox had spent his last evening on earth before being dispatched to whatever circle of hell was reserved for racists. Why on earth did it matter who had killed him, or why? Banks wondered as he walked on. Wasn't it good enough that he was dead? Was it only Banks's insatiable bloody curiosity that made it so important, or was there some absolute standard of justice and truth to be served?

Banks had no answer. All he knew was that if he didn't get to spin it out until he thought it was all over, then it would stay with him like a sore that won't heal. And he knew that, in some way, it was the murder of Frank Hepplethwaite he was out to avenge, not Jason Fox's.

One or two pairs of curious eyes followed him up the stairs at the station, but nobody said anything. Susan was in her office waiting for him with a thick pile of papers in front of her.

"I feel like a schoolboy sneaking a look at naughty pictures," Banks said. "Can I take them to my office?"

"Of course," said Susan. "You don't have to ask *my* permission." She stood up.

"Look, I appreciate this."

"No problem."

"Susan, is—"

"Sorry, sir. I've got to go."

She dashed out and left him standing in her office. Well, he thought, it didn't take long to become a pariah around here, did it? But he could hardly blame Susan for wanting to put a bit of distance between them. Not after all that had happened. And she *had* put herself out to help him.

Checking to see that the coast was clear, he tiptoed across the corridor to his own office with the papers and shut the door behind him. Nothing had changed. Even the desk was still at the same odd angle after Riddle had fallen back on it. Embarrassed at the memory of what he'd done, Banks straightened it, sat down with the pile of papers, packet of cigarettes and ashtray beside him, window a couple of inches open, and settled in to read.

II

What the hell am I doing here? Susan wondered, as Banks stood aside and held the door of the Duck and Drake open for her. Why did I agree to this? *I must be insane.*

The Duck and Drake was a small hideaway in Skinner's Yard, one of the many alleys off King Street. Wedged between an antiquarian bookshop and the Victoria wineshop, it had a narrow frontage and not much more room inside. One advantage was that it was one of the few pubs that still had a snug, a tiny room handy for private conversations. The doorway was so low that even Banks had to stoop. Inside, the snug was all dark wood beams and whitewashed stone walls hung with brass ornaments. An old black-leaded fireplace took up almost one entire wall. Above it ran a long wooden mantelpiece with a few tattered leather-bound books.

They had the snug to themselves. Banks bought the drinks and sat against the wall, opposite her, a small table between them.

Sipping her St. Clement's, Susan could hear the occasional *ker-chunk* of the fruit machine and chink of the cash register coming from the other rooms. If they wanted the barman's attention, they had to ring a little bell on the bar. It was an altogether too intimate and cozy setup for Susan, but there was nothing she could do about it. Banks had been right in that the Queen's Arms was far too public a place for them to meet. And he was clearly oblivious to her discomfort, drinking his Sam Smith's Old Brewery Bitter and chewing on a cheese-and-onion sandwich. Susan had no appetite at all. Between mouthfuls, he told her about what he had discovered in Amsterdam.

Susan listened, frowning and biting her lower lip in concentration. When Banks had finished, she said, "It makes sense, sir, but how does it change things? We already know Mark Wood killed Jason. He admitted it."

Banks finished his sandwich, sipped some Sam Smith's and reached for his cigarettes.

"Yes," he said. "I've just read through his statements. The kid's a pathological liar. He's confessed to manslaughter, but if I'm right, it was murder. Premeditated murder."

"I don't see how you can prove that."

"There's the rub. According to the postmortem report, Jason Fox was hit *on the back of the head* with the beer bottle, right?"

Susan nodded. "That's where Dr. Glendenning found the most damage to the skull, and the glass fragments."

"But in his statement, Mark Wood said he hit Jason *on the side of the head*."

"I noticed that," said Susan, "but, quite honestly, sir, I didn't think much of it. He was confused, under pressure. Basically, he was saying he just lashed out."

"Yes, I understand that. The point is, that doesn't happen in a fight."

"Sir?"

"Stand up."

Banks edged out from the bench. The room itself was just about high enough for him to stand up in. There was no one else around. Susan got to her feet and stood facing him, almost close enough to feel the warmth of his body.

She concentrated on the demonstration, focusing on little details. He didn't look well, she noticed. He had dark bags under his eyes, and his face was pale. There was also a deep sadness in him that she had never noticed before.

"Pretend to hit me on the back of the head with an imaginary beer bottle," he said.

"I can't, sir," Susan said. "Not from this angle. Jason must have had his back to Wood, walking either in front of or beside him. Or he must at least have been partly turned sideways."

"Like this?" Banks turned sideways.

"Yes, sir."

Banks went back to his seat and lit a cigarette. "Been in many fights?" he asked.

"No, sir. But that—"

"Let me finish. I have. At school. And, believe me, you would never get your opponent to stand in that position. Not willingly. Not unless you'd hit him with your fist first and knocked him sideways."

"Maybe that's what happened?"

Banks shook his head again. "Listen to what you're saying, Susan. To do that, he'd have to have been holding the beer bottle in the same hand he punched Fox with and then swung back very quickly and hit him before he moved. Even if he had the beer bottle in the other hand and switched after he'd hit him, it still doesn't make sense. And remember, Jason was no slouch when it came to physical strength. You'd need every advantage to get the better of him. Let me ask you a question."

"Yes, sir."

"Was Mark Wood bruised in any way? Did he have a black eye or a cauliflower ear?"

"No."

"You'd expect something like that, wouldn't you, if he'd been in an actual fight? Especially with as tough a customer as Jason Fox. Are you telling me Jason didn't even get one punch in?"

"I don't know, sir. Perhaps he hit Wood in the body, where it wouldn't show, and not in the face? I mean, we didn't do a strip search or anything."

Banks shook his head. "I'm sorry, but it's just not on. I had another good look at the crime-scene photographs as well, and I reread Dr. Glendenning's postmortem report. It just couldn't have happened the way Mark Wood said it did."

"Well," Susan said slowly, "Superintendent Gristhorpe wasn't entirely convinced, either. But Mark said Jason Fox was goading him about his wife and kid. They needn't have faced off to start fighting. Mark probably just lashed out when he'd had enough. I suppose you saw it for yourself in the statement, but when we pushed Wood on exactly how and when it happened, he said it was all a blur, he couldn't remember."

"How very convenient. He also denied emptying Jason Fox's pockets. Two loose ends."

"That's the thing that bothered me most, sir. But we just assumed that either he lied because it would look bad for him, too deliberate, stopping to empty Jason's pockets instead of running off in a panic. Or maybe someone else came along later and robbed Fox while he was lying there."

"I'd go for the first explanation, myself. It just didn't fit with the scenario he was painting for you. But why take his keys as well, unless they might have led to easier identification? I think whoever did this wanted to keep the victim's identity from us until they had a chance to clear out the Rawdon house of any dodgy files or notes he might have kept there, and they weren't taking any chances."

"We just thought that if some opportunist came along and did it, he simply took everything. You know, just sort of scooped it all up quickly without pausing to separate the keys from the loose change." Susan shrugged. "Chief Constable Riddle didn't seem to be worried by any of this. And by then we had him breathing right down our necks."

"It's still two loose ends too many for me."

"Then I don't know where that leaves us, sir. What about motive?"

Banks told her about Mark's connection with Motcombe's drug deal, and Jason's disapproval.

"So you think Motcombe's behind it?" she said.

"I do. But proving it is another matter. Officially the case is closed. You got an easy conviction. That pleased Jimmy Riddle. That and the opportunity to suspend me. I made a mistake there. I didn't expect you'd solve the case so quickly that he'd be buzzing round the station all weekend. To be honest, I didn't expect he'd find out where I'd gone."

"Sir," Susan blurted out, feeling her heart lurch into her throat. "Can I tell you something?"

Banks frowned and lit another cigarette. "Yes, of course. What is it?"

Susan chewed on her lip for a while, just looking at him, unsure now whether she dare speak out or not. Then she took a deep breath and told him all about Gavin's betrayal.

When she had finished, Banks just sat quietly staring down at the table. She was afraid of what he might say, especially as she could no longer deny to herself the way she felt about him. Please God, she prayed, let him never find out about *that*.

"I'm sorry, sir," she said.

Banks looked at her, a sad, crooked smile on his face. "Never mind. It wasn't your fault. How were you to know your boyfriend would run off and tell tales to Jimmy Riddle?"

"Whichever way you look at it, sir, I still betrayed a confidence."

"Forget it."

"How can I do that? Look how it's turned out."

"It isn't over yet, Susan. I'm far from finished. It must have hurt you, this betrayal. I'm sorry."

Susan looked down, into her empty glass.

"Fancy another drink?" Banks asked.

"No, sir. I'm fine. Really."

"Well, I fancy another pint."

Banks went to the bar and rang the bell. While he was waiting to get served, Susan sat hunched in on herself, feeling miserable. No matter how bloody kind and forgiving Banks might be, she could never forgive herself for what she had done. It wasn't so much the betrayal itself, as the humiliation of letting herself be fooled and used by a bastard like Gavin.

"So what do you want to do?" she asked when he came back. "I mean about Mark Wood."

"I see from the paperwork that Wood's solicitor was called Giles Varney?"

"That's right. A real arrogant bastard. Expensive, too. It seemed a bit odd at the time, that he would get Varney to come all the way from Leeds."

"Yes."

"Wood also said something about him being Jason's solicitor, too—the one who helped them get the business set up. He didn't want a duty solicitor. He was adamant about that."

"Interesting." Banks sipped his pint, wiped his lips and said, "And fishy. You know, I wouldn't be at all surprised if Varney is Motcombe's solicitor, too, or at least works for the same firm. I'll have to give Ken Blackstone a call and check. Now, according to the reports, it was only when the blood evidence came back that Wood confessed, right?"

"Yes, sir. It would have been pretty difficult to lie his way out of that one."

"Did he have a private conference with Varney? Make phone calls?"

"Yes, sir. We did it all strictly according to PACE."

Banks nodded. "So Wood talked to Varney, then he made a telephone call, then he confessed."

"Yes, sir."

"Who did he call?"

"I don't know. It was made in private."

"We should be able to find a record of the number. I'll bet you a pound to a penny it was Neville Motcombe. I'll bet he told Motcombe he was well and truly up shit creek, and Motcombe talked to Varney, who then told him to plead manslaughter."

"But why would he do that?"

"Isn't it obvious? You had him against the ropes. I mean, fine, early blood evidence doesn't necessarily mean a hell of a lot, but Wood *knew* he'd done it, and both he and Varney probably knew it was just a matter of time before we got results from DNA test-

ing. And that they'd be positive. In the meantime, if Mark Wood
admits to a lesser charge of manslaughter, denying that he's ever
even met Motcombe, then the heat's off. It was just a fight that
went wrong.

"And you can also bet that Varney will milk as much sympathy from the jury as he can from the fact that the fight started
over Jason Fox making racist remarks about Mark Wood's wife
and child. All Motcombe has to promise is that Wood will get a
short sentence *and* that his family will be financially taken care of
while he's inside. That and a nice bonus when he gets out. I think
it's an offer I'd probably take if my balls were in the wringer like
Wood's are."

"*If* he pays a penny."

"Yes. I suppose he could renege. And arrange for an accident in
jail. I'm assuming he's not doing all this out of the kindness of his
heart. He's doing it because Wood has something on him. Like the
truth about what happened."

"What can we do about it, if you're right?"

"*We* can't do anything, Susan. Remember, you're still on the
force, but you're off the case. I, on the other hand, can do whatever
I want."

"But—"

Banks held his hand up. "Susan, I appreciate what you've done
so far, but I don't want to risk getting you into trouble again. Even
Superintendent Gristhorpe wouldn't approve if he knew what I
was up to."

"He would if you told him, sir. I told you he had his doubts, too.
But Jimmy Riddle just barged in and steam-rollered everything."

"I know. But the super's not here. It's better this way for the
time being. Believe me."

"What next, then?"

Banks looked at his watch. "Next, I think I'll get right back to
basics and pay George Mahmood another visit. There's something
missing from those statements. Some connection I'm missing, and

it's starting to irritate me. It might be worth eating a mouthful or two of humble pie to find out what it is."

III

Banks walked down King Street toward the Mahmoods' shop. As he passed School Lane, he could hear kids shouting on the rugby pitch and was almost tempted to go and watch. He had enjoyed rugby at school, and when he first joined the Met. He'd been a pretty good winger, if he said so himself. Strong, slippery and fast.

Is this what private eyes feel like? he wondered as he cut down along Tulip Street, on the northern edge of the Leaview Estate. Walking the mean streets of Eastvale? He didn't even have a license to validate what he was doing. How did you go about getting a private-eye license in Yorkshire? Did you even need a license?

He did, however, still have his warrant card. Riddle hadn't had the chance to ask for it, and Banks hadn't managed the cliché of slapping it down on the table. He supposed it would be an offense to use it while under suspension, but that was the least of his worries.

The builders were busy at work in the fields around Gallows View, mixing concrete, climbing ladders with hods resting on their shoulders, or just idling around chatting and smoking cigarettes. Soon, the row of old cottages would be swallowed up. Banks wondered if they'd change the name of the street and the fields when the new estate was finished. *Gallows Estate* probably wouldn't sit too well with the local council.

For Banks, approaching the Mahmoods' shop felt like coming full circle. Not only had the Jason Fox case led him there, but his first case in Eastvale had involved the previous owner. And the way things looked, this might be his last case.

George stood behind the counter, wearing his white shirt with its Nehru collar, serving a young woman with a baby strapped to her breast. When he saw Banks, he scowled. His mother, Shazia, came over from the freezer area, where she'd been stamping prices on packages of frozen pizza.

Though she only came up to Banks's shoulders, her eyes challenged him. "What do you want this time, Mr. Banks? Haven't you caused enough trouble around here?"

"As far as I know, I haven't caused any trouble, Mrs. Mahmood. Not intentionally, at any rate. I have a job to do." A small lie, he realized. *Had* a job would be more like it. "I have a job to do, and it's sometimes difficult. I'm sorry it has caused you pain."

"Oh, are you? Such as throwing my son in a cell overnight, worrying his poor parents to death?"

"Mrs. Mahmood, George wasn't *thrown* anywhere, and he exercised his right to make a telephone call. If he didn't ring you—"

She waved her hand impatiently. "Oh, yes, he rang us, all right. But we still worried. A young boy being put in jail with all those criminals."

"He was in a cell by himself. Look, I don't know where you've got this from—"

"And only because of his color. Don't think we don't know that's why you pick on us."

Banks took a deep breath. "Look, Mrs. Mahmood, I'm getting sick of this. We took your son in because he and his friends had an altercation with the victim's party on the night of the killing, because they live in pretty much the same area of town, because they refused to cooperate with us and because we found something suspicious on George's trainer."

"Suspicious? Animal blood?"

"We didn't know that at the time. It *could* have been human blood."

She shook her head. "My son would never hurt anyone."

"I'm sorry, but my business isn't always as trusting as it might be."

"And what about the second time? Wasn't that persecution?"

"My colleagues turned up a witness who said he *saw* George and his two friends beat up Jason Fox. What could they do?"

"But he was lying."

"Yes. But again, we didn't know that at the time."

"So why have you come here pestering us all over again?"

"It's all right, Mother," George said, walking over. The woman with the baby seemed torn between leaving and staying to eavesdrop on the conversation. She took a long time putting her change back in her purse, then Banks gave her a sharp glance and she scurried out murmuring comforting sounds to the baby, who had started to cry.

"Can we go somewhere and talk, Mohammed?" Banks asked.

George nodded toward the stockroom in the back of the shop.

"I'm going to call a solicitor," Mrs. Mahmood said.

"No need to, Mum," said George. "I can handle this."

Banks followed him into the back. The stockroom was full of boxes and smelled of cumin and shoe polish. There were no windows, or if there were, they were covered by the stacks of boxes. A bare bulb shone in the center of the room. Banks fancied it looked rather like a filmmaker's idea of one of those interrogation rooms from the old days. He'd seen a film not too long ago in which two detectives had actually sat a woman in a chair with two bright desk lights pointed at her. He'd never tried that in interrogations himself; he wondered if it worked.

"What do you want?" George said. There wasn't a trace of friendliness in his voice. Whatever friendship there had ever been, through Brian, was gone now.

"I need your help."

George snorted and leaned against a stack of crates, arms crossed. "That's a laugh. Why should I help you?"

"To find out who really killed Jason Fox."

"Who cares? From what I've heard, the racist bastard deserved everything he got. Besides, I read in the paper that his mate confessed. Isn't that good enough for you?"

"I'm not going to argue with you. Will you just answer a few straightforward questions, please?"

He shrugged. "All right. No skin off my nose. But hurry up."

"Cast your mind back to that Saturday night at the Jubilee. Why were you there?"

George frowned. "Why? To listen to the band. Why else? Kobir was up visiting from Bradford, like I said, so Asim and me thought he'd enjoy it."

"I understand the Jubilee has a good reputation for music?"

"Yeah."

"Girls?"

"Yeah, it's a good place to meet girls."

"And drugs?"

"If you're interested in that sort of thing. I'm not."

"People come from miles around."

"So?"

"And it was really busy that night?"

"Yeah. Well, Scattered Dreams are really popular. They're pretty new on the scene and they haven't got to the really expensive venues yet. But they're already recording for an independent label. Pretty soon you'll be paying through the nose to go see them at Wembley or somewhere."

"Okay. Now, apart from that little contretemps you had with Jason, did you notice anything else about him and his pal?"

"Never paid any attention, really. Except that they seemed to be talking pretty intensely a lot of the time."

"Arguing?"

"Not loudly, not so's you'd notice. But they didn't look too happy with one another."

"Did they try to chat up any girls?"

"Not that I saw."

"They weren't listening to the music?"

"Not really. Some of the time. But they were sitting toward the back, closer to the bar. We were near the front, but the way the chairs were angled around the table, they were pretty much in my line of vision. When they weren't talking, the other one, the one that killed him, would seem to be listening, but the one that got killed even put his fingers in his ears every now and then."

"What kind of music was it?"

George shifted position and put his hands in his pockets. "Hard to describe, really. Sort of a mix between rap, reggae and acid rock. That's about the best I can do."

No wonder Jason had put his fingers in his ears, Banks thought. He obviously hadn't known what kind of music to expect. But Mark Wood probably had.

"Did you see either of them talk to anyone else?"

George frowned. "No. I was far more interested in the music than in those two pillocks." The shop bell pinged. "I'd better get back and help my mum. My dad's down at the cash-and-carry."

"Just a couple more questions. Please."

"Okay. But hurry up."

"What about those Jamaicans selling drugs you mentioned when I first talked to you?"

"What about them?"

"Was that true?"

"Yes, of course it was. I suppose I should admit I don't know for certain they were from Jamaica, but they looked like Rastas, and one of them had dreadlocks."

"And the drugs?"

"I saw a bit of money change hands now and then, then one of them would talk on his mobile. A while later he'd nip outside and bring back the Ecstasy or crack or hash or whatever from the person who was carrying it. They don't carry it on them. That's how they usually do it."

"And you saw them doing that?"

"Sure. You think I should have reported it? You think the police don't know what's going on? You told me yourself the Jube has a reputation for drugs."

"I'm sure the Drugs Squad are quite well aware of what's going on. It doesn't sound as if these lads are major dealers, though. Were they regulars?"

"I'd never seen them before."

"Doing good business?"

"By the looks of it." George sneered. "Some of the white kids think it's cool to buy from spades."

"Were they with anyone?"

"They were with the band as far as I could tell."

A few connections started to form in Banks's mind. This was the link that had been eluding him. "Were they actually playing with the band?"

George shrugged. "No, maybe roadies or something. Hangers-on." The bell pinged again. "Look, I'd better get back. Really."

"Right. Just one more thing. Did you see any contact at all between the Jamaicans and Jason, or Mark?"

"What? That would have been hardly likely, would it? I mean . . . wait a minute . . ."

"What?"

"Once, when I was going for a piss, I saw them pass one another in the corridor. Anyway, now I think of it, they sort of nodded at each other. Very quick, like, and expressionless. I thought it was a bit weird at the time, then I forgot about it."

"Who nodded at whom?"

"The kid who confessed. He nodded at one of the Jamaicans. Like I said, I thought it was odd because he was with the bloke who called me a 'Paki bastard' and there he was, on nodding terms with a Rasta."

"So this was *after* your little conflict with Jason Fox?"

"Yes."

"That makes sense," Banks muttered, mostly to himself. "You were very nicely set up."

"Come again?"

"Oh, nothing. Just thinking out loud." Banks followed George back into the shop. "Thanks for your time, Mohammed." He became aware of Shazia Mahmood glaring at him as he walked out onto the street.

For a moment, Banks just stood there on Gallows View as the chaotic thoughts settled into some sort of pattern, like iron filings when you hold a magnet under them. Motcombe's drug deal with the Turk and Devon, using Mark Wood as a go-between. Mark Wood's Jamaican wife, Mark's connection with a reggae band and with drug dealing. Scattered Dreams. That signal between Wood and the drug dealer. Jason's death warrant. There was a pattern all right, but now he had to come up with a way of *proving* it.

Banks set off toward King Street. A pneumatic drill from the building site broke the silence and sent a pack of scavenging sparrows spiraling off into the sky.

FOURTEEN

I

"Ken, you're a mate," said Banks, "so I want to let you know before you agree to anything that I'm under suspension."

"Bloody hell!" Blackstone nearly spilled his drink. It was Thursday lunchtime, and they were in the City of Mabgate, a pub near Millgarth, finishing bowls of chili. "What's it all about?" Blackstone asked when he'd recovered his equilibrium.

Banks told him.

Blackstone shook his head. "They can't make it stick," he said. "It sounds like a personal vendetta to me."

"It is. But don't underestimate personal vendettas, Ken. Especially when Chief Constable Jimmy Riddle's the one carrying them out. And for the record, I'd appreciate it if you didn't tell anyone else around here where I was over the weekend. It could mean real trouble for Craig McKeracher."

Blackstone tilted his head and squinted at Banks. "Are you hinting that one of our lads is bent?"

Banks sighed. "Look, there's no evidence, but it seems clear that someone, most likely someone from West Yorkshire, is doing a few little favors for Neville Motcombe and his league of merry men."

Blackstone's expression hardened. "Are you certain?"

"No, not certain. It just seems to be the most obvious explanation. As far as I know, so far it's just been a matter of accessing criminal records. If you use the PNC, you wouldn't have to be in West Yorkshire to do that, I'll admit, but that's where Motcombe lives. Logical deduction."

"Brilliant, my dear Holmes," said Blackstone. "But ve haff vays of finding out who's been using the PNC, and what they've been looking for. I'll catch the bastard and have his bollocks for golf balls."

"Maybe it's a 'her'?"

"Maybe. But how many women do you find hanging around with these white-power groups? Not a lot. It inclines me to believe they've got more sense."

"Well, not many of them like playing soldiers, that's for certain. I don't know what odds I'd take against how many of them actually *agree* with some of the stuff Motcombe's lot comes out with, though. Anyway, can I ask you one more favor, Ken?"

"Go ahead. You're doing pretty well for a suspended copper so far."

"Thanks. Don't move on the mole until I've played out my hand."

"Why not?"

"Same reason I asked you to keep quiet about Amsterdam. It could jeopardize Craig's cover as Rupert Francis. Or even his life. I don't think Motcombe's the forgiving sort."

Blackstone squirmed and scratched the back of his neck. "Okay. My lips are sealed. Want to tell me more?"

Banks told him about Motcombe's gangs of steamers and muggers, then about the Turkish connection and the possible heroin deal with Devon, the deal that Mark Wood was to play such a big part in. Blackstone listened without comment, shaking his head every now and then.

"That's quite a conspiracy," he said finally. "It makes me wonder about this suspension business. Do you think there's anything more to it?"

"Like what?"

Blackstone paused a moment. "More sinister. Remember when John Stalker got taken off that investigation into the RUC's shoot-to-kill policy in Northern Ireland a few years back?"

"Yes."

"I seem to remember they mocked up some story about him consorting with criminals just to shut him up and stop him embarrassing them. It was all political."

Banks shook his head. "A week or two ago I might have been paranoid enough to agree with you," he said. "The old conspiracy theory has its appeal. Especially when Dirty Dick Burgess appeared on the scene. And it wouldn't have surprised me if Jimmy Riddle had been in the BNP at the very least. But I don't think so. Whatever he is, Riddle isn't a card-carrying fascist. He's just a pushy, bullheaded arsehole, a frustrated headmaster with a mean streak. Put him on the inner-city streets where the real coppers work and he'd shit himself in five minutes."

"Maybe so. But you're certain there's nothing more to it?"

"Pretty much. He's been looking for an excuse to nobble me ever since he took the job, and now he thinks he's found it."

"Okay. So how can I help?"

"I'm going to ask you a couple more favors and I want to give you the chance to say no. I don't want you to stick your neck out for me. I'm giving you fair warning."

Blackstone paused, then said, "Go ahead. I'll tell you if I don't want to hear any more. Or when."

"Fair enough." Banks lit a cigarette. "The way I see it, though, is that most of what's going on here is on *your* patch anyway, so you can regard me as informant, consultant, whatever the hell you like, as far as official records go."

Blackstone laughed. "Clever bugger. Thought it all out, haven't you? You'd have made a good lawyer. All right. I'm interested. I only hope you don't expect paying, that's all."

Banks smiled. "This is for free, Ken. First off, I'd like to know whether a solicitor called Giles Varney has ever acted for Neville Motcombe. There might be some record in the paperwork on that receiving charge. Or, better still, last Thursday, after that fracas at Frank Hepplethwaite's funeral. Someone got Motcombe out of Halifax nick pretty damn quickly."

Blackstone got his notebook out. "How d'you spell that?"

Banks spelled "Varney" for him.

Blackstone smiled. "Well, that ought to be easy enough to do without compromising my career."

"The next request might be a bit tougher, and I'll understand if you say no. There was a band from Leeds playing at the Jubilee in Eastvale on the Saturday Jason Fox was killed. They're called Scattered Dreams. Someone who was there told me that there were a couple of Jamaicans dealing small quantities of hash, crack and Ecstasy. Apparently, they might have been with the band in some capacity. Roadies, hangers-on, what have you."

Blackstone nodded. "A lot of small dealers are mobile now they've saturated the urban markets. And it makes sense they'd target places where there's loud music and lots of kids. I think I've heard of the Jubilee. Is that the one that advertises in the *Evening Post?*"

"That's the one. I suppose the Drugs Squad keeps tabs on these bands and their itinerant dealers?"

"I hope so," said Blackstone. "Though you never quite know what the DS is up to. They're a law unto themselves half the time."

"Anyway," Banks went on, ticking off on his fingers, "Mark Wood had passing contact with one of these lads at the Jubilee. My thinking is that they might have been in this together. First off, I need to know if this band is the same one Mark Wood roadied for a couple of years back, when he was arrested on the drugs charge."

Blackstone nodded.

"And then I'd like the names of the Jamaicans who were on the fringes of Scattered Dreams that night, if you can get them. I know that might be a bit more difficult."

"I can only try," said Blackstone. "Actually, I know a bloke on the Drugs Squad who can keep his mouth shut. We did some courses at Bramshill together a few years back. Bloke called Richie Hall. He's a Jamaican himself, and he's done a fair bit of undercover work over the years. Anyway, the point is, he knows the music and drugs scene up north better than anyone I know. If he doesn't know who they are, nobody does."

"Great. There might even be a short cut. Mark Wood's wife's Jamaican. Her maiden name is Shirelle Jade Campbell. They seem to have met up around the time Wood got involved with the band, and I'm wondering if there isn't maybe a family connection. A brother, cousin or something. At least that gives you a name to work on."

"I'll pass it on to Richie. Like I said, if anyone knows, Richie does."

"You sure you don't mind doing this, Ken?"

Blackstone shook his head. "Nah. What are mates for. I'll warn you, though, you'll be bloody lucky to get anything out of these lads even if we do track them down."

"I know that. Actually, if I'm right, I was thinking of a slightly more devious approach to the truth. But let's wait and see, shall we?"

"Just as long as your expectations aren't too high. Who knows, there might even be a bit of glory in this for me."

Banks smiled. "Maybe. Whatever happens, there'll be no Brownie points for me from Jimmy Riddle. But I promise you, if there's any credit to be taken, it's yours. And lunch is on me."

"Will you do *me* one small favor, Alan?"

"Name it."

"Just be bloody careful, that's all."

II

By nine o'clock on Friday morning, Banks felt edgy and restless alone in the house. He was pleased with himself, however,
for avoiding the booze completely on Thursday evening, and for
actually managing to finish *The Power and the Glory* as he listened to Beethoven's late quartets. So he felt full of energy when
he woke up on Friday. There was nothing he could do until he
heard from Ken Blackstone except pace the floor.

When his phone rang at about half past nine, he grabbed the
receiver on the first ring. "Yes? Banks here."

"Alan, it's Ken."

"What have you got?"

"Some answers for you. I hope. In answer to your first question,
yes, Giles Varney is Neville Motcombe's solicitor and has acted
for him on a number of occasions. Their professional relationship
goes back to the time Motcombe started buying property in the
Leeds area, about four years ago. It seems like they've been bosom
buddies ever since."

"Does Varney have any other known right-wing connections?"

"Yes. I checked around and he's pretty well known in some of
the more extreme right circles."

"Great. That would seem to indicate that Mark Wood did a deal
with Motcombe through Varney. Anything else?"

"This is where it gets a bit more complicated, I'm afraid. And
you owe me. I had to spend yesterday evening in a pub with Richie
Hall, and he drinks like a bloody fish. I'll be sending you the bill."

Banks laughed. "Find anything out?"

"Yes. The band Mark Wood worked with at the time of his
first arrest was called Cloth Ears. They split up shortly after the
drug bust. But this Scattered Dreams was formed partly from the
ashes. Phoenix-like, you might say. Apparently the blokes you're
interested in used to play with Cloth Ears, but now they just hang
around the fringes of Scattered Dreams and sell dope. Seems

drugs have sapped whatever talents they might once have had, and most of the time they're too stoned to strum a chord. And you were right about the family connection. The one with the dreadlocks is Shirelle Wood's brother, Wesley Campbell, and the other's a mate of his called Francis Robertson. 'Wes' and 'Frankie,' as they're known locally. Both of them have been seen to associate with Devon recently, according to Richie."

"Low-level dealers?"

"Looks that way."

"Excellent."

"And in Shirelle Wood's favor, Richie says she's not connected with any of this. In fact, she stopped talking to her brother Wes as soon as she discovered he was involved in getting Mark busted the first time, and she hasn't talked to him since. Cut him off completely."

Good for her, Banks thought. There were very few people he had come to have respect for in this whole business. Frank Hepple-thwaite was one of them, and Shirelle Jade Wood was another. Pity about her husband. He should have followed her lead and cut off communications with Wesley Campbell, too. But no, Mark Wood thought he could make an easy fortune. And it was a sad thought that Shirelle and Connor would be the ones to suffer the most if the truth did come out.

"Thanks, Ken," Banks said. "You've done a great job."

"No problem."

"Now for the hard part."

He heard Blackstone sigh. "Somehow I had a feeling there might be more to it than this. I assume this is your 'cunning plan' for getting to the truth?"

Banks laughed. "Hear me out, Ken, then let me know if you think we can do it."

III

About an hour later, Banks drove down to Leeds alone. There was no point involving Susan Gay or Jim Hatchley in his scheme. It was risky and could backfire, then he'd have their jobs on his conscience, too. Ken Blackstone would be fine; he was simply carrying out an investigation on his own patch, based on information received. The fact that Banks was along for the ride really didn't matter.

Banks lit a cigarette and turned up the volume on Bryn Terfel's renditions of Robert Louis Stevenson's *Songs of Travel*. He looked at the digital clock. Eleven o'clock. Plenty of time to do what he had to and pick up Tracy at the residence by six o'clock.

As he pulled up behind Millgarth, he looked at his watch. Just after twelve. If Ken Blackstone had done his work, everything ought to be set up and ready to roll by now. He checked at the front desk and went straight up to Blackstone's office. In the corridor outside the CID offices, as arranged, sat Mark Wood, who had been brought in from Armley Jail shortly after Banks's nine-thirty talk with Ken Blackstone, just to answer a few more questions and help make the paperwork flow more smoothly.

Apparently, Wood had been more than willing to show his cooperation. And even though he'd been sitting there for probably a couple of hours already, he hadn't asked for Giles Varney yet. If he did, they'd have to lie and tell him they couldn't get in touch. With Varney present, the plan would be useless.

Mark Wood didn't look like much, Banks thought. Muscular, yes, but basically just another sullen, nervous kid chewing his fingernails in a police station.

Banks introduced himself. They hadn't met before, and it was important that Wood know *someone* from Eastvale was involved in all this. As expected, Wood looked puzzled and confused. When he asked Banks why he had come down all this way, Banks said it was nothing to worry about, he would find out in a while.

He sounded like a doctor about to tell a patient he has a terminal illness.

Leaving Wood under guard in the corridor, they went into Ken Blackstone's office, where Wood could watch them through the glass partition if he wanted, though he couldn't hear what they were saying. That would make him even more nervous. Especially if they glanced his way once in a while as they spoke.

They had been standing behind the glass chatting about Leeds United's abysmal season and occasionally looking at Mark for about fifteen minutes, when three large uniformed officers led Wesley Campbell and Francis Robertson along the corridor, as arranged. The two had been passive and compliant when picked up over an hour earlier, Ken said. That was either a mark of confidence that they'd be out again in two shakes of a lamb's tail, Banks thought, or they were too stoned to care. Both had been found in possession of small amounts of marijuana, and neither had had time to flush it down the toilet, so they had been languishing in the charge room for a while. By now, they weren't quite as complacent.

As they passed Mark Wood, they glanced down at him, and Mark looked even more confused. His eyes widened with fear. Campbell actually struggled against his guards for a moment and tried to get closer to Wood, as if he wanted to warn or threaten him. But the guards held on. Campbell and Robertson were taken to separate interview rooms around the corner. Both seemed to know the PACE regulations by heart, and they asked to make their phone calls immediately.

At about two o'clock, after Banks and Blackstone had enjoyed a leisurely lunch across the road, it was time to start. They went back upstairs and took Mark into an interview room. It was agreed that Banks, being more familiar with the case, would do most of the questioning. Blackstone would give the occasional prod if things got slow. They weren't taping this one. There would be time for formalities later, with Banks well out of the way, if the plan worked. If it didn't, then all hell might break loose as far as disciplinary actions were concerned. Banks had already warned Ken and given him the option of staying well away, but Ken had insisted on being involved.

"Well, Mark," said Banks, "I know we haven't met until today, but I've had a great interest in you ever since I saw Jason Fox's body a couple of weeks ago."

"I've told the police all about that," Wood said. "I've pleaded guilty to manslaughter. What's all this about?"

Banks raised an eyebrow. "It's not quite settled yet," he said. "Not to *my* satisfaction, anyway."

Wood folded his arms. "I don't know what you mean. First you leave me hanging about in the corridor for hours, now you start interrogating me. I'm not saying anything. I want my solicitor."

"Mr. Varney? Well, we'll see what we can do. For the moment, though, I suggest you hold your horses, Mark, and listen to me. Certain new evidence has come to light that puts an entirely different complexion on the Jason Fox killing."

"Oh? What's that, then?"

Banks jerked his head toward the door. "We've just had a long chat with Mr. Campbell and Mr. Robertson, and they've told us some very interesting things."

"Like what?"

"Like the truth about what you did to Jason Fox."

"I don't know what you're talking about."

"Oh, come on, Mark, surely you can do much better than that?"

"I'm not saying a word."

"Listen to me, then. According to your brother-in-law, Mr. Campbell, an old mate of yours from the Cloth Ears days, the two of you were commissioned by Neville Motcombe to get rid of Jason Fox. Jason had become a major risk in a heroin deal you were planning, and a serious threat to Motcombe's power. Motcombe couldn't get any of his own members to do it because Jason was too popular with them. Instead, he got two of the people who were already involved in the drug deal—one from each side, so to speak—two people who also stood to gain a lot. I should imagine Devon wanted one or two of his own lads along just to make sure you did what you agreed, didn't he? From what I hear, he's not the kind of bloke to take undue risks. How am I doing so far?"

Wood's eyes widened. "You know about Devon? Jesus Christ, does he know about this? Does he know I'm here? Have Wes and Frankie been talking to him? Shit, if Devon thinks I'm talking to the coppers, he'll fucking kill me."

Banks ignored him. "When Scattered Dreams played at the Jubilee, it gave you the perfect opportunity. Jason was going to be in Eastvale anyway—he had a football match in the afternoon—so you told him you were coming up and that the two of you could go see the band. Maybe it would be a chance to settle your differences and talk a bit of business, try to save the partnership somehow. I'd imagine you were compliant, more than willing to make compromises. You knew Scattered Dreams weren't Jason's cup of tea, but suggested he might like to broaden his horizons a bit. Who knows, maybe you promised to go to the next Celtic Warrior concert if he gave your lot a try. Jason had been to the Jubilee before, and he had mentioned that a couple of Pakistani youths went there on a fairly regular basis. I'm only guessing at this part, but I think he'd already chucked a brick through one of their windows, and he'd said he was looking for trouble with them. Perfect for you, if something like that happened in public, wasn't it? A bonus. As long as it was just a minor incident, enough to draw just a bit of attention.

"Anyway, according to Mr. Campbell, you accompanied Jason toward the ginnel, where he and Mr. Robertson were waiting at the other end to render any necessary assistance. According to them, you whacked Jason on the back of the head with the bottle a couple of times, and he went down. After that, you managed to kick him to death all by yourself. They didn't have to do a thing. And that, Mark, with two eyewitnesses to testify against you, makes it murder."

Wood turned pale. "That's not true," he said. "It didn't happen like that at all. They're lying."

Banks leaned forward. "What didn't happen like what, Mark?"

"It was like I said. There was just me and Jason. We got into a fight. He slagged off Sheri and Connor. I didn't mean for him to die."

Banks shook his head. "I'm afraid that story's gone right down the toilet now, Mark, along with all your other stories. Let me see if I can get them right." He began counting them off on his fingers, looking toward Ken Blackstone, who nodded at each one. "First, you weren't anywhere near Eastvale the night Jason got killed. Second, you were at the Jubilee but you never went anywhere near the ginnel. Third, you *were* there and you saw George Mahmood and his mates kill Jason. And, fourth, you killed him yourself in a fair fight. How am I doing so far?"

Wood licked his lips and shifted in his chair.

"Problem is, Mark," Banks went on, "you're a liar. The only version we have any independent corroboration of is the one I just put to you, the one Mr. Campbell told us about. So it looks as if that's the way it's going to go down now." He paused, then went on. "After this interview, DI Blackstone and I will be having a word with Crown Prosecution Service about changing the charges from manslaughter to murder. That carries a much longer jail sentence, as I'm sure you know."

"You can't be serious? You can't believe those bastards."

"Why not? I certainly can't believe *you*. Look at your track record, Mark. No, I'm afraid this is the end of the line for you. You get charged with murder now, and you don't get out of jail for a long, long time. In fact, by the time you get out, your wife will have run off with another bloke long since, and your kid will have grown up and forgotten you. In the meantime, you'll be fending off the arse-bandits in Wormwood Scrubs or Strangeways. And that's *if* you last that long. I suspect both Devon and Neville Motcombe have long reaches."

Wood seemed to shrivel, to draw in on himself like a bank of ashes collapsing. Banks could tell he was trapped. He knew lies wouldn't save him now, but he didn't know the best course of action. Time to tell him, time to give him a ray of hope. After pulling the carpet from under him, give him a foam mattress to land on.

"There's only one way out for you, Mark," he said.

"What's that?" Mark's voice was no louder than a whisper.

"The truth. Right from the top."

"How will that help?"

"I'm not saying it'll get you off scot-free. Nothing will do that. We don't have the power to make deals with criminals, reduce their sentences in exchange for information. That only happens on American TV shows. But I can guarantee it'll make things easier for you."

Wood chewed on his knuckles for a few seconds, then said, "I need protection. They'll kill me. My family, too."

"We can help you with that, Mark. If you help us."

Mark rubbed his nose with the back of his hand. "I never meant to kill him," he said. "Honest, I didn't. It was those two." He was close to tears.

"Who?"

"Frankie and Wes."

"What happened, Mark? Right from the beginning."

Banks took out his cigarettes and offered Mark one. He took it with a shaking hand. "All right," he said. "But what guarantee have I got that things will go easier for me if I tell you the truth? What are you offering me?"

"You've got my word," said Banks.

"For what?"

"That you and your family will be protected and that your co-operation will be considered."

"I want relocation for me and Sheri," he said. "And new identities. The Witness Protection Program. That's what I want."

"I've already told you, this isn't America, Mark. We don't do things that way in England. Look, like I said, I'm not telling you you're going to walk out of here a free man. You're not. One way or another, you'll serve some time. What I'm saying is that if you give us what we want, the charge can remain manslaughter, not murder."

"It doesn't sound like that good a deal to me."

"Well, it is," Ken Blackstone chipped in. "The difference is between, say, twenty-five years in a very nasty place—where you'll be vulnerable to anyone Devon or Motcombe cares to send along—and maybe five in minimum-security prison. Protected environment. Telly and conjugal visits thrown in." He glanced at Banks, who nodded. "Your choice, Mark. It's as simple as that."

Wood looked between the two of them and his gaze finally settled on Banks again. "What about Sheri and Connor?"

"We'll take care of them, make sure they're safe," said Banks. "You have my word. What about it?"

Wood looked at Blackstone again, who assured him that Banks was right, then he rested back in his chair and said, "All right. Okay. Neville Motcombe approached me several weeks ago and said he knew about my record for drugs offenses. At first I didn't know what he was getting at, then it became clear that he'd made a contact for getting his hands on some pretty large amounts of heroin through Turkey at a rock-bottom price, and he hadn't a clue what to do about it. Drugs just weren't part of his gig, but he saw a way to make a lot of money and fuck up the 'niggers' in the bargain, as he put it. He really does talk like that. Makes you sick. Anyway, he found out about my drug bust and decided I was to be the go-between."

"What was in it for you?"

"Something in the region of fifty thousand quid over a period of a few months, if all went well. Maybe more in the future, if the supply didn't dry up." He leaned forward and gripped the sides of the chair. "Look, you can judge me all you like, but have you any idea what that would have meant to Sheri and me? It would have got us out of that fucking prefab, for a start, and it would have given me a good chance at expanding the business, buying some up-to-date equipment, making something out of it. And all I had to do was play go-between for Motcombe and Devon." He laughed. "It was a bit of a joke on Motcombe, too. He didn't know Sheri's Jamaican and that his money would actually be going to help one of the people he wanted to destroy."

"Didn't that bother you, Mark? That he was intending to cause so much suffering in the West Indian community?"

"That was just a load of bollocks he came up with for Jason's benefit. He was after profits, pure and simple."

"Takes one to know one?"

"Something like that. Anyway, once you get heroin out on the streets, there's no telling what color your buyers will be, is there? There's no color bar on H. Even Jason knew that. Like I said, I thought it was funny that Sheri and Connor were going to get some benefit from this."

Banks shook his head. "So you agreed?"

Wood nodded. "Under Motcombe's instructions, I met with Wes, then with Devon. They never met Neville, didn't know who he was. I called him Mr. H. Anyway, we talked about prices, delivery schedules, methods of getting the stuff into the country, the lot. Then Devon said he'd think about it. A few days later he got in touch with me through Wes and told me to let Mr. H know we were in business. I suppose Motcombe got in touch with his blokes in Turkey—I didn't have anything to do with that end of the operation—and they set things in motion. There were huge profits in it for everyone. Devon wouldn't stop at Leeds—he'd be shifting stuff to Bradford, Sheffield, Manchester, Birmingham, you name it. Somehow or other, that seemed to resolve the problems on both sides. Motcombe's about dealing with darkies and Devon's about dealing with a whitey like me." Mark snorted. "Great healer of race relations, greed, isn't it?"

"And where does Jason come in?"

"Motcombe made a big mistake there. I could have told him, but he didn't ask. He seemed to think Jason would just love the idea. I mean, I don't think they'd ever talked about drugs or anything other than league business before. But Jason was straight. Even with Motcombe's justification, he wouldn't go for it. Motcombe got worried that Jason would spread the word among his colleagues in the movement and they'd chuck him out and put Jason in charge instead. I suppose you know neo-Nazis aren't really supposed to be into drugs?"

Banks nodded.

"Then there was the matter of the money to be made. Anyway, Motcombe got paranoid, especially as Jason had gained a lot of respect in the movement and people looked up to him for guidance and leadership. Jason was fast becoming a loose cannon on the deck. So Motcombe decided things would be better all around with Jason out of the way. He knew I was desperate for the money, and he also knew me and Jason didn't get along, so he asked me if I could arrange for the Jamaicans to do away with him. That way, he said, if they happened to get caught, it'd only be two less 'niggers' to worry about. You have to give the guy credit, at least he's consistent. I didn't want to do it. I mean, I'm no killer. I know Jason and me had our problems, but I didn't want to see him dead. You have to believe that. I had no choice."

"What happened?" Banks asked.

Mark ran his hand over his head. "Like Motcombe asked, I talked to Wes and I told him Jason was involved in the Turkish end of the deal and that he was planning to rip Devon off. I also said he turned out to be a racist bastard, a member of some loony fringe group. Well, I couldn't tell him the truth, could I? I had to make something up pretty quick, and it had to cover whatever publicity might come about when you found out who Jason was. Wes went back to Devon, who ordered it done. Just like that. No questions asked. And he also stipulated that I had to be in it with them. A sort of test of faith, I suppose. I didn't want to do it. I just didn't have any fucking choice."

"There's always a choice, Mark."

"Right. Sure. Easy for you to say that. It came down to me over Jason. Sheri and Connor over Jason. What would you have done? Like I said, Jason and me weren't close, and the bastard did get on my nerves with all that Nazi shit."

"Who came up with the plan?"

"That was down to me. You know the rest. Motcombe wanted it done out of the way. I mean, he knew you'd find out who the victim was eventually, and what organization he belonged to, but he needed time to get his files out of Jason's house. He sent two of his blokes to do that. Anyway, Scattered Dreams were playing in Eastvale and Jason had mentioned possible trouble with some Pakistani kids who went there. Told me he'd already chucked a brick through one of their windows. It couldn't have been better."

"What about the actual killing? How did it happen?"

Wood swallowed. "Frankie and Wes were waiting at the other end of the ginnel, as we'd arranged, and when I hit Jason with the bottle they came forward and started booting him. I kicked him a couple of times, to make it look like I was with them all the way. But only a couple of times. And not very hard. He—" Wood stopped for a moment and put his head in his hands. "Christ, he *begged* us to stop. I just thought about Connor and the damp walls and the yobs that taunt Sheri, call her a black bitch and threaten to gang-bang her every time she goes to the shops. I didn't think about Jason lying there till it was too late. You have to believe me, I didn't mean to kill him. It was Wes and Frankie. They're fucking maniacs. They'd been out in the van smoking crack."

"All right, Mark," said Banks. "Calm down. Tell me, what happened when we first arrested you? Why did you change your story?"

Mark shifted in his chair. "Well, the evidence. It was getting pretty strong against me. I was up shit creek. So when Varney took me aside, I phoned Motcombe and basically explained the situation."

"What did he say?"

"To tell you it was just a fight between the two of us, to leave him out of it, and he'd see I got the best legal help available. He'd also take care of Sheri and Connor financially while I was inside, if it came to that. What a laugh, Motcombe taking care of a black woman and a mixed-race kid."

"But he didn't know that."

"No. And I didn't tell him."

"Have you talked to him from jail?"

"A couple of times. But even then he seemed very nervous."

"What did you talk about?"

"Getting my story right when it came to court."

"Did you talk to Devon?"

"No. He's keeping a low profile. I phoned my brother-in-law, though, Wes."

"What did you talk to him about?"

"I told him who Mr. H was, where he lived. Just in case something went wrong and Motcombe didn't keep up his end of the bargain. You know, like maybe when he *did* find out Sheri's black and all, then he wouldn't help them. I needed some sort of insurance."

"Okay, Mark, I need to know just one more thing before we start taking fresh statements and making this all official."

"Yes?"

"Will you testify that Neville Motcombe instigated this conspiracy to murder Jason Fox?"

Wood's lips curled. "Motcombe? Bloody right I will. No way that bastard's going to get away with it."

"And Devon?"

Mark looked away. "I don't know. That's different. I'd need some sort—"

"We'll see you and family are protected, Mark, like I told you earlier."

"I'll think about it. Okay?"

"Okay." Banks smiled. "I think that just about wraps it up for now. Thanks, Mark, you've been a great help."

"What happens to me now?"

"You make your official statement, then you go back to Armley. Eventually, there'll be committal proceedings and a trial, but we'll cross those bridges when we get to them. In the meantime, we'll make sure you're protected." Banks looked at his watch. Just after three-thirty. Then he turned to Ken Blackstone. "For the moment, though, I think it's about time we paid Mr. Motcombe another visit."

IV

Leaving one of Blackstone's most trusted DCs to take Mark Wood's official statement, Banks and Blackstone set off in the Cavalier for Motcombe's house. Most of the journey, they talked about getting enough evidence together for the CPS to take on Motcombe.

"I'm still not sure about this," Banks said, driving along through Pudsey. "I can't help feeling I'm jumping the gun. How bloody long's Motcombe likely to get for conspiracy to commit murder? That's assuming we can prove it. Giles Varney will whittle it down to conspiracy to assault, if he's got any brains. We might be better off leaving him to the Drugs Squad. He'd get longer for dealing heroin. And I promised Craig McKeracher I'd wait till I had something really solid before I moved in."

Ken Blackstone shook his head. "At this point, I don't think we have much choice. We've got evidence we have to act on. Mark Wood has actually *named* Motcombe as one of the blokes who requested Jason Fox's murder. Now Wood's blurted it all out, we *have* to go ahead. I don't think he'll get such a light sentence. And this way we also get Wes and Frankie in the bargain, and maybe even Devon, too. That'd be a real plus."

"Maybe so," said Banks. "I hope you're right."

"Besides," Blackstone added, "I'd say we're best getting Motcombe off the streets as soon as possible. And none of what we're doing blows Craig McKeracher's cover. What we've got all came from Mark Wood."

Banks turned down the hill to Motcombe's house and they got out of the car. The sky was clear and the countryside shone green and gold and silver. A chill wind from the valley whistled around their ears as they stood and knocked at the front door.

No answer.

"What's that noise?" Blackstone asked.

Straining his ears, Banks could detect a faint whining above the sound of the wind. "Sounds like an electric drill or something. He must be down in the workshop. That's why he can't hear us."

"Let's try the back."

They walked around to the back of the house, which overlooked the valley and parkland. The sound of the drill was louder now.

Banks hammered on the back door. Still nothing. Just on the off chance, he tried the doorknob. It opened.

"Mr. Motcombe!" he called out as the two of them walked down the stairs to the workshop. "We're coming in." He began to feel a slight shiver of trepidation. It looked dark at the bottom, and they could be walking into a trap. Motcombe could have a Kalishnikov or an Uzi with him. He might be hiding in a dark corner ready to start blasting away at them.

But still they advanced slowly toward where the sound was coming from. Then Banks noticed something odd. The high-pitched whine the drill was making hadn't changed the entire time they'd been there. Surely if Motcombe was working on something and really couldn't hear them, there would be variations in the pitch of the drill—when he stuck it into a piece of wood, for example. And if he was making so much noise when he worked, he would hardly leave the back door unlocked so that anyone could walk in, would he? Banks felt the back of his neck tingle.

At last, they approached the workroom and pushed the door open slowly on the brightly lit room.

Motcombe was there all right.

His body hung at an awkward angle, naked to the waist, his polo-neck tunic hanging in shreds around his hips as if it had been ripped or cut off. His left wrist had been wedged in a vise, which had been tightened until the bones cracked and poked through the flesh. Blood caked the oiled metal. The smell of blood and sweat mixed with iron filings, shaved wood and linseed oil. And cordite. The room felt crowded, claustrophobic, even with only the two of them there. Three, if you counted the dead man.

The drill lay on the workbench. Banks didn't want to touch it, but he wanted the sound to stop. He went over to the wall and pulled out the plug, using a handkerchief carefully, and hoping he wasn't smudging any valuable prints. Old habits die hard. Somehow, he doubted that there would be any. People who do things like this don't leave fingerprints.

The scene was a gruesome one. More so because of the unnaturally bright lights that Motcombe had rigged up so he could see clearly what he was working on. What Banks at first took to be bullet holes in Motcombe's chest and stomach turned out, on further examination, to be spots where the drill had been inserted. When the bit stopped spinning, he could see it was clogged with blood and tissue.

Motcombe's right arm was practically in shreds, striped with lacerations, patches of skin hanging off as if he'd been flayed. Someone had obviously shredded the flesh with a saw, cutting deep into the muscle and bone. Banks noticed the blood and chips of bone on the edge of a circular saw that lay on the floor beside the body.

The coup de grâce looked like two gunshot wounds to the head, one through the left eye and the other in the middle of the temple, both leaving large exit wounds.

"Well, Ken," said Banks finally, backing away from the scene, "I can't say I envy you sorting this little lot out."

"No," said Blackstone, visibly pale. "Let's get outside. I don't think I can stand being in here much longer."

They stood outside the back door overlooking the valley and the peaceful village of Tong in the distance. Three large crows circled high in the blue air. Banks lit a cigarette to take the taste and smell of the workshop out of his mouth. "Want to call it in?" he asked.

"Yes. Just give me a minute."

"What do you think?"

Blackstone took a deep breath before answering. "You probably know as well as I do, Alan," he said. "Either Wes Campbell or Frankie Robertson phoned Devon the minute they saw Mark Wood at Millgarth. That was what?—over four hours ago now. This pisses Devon off mightily, and he sends a couple of lads over right away to help him vent his rage. You don't get far in Devon's business unless you're seen to act, and to act *fast*. He relies heavily on pure fear. Who knows, maybe he's even made a down payment to Motcombe and wants his money back, too? So they either torture him to find out where the money is, or they do it for fun, just to teach him a lesson. Then they execute him. Bang, bang."

Banks nodded. "Either that or they decided they didn't like Mr. H's politics when Mark told them who he really was."

"It's Devon's style, Alan," Blackstone went on. "Two head shots with a thirty-eight, by the looks of it. Remember those murders I told you about in New York, Toronto, Chapeltown?"

"Uh-huh."

"Same MO. Torture and two head shots. It still doesn't help us prove anything. I don't suppose anyone can tie Devon to the scene. He'll have an alibi you can't break, and there'll never be any trace of a murder weapon."

"We've still got Mark Wood to use against him."

"If he doesn't suddenly lose his memory the minute he

hears about what happened to Motcombe. I probably would if I were him."

"And don't forget Campbell and Robertson. You've got them, too. They might not be quite as tough as they seem once you put the pressure on. Especially if they're deprived of their narcotic sustenance. And I'll bet you've got records of any telephone calls they made from Millgarth."

Blackstone nodded and looked around, then he sighed. "Well, we'd better set things in motion. Can I use your mobile?"

"Be my guest."

They walked around to Banks's car at the front of the house and Banks handed him the phone. Blackstone tapped in the numbers, gave the details and requested more police, a murder van and a SOCO team.

"I'll tell you something," he said when he'd finished. "Your chief constable isn't going to like it, is he? Remember the song and dance he made in the paper about solving the murder, keeping race out of it?"

"Bugger Jimmy Riddle," said Banks. "This isn't a matter of race, it's drugs and greed. Anyway, they're West Yorkshire's Jamaicans, not ours. And I wasn't even here."

"What do you think now?" Blackstone asked, handing Banks the phone. "Still want to come and work for West Yorkshire?"

Banks stubbed out his cigarette on the wall and put the butt in his pocket to avoid contaminating the scene. "I don't know, Ken. I really don't know. I might not have much choice, might I? Anyway, right now, I think I'd better make myself scarce before the troops arrive and all hell breaks loose. You'll be okay?"

"I'll be fine. I'll catch a lift back to Millgarth from one of the patrol cars. Go. Go."

Banks shook Blackstone's hand. "Thanks, Ken. I'd be interested to hear you tell them why you're here and how you got here, but I really can't stay."

"I'll tell them I got the bus," said Blackstone. "Now be a good lad, Alan, and bugger off back to Eastvale. I think I hear the sound of sirens."

Banks got in his car. He couldn't hear sirens, but the sound of Neville Motcombe's electric drill still whined in his ears.

A mile or so down the road, the first patrol cars passed him, lights and sirens going. No hurry, Banks thought. No hurry at all. He lit another cigarette and switched on the tape player. Robert Louis Stevenson, sung by Bryn Terfel:

Now when day dawns on the brow of the moorland,
Lone stands the house, and the chimney-stone is cold.
Lone let it stand, now the friends are all departed,
The kind hearts, the true hearts, that loved the place of old.

Banks looked at his watch. Just gone half past four. Hard to believe, but they had hardly been half an hour at Motcombe's house. He still had plenty of time to go and pick up Tracy for the weekend, even with the rush-hour traffic. Plenty of time.

Here is a chilling excerpt from
Peter Robinson's Inspector Banks novel

WHEN THE MUSIC'S OVER

Coming Summer 2016

PROLOGUE

They threw the naked girl out of the van on the darkest stretch of road. First she felt the wind whip as one of them slid open the door, then she was in free fall, tumbling through space. Her hip bounced on the hard road surface and she felt something crack. Then she hit damp grass and rolled into a ditch full of stagnant water. She could hear their laughter and whooping over the loud music, but soon even the music had faded into the distance and there was nothing left but silence.

She lay in the ditch winded, her hip hurting, head spinning, and tried to take stock of her situation. She had no idea where she was. Somewhere in the countryside, obviously, miles from civilization. She struggled to push herself up out of the foul, muddy water. As soon as she moved, she gasped at the pain, which shot first through her hip, then seemed to diffuse through every atom of her body, as if someone were pushing red-hot needles into her flesh. The stuff they'd given her back in the van was wearing off, the last couple of hours fading like a dream as she awoke into pain, but even as it faded it rushed through her when she least expected it, distorting her senses. There was a whooshing sound in her ears, like big waves crashing, and her vision was blurry.

She had also cut her shoulder on something, a broken bottle in the ditch, perhaps, and she became aware of other cuts and bruises as the pain started to focus on more specific parts of her body. She tried to clean the mud and blood off her skin as best she could with water from the ditch, but it was too dirty, and she only succeeded in spreading the filth all over her body. She felt that she resembled some primeval creature crawling out of the slime.

She limped into the darkness and stumbled in the direction from which the van had traveled. There was nothing she could do about her nakedness except hope someone decent came along, someone who would wrap her in a blanket and take her to the hospital. Being naked and muddy were the least of her problems. Her brain wasn't working properly, for a start. The road surface seemed to be undulating beneath her, and the overhanging trees were assuming threatening shapes. She shook her head to try to make it all go away, but that only made things worse. She felt dizzy and had to support herself against a tree trunk for a moment. The bark was pulsing under her fingers like the dry scaly skin of a reptile. Her hip hurt so much that she was certain it was broken. And she felt terribly torn up inside. She was certain she was bleeding internally. She needed a doctor. He would give her painkillers, maybe even morphine. Then her pain would disappear and she would drift on warm soft pillows without a care in the world. But they would want to take swabs and samples. They'd call the police and then she would really be in trouble. The police wouldn't believe her. They never believed people like her. Besides, in her experience, such kindness was unlikely. No Good Samaritan would come along and give a lift to a naked girl covered in mud. That wasn't what the sort of people she knew did with naked girls. It wasn't the kind of thing that happened in her life.

It was late July, but a long week of rain had just ended. The night was muggy, and a gauzy mist hung over the dark landscape. No street lamps, only the hazy light of a haloed half-moon. Somewhere in the field beyond the drystone wall a sheep bleated, and she thought she could see a lone light shining in a farmhouse upper window. Should she head for that? Would they help her? There was the ditch and a stone wall topped with barbed wire in her way, but there might be an entrance farther ahead. If she found a gate, she decided, or a gap in the wall, that's what she would do. Head over the field toward the light.

How late was it? Or how early? She had no phone or watch. She couldn't remember how long she had been in the van. Surely dawn couldn't be far off. The sun rose early these days. But everything was still dark, and the trees and walls were silhouettes of scarecrows and demons closing in on her. The road was narrow, and there was no pavement, so she walked on the hard surface. Stones dug into the soles of her feet with almost every step. If a car came she would have plenty of warning. She would hear it and see its headlights from far away. If a car came . . .

She hadn't been walking for more than ten or fifteen minutes when she thought she heard the distant drone of an engine and saw lights playing between the shadows and trees ahead, refracted in the mist down the winding road. A car! It was traveling in the opposite direction she was walking, the same direction the van had been heading, but that didn't matter. As the car came closer, she at least had enough sense to stand back, near the edge of the ditch, so it wouldn't hit her by accident. She threw away her dignity and waved her arms in the air. The headlights dazzled her, and the small van shot straight past. She watched it in despair, then she saw it stop with a screeching of rubber about a hundred yards ahead. She couldn't make out what sort of van it was. The engine purred and the red brake lights glowed like a demon's eyes in the mist. Shaking off the feeling of apprehension that came over her, she started hobbling toward the van as quickly as she could.

ONE

Detective Superintendent Alan Banks stood in front of the mirror in the gents and studied his reflection. Not bad, he thought, tightening his mauve-and-gold-striped tie so that it didn't look as if the top button of his shirt was undone, which it always was. He couldn't stand that claustrophobic feeling he got when both button and tie pressed on his Adam's apple. There was no dandruff on the collar or shoulders of his suit jacket, and his dark hair was neatly cropped, showing a hint of gray, like a scattering of ash, around the temples. He had no shaving cuts, no shred of tissue hanging off his chin, and he wore just a faint hint of classic Old Spice aftershave. He straightened his shoulders and spine, noting that there were no bulges in his jacket pockets to spoil the line of his new suit. His wallet and warrant card were all he carried, and both were slim. He fastened the middle button, so the jacket hung just right, and decided he was ready to face the world.

He glanced at his watch. The meeting was due to begin at nine sharp, and it was about three minutes to. He left the gents and took the stairs two at a time up to the conference room on the top floor of the old mock-Tudor building. Timing was an issue. Banks didn't want to be the first to arrive, but he didn't want to be the last, either. As it happened, he ended up somewhere in the middle. Detective Chief Superintendent Gervaise and Assistant Chief Constable McLaughlin stood outside the room chatting as they waited outside. Banks could see through the open door that some people were already seated.

"Alan," said McLaughlin. "New duties not proving too much of a burden, I hope?"

Banks's promotion to detective superintendent had come through a short while ago—a bloody miracle in this day and age, or so he had been told—and he had spent the last few weeks learning the ropes. "Not at all, sir," he said. "I had no idea how much I was getting away with before."

Gervaise and McLaughlin laughed. "Welcome to the real world," said the latter. "Shall we go in?"

McLaughlin went ahead. Banks turned to Gervaise and whispered, "Any idea what this is about?"

She gave a quick shake of her head. "Very hush-hush," she said. "Rumor has it that the chief constable himself is going to be here."

"Not crime stats or more budget cuts, then?"

Gervaise smiled. "Somehow, I doubt it."

The conference room was sparsely furnished, nothing but an oval table, tubular chairs and institutional cream walls. They took their seats around the table, and a few minutes later Chief Constable Frank Sampson—soon, it was whispered, to be *Sir* Frank Sampson—did indeed arrive. When he was followed shortly by the new police and crime commissioner, Margaret Bingham, Banks knew that something important must be brewing.

But the last person to arrive, a minute or so after everyone else, was the biggest surprise of all.

Dirty Dick Burgess was now some sort of deputy director or special agent at the National Crime Agency. More commonly known as the British FBI, the NCA dealt mostly with organized crime and border security, but it also worked against cyber crime and the sexual exploitation and abuse of children and young people. Burgess flipped Banks a wink before sitting down. Even he was wearing a suit and a crisp white shirt instead of his trademark scuffed leather jacket, though he could have done with a shave and a haircut, and he had foregone the tie completely. Clearly the British FBI didn't bother dressing up for a visit to the provinces.

There were eight people seated around the table when the chief constable opened proceedings by introducing them all to one another. One of the people Banks didn't know, by either name or sight, was the lawyer from the Crown Prosecution Service. Her name was Janine Francis, and she was not one of the CPS lawyers that he usually dealt with. The eighth person, still only vaguely familiar to Banks, was the county force's new media liaison officer, Adrian Moss, an ex-advertising agency up-and-comer and political spin doctor with a flowered tie, fresh-scrubbed youthful appearance and a breezy, confident manner. A motley crew, indeed, Banks thought, as he tried to imagine why they might all have been brought together under one roof. It had to be something big.

"I know some of you must be wondering what all this is about," said the chief constable, "so I'll make it simple and get straight to the point. I assume you're all familiar with Operation Yewtree and its investigations into sexual abuse, predominantly against children and primarily by media personalities? In the wake of the Jimmy Savile business and the successful convictions of Rolf Harris, Gary Glitter, Dave Lee Travis and Max Clifford, among others, I'm sure you can imagine that a lot of past victims have been encouraged to come into the open over the matter of historical sexual abuse."

Historical abuse. The words brought about an immediate sinking feeling in Banks's gut. A function of the political correctness of the times, historical abuse investigations were intended to right the wrongs of the past and to send the message that no matter how many years had gone by, if enough people cried foul, someone would be sent off. They were also a way of appeasing the victims of such crimes, of giving them a voice some of them had been seeking for years, and perhaps even that much overused word "closure," both things of which Banks approved in principle. In practice, however, it often turned out to be a different matter, a witch hunt where victims were often disappointed, and the reputations of innocent people sometimes went down in tatters. No detective in his right mind wanted to be part of a historical abuse investigation. Banks checked the faces of the others. Their expressions gave away nothing. Was he the only one who thought this way? Did it show?

"I'd like to think we've all learned a thing or two from the way these incidents have been handled over the past couple of years," the CC went on, "and one of the things we should have learned by now is to keep things close to our chests. I ask you all not to speak of what's said in here to anyone outside this office. Not even to your colleagues. Adrian."

Moss glanced from face to face. "Yes," he said. "No doubt you all know there's no way we can keep this from the media forever. They'll get hold of it eventually, if they haven't already. It's my job to make sure that nothing gets said to them by anyone involved unless it goes through me first. Am I clear?"

He was obviously enjoying his temporary power over such an eminent gathering, Banks could tell from the triumphant expression on his face and the undertones of evangelistic delivery in his speech. And Banks didn't even know what "this" was yet.

"Mistakes have been made in the past," Moss went on. "That business with the BBC cameras in position to film the raid on Cliff Richards's home before Sir Cliff knew about the search himself, for example—and we don't want any of that sort of behavior dogging our footsteps. As you know, the investigation into Sir Cliff was dropped, and Paul Gambaccini had some harsh words to say about the way he was treated by the police. We've ended up with egg on our faces often enough, and we have to make sure that doesn't happen this time. When the media do come knocking, as they will, we want everything calm and by the book. Nothing they can get between their teeth and run with. Naturally, celebrities are of interest to them, and celebrity misdeeds are manna for them. We not only have to prosecute this, but we need to be seen prosecuting it. It won't take them long to gets their nibs sharpened. I can tell you now, there's a media shit storm due in the near future. My job, ladies and gentleman, is to manage the flow of information, and to do that I will need the cooperation of all of you. Everything goes through the press office. Is that clear?" He had a sheen of sweat on his forehead as he scanned the room. Most of those present beamed back at him. Moss was one of the chief constable's and the police commissioner's golden boys. Now that the brass seemed far more concerned with publicity and image, people like him were more important to them than detectives, Banks thought. Burgess was the only one to appear unimpressed, the beginnings of that characteristic cynical, seen-it-all smile appearing in the twist of his lips.

"Thank you, Adrian," said the chief constable. "Now we all know where we stand, let's get down to brass tacks. You are all here because from now on you're going to be working together in one capacity or another on the same case. Assistant Chief Constable McLaughlin will enlighten you."

Red Ron cleared his throat and shuffled his papers. "You're here because we're going to be conducting an investigation into Danny Caxton," he said, pausing for a moment to let the name sink in.

Danny Caxton, thought Banks. Shit. Celebrity, personality, presenter before presenters had even been invented. Household name. The Man with the Big Smile. Caxton had started his career in the late fifties with a few pop hits. He wasn't a rock and roller, more of a crooner, a part of the Jim Reeves, Val Doonican and Matt Monroe crowd. Perhaps the girls didn't scream at him the same way they did for Elvis or the Beatles, but plenty drooled over him as their parents had drooled over Johnnie Ray or Frank Sinatra. From what Banks could remember, Caxton obviously had good business sense and he must have realized early on that a career in pop balladry doesn't last for ever. In the early sixties, he started to diversify. He had always had good comic timing and a knack for impersonating famous people, in addition to having the personality of an affable host. He hosted variety shows, both live around the country and on television, cut the tapes at supermarket openings, judged beauty contests and quickly became the regular host of a popular talent-spotting program called Do Your Own Thing! which lasted well into the late eighties. That was his catchphrase, too: "Do your own thing." Spoken with a tongue-in-cheek knowingness that tipped a wink toward its hippie origins. Even during the sixties and seventies he had the occasional novelty hit record, and he made a couple of dreadful swinging sixties films when he was already too old and square for such roles. He would have known Jimmy Savile, Banks realized. They were of the same generation. Caxton went from strength to strength: summer seasons, Christmas pantomimes, a successful West End musical comedy. He had married a pop singer at some point, Banks remembered, and there had been an acrimonious and public divorce not long after. His career had slowed down in the early nineties, but he still appeared occasionally as a guest on chat shows and had even hosted the odd Christmas variety special in the noughties.

"I'm surprised to hear he's still alive," said Banks.

"Very much so," said McLaughlin. "At eighty-five years of age."

"And what does the CPS think?" Banks asked, glancing at the lawyer. He knew there had been some confusion in the Savile business as to whether the CPS hadn't gone ahead with a prosecution because he was too old and infirm, or because they thought the police had insufficient evidence. Banks knew the CPS had already been criticized for not acting sooner over Sir Cyril Smith, the Rochdale MP, who had been abusing young boys for years until his death in 2010. Now, no doubt, they were eager to show the public they were taking the lead on child sexual abuse and exploitation.

"He's fair game as far as we're concerned," Janine Francis answered.

"And when did the offence take place, sir?" Banks asked Red Ron.

"Summer 1967."

Danny Caxton was almost at the height of his success by 1967, Banks remembered. Everyone knew who he was. He was still a handsome devil, too, or so hundreds of mums thought. Christ, even Banks's own mother had sat fixated in front of the screen drooling over him while his father snorted and Banks disappeared upstairs to listen to his Rolling Stones and Who records.

"I'll give you a brief outline," McLaughlin went on. "There's a useful bio and a summary of events so far in the folder before you. Take it away and study it later. He certainly had an eventful sort of early life. Overcame a lot of adversity. He was born in Warsaw in 1930. His parents saw the writing on the wall and got Danny and his brothers and sisters out in 1933. They got split up, and he grew up with distant relatives in Heckmondwike."

"That could have a serious effect on a person's mental health," said Banks. "I mean, just trying to pronounce it."

There was a brief ripple of laughter, then DCS Gervaise said, "Be careful, Alan. My dad came from Heckmondwike. Anyway, it wouldn't be too hard. Just omit the vowels and it'd be perfect in Polish."

McLaughlin waited for the laughter to die down, then went on. "For the moment, I want you to consider the following. The complainant in this case is a woman called Linda Palmer. She was fourteen years old at the time of the alleged assault."

Banks had heard of Linda Palmer. She was a poet, lived locally, had been written up in the paper once or twice. Been on BBC2 and Radio 4. Won awards. "The poet?" he said.

"One and the same. She first called Childline, and they told her to get in touch with us."

"And why do we believe her?" asked Gervaise.

"Same reason we believe any claim of historical abuse," said McLaughlin. "Her story's convincing, and we hope it will be even more so after you have all finished your tasks." He glanced toward Janine Francis. "The CPS has given a green light to continue with this, even on what little we have so far. That's why what Mr. Moss said about managing the media is so important. We don't want to draw flack the way some other county forces have done. On the other hand, we don't want to appear to be operating in secret. And we know how difficult it is to keep a low profile with a case of this magnitude. You'll just have to do your best for as long as you can."

"What are the facts?" Banks asked. "Briefly."

"That's what we want you to find out, Alan. You'll be conducting the initial interview with Linda Palmer. You'll also be interviewing Danny Caxton. Mr. Burgess here will be monitoring the case nationwide."

"Surely it would be protocol to send a female officer to interview Linda Palmer?" asked Banks.

"Not necessarily," said McLaughlin. "The detective she talked to when she first called in is a female, a DI MacDonald, and she asked the same question, but Ms. Palmer said she didn't care as long as it was someone who would believe her. She doesn't want any special treatment. That having been said, you have three extremely competent female officers on your team."

"What did Linda Palmer accuse Caxton of doing, exactly?" Banks asked.

"According to Ms. Palmer, Danny Caxton raped her."

"And she's just come out with this story?"

McLaughlin sighed and glanced at the police and crime commissioner.

"That's irrelevant," Margaret Bingham said. "The reasons women have for coming forward so many years after a traumatic event are complex. It's not, at the moment, your job to question these motives, merely to ascertain their veracity."

"And how do we do that?" Banks asked.

"The way you usually do it," McLaughlin answered. "Use your

detective skills. We also have trained child protection officers who specialize in knowing the sort of details true victims are likely to remember, and whether they are telling the truth. If you have any doubts after you've talked to her, you're welcome to go over her statement with one of them, if you wish. And if it makes you feel any better, Ms. Palmer did report the incident shortly after it occurred in 1967."

"And what happened to that investigation?" Banks asked.

"That will be another aspect of the case for you to determine," said McLaughlin. "Clearly it was derailed at some point, for some reason, as Mr. Caxton wasn't brought to justice at the time, and he's never been charged with raping Linda Palmer or anything else since."

"Don't you think that might be because he never did anything?" asked Banks. "I mean . . . nearly fifty years ago . . . It's about as cold a case as you can get."

"I know," said McLaughlin, "and I sympathize, Alan. But some of Jimmy Savile's crimes went back further than that. We've got historical abuse going back to the early sixties and before."

"I get that you don't like it," Margaret Bingham interrupted. "But you'd better get used to it. All of you. We might have dropped the ball in the past, but not again. Not on my watch. There's going to be more and more cases of historical abuse coming up over the next few years. People who think they've got away with something forever. Men who think they've got away with something forever because of their fame or their wealth or their power. Or just because they're men. This was the brutal rape of an underage girl by a man of thirty-seven, and I expect you to go about it investigating it as you would if it had happened yesterday."

"That's not possible," said Banks.

"Oh? And why not, Superintendent Banks?"

"No physical evidence. Dodgy memories. Missing statements. With all due respect, ma'am," Banks went on, "you're a civilian. So is Mr. Moss. Most of the people you're talking to here are veterans of many investigations, and the fact of the matter is that you simply can't investigate a crime that happened almost fifty years ago in the same manner as you can investigate one that happened yesterday. All you have to go on is the accuser's statement. I understand all about cold cases solved by new DNA evidence. They're the ones that make the news, and I've seen New Tricks, but those are the exceptions. Do we even have any DNA in this case, for example?"

"I have no idea," said Margaret Bingham, clearly irritated by Banks's objections. "That's for you to determine. And I may be a civilian, as you say, but I am the police and crime commissioner, and I have every right to ask my officers for their best efforts. That's what I'm asking. You put as much time, effort, intelligence and investigative skills into this as you would into a sexual assault that happened yesterday. Believe me, you'll have all the resources you need at your disposal."

That was a good opening move on his part, Banks thought. Piss off the bosses and the crime commissioner at the first big meeting of the new job. But he'd never had much time for Margaret Bingham and her agendas. She and Adrian Moss would make a fine team. "Yes, ma'am," he muttered.

McLaughlin cleared his throat again. "Though the Met is technically in charge of Operation Yewtree, Mr. Burgess here from the NCA will be bringing his expertise of the Child Exploitation and Online Protection command to bear on the case."

Burgess tipped his hand in a mock salute. "At your service," he said.

"What will your role be?" Banks asked.

"Co-coordinating between you and the Met, mostly," said Burgess. "I'll be trying to make sure that the left hand knows what the right hand is doing. The case is unwieldy enough already. Linda Palmer was living with her parents in Leeds in 1967, but the assault took place in Blackpool. She now lives near Eastvale, a village called Minton-on-Swain, and Danny Caxton lives out on the coast, as you probably know already, though he lived in West Yorkshire for some years. In Otley. If we involved all the local forces—not to mention the rest that will soon come into play as the complaints add up—you can imagine what a mess we'd have on our hands. That's why we decided on one SIO for Linda Palmer, one team manager, and that's you. It's your job to keep a firm hand on the rudder. I'm available to provide updates and background intelligence from other sources wherever possible. Believe me, in this investigation, the different county forces involved will be talking to one another, and complete records will be kept of every interview, every allegation, every scrap of evidence. We have several complaints about Caxton from around the country already. The one thing you can be certain of is that there will be more complainants coming forward once the news gets out, and there's strength in numbers as far as we're concerned. How many depends very much on the access and opportunity Caxton had to satisfy his needs. It's my feeling, given his long and wide-ranging career, that he had plenty. They'll all have to be traced and investigated. Possible witnesses tracked down. Locations probed. I'll be searching for similarities in the complainant accounts."

"Just how wide is this investigation?" asked Gervaise.

Burgess looked at Chief Constable Sampson, who put on a suitably grim expression and said, "So far, according to the NCA, we have seven independent complaints about Danny Caxton spanning the years between 1961 and 1989. All from females between the ages of fourteen and sixteen at the time. The county forces involved have done as much background checking and taken as many preliminary statements as necessary so far, but we, and the CPS, feel it's time to move quickly now. The CPS also happens to feel that this is one of the crucial cases, that it has a better than most chance of netting a positive result."

"Why is that?" asked Banks. "As far as I've heard so far it's no different from any other such case. One person's word against another's. What gives us a better chance of making a charge that sticks?"

"Simply this," said Chief Constable Sampson. "Linda Palmer has informed us that, in her case, there was someone else present. There was a witness."

When DI Annie Cabbot and DC Geraldine Masterson arrived on the scene around half past nine that Wednesday morning, the whole eight miles of Bradham Lane were already sealed off from where it began at a T-junction two miles west of Eastvale to where it ended beside a bridge over the River Ure.

"It would be bloody miles from nowhere," said Annie. "We'll have to get a mobile unit out here and find the bodies to man it. And we'll have to run the Major Incident Room from HQ. There aren't enough facilities out here."

The uniformed constable standing by the police tape bent to talk to them. "There's an officer and a patrol car down by the bridge at the far end, and two officers at the scene," she said, then pointed. "The crime scene is three miles down there."

"Thanks," said Annie. "As long as we don't have to walk."

"It's a hard road surface, ma'am," said the officer. "And a rough one at that. Not much chance of tire tracks, but you never know what the CSIs might find. I'd go carefully."

"We will. I know those CSIs."

The patrol officer untied the tape at one end, and Gerry drove slowly along the narrow road.

Annie was intrigued by the shapes of the trees. Some seemed dead and stunted, standing there like men doing handstands, or the twisted and darkened shapes of burned bodies in a pugilistic stance. Others made a dazzling symphony of green in the breeze after last week's rains, leaves glistening and dancing in the morning sun. The road meandered, and on a couple of occasions, there were narrow unsurfaced lanes leading off, signposted to villages or farms Annie had never heard of. It would be easy to get lost here if you took a wrong turn, she thought. Here and there was a passing place in case you met someone coming the other way.

The first sign that they were close to their destination was a patrol car blocking the road ahead and a cyclist in bright purple Lycra leaning against the bonnet, head in his hands. A female PC stood next to him, notebook in her hand. A male officer, also making notes, sat in the car. The sleek bicycle leaned against the drystone wall. Annie bet it weighed about two ounces, cost a fortune and went like the clappers. So many cyclists had been inspired by the Tour de France's Grand Départ in Yorkshire that you could hardly move for them on the roads these days. Some of them looked quite fit in their Lycra, too, Annie thought, though not this one. He needed a few more thousand miles on his odometer to get up to snuff.

"This is Mr. Roger Stanford," said the PC. Then she gestured toward the misshapen bundle lying in a cordoned off area several yards further along the road. "He found the . . . er . . . her."

"Thanks," said Annie. "And you are?"

"PC Mellors, ma'am. Stephanie Mellors. Most people just call me Steph."

Annie gestured for PC Mellors to follow her a short distance from Roger Stanford. "Tell me, Steph," she said, "what do you think? First impressions?"

"You mean did he do it?"

"Well, if that's where you want to start."

Steph shook her head. "He's gutted, ma'am. A blubbering wreck. You can tell. I don't think he's faking it."

"You look a bit peaky, yourself."

"You haven't seen her yet, ma'am. It's never easy, something like this."

"Too true. What do you think happened?"

"From my limited experience, I'd say she was either hit by a car or beaten to death."

"Have you any idea who she is?"

"No. There's no ID, and as far as I can tell from . . . you know . . . I've never seen her before in my life. It's such a strange thing. She's not wearing a stitch of clothing."

"OK. Let's have a word with Mr. Stanford."

Roger Stanford was still leaning on the bonnet of the patrol car with his head in his hands. He wasn't crying, Annie noticed, just propping his head up as if were too heavy with images of violent death to hold itself up. He would need to be investigated, being the person who had found the body, but he didn't need to be treated like a suspect. "Mr. Stanford," she said, touching his arm. He raised his head, a blank expression on his face, as if he had been startled out of a deep sleep. Annie introduced herself. Gerry stood beside her, notebook at the ready. "What time did you find the body?" Annie asked.

"It would have been about a quarter to nine."

"Is this journey part of a routine, or are you on holiday?"

"Daily routine. I live in Bradham and I work in Eastvale. Clinton Estate Agents. I usually pass here about a quarter to nine. That's how I know. I keep track of my times."

"There are quicker ways."

"No nicer ones, though. I always make sure I have plenty of time."

Annie looked him up and down. "You go to work dressed like that?"

"Oh, no." He pointed to the little bundle strapped to back of his saddle. "I change at the office. We have a shower there, too."

"Very civilized." Annie made a mental note to take in the bundle of work clothes for forensic analysis. Maybe he didn't do it, but she couldn't go around letting things like that slip by. "So you make this same journey every morning?"

"And evening. More or less. Every weekday."

"Do you ever notice anyone else using the road?"

"No. I mean, once or twice I've seen a tractor out early, pulling a few bales of hay or something from one field to another, and once there was farmer shifting some cows over the road, blocking the way. Maybe the occasional car, but they're few and far between, thank the Lord. Cars are . . . well let's just say they're not always sympathetic toward cyclists. Usually the lane is deserted. That's why I like it. Nice and quiet."

Yeah, thought Annie, and cyclists are a pain in the ass as far as motorists and pedestrians are concerned. They don't stop at red lights, they go the wrong way up one-way streets, they ride on the pavements when it suits them, and the list went on. But she said nothing. "Let's go back to this morning. Anything unusual at all?"

"No," said Stanford. "I set off the same time I always do, around a quarter past eight, and I got here as I said, about a quarter to nine. It's only about six miles, but there's a tough uphill stretch, and I wasn't really pushing my speed."

"Did any cars pass you?"

"No."

"See anyone on foot?"

"No one. It was a perfectly ordinary morning—until I got here." He put his head in his hands again. "The first thing I saw was the crows. That poor, poor girl . . ."

"I'm sorry I have to ask these questions Mr. Stanford, but the sooner I'm done, the sooner you can go home."

"Home? But I haven't . . . I have to . . ."

"I'd go home if I were you, Mr. Stanford. Phone your work. They'll understand. Delayed shock and all that. We'll have someone come around and take a statement from you this afternoon. Who knows, you may have remembered something else by then."

"He's already given his address," said Steph.

Annie nodded. "You're free to go, Mr. Stanford. If I have any more questions, I'll be in touch. But I'd like to take the clothes you're carrying to our lab. We'll let you have them back good as new. Is that a problem?"

"My clothes? But . . .? Oh, I see. But surely you can't think I did it?"

"Just for purposes of elimination, Mr. Stanford."

"Of course." Stanford walked over to his bike, still stunned, unbuckled the bag and handed it over. Then he got on the bike and rode back, rather wobbly, down the lane.

"Where are the nearest houses?" Annie asked PC Mellors.

She pointed. "Nearest farmhouse is over there, at the other side of that field."

Annie could see the house in the distance. "Unlikely they'll have witnessed anything," she said, "though it's not so far away. Someone might have heard a car, for example, especially as the lane is little used by traffic." No houses lined its sides, she noticed, only trees and fields of grazing sheep beyond the ditch and the drystone walls. That said, it was certainly a scenic route if you weren't in a hurry. But it's hard to see pretty landscapes at night. On the other hand, she realized, if you wanted to avoid the Automated Number Plate Recognition cameras, the speed cameras and all the rest of the Big Brother paraphernalia that makes any road trip practically a public event these days, then Bradham Lane was your route of choice.

Annie glanced over at the body by the roadside and took a deep breath. No sense putting it off any longer. "Come on, Gerry," she said. "Let's go have a butcher's at what we've got."

The girl lay curled up in the fetal position, half in the long grass that edged a ditch, hands covering her face, as if to protect it. She was naked, and her body was streaked with mud, dirty water and blood. The soles of her feet were crusted with dried blood, and small stones from the road were embedded in the skin. There were no obvious bullet holes or stab wounds, and her throat seemed unscathed. Not so the rest of her. She could have been hit by a car, Annie supposed, but it would be up to the medical professionals to determine that. It was hard to see her features because of the position of her hands, but Annie noticed between the fingers that one eye was swollen shut, her lips were split and bloody, with a tooth protruding through the lower one, and her nose was crooked. Squatting to examine the rest of the body again, Annie noticed signs of bruising around the ribs, stomach and left hip. There were also signs of a scuffle in the earth around the body and, not so far away, the only obvious skid marks on the road surface, far too faint and blurred to give a decent tire impression. In the absence of a medical and CSI opinion, Annie was convinced that this girl had been beaten to death, kicked, perhaps even jumped on. And girl she was. Despite the injuries, Annie could see that the victim was hardly any older than fifteen or sixteen. She sensed Gerry's presence beside her and stood up.

"My God," said Gerry, hand to her mouth.

Annie put a friendly hand on her shoulder. "I don't think God had much to do with it, do you? And I'd like to say you get used to it, but you don't." Not so used to it, Annie thought, that you become indifferent to it, that you don't feel that tightening in your gut and that surge of anger that someone had done this to a fellow human being, or don't feel you're going to put your all into catching the bastard who did it.

"But she's so young. She's just a girl."

"I know." Gently directing a pale and trembling Gerry away with an arm around her shoulder, Annie headed back toward the uniformed officers. "Come on," she said. "It's time to call in the heavy brigade."

"Well, Banksy, what a turn up for the book. You and me working together again. Just like old times. Congratulations, by the way. The promotion. Long overdue."

They were basking in the sunshine at one of the tables outside at the Queen's Arms, eating lunch: monster fish and chips and mushy peas, with a pint of Timothy Taylor's for Banks and a cheap lager for Burgess. Cyril, the landlord, had taken on a new barmaid to deal with the summer rush, an attractive blond Australian called Pat, to whom Burgess had already taken a shine. Luckily, Cyril wasn't around, as he and Burgess had history.

"So what's your official title these days?" Banks asked. "What do I call you?"

"I always fancied 'Special Agent.' It has a ring to it. But in actual fact I'm a non-executive director. Sounds like a dull second-rate businessman. Mostly I go by plain 'Mr. Burgess' these days."

"Like a surgeon."

"Exactly. It's got class, don't you think?"

The cobbled market square was buzzing with shoppers and tourists, and clogged with parked cars. Young girls in vests and tight denim cut-offs over black tights hung out around Greggs eating pasties, then disappeared into the amusement arcade next door. A gaggle of serious ramblers, with walking-sticks like ski poles, expensive boots, baggy shorts and maps in plastic bags around their necks gathered by the market cross. A few people sat on the plinth around the market cross waiting for a local bus. Not far from Banks and Burgess sat a group of bloke-ish tourists in garish shorts and even more garish shirts, their faces flushed and eyes glazed from sunburn and beer. They were talking and laughing loudly enough that nothing Banks and Burgess spoke of could be overheard.

"Have you done this sort of thing before?" Banks asked.

"Once or twice." Burgess sat back and sipped his drink, studying Banks over the rim of his glass. "I was peripherally involved in Operation Yewtree when I was back at the Yard, so I know the way things go. Look, Banksy, you probably thought the same as I did when all this stuff started coming out. You thought it was some sort of witch hunt, wondering who'd be the next celebrity to be accused of groping a young publicist fifty years ago. Different times, you'd say, and you'd be right." He leaned forward and tapped Banks on the chest. "You probably even thought, what's so wrong with pinching the office girl's bum, maybe suggesting a hotel room after work for a bit of hanky panky? Right? I might even have a go with young Pat here, given half the chance. After all, I'm only human, and if you don't ask . . . But that's not what this is about. We're not talking about a bit of 'how's your father' in a dark corner at the office Christmas party. A hand casually resting on a knee in a restaurant. A surreptitious brushing up against a nice pair of tits. We've all done that, all had a kiss and cuddle in the broom cupboard and a bit of slap and tickle under the stairwell with that secretary we fancied all year."

"Speak for yourself," said Banks. But he remembered. It was just such an indulgence in a dark corner under the mistletoe at an office Christmas party that had led to the only affair of his married life. He didn't much care to be reminded of it now, though at the time it had seemed exciting and dangerous; it had made him feel alive at a time when he had felt the world and his marriage were falling apart around him. Looking back, it just made him feel guilty. Maybe it was some kind of poetic justice that his ex-wife Sandra had finally left him for another man.

"But this is something else," Burgess went on. "It's not even a matter of someone sticking his tongue down a girl's throat or squeezing a breast. Believe me, I've had enough access to statements that I can say what we're talking about here is the delilerate, arrogant and systemic abuse of innocent young girls—underage girls—by people who believe they're above the law. People so blessed and so famous that in the general run of things they probably get more free pussy than they can shake a stick at. And what do they do? They pick on vulnerable thirteen-, fourteen-, fifteen-year-olds, and they assault them and rape them, force them to do vile stuff, and then tell them they ought to be jolly grateful for getting raped by Danny Caxton or whoever. These girls end up so terrified, so fucked up, that often the rest of their lives are blighted. They see themselves as natural victims and that's what they become. All their lives, people abuse them just the way Caxton or whoever did all those years ago, and they can't stop it. They can't even figure out why. But even that's not the point. The point is that these bastards, and I mean bastards like Danny Caxton, have been getting away with it for years and making us look like the fucking Keystone Cops. They've abused these girls and boys, just like those Pakistani grooming gangs in Rochdale and Rotherham, and nobody did a fucking thing about it. Not the parents. Not the social workers. Not us. Well, times have changed, mate, because here comes the cavalry, with a vengeance."

"I never did think that," said Banks.

"Think what?"

"That this business is insignificant, that what we've been asked to do doesn't matter. And I'd certainly agree that some very influential people have got away with a lot of serious crimes over the years. Nothing new about that. It's just so bloody difficult to put a good case together after so long, like I said at the meeting. That's all. Memories change; evidence gets lost. People become convinced that something happened when it didn't, or that things happened differently. It's damn near impossible to sort out who's right in most cases. All you end up with is a shifting sandstorm of accusations, lies, half-truths, minor transgressions and full-blown felonies. Nobody knows what the truth is, in the end."

Burgess ran his hand over his unruly hair. "Too true. Too true. But we're getting better. The CPS are building stronger cases, they're more willing to prosecute, getting more convictions."

"So we ride their wave of success?"

"Why not? Isn't it better than riding a wave of failure? Besides, since when have you not risen to a challenge? This time they think we're in with a chance. They rate this Linda Palmer as a credible complainant. According to them, she's definitely not some fucked-up alcoholic with a chip on her shoulder."

"That's good to know," said Banks. "Does Caxton know we're on to him?"

"Probably. He shouldn't, but I wouldn't be surprised. He's still got friends in high places. I want you to go and talk to him tomorrow. After that, we'll get a team in to search his premises before he gets a chance to destroy any evidence there might be in his papers and on his computer. You can talk to Linda Palmer today. I trust your instinct enough to know that you won't need a child protection expert to figure out whether she's telling the truth. I know you, Banksy. I think once you get the bit between your teeth, you'll take to it like a duck to water, if you'll forgive the mixed metaphor, and you'll be only too glad to bring down the wrath of God on arrogant bastards like Danny Caxton."

"I will?"

"I think so." Burgess finished his pint. "Another? I wouldn't mind having another word with that buxom Australian barmaid. I like the way she pulls a pint."

"You need real cask ale to get a full show of flexed muscle, not that piss you drink. All she has to do is flick the lever."

"She can flick my lever any time. Why do you think I'm offering to buy you another one? Out of the goodness of my heart?"

Banks rolled his eyes. "I'd better not," he said. "Not if I've got to get this crusade off the ground and talk to Linda Palmer this afternoon. Can you tell me anything about her, other than that she's a poet and claims to be a victim of Caxton's?"

"I've never met her," said Burgess, "but from what I understand, she's got her head screwed on right. I've talked to plenty of others who've been in her position. Memories are unreliable, you're right about that, very vague sometimes. Like chasing shadows of shadows. You just have to keep at it. Gently, mind. They're sensitive souls, these victims of historical abuse. Especially poets. Some of the girls buried it right away. Really deep. They were just kids, after all. Some went through years of analysis and therapy without really knowing why—why they couldn't hold down a job, why they couldn't handle a relationship, why they couldn't bring up their kids properly. Some of them just turned to drugs and booze to help them forget. Some even committed suicide. But Linda

Palmer isn't like that, from what I understand. She's different. She's got her shit together."

Banks finished his drink and stood up. "OK," he said. "Thanks for the pep talk."

Burgess gave a mock salute. "My pleasure."

As Banks walked away, he turned and saw Burgess disappear inside the pub with his empty glass and a spring in his step.

BOOKS BY PETER ROBINSON

 NO CURE FOR LOVE

 BAD BOY

 IN THE DARK PLACES

 THE PRICE OF LOVE AND OTHER STORIES

 CHILDREN OF THE REVOLUTION

 ALL THE COLORS OF DARKNESS

 WATCHING THE DARK

 FRIEND OF THE DEVIL

 BEFORE THE POISON

 PIECE OF MY HEART

STRANGE AFFAIR

 COLD IS THE GRAVE

 PLAYING WITH FIRE

 IN A DRY SEASON

 THE FIRST CUT

 BLOOD AT THE ROOT

 CLOSE TO HOME

 INNOCENT GRAVES

 AFTERMATH

 FINAL ACCOUNT

WEDNESDAY'S CHILD

A NECESSARY END

PAST REASON HATED

A DEDICATED MAN

THE HANGING VALLEY

GALLOWS VIEW